JAGGER

PIPER STONE

Published by Stormy Night Publications and Design, LLC.
www.StormyNightPublications.com

Stone, Piper
Jagger

Cover Design by Korey Mae Johnson

CHAPTER 1

"*The quiet but inexorable breaking down of self-esteem is much more sinister—it's a violation of the soul.*"

—*Rachel Abbott*

Bella

"I have the perfect idea," Esme said as she lifted her glass of wine. "I'll hire a dude to run him over with a Hummer."

I almost choked on my merlot. I'd been thinking about similar methods of offing my ex. Each one a much more painful death than the idea before. "Not a bad idea, but messy."

"Maybe, but it would be fun. Even better if you were behind the wheel. There must be fifty plus a million ways to kill your lover," she continued, belting out the old country tune with updated phrasing.

"Yes, there definitely is." I knew that well. I could never count the number of poisons Joel could ingest where no one would be the wiser. I'd easily be able to get away with murder given my current profession. What physician didn't know about poisons? Although I was beginning to wonder how long I'd have my medical license so I could gain access to any toxic concoction.

I dug my fingernails into my palms, reminding myself I was escaping his tyranny.

"How about you bring him by the restaurant and I'll add the poison to his food." She was pleased with herself, shifting back and forth on the floor in a happy dance. "I'm also very good with a filet knife, remember."

Bloody images filled my mind.

"I don't think that's the best thing for your successful career as a chef. Do you?" At least she could make me laugh.

"Party pooper," she hissed and shook her head. Suddenly, it was like a light bulb went off inside that wacky brain of hers. "Why don't I cut to the chase? My cousin knows some people. You know what I mean. *People*. They don't necessarily follow the letter of the law. With a single phone call and a little bit of cash, your issue will vanish. Unless you'd prefer it like in *The Sopranos* series where the bloodied, chopped-up body washes up on the shore. Oh, I know, his body could be sent to his asshole father via Fed-Ex. That should do the trick."

It would do the trick alright, including landing our asses in jail.

The woman was not only my best friend but my cheerleader through this… disaster of a life I currently had. As soon as my best friend leaned over, she sloshed wine on her pants and didn't even seem to notice. I had to steady her with her arm to keep her from falling over. "You're drunk, girl. I love you for all your magnificent thoughts, but I honestly don't think I'd do well in prison."

She snorted. "I beg to differ. You'd be the belle of the ball and it would be worth it to carve Joel up into teensy-tiny pieces. He's a bastard. He hurt you."

"Yeah, I know." My knight in shining armor had turned into a gaslighting prick with a God complex. That was being kind.

That had been established even before I'd walked into my bedroom finding him in bed with my former friend, a woman from work I'd thought I could trust. Susie had been doing nothing more than playing a game with me while fucking my husband. Another wave of anger boiled my blood. "You haven't even mentioned Susie's demise."

Her laugh was filled with an evil tone. "Oh, girl. I've written down on paper how that bitch will be terminated. Maybe thin razor wire."

Now she sounded like Arnold in a famous sci-fi movie. After everything I'd been through, all the horrible threats and innuendoes as well as recent efforts to derail my career, at least I could count on Esme to make things seem less horrible. "I'm going to miss you, girl."

"Then why are you going? Stand up for your rights!"

My rights were to get the hell out of Baltimore to somewhere I could start over without a rich dickhead breathing down my neck, acting as if he was going to take my daughter away from me. He wasn't even her sperm donor, let alone her father. Granted, Joel had been the only father Cally had ever known, but he'd shown very little interest in her until I'd tossed him from the house.

"I've tried. You know that. I have a little girl and a career to try and salvage." The video my ex had sent only a week before had reminded me quite painfully of the power and influence he had in Baltimore. His family was rich and could easily ruin me by making a few phone calls.

"Why is that bastard rearing his ugly head after you filed for divorce almost six months ago?" Esme scoffed. She tossed her hair in my direction, another highlight of her contempt for the man.

"Because he fucked up on a surgery and I was asked to take over. He blames me." He was even reprimanded by the hospital administrator. The man didn't like my ex very much and made it quite apparent whose corner he was in. That's when things had gotten really ugly, his last visit leaving bruises. I couldn't tell Esme the worst of it or I had no what she would do.

"Take him down. Go to the press. Make it known how he treated you and baby Cally."

I shifted against the couch, avoiding another round of tears like the plague. I'd cried enough over the loss of my marriage. I'd thought it a fairytale, not a nightmare. "I just can't do that to Cally." My daughter was the best thing that had ever happened in my life. I was determined to provide her with a better life.

"I get it, but this isn't like you. Running away?"

Maybe I was, but after going through all the scenarios, I knew there was no other chance at finding happiness. "What other choice do I have?"

Not that her influence over a man who had ties to some pretty bad people didn't sound appealing.

She huffed and jerked up, her body swaying from the amount of wine we'd consumed. "More wine and ice cream. That's what the doctor ordered."

"I need to go home."

"Cally is already asleep and I refuse to allow you to drive. Besides, with you determined to leave in the morning, I need to spend as much time with my bestie as possible. Where the hell are you going again?"

"Just someplace special." I'd thrown a dart at a map of the surrounding states, hoping to land somewhere I'd find happiness.

If that was possible.

"Well, you've got guts, lady. I'll give you that, but my offer to have him taken out like the bastard he is still stands."

"And I love you for it."

After she walked from the room, I pulled my phone from my jeans pocket. I'd watched the ugly video at least fifty times and every time pulled me further into darkness and hatred. If he released the raunchy video to the press or the hospital administrators, my career would be over anyway. I'd been so stupid to trust him. I'd been blinded by his wealth and good looks, falling into the predator's lair.

The only thing I could do was to start a new life.

And pray my past wouldn't follow.

CHAPTER 2

Jagger

"I fucking hate holidays," I snarled as Shephard and I walked from the elevator toward the lobby of the resort. Foxhead Resort and Winery was exploding with business, which did little more than irritate the hell out of me.

I hadn't been born or raised to be responsible for the financials of a multimillion-dollar operation.

I'd been born to fight.

And to kill.

"All of them in general or just Christmas?" My older brother Shephard had amusement in his tone.

The Fox brothers had been mandated to leave our lives, accepting our father's 'gift' of controlling the business in exchange for our full inheritance. It was basic blackmail, but the three of us, who'd barely gotten along as kids as it was, had been forced to work together.

I'd loathed almost every day since.

I gritted my teeth as we moved through a large group of guests. They'd all headed for the resort for the winter festivities and the goddamn festive atmosphere in the tiny town. We were packed to the gills, every snow lover in the world landing in Danger Falls.

"Every single one of them," I answered. I was used to traveling the world, indulging in the finest foods and liquors, not babysitting tourists determined to get lost in the mountains or break a fucking leg. Plus, I'd lived alone, never forced to deal with people.

At least as long as they were alive.

"What's his problem?" Hunter asked as he walked toward us from another direction.

My younger brother had sipped too much of the small town's Kool-Aid, enjoying living in such a confining space. It shouldn't piss me off that he'd sold out for a better way of life, but it did. We weren't close, barely burying the hatchet, but agreeing to run the resort and winery. But they both thought they could butt in whenever they felt like it.

Fuck them.

"He's grousing about the decorations and the lively guests, I'm assuming," Shephard told him.

Hunter laughed. "He's more of a pessimist than you are."

"Stop fucking with me. I don't need to like shit." Yeah, I was grumpier than ever. Maybe it was because some kid had run into me with his damn hot chocolate, nearly scalding my arm. I smelled like one big chocolate factory.

"Oh, come on. The snow has brought us more guests than ever." Shephard had become the head of the resort, his adoration of the place driving me bat shit crazy. "Plus, our profits are up fifteen percent. According to the financials you just provided anyway."

I glanced in his direction, shaking my head. "Yes. We are making money hand over fist at this point."

"Then what's the problem?"

"The problem? I feel like a boulder is going to drop on our heads." I had been feeling like that for a couple of months. There was no legitimate reason for my glass half empty thoughts, but my instincts were kicking into high gear. There were people who hated us in this town, including the Young family, who up until our father's arrival had been the richest family in town. That meant the lot of them could lord their wealth over everyone else living within the city limits.

"Always the pessimist." Hunter shook his head. "I hear you, bro, but you need to stop looking at everything as if it were half empty."

"Nope," I countered. "The glass is going to be shattered."

Shephard was forced to stop moving as an employee approached with whatever paperwork he needed to sign.

Hunter lagged with him, asking questions of one of the restaurant employees.

I kept walking and I didn't care if they tried to keep up.

Suddenly, Shep was right there by my side once again. Sometimes, I thought the man had a death wish.

"Seriously, what's up? You're grouchier than usual."

I threw a hateful glance toward Shephard and stopped in the middle of the lobby. People were everywhere, loud Christmas music playing. Hell, there was even a jazz band with a singer belting out holiday tunes in the lobby bar. Fuck this shit. "We have the storm of the century rolling in. And I have my reasons." The story was something my brothers hadn't heard and I wasn't going to talk about the experience.

The holidays would always remind me of the worst time in my life.

"Uh-huh. So what about the storm? Good for business. Fresh snow on the ground," Shephard declared. "Most of the guests are here for an extended period of time. They can enjoy the snowy world of adventure, which should provide additional business in the future."

My brother had gone from a brutal assassin working for an undisclosed organization meant on ridding the world of savages to a small-town family man. I was happy he was enjoying his life with the woman who'd captured his heart, but I wasn't at that point.

Nor would I ever be.

I missed the action, working alone, eliminating a threat while enjoying the sights and sounds of other countries. I was a danger junkie, fueled by the rocketed levels of adrenaline and the stench of fresh blood. Now I was subject to boring days sitting in front of a computer ensuring contracts were in place, money coming in.

All because our father had insisted his three sons take the helm of the now profitable business in the middle of fucking nowhere. Or we would have lost our share of the profit had he sold. Months after accepting his toxic demand, I was miserable.

Hunter snickered. "He needs to get laid." He flanked my other side. What was this, some bullshit intervention?

"Shut the fuck up," I told him. So he'd decided to be the playboy of the Shenandoah Valley. That wasn't me. Not by a long shot.

"You're a grumpy son of a bitch," Shephard said with disdain in his tone. "You need to get out more, enjoy the Shenandoah Mountains. Take up a damn hobby. Chase women. Do something to alter your nasty moods."

"Yeah, well, go home to your lovely woman and handsome dog. Just leave me alone."

Shephard stopped short and I kept walking. "In other words, brother. Get a life."

"By the way. I like the new aftershave," Hunter called after me. "Heavy on the chocolate and marshmallows."

I threw my hand out, shoving him aside as I headed into the lobby. My two brothers continuously got on my freaking nerves. Shephard was worse, with his new, sunny disposition because of having a woman in his life. Good for him. I wanted no part of it.

"I'm sorry, but there's nothing we can do. I can suggest another hotel, but they could be booked."

The loud voice was coming from one of the front desk employees. Mark was usually extremely polite, going the distance to provide whatever a guest needed. I glanced in his direction, noticing a woman and a little girl, who was hanging on her mother's jacket, whimpering and whining like small kids did.

"You don't understand," the woman said in return. I had a feeling she was repeating herself. "I need this room. Just for one night."

"Not only are we booked up, but you have no identification. Our rules will not allow us to rent a single room without the guest producing identification or a valid credit card."

Sighing, I had the distinct feeling I'd need to intervene. I walked closer, noticing the woman appeared haggard, dirt covering her light jacket. Had she not prepared for the elements? Even the kid wasn't dressed warmly enough.

"Is there something wrong, Mark?" I asked as I leaned against the counter, studying the woman in question from several inches away.

She certainly didn't want to look me in the eye. Given my former profession, I knew that generally meant she was guilty of something.

However, she was also beautiful. Even the dark circles under her eyes couldn't diminish her stunning good looks. But there was a level of sadness exuding from her that heightened my curiosity.

"Yes, this woman doesn't understand I can't rent her a room. She has no identity and two credit cards were denied." Mark was almost as harried as the mysterious woman was. "That is not allowed in this resort. It's against our very strict rules."

The guy was actually schooling me in the regulations of the resort? Was he kidding me? Now I was past being irritated, moving into full-blown rage.

"You know what, Mark? I'm certain we can make an exception," I told him. I wasn't typically the kind of man who gave a shit about someone, but I could tell by the woman's pinched face she was in dire straits.

"As I told the woman, we're booked. Solid. Not one room to be found," Mark insisted. The young man was glaring at me as if I was the problem.

I resisted snapping at him, trying to learn from Shephard by taking the high road. "Our potential guest has a name. Now talk to me. What about our cabins? Are they all filled?" He was a complete asshole as far as I was concerned.

The woman turned to me, her brow furrowed. "I can't afford a cabin. I just..."

"Mommy. I'm hungry." The little girl continued tugging on her mother's jacket, even stamping her feet for emphasis. I could tell whoever the mother was, she was doing her best to remain calm.

"Honey. I'll get you some graham crackers in a little bit," she said.

Graham crackers?

Mark snapped a hateful look at me. "Let me check." His fingers flew across his computer's keyboard and I made a mental note to rake the shithead over the coals later. "Yes, the Wyoming cabin is available. But it's *very* expensive."

Her face fell.

He was telling me this as if I didn't know? The resort's accountant? I was close to being livid, which wasn't good for anyone. "We're comping her the cabin for as long as she needs."

"But sir—"

"Don't 'but sir' me," I interrupted. "You heard me. You work for me. Remember? Not the other way around. Make it happen. Identification or not. It's on me."

"Yes, sir," Mark said, but he wasn't a happy camper.

As if I cared.

The woman appeared shocked, but her expression changed quickly into more than a slight hint of anger. "I don't take charity. Thank you very much, but I'm not that kind of woman."

I could tell she was the kind of person who didn't appreciate anyone providing assistance. "A storm is coming."

"I'll go to another hotel," she said.

"The two other inns are completely booked given the damn season and the upcoming snow event. It's late and your daughter is hungry. Accept my generosity. I don't usually offer any." I started to turn away until she touched my arm.

As soon as she did, a huge jolt of current rushed through every cell in my body. Shock followed, the kind that caught my breath in my throat.

"You didn't need to do that," she said more softly this time.

"It would appear you needed a little help. I have the ability to make that happen."

"Mommy. I'm so hungry. Pwease."

The little girl was now begging, which struck at the heart-strings I hadn't known I had any longer. I rubbed my eyes, already hating what I was about to do.

"Why don't we grab some dinner? The chef makes a tasty cheeseburger." I was shocked by how generous I was being. I was the Fox brother who argued against a single freebie.

"Mommy. A cheeseburger."

"No, Cally. We can't do that." Cally's mother was at the point of losing some sense of control. I could tell from her face and by her body language.

"Nonsense," I told her. "I was going to grab a bite and I hate eating alone." It was just a lie since I preferred being entirely alone.

PIPER STONE

The woman's face as she peered at me yanked at something else, desire that I'd long since thought dead. She was also distrusting, questioning whether I was a good guy or bad guy.

I knew the answer and I doubted she would feel more comfortable knowing.

"I don't bite," I told her, although that was no more the truth than anything else I'd said.

"What's your name at least so I can place you into our system?" Mark asked, his tone prompting another expression of displeasure from me. Since when did our employees judge a single guest?

Not allowed.

She bit her lower lip and I could tell she was still deciding whether to accept the offer.

I wasn't the kind of man to beg for anything.

"Bella Winters," she said in a tone suggesting defeat. She had a story to tell, but one I didn't care to hear.

I'd done my good deed for the year, dinner just icing on the cake. As she signed a piece of paper for the hotel, I took more time paying attention to how she was dressed, her daughter as well. I was a damn good judge of character, my former life requiring me to be observant with the smallest details about a person.

Bella's lower lip was quivering, but she was doing her best to remain strong. She'd obviously been through some kind of ordeal, doing an excellent job of hiding it from her daughter. She was also the most beautiful woman I'd ever set eyes on.

I'd had my share of affairs over the years, none of which I could call a relationship. However, I was more attracted to Bella than I had been with anyone in as long as I could remember. With her long blonde hair, striking violet eyes, soft rosy lips, and an hourglass figure unable to be hidden by her jacket, she was the epitome of stunning.

Even my cock registered just how insanely gorgeous she was, my shaft pushing hard against my trousers.

"Here are the keys to the Wyoming cabin and a map to show you how to get there. Enjoy your stay." I didn't like the look on Mark's face. He was definitely pushing the envelope in my world and he wouldn't like me getting angry.

I'd been called a son of a bitch more than once, the title held with pride.

With the keys in her hand, Bella was still debating. "I will pay you back."

"Don't worry about it. Now, how about those cheeseburgers?"

Cally smiled at me and her small gesture could light up the dreary night. "Thank you, mister." The kid couldn't have been more than three, maybe four, yet she'd already been taught manners.

"You can call me Jagger."

The little girl's eyes opened wide and she clapped. Maybe

the kid thought I was some kind of superhero in a world that held few.

"Jagger," Bella repeated. "A good name."

A dangerous one. If only she knew the moniker provided by the last people I'd worked for.

If she learned, she'd leave the resort and never return.

ella

Charity.

I'd never thought since reaching adulthood that I'd be forced to accept anyone's charity again. I wasn't that kind of woman, priding myself on climbing from the depths of hell, my hard work allowing me a lucrative career.

But that had been before.

Before my life had fallen apart in a few days.

I'd followed my GPS, heading for the location I'd selected at random, uncertain of the name of the town or the resort. What I did know by the festive and posh interior including marble floors and gleaming brass accents was that I was in way over my head.

With little cash available at this point, and my credit cards cut off, I had few options. Being despondent wasn't going to get me anywhere, but tears had formed more than once during the trip. The bastard I'd left had worked quickly, no doubt eliminating any chances for resuming my old life or being able to afford much of anything.

So charity it was.

Cally was starving, the few bites of food I'd provided screaming I was a bad mother.

Jagger was staring at me. I had a feeling he sensed I was on the ropes. That was putting it mildly. His kind gesture was something I never would have gotten back in Baltimore. Maybe that's why I couldn't find the right words.

The man towered over me. He had a look about him that reminded me of a grizzly bear crossed with a mountain man. His thick, curly dark brown hair was unruly as if he'd been running his fingers through it all evening long. In my world, men either wore expensive suits in an effort to appear rich to lure ladies into a night of passion or they were wearing scrubs, hiding their natural physique.

Not that many of them were anything to write home about. They'd likely never gotten dirt under their fingernails. Not like Jagger. He was the epitome of rough and tumble, his scruffy beard creating a slightly dangerous persona. But it was his piercing eyes I couldn't seem to glance away from. The man was a definite breath of fresh air and I needed that desperately right now.

"Okay. Let's get some food for Cally. Thank you."

"Good, but no need for thanks," Jagger told me. "I don't like seeing a pretty young lady starving to death."

I sensed Jagger wasn't used to dealing with people, his stilted words giving him away. But he was trying and for that, I would be forever grateful. Cally had already been through a lot, her entire life disrupted. I hated myself for being forced to do so and about a dozen other things.

"Come on," he suggested. "We'll head to the grill. They make the best burgers this side of the Mississippi."

He was trying harder to seem more likable, yet his jaw was as clenched as before. His vibes were electric, his gruff demeanor likely turning off everyone who didn't know him. But with me, I felt an odd sense of connection. Why? I had no clue and I couldn't allow that to cloud my judgment.

Never trust anyone ever again.

As he led the way, I realized I'd never felt so uncomfortable with a stranger in my life. He was sexy, very much so in a rugged, almost mountain man kind of way. I had a tough time not throwing him glances, feeling tiny next to his six foot something muscular body. His dark, very thick shoulder-length hair couldn't hold a candle to his whiskey-colored eyes. But they were pained, haunted.

Almost dead.

Still, my bestie would call him eye candy for the soul.

Maybe former best friend. Would I ever see her again, enjoying a night of my favorite treats including mojitos? I reminded myself for the tenth time this was best for my little girl's life.

As well as mine.

"Who are you, Jagger? If you don't mind me asking?"

"Meaning what?" he asked as he glanced in my direction.

"Are you the resort manager?"

He laughed at my question, shaking his head. "One-third owner."

"Who owns the other two-thirds?"

"My brothers."

"There are two more of you?" I realized my question could seem flirtatious and that was the last thing on my mind. No matter how hot he was or how lonely I felt already, men were completely off the radar.

At least he finally smiled. "My father might say unfortunately so."

"Oh, cold."

"Trust me. The man is ice cold. I took after him."

"What a pity."

The moment we walked into the restaurant my stomach growled so loudly Jagger looked over at me. I couldn't remember the last time I'd eaten. He said nothing while my face flushed. I felt the heat and was embarrassed, tugging down on the sleeves of my jacket. I must look like some homeless person looking for freebies. I had to remind myself I was close to that and would be if I wasn't extremely careful with my money.

Several of the employees greeted him as we passed, although I wasn't certain if their extended glances were out of respect or hatred.

He headed directly for a table, pulling out the chair for my daughter. I helped her remove her jacket, putting it on the back of the chair before she sat down. Her little giggles were a wonderful sound to a mother who felt like Mommy Dearest. She'd acted like a big girl the entire trip, napping a good portion of the way. I could tell she was close to shutting down, the ache in her tummy just another reminder of the horrific actions I'd taken.

Everything was aching straight to my bones. Even my pulse had increased from continued anxiety. I yanked off my jacket, shivering almost immediately. I remained turned away from him, pulling on the three-quarter sleeves of my sweater. I hadn't expected seeing anyone who might ask questions.

"The jackets you have are too thin for the area." His words sounded like he was chastising me, but I didn't take the bait. He studied me intently, including allowing his eyes to fall to my arms.

Dropping my arms into my lap, I almost told him I could be pretty nasty myself when shoved into a corner.

I shouldn't have been surprised when a waitress appeared almost immediately, but I was.

"Samantha, these young ladies are my guests so anything they'd like is on the house," Jagger told her.

"Yes, sir."

"What would you like to drink?" he asked me. When I hesitated, he lifted his eyebrows. "White wine?"

"I'm not a white wine kind of girl. Merlot? Cabernet?" I still felt guilty, but the thought of a glass of wine seemed like a small slice of heaven right now.

He nodded as if appreciative. "Bring my guest a glass of our finest cabernet and reserve the bottle. And for the little lady?"

I wouldn't have thought a man as gruff as he appeared to be would allow my little girl to feel more comfortable in strange surroundings.

"Milk for the little princess," I told them both. Her nose wrinkled, but she knew better than to ask for her favorite soda. Although I could tell she was going to try to twist his arm.

"And you, Mr. Fox?" Samantha asked.

"I'll have a bourbon. Neat. We'll also have three juicy cheeseburgers with all the trimmings, including crispy fries."

I would ordinarily be pissed when a man dared order for me, but this time, I was honestly grateful. Exhaustion was taking a toll, the stress of worrying and wondering sapping my energy.

"Coming right up, sir."

Being comfortable around a stranger wasn't possible and I sensed he wasn't interested in chitchatting. At least Cally did it for us, jabbering about deer she'd seen on the way. She loved animals, constantly asking for a guinea pig or a puppy, neither of which she'd been allowed to have.

Jagger tried to engage, his uncomfortable demeanor apparent by the tenseness in his body and the pulsing of the thick cords in his neck. He was ruggedly handsome, completely unlike the men I was used to dealing with. Especially with the beard and mustache. I could see him in jeans and holding an ax, a flannel shirt tossed over a log after he'd gotten sweaty. The thought and the naughty images forced me to bite back a laugh. He was also doing everything not to look in my direction.

After the milk was brought, Cally stopped talking long enough for me to get a word in edgewise. I was just as uncomfortable doing so as he was talking. "It's pretty here."

"Yeah," he said quietly. "Real pretty in Danger Falls this time of year. Like I give a…" He caught himself before cursing in front of my daughter, which prompted me to laugh.

His brow furrowed, making him look even more dangerous. "What?"

"Nothing. Danger Falls. That's the name of the town?"

"Yep. Did you get lost coming up the mountain?" His question was almost accusatory.

"Not really. I just didn't remember the name." I was a terrible liar. I'd forgotten it the moment I'd tossed our things into the back of the SUV, screeching out of the driveway before Joel returned to a house he no longer belonged in.

Neither did I.

"Mmm… Well, it's a quaint and happy little town in a beautiful part of the country. So I'm told."

"You don't like it here?" I took a sip of wine and thought it to be as close to heaven as I'd ever experienced. "This is delicious. Thank you."

"Not particularly," he answered, giving a slight nod. The man was as closed off as anyone I'd ever met.

"Then why are you here?"

I had a suspicion the man didn't like being hassled with questions. The expression he wore screamed of a shutdown. Maybe even a warning to let it go.

Fortunately, the food arrived a few seconds later.

I was too busy paying attention to keeping Cally eating to notice until much later that he'd been staring at me. When I finally caught a glimpse of his pensive face, I was instantly on alert. What if he was going to report where I was?

That was ridiculous. The odds of that were slim to zero.

My deep breath was scattered and he caught the sound, tilting his head as he continued studying me. We munched in silence and I was grateful my daughter wasn't shy. She'd managed to shut down some of the awkwardness.

A flash caught my eye as a different waitress rushed in our direction.

"I'm sorry to interrupt, Mr. Fox, but Carlos is hurt pretty badly. There's blood everywhere."

The girl was almost panicking. I could tell he was annoyed by the deep sound rumbling up from his throat.

"Did you grab the first aid kit?" he asked.

"The cut is too bad. I think he's going to need stiches and I tried Doc Welby, but he's not answering. I don't know what to do. Carlos is losing a lot of blood."

"Where is the cut?" I asked,

"His hand and wrist. It was a sharp knife."

"Did the blade cut the major artery on his wrist?"

The girl's eyes opened wide. "I think the knife nicked it."

Shit. I bit my lower lip and shifted my gaze toward Jagger. This was the absolute last thing I needed, but I wasn't able to let an injured man go unattended. "Can you watch Cally while I see what I can do to help?" I realized as soon as the words slipped from my mouth naturally how idiotic they sounded. Why would I leave my daughter with a stranger and how the hell could I help in any way? "I have some first aid training. You know because I was once a camp counselor."

I was racking up the lies today.

"Abby, why don't you take our little guest here to my office and keep her company while we take a look at Carlos. Cally. Abby is going to take you to a special place. Call it a little adventure. Will you go with her?"

"Of course, Mr. Fox."

My daughter had been taught as early as she could understand never to talk to a stranger let alone go anywhere with one. Yet she stuck out her little hand as if we were all best friends or family.

"You don't need to go with me," I stated through gritted teeth. If he did, he'd possibly suspect I was lying.

Not that I'd told him anything about myself.

"It's my hotel," he said with more than a harsh tone.

"Come on, Cally. Let's go on that adventure." Abby didn't miss a beat, taking Cally by the hand.

Once she was gone, I pushed back the chair. "We need to attend to your employee quickly. A cut in that area could be life threatening."

"I'll take you to the kitchen." Jagger led the way, taking long strides as he headed to where we were going.

There was near pandemonium inside, the entire staff freaking out about the amount of blood. One of the men was close to yelling at them. I wanted to tell him to shut the fuck up as he wasn't helping the situation. Carlos was close to panic mode, his face far too pale. He was holding his wrist, blood seeping through his fingers. His white jacket was stained, his body swaying even though he was seated.

I immediately snatched a couple of clean towels folded on a rack, rushing toward him and kneeling down. "Hi, Carlos. I'm Bella and I'm going to try and help you. I promise I'll be very gentle, but I need to take a look."

He wasn't any more trusting than Jagger was, but finally agreed. I held my breath, expecting the worst. Fortunately, I was wrong.

"How bad?" he asked in broken English.

"Not as bad as I thought, but you'll need stitches. Okay? Jagger, I have my old counselor bag in my vehicle. Let me get it. You need to keep pressure on the wound and maybe find us a quiet space. Can you do that?"

I knew the man wasn't used to taking orders or even suggestions from a woman. His eyes reflected a hint of anger. I responded with defiance in mine.

"Jagger. I can help this man if you'll trust me and do as I say."

He huffed, but finally nodded. "Come on, Carlos. Let's get you comfortable."

Nodding my thanks, I yanked a clean towel for myself so I could wipe my bloodied hands, heading out of the kitchen quickly. I managed to grab my coat and purse, fumbling to find my keys, my fingers were shaking so badly. Once outside into the frigid air, I took a deep breath.

"What the hell are you doing?" My words barely registered in the wind. But I heard them. I had no decent answer either. I couldn't allow the man to remain hurt. I'd taken the Hippocratic Oath years before. Maybe Jagger wasn't the kind of man to ask any questions.

I weaved my way to my vehicle, grabbing my doctor's bag. I'd always seen myself as a house doctor. As soon as I'd had my medical license, I'd purchased a special leather bag, equipping it with all the goodies that I'd seen on television growing up. Fortunately, my doctor instincts had pushed me into making the kit useful instead of a piece used for reminiscing.

That included a suture kit. Bandages. A stethoscope and other implements for a basic first aid adventure.

Not that I'd needed another one.

I rushed back inside and into the kitchen, a couple of the employees pointing the direction of where Carlos had been taken.

Jagger was still holding the man's arm, talking to him in a low voice to keep him calm. I was pleasantly surprised he'd known what to do.

"Let's get this washed off so I can get you all cleaned up," I told Carlos, giving Jagger a nonverbal thank you. I took over talking to Carlos as I worked, finding out he had a wife and two little girls, working in the resort his only income.

I sensed the poor guy was terrified he'd lose his job. He continuously glanced at Jagger. There was no mistaking fear in a man's eyes.

When I was finished stitching him up, I offered him as bright a smile as I could handle. "You're going to need to take a couple days off and have your wrist looked at by a qualified doctor."

"I cannot do that," Carlos exclaimed. I was certain the guy was going to go into a panic attack. "I need money. Bills. Food."

"I'm certain Mr. Fox is prepared to pay you for your down time. You were injured on the job." I threw a look over my shoulder at Jagger's smug face. He knew the rules. He couldn't deny time off or fire the man.

If he dared try either one or not to pay him, I'd turn his ass in to the Employment Commission myself. There were several crackles of electricity and I was surprised Carlos didn't react to them.

Maybe it was the only real language Jagger and I could share. He was glaring at me as he'd done before. For a hot as sin man, he could get under a person's skin by his looks alone.

Let alone his gruff attitude.

"Won't you, Mr. Fox?" I repeated.

Jagger sighed. "Take as much time as you need, Carlos. Your job is secure and you'll be receiving your paycheck plus a bonus."

"Thank you, Mr. Fox. Thank you, Doctor."

"Oh, I'm not a doctor," I told Carlos. How many lies was I going to tell in a single day? "You should be good as new."

"Go home, Carlos," Jagger told him.

I headed to the sink to wash up, trying to ignore the flashes of heat I felt surrounding me. The stings were prickly, red-hot, and unwanted. How could I be so attracted to a man whose picture was likely in the dictionary under grumpy?

As soon as I dried off my hands, I turned around. "Thank

you for the room, dinner, and the excitement this evening. I haven't had so much fun in years. I should get going."

Yes, there was some sarcasm in my voice, but it seemed Jagger brought that out in me. Or maybe I was just tired. Either way, this wasn't leading anywhere but to a bad place for both of us.

I found myself holding my breath as he walked closer. I was struck that I hadn't noticed his aftershave before. The scent was as rugged as the man full of the scent of timber and moss, fresh rain and sunshine. Wasn't I suddenly the little romantic?

As he came closer, I was still holding my breath. He threw a heated gaze all the way down to the old pair of tennis shoes I'd shoved my feet into. He also took a deep breath as if catching that I'd been indulging in his manly fragrance.

A wry smile crossed his face and I sensed he was about to say something. For a couple of different reasons, I gripped the edge of the stainless-steel sink with one hand.

"You sure could have fooled me about you not being a doctor, Bella. I'm wondering what else you're hiding."

CHAPTER 4

Telling a beautiful woman that she was lying was as much a Neanderthal thing as commenting on her weight. Even I knew better than to do something so stupid. However, I'd watched how she'd handled Carlos. She was a damn doctor. I could feel that to my bones.

She'd also suffered some abuse at the hands of an asshole. I'd caught sight of a couple of bruises on her arm. There was no way an accident could have caused them. Right now, it was not my damn place to ask who the jerk was. Nor should I care.

"You didn't need to carry Cally. She's still small enough I can do that," Bella told me as I walked with her to her vehicle.

"It's fine. You're exhausted. I need to lead you to the cabin. The map is decent by daylight, but at night it's shit."

She chuckled. "I'm a big girl. I'm pretty good with directions." The woman already had her car keys in her hand. What did she think I was going to do?

"Not if you didn't know where you were going in coming here in the first place. It was a dangerous thing to do."

"You're not a very nice man. Are you?" She pressed a button on her key fob and headlights flashed from only a few car lengths away.

"What makes you think that?"

"I could tell by the way the employees were looking at you and by the actions of the two girls that came up to the table. It appeared they were terrified of how you'd react."

The lights in the parking lot were damn good. It allowed me to see the make and model of the vehicle she was driving. A Mercedes Visionary SUV. I wasn't a fan of the brand, but I knew it well enough to realize not only was it less than a year old, but it was also priced over one hundred and thirty k without being loaded.

Why had her credit cards been declined?

More than one mystery enshrouded the beautiful woman.

"I'm not here to make friends," I told her as I eased Cally into the car seat in the back passenger seat.

A moment of silence fell between us.

"How about trying not to make enemies?" Bella adjusted the straps, finishing by stroking her daughter's cheek.

"I don't need anyone to like me."

She folded her arms out of frustration and a chill from the wind. "Well, then you're meeting your goals." Without saying another word, she moved to the driver's side, climbing in and shutting the door.

My mouth twitched in my own level of frustration. No one challenged me that way. Not a single soul.

Huffing, I headed to my Range Rover, jumping inside and starting the engine with enough ferocity I almost flooded it. Who the hell did she think she was, anyway?

I jerked out of the parking lot, waiting until she figured out where I was. Once she was behind me, I took off, twisting my hands around the steering wheel. Why did she get to me so much? Because she'd called out my bad behavior? Maybe.

I'd felt far too much chemistry between us, which was almost as irritating as her attitude.

Yeah, I'd done the right thing and she'd paid me back by offering her help. With the town's damn doctor retiring and a snowstorm rolling in, I sure as hell hoped the next few days were quiet.

I forced myself to concentrate on the road instead of thinking about her long legs or the shimmer on her flushed cheeks. Damn, my cock was aching.

There were several cabins surrounding the property, some used for family members like my parents and others meant for larger families. Wyoming was a smaller cabin, but one with pristine views and a massive stone fireplace. They'd all been renovated thanks to my dad. My cabin was also far enough away I wouldn't run into her without trying.

And I had no plans of doing so.

For however long she was here, it was best to keep my distance. Complications I didn't need nor want.

The snow had started to fall in small flakes. That would establish the groundwork for the foot plus that I'd heard the lower lying areas were getting, with eighteen inches to two feet in the mountains. It was crazy to think we'd get that much at the start of December in Virginia. I was reminded already why I preferred warmer climates.

The winding roads leading to the various cabins could be treacherous by the morning.

I pulled into the driveway leading to the Wyoming cabin, allowing her to take the better parking location right in front.

Bella seemed hesitant to turn off her engine or climb out. I didn't know anything about her except that she didn't like taking handouts and had suffered some kind of attack. Maybe now I knew why. She was on the run from something or someone. That much was clear.

She remained tentative with all her actions, finally cutting the engine and opening her door. I did the same, waiting to see what she'd do. She really didn't need help from here, but at least my mama had taught me manners and those had stuck. Just about everything else regarding being a nice guy had been beaten, prodded, or tortured out of me.

After checking on her daughter, Bella climbed out, leaving the door open and her headlights shining on the front door while she walked onto the porch. The girl was definitely scared of something, completely untrusting of anyone offering assistance. I stayed where I was, hugging my jacket more tightly around my chest.

Goddamn, I hated this time of year. My leg ached more than usual. It was going to be a rocky night.

I couldn't believe how long she was taking to open the door. When she was finally inside, it took her an equal amount of time to find a light. Not just one. She turned on at least six, including the outside floodlights. One scared lady.

She had her hands in her pockets as she walked back out, heading toward me after closing the driver's door.

"The place alright?" I asked.

"It's beautiful. Too much, but just… amazing." Her sigh was exaggerated.

"Food. We usually have a welcome basket for guests, but this was different."

Bella laughed nervously. "Yes, I kinda intruded."

A very awkward silence settled between us and I had no freaking clue what to say to her.

"Anyway, I was a little rough on you earlier. I don't know you and it wasn't fair to act as if I did."

She was apologizing to me? My normal self, the one that had been called an asshole thousands of times had a retort readily, but I couldn't say it. Not to her. Not now.

Maybe never.

I shrugged instead like some ah-shucks backwoods mountain man. "No biggie. I'm sure you're tired from your trip. There's nothing in the cabin unless you can find a bottle of wine or two, which you're welcome to have. I'll have a few things dropped off in the morning for you. Food and beverages. Okay?"

"You don't need to."

"Not a problem. Why don't I at least carry in your bags?"

I didn't need much light to read her expression. Utter fear.

"You already pointed out a couple of my faults, Bella, but I'm not a serial killer."

Maybe a mercy killer, definitely an assassin, but there'd been reasons behind the men I'd killed.

Her laugh was as nervous as a kitty cat. "I know that. I would appreciate your help." She unlocked the back so I could grab her things.

"You'll find, I think, three bedrooms upstairs. Pick any one you want."

She nodded before gathering Cally into her arms. I waited until she was inside before opening the hatch, standing back for a few seconds before grabbing anything. There were only four suitcases, none of them I'd considered large enough to hold enough clothes. There was a single stuffed animal and unless some were buried in one of the bags, there were no toys.

Even more startling was the long duffle bag positioned on the side. I recognized the look of it. After looking up toward the house and seeing no one, I allowed my curiosity to kill the cat. Snooping wasn't in my job description, but I had to know what I might have brought into the resort. Assassins came in all shapes, sizes, and genres.

My brothers would tell me I was still living in my past, but there was no way to avoid it. Not after everything I'd been through. I tugged the bag closer, immediately pulling the zipper. The contents weren't what I thought; no assault rifles or handguns and correlating ammunition. But the weapon was just as deadly when used by a skilled marksman.

A crossbow.

What in God's name was she doing with a crossbow?

"Whew," I whispered, lifting it from the bag for a few seconds. The damn thing was a professional model. Now I knew Miss Bella Winters wasn't who she said she was. I couldn't take any longer for fear of discovery. I hurriedly returned the weapon, zipping and grabbing all the bags. I couldn't pick and choose, or she'd become suspicious.

I placed them just inside, closing the door behind me. While I'd been in all the cabins at least once, it struck me all over again how much money my parents had invested. My father was many things, including an ex-Marine. He was also hiding more secrets than he'd wanted his kids to learn. I'd learned a long time ago how to recognize when someone was hiding behind a lie.

The three of us had stopped pressing our dad for how he'd gotten so much money, none of us believing he'd squirreled away money from a now dead and once corrupt organization. But the man was dying and the three of us had made a determination to let our questions drop.

That didn't mean I wasn't still curious, occasionally surfing the internet for any clues.

I headed for the fireplace, happy to see leftover wood. After opening the flue, I spent my time starting a fire. No matter how well insulated the house, the brisk wind could still cause a chill. It was funny that I didn't care about that at my own place.

Her approach minutes later was nearly silent, but I sensed her before she cleared her throat.

"You didn't need to do that," she said. The animosity was gone from her tone.

"Yeah, I felt like I did. It'll be cold." With the fire roaring, I stood.

"Thanks again for bringing in my bags."

"You don't have much." I walked closer.

She backed away. "I don't know how long I'll be away from… home."

The word was tough for her to say as if she didn't have a home. "Well, since you're on vacation, if you need anything, the town isn't too far away. You'll find most things there. Just beware of the weather. I think there's a weather station in the kitchen. They were installed in every cabin."

"Oh, okay. I got it." Bella wasn't going to be but so forthcoming. "You're limping. Is there anything I can do?"

"It's nothing. An old injury." Injury, my ass. I was lucky I had use of the one leg.

"Don't forget a heating pad will help and since I guess there are sporting goods shops around here, the cheap gel hand warmers work really well." She laughed. "I don't mean to intrude."

"Nah. It's fine. Good thoughts."

She nodded, but remained silent.

I took a step toward her again and she tensed. "Okay. It's time for me to leave you alone."

"Thank you for everything."

"No problem." There was something to be said for a pregnant pause in business, but not in this case. I found myself walking even closer, trying to corral my raging libido.

Bella was more nervous than before, still unable to look me fully in the eyes. "I just need a good night's rest."

When I was standing only a few inches from her, I expected her to bolt away like a terrified filly.

She didn't.

She finally locked eyes with mine and I sensed so much of her life had been painful. Well, I wasn't the man who could comfort her. "Thank you again. I really do appreciate all you've done."

Her repetitiveness indicated continued trepidation.

I'd been a man who hadn't been able to express any emotion but anger for so long that when I brushed my knuckles across her face, I was more shocked than she was. She didn't flee, didn't strike me with her hand. She looked hopeful, but not for a night of romance. One of peace instead.

I knew I needed to get the hell out before lines were crossed and something occurred we'd both regret. Sadly, being around her meant a loss of my control and a need that furrowed so deeply inside I was completely and utterly lost in the heat of the moment.

The moment I lowered my head, we both stiffened, but without thinking about it too much, I pressed my lips against hers. The electricity we'd already experienced was definitely still there, but the hesitation coming from two people who didn't know each other clawed at the surface. The taste of her was sweet, her slight moan jerking at the man inside of me.

Only a few seconds later, Bella pushed one hand against my chest. Not angrily. Certainly not because she was repulsed at my actions. Just because she was hurting from something that had nothing to do with me.

My gut told me that.

I didn't apologize although I took a step away. Her incredible scent lingered and would for some time.

The warm glow of the firelight highlighted a slight blush on her cheeks and that was the moment I felt like a shit. "I should go."

"Yes, you should."

Sighing, I headed for the door, stopping the moment I wrapped my fingers around the handle. "I think you're in some kind of trouble. I'm no hero, but if I can help with anything, just let me know."

"I'm in no trouble, Jagger. If you don't mind, stop butting in. I can take care of myself. I have for a very long time."

That was a kiss-off if I ever heard one. "Fine, lady. No problem. I'll try not to bother you. Enjoy your stay." Maybe my male ego was crushed or maybe I was just in a pissy mood, but I closed the door on my way out a little too hard.

CHAPTER 5

ella

The hard slam of the door made me wince.

Jagger was angry with me.

What should I care? Okay, so he'd provided me with a fabulous place to stay at least for a couple of nights. He hadn't hassled me about who I was and why I was here. I pressed my fingers across my lips, even laughing a little. I hadn't done that in so long and it felt good.

Just like his touch.

My mind shifted to a few additional naughtier visions, images that shouldn't be entering my mind.

However, the thought of seeing his body devoid of clothing left a slight flutter in my heart and a wave of heat in my pussy. I had to be exhausted. There was no other excuse for my thoughts.

But whew.

Rugged.

Chiseled.

Buff body.

What more could a girl ask for?

"What are you doing here, girl?" I'd been impetuous in my decision, emailing my resignation to my boss like some coward. I'd felt I'd had no other choice. Yet I kept asking myself: What now? I didn't have any answers. At least we were safe.

For now.

With Cally sound asleep, I headed into the kitchen, opening every cabinet and the pantry door. When I noticed a couple of bottles of red wine, I almost jumped for joy. Maybe the last thing I needed was alcohol, but my nerves were still on edge. Using my maiden name wouldn't mean anything to a man like Joel Brockford.

Maybe Susie would keep his sorry ass busy and he'd forget about me.

At least I could hope for miracles.

I tugged my phone from my purse, grateful to see I had internet service. Checking in with my bestie was at least a hold onto my past. The furnishings inside the A-frame cottage were incredible, comfortable with a flair of color.

One wall was painted a bright turquoise, which complemented the artwork adorning the walls. The leather furniture wasn't something you usually saw in a rented facility unless it was a posh hotel in the penthouse suite.

I'd stayed in a couple during my marriage, the vacations we'd shared meant for a king and queen.

But all of it had been a lie.

I eased down on the couch and the sadness of my ordeal almost overwhelmed me all over again. No matter how many promises I made to myself I wouldn't allow Joel to hurt me any longer, I'd resorted to extreme sadness almost every night.

The feeling of Jagger's kiss lingered as I dialed Esme's number. Even the heat of his body when he'd been so close to me had been a welcome change in the iciness I'd felt for months. Just to imagine for a few seconds what it would be like to have a man embrace me with passion in his heart instead of anger was an excellent reminder of why I'd left.

I closed my eyes, envisioning the kiss in front of the fire.

If only things had been different and I'd been able to let go.

That wasn't going to happen for a long time if ever. I'd learned my lesson about trusting a man with sexy dimples and a killer smile.

"Well, hello, sunshine," Esme said as she answered. "I was beginning to wonder about you. What took you so long?"

"You don't even know where I landed."

"So why don't you tell me?"

What was the harm in letting my best friend know where I was? She'd been a good friend for years, my maid of honor at my wedding. I obviously had trust issues because I didn't answer her right away. It was silly. No, my hesitation was ridiculous. Esme would never betray me.

"Some small town called Danger Falls."

She burst into laughter. "You ended up at a place called Danger Falls? You're pushing karma. Aren't you? You are one gutsy lady though."

I hadn't thought of it that way. "Maybe, but karma made my choice for me."

"At least you still have a sense of adventure. So, where are you staying?"

"A sinfully gorgeous cabin in the mountains."

"Wow. You spared no expense. Good for you. Now, you just need to find a hot man and everything will be better."

I almost choked. She almost always caused that reaction in me. The woman had no filter, which I adored about her. I'd learned a long time ago to keep my mouth shut, never making waves. Being noticed wasn't always a good thing, which was one reason I'd been shocked Joel had sought me out at a bar. I wasn't flashy and hated sexy dresses. It was better to remain in the background.

"You know what they say about getting under a man to get over one?" My bestie added insult to injury, which prompted a few sexy and totally inappropriate images about Jagger.

"Not in this lifetime."

"Then you'll die old and lonely."

"Why, thank you very much," I told her.

"I'm serious. There must be a hot dude where you're staying?"

I glanced around the living room, more impressed by my surroundings than before. I could only imagine what the views looked like in the daylight. One wall was entirely made of windows and wood beams. With the huge stone fireplace and raised hearth, I could seriously learn to relax.

"A few of them, but it doesn't matter."

The moment I made the statement, I knew I'd made a mistake. "You met a hot guy. I can tell!"

She was way too excited.

"He just helped me get the cabin. Nothing more. He's a grumpy bastard anyway." Why was I providing any ammunition to the woman?

"Uh-huh. I know you better than you think I do. Is he a dreamboat?"

The answer was a profound yes, but I refused to get carried away on her slow boat to China. "He's okay. But a total ass."

"You know what they say…"

"Don't you dare. I didn't leave town to hook up with some grumpy asshole."

"Me thinks you doth protest too heartedly."

"Stop it. I'm going to sleep now." After I consumed at least one glass of wine.

"Fine, but think about what I said."

"Never," I told her.

"You will die so lonely. So very lonely." We both laughed and I could tell she had more on her mind.

"Just say it."

"It's really nothing, but…"

"But what?"

"Just be careful, Bella. I don't want to see you get hurt again."

"I have no intention of allowing that to happen, girlie. I'll call you in a couple days."

"You better. Look, do you need some money? I know the bastard froze your accounts. I'll wire you some if you need it."

She had a trust fund she tried not to use so money wouldn't be an issue, but I just couldn't stand the thought of borrowing from her. "I'm okay for now."

"Are you sure I can't get my cousin to convince Joel he needs to unfreeze those accounts?"

A nervous laugh popped from my lips. "Just hold onto that thought."

"I will. Good night, girl. I'm going to remain worried. Call me."

"Yes, Mother."

I tossed the phone onto the couch, leaning back and trying to absorb what I'd actually done. My actions had taken courage and a little of the chutzpa that had been robbed from me. Just surviving wasn't an option. Neither was just building a new life. I'd done so a dozen times before. It was old hat.

Although with Cally in tow, whatever decisions I made would have her best interest at heart. Plus, I had to make money. Everything was so complicated: name, my credentials, everything.

Hopefully, time would allow me to figure out how to handle the huge mess.

As I closed my eyes, my mind played tricks on me as usual and I almost jerked up from the couch, certain he was in the room. As usual, the bastard won a small battle once again. A single tear slipped down my cheek.

What bothered me even more than being here alone in an unknown location was the sick feeling that something was coming, something dark and scary. Maybe I was certain Joel would make good on his threats.

But what if it was something else, something equally as terrifying?

 agger

"What do you mean you can't deliver?" I barked into the phone. I was furious I'd counted on a service that I'd considered sketchy in the first place.

"Have you looked outside, buddy?" Bronco asked. With a name like Bronco, one would expect him to be a linebacker or a hired gun. Maybe a bouncer. He had the deep, cigarette-laden voice, but standing at just five foot seven and weighing barely one hundred and ten pounds, he'd never win a fight.

He certainly didn't want to enter a boxing ring with me.

The thought had always made me smile. Today, I was pissed at the dude. "It's snowing. It does that in the mountains. So the fuck what?"

"So, it's called the storm of the century for a damn reason. I have two drivers out due to the weather, the wife of another going into premature labor. I got no one to bring your shit to the resort."

"I pay you top dollar." Somehow, I'd allowed myself to become involved with ensuring our deliveries were made on time. Hunter had managed to rope me into that duty two months before.

The asshole.

"Maybe, if I'm damn lucky, I can get that to you late today. But I ain't makin' no promises."

"Late today? Not good enough. After this storm, you and I are talking about your current contract." My signature was hanging up on people. I couldn't stand excuses or bullshit, which I was forced to experience more often outside of my former regiment. The world of hospitality was entirely different than what I was used to.

I stormed toward the window, throwing back the curtains. I'd managed to get the cabin that had obviously been decorated by a woman. Frilly curtains. Bold colors on the walls. I'd been in Danger Falls for months and all I'd managed to do was toss out the corny pillows and artwork of cows on the walls.

The goddamn curtains were next.

Yes, it was snowing. More than I'd seen since the mission I'd accepted in upper Alaska. I'd nearly frozen my nuts off as I'd waited for sign of the target. At least four inches were on the ground already, the fall rate about an inch an hour and expected to rise. It was nothing my Range Rover couldn't withstand.

I'd purchase the goddamn groceries myself. It was only a few miles into town.

My second cup of coffee left untouched, I grabbed my parka and keys, heading for the door. It wasn't in anyone's best interest to infuriate me this early in the day. I didn't make it to my damn vehicle before Hunter pulled up, barely getting the gear into park before jumping out.

"You headed to the resort?" he asked. My younger brother had adapted more than Shep or I had done, enjoying his work handling the restaurant and winery.

"After I run an errand. I wouldn't expect the produce delivery any time soon. Fuckin' Bronco and his shitty staff."

"Someone woke up on the wrong side of the bed. Does it have anything to do with that unexpected guest dropping in last night?"

How many times had I wanted to punch the smug look off the man's face? He chided me about everything. Sure, I'd done that to him when I was younger, but that was two plus freaking decades before. "I have shit to do. Are you here for a reason?"

His damn smile remained. "Shep mentioned the park rangers are real concerned about the storm with the wind speed and amount of snow we're expecting."

"And that matters to us why?"

"We need to keep the weather alert systems on. That's your baby. Plus, the resort is considered a safe haven in storms."

"Why the hell is that?" Yeah, it had been my idea to install a sophisticated weather system instead of the shit I'd found when we'd arrived. I hoped I wouldn't regret it.

"Because we have fully operational generators and the power goes out to half the town way too often."

I glanced toward the sky, the light pelting I felt indicating the snow was laced with ice crystals. "I'll be there in an hour or so."

"Good deal. I'll let Shep know."

Shephard wasn't our boss. We were equal partners, but he'd acted like papa dog since we'd arrived. Fuck him. I didn't need anyone looking over my shoulder telling me how to do my job. Hunter continued studying me, searching for answers I didn't have. He'd wanted to talk about our respective pasts and I'd shot him down every time. If he needed a shrink, he should hire one.

He knew I wasn't the comforting type. Plus, our secret missions were required to be kept private. Forever.

"Well," he said. "I'll get out of your hair."

"You do that." I didn't wait for him before hopping into my vehicle, starting and revving the engine. I followed closely behind his truck as he headed down the driveway, only turning the opposite way toward town. It was an exercise I didn't take very often. I went into town once a month to get supplies and no more.

I handled repairs at the cabin myself, spending my days off chopping wood or hiding in the mountains. I preferred being very much alone, only putting on a fake plastic smile when required. Being the controller allowed me to work in an office instead of walking the resort, but I still had been forced to deal with the staff.

They'd learned quickly that I wasn't a people person, choosing to stay out of my way whenever possible.

The ride into town would be treacherous for anyone without a four-wheel drive. The roads were slick and it wouldn't be long until they became impassable. As I made the last turn, heading into town, I realized just how important the Christmas holidays were to the townies. They went all out with decorations, a damn parade and Santa being a huge deal for the kiddies.

The resort was bad enough with huge Christmas trees and wreaths on every door. Seeing the huge fake Santas and reindeer everywhere, the main square lit up with thousands of twinkling lights was enough to make me sick. Danger Falls looked like a Hallmark movie on steroids.

I passed by the bakery, the old fountain store still serving ice cream cones in the winter, a quaint bookstore that was always busy, the farmer's market, which was still open even on a day like today, and the fish and bait tackle store run by two old-timer brothers. There was a smattering of small clothing stores, a decent hardware place, and plenty of delicious eateries where I'd never eaten a single bite.

Hell, other than going to Rutherford's General Store for

groceries, I could count on one hand the number of times I'd been in any of the other locations.

I knew where I was going, the grocery store the only one I shopped at. The manager usually gave me a quick wave before turning away. My gruff reputation preceded me, but the locals had become insistent on making me a part of the community. You couldn't walk anywhere without a few of them waving. Even if they didn't know who you were, they nodded in recognition, most offering a small-town smile.

Still, they liked to gossip about the dangerous Fox brothers, a notion stuck into their head after the local sheriff had called us enemies of the state in front of one too many people. The angry dude had been watching too many movies.

This was the kind of place where manners still applied, kids taught to respect their elders. Hell, I'd learned it was disrespectful not to open a door for a lady, schooled by the owner of the popular diner. Poppy Danfield had been around since the beginning of time, friendly to a fault to everyone, myself included. But her sharp wit and sassy mouth had issued a clear warning that if I wanted to be liked in this town, I needed to relearn my manners.

I tossed items into the grocery basket, already gritting my teeth from accepting the job myself. I had no clue what Bella or Cally liked. What the hell did a kid eat for breakfast or for a snack? I was standing in the cereal aisle when Denise Parker came over. She was the love of Shep's life, a park ranger with an attitude. She was damn good at her job, not only because she loved what she did. She'd also been a former detective in a big city.

I still had no clue what the hell she was doing here and what she saw in my brother.

"Stocking up for the big storm?" she asked.

I happened to notice her cart was filled with bottled water and dehydrated beef products. "I guess you're preparing for the apocalypse."

"Something like that. It's supposed to be a bad one." She was studying me carefully. "What are you looking for?"

I'd picked up eight boxes of kids' type cereal, grimacing at the sugar content. "Something a damn kid would eat."

Her sarcastic laugh was one of the things Shephard adored about her. She reached over me, selecting a box of Cinnamon Chex. "Nutritious and sweet. Is there something you're not telling me?"

She knew I'd glare at her since she turned her evil grin away from me.

"Just a guest who needs help."

"In this weather? Whew. I hope they know they're going to be snowed in for a while."

I nodded and took her suggestion, trying to move around her. "Yeah. I'll tell her."

"Jagger. You know Shephard really wants you to be his best man."

It had been a conversation I'd avoided. They were planning their wedding. I was happy for them, but I had no desire to be a part of the festivities. Sure, I'd buy them a present, but that was the extent of it. Being his best man seemed like the last thing my brother would want. "Tell him to pick Hunter."

"He doesn't want Hunter. He wants you."

I didn't turn around or say anything else. There was nothing to say, the subject between me and my brother. "Yeah, well, we can't all have what we want, Denise. It doesn't work that way."

"When are you going to stop feeling sorry for yourself, Jagger? You have two brothers who give a damn about you. Why don't you show them some love in return? At least some respect."

I'd tried to be more of a friend, especially to Shep, but our bullheaded personalities continued to keep us at arm's length.

I knew she continued to stare at me. She'd tried to become my friend, maybe because she'd be considered family soon enough. I had no interest and not because of her. She was a nice girl with enough balls to keep my brother on his toes.

I had my reasons and that was final.

She finally knew it was no use and walked away. I'd hear about it from my brother, but as with most things, I just didn't care.

After finishing my shopping, including grabbing a few bottles of wine and a couple of bottles of booze for myself, I knew it was time to get going. At least Bella and the cute kid would have enough food for at least a week. The number of items I'd purchased was four times what I had in my house if not more. The money wasn't the issue. Cooking for myself simply didn't have appeal.

On the way out of town, I noticed the small toy store was still open. Slowing down, I stared at the storefront window, debating if I should go in. It was impetuous of me to think I had any better idea what kind of toys a little girl would like than a box of cereal. However, I felt compelled.

As I'd seen with so many quaint towns, there was on-street parking. I found a parking place a couple of blocks down. The tourists were out in droves, taking pictures and enjoying the constant holiday music being piped from unseen speakers. With the snow covering the ground, I cringed as I headed down the sidewalk.

As usual, I was waved to by just about everyone, some recognition in a few pairs of eyes, but mostly, it was all about being nice to a stranger. I did my best to keep my head down. A chill shifted down my spine the moment I walked in. I must have looked helpless since a young woman appeared from behind the counter.

"Can I help you?" she asked. "You look lost." Her smile was genuine and she offered me an appreciative glance all the way to my boots. When I was younger, I would have toyed with a woman's flirtatiousness, enjoying the banter. Not any longer. The thought of a relationship left a bad taste in my mouth.

"I need some toys for a little girl." My voice sounded even rougher than before. Impatient.

She lost her smile. "How old?"

"I don't know. She's about this big." I placed my open palm about three feet or so off the floor.

The woman narrowed her eyes. "Well, if you don't know then I'm just guessing and could be totally wrong."

"I won't shoot you if you are."

For the first time, her gaze held a hint of fear, but she managed to blow it off. Yeah, I was being an asshole. Being in this town around these people had forced me to retreat further into my shell. What I knew and few others did was being an asshole that was feared by some and loathed by others was a much better alternative for everyone involved.

No one would get me to change, including some woman with an intent on brightening the world after saving it.

Or even one so beautiful I'd remained awake all freaking night long thinking about her.

Truth be told, I'd fantasized about her. Bella was refreshing to a man who'd given up on life. Still, I'd do my good deed and walk the fuck away. That was best for everyone.

I was a fuckup and caring meant suffering, which in turn would mean I'd create agony for others. No, it was better to be this way.

"I'd say maybe three or four. Let me gather a few items for you to choose from."

"I'll take whatever you got."

Her eyes opened wide and she blew out a heavy breath. "Well, okay then. Let me get your order together. It'll take a few minutes."

I had all the time in the world.

As I stood and waited, I couldn't avoid thinking about Bella. However, I had to get her out of my mind.

Nothing could happen between us. If it did, I'd place her in harm's way.

From me.

CHAPTER 7

 ella

Frustration.

Anger.

Sadness.

I'd experienced every emotion over the last few months, the darkest ones more concentrated over the last few days. My mind was still finding it difficult to process that Joel hated me to the point of ruining my career and my reputation. How and when had things gotten so repulsive?

I stared out the window at the snow, my jaw clenched. Thankfully, I'd found a box of PopTarts that hadn't been opened and a toaster. Cally was happy with her breakfast. But there was no other food to be found.

Baltimore had its share of snow-filled events, but given the fancy house I'd once lived in, the adjoining roads had been plowed continuously. The rich people could never be inconvenienced. This was entirely different, the light of day providing a beautiful but eerie reminder I was in the mountains.

Still, I'd need to find a grocery store if I had any hopes of lasting through the storm. I'd counted the money I'd managed to grab before leaving. The exercise had left me with a sick feeling inside. I'd been stupid not to stop at an ATM prior to climbing the steep roads. My fear that Joel had somehow managed to obtain access was the reason. He would have been able to trace the direction I'd headed out of town.

I was such a fool.

At least I could take Esme up on her offer, but only if absolutely necessary.

With my little girl happily munching and enjoying her coloring book, I was free to try to breathe. And think. And plan.

What in God's name was I going to do?

My phone chirped and I anticipated seeing Esme's number. Instead, it was Joel's. The bastard had found my new number for a second time. Shit. He'd likely coerced the woman in the business office at the hospital. Another mistake. I should have picked up a burner phone.

"What do you want, Joel?" I hissed.

"Is that any way to talk to your husband?"

"You're not my husband any longer. You ceased to be that the moment you stuck your dick into Susie. Remember?"

"I can't believe you are holding that against me, but last I checked, we're still married."

"Are you kidding me? Aren't you the biggest asshole in the world. Stop calling me. We are finished."

"You have my daughter."

"She's not your daughter."

"The adoption was almost final and wouldn't you know, my father knows someone who is ensuring the adoption papers are signed."

A wave of nausea hit me hard and immediately.

I was sicker inside than before. I'd stopped the adoption process almost immediately after we'd met with a divorce attorney. It was even in the separation arrangement. But I couldn't put anything past Joel. He wanted to destroy my life.

What had I ever done to him other than find the courage to walk out? I'd found out his father had insisted his son marry. Why I didn't know and had no care to find out. That's the only reason Joel had shown me any interest. I'd had enough of a pedigree being a surgeon I wouldn't embarrass him.

And I'd been stupid enough to fall for every line of bullshit he'd dished out.

"I'm going to tell you this just once, Joel. Stay out my life and my daughter's life. You will never get your slimy hands on her. Not for a meeting. Not for a visit. Nothing. Am I clear enough for you?"

He snickered. "You're clear, my darling. However, you seem to underestimate me. If you fight me on the custody, I'll do what's necessary to ensure the courts see how damaging you are to a young child in her developmental years. I'm just itching for everyone to see how beautiful you are in the porn film."

The entire video had been shot exactly that way. He'd planned on using it as blackmail or to keep me in line. My stomach lurched and it was all I could do to keep from vomiting. No. He wanted me upset. He wasn't going to win. I wouldn't let him.

"You cruel son of a bitch." While I tried to keep my voice down because of Cally, I was so angry I couldn't think straight. "Don't contact me again or I will talk with my attorney to get a restraining order."

I had no attorney.

He'd made certain I couldn't afford one. I'd talked to one who'd wanted ten thousand dollars up front before he'd speak to me. I didn't currently have ten grand. After I'd spoken with the second and the jerk had wanted fifteen, half laughing that I had a case to win, I'd all but given up. I needed space and time to figure out what the hell I was going to do.

With all the money I'd made, I'd placed my trust in a man who'd professed to love me and he'd fucked me over. Just like everyone else had in my life. I'd thought for once, one time I could let go of keeping so much control. Being a fool didn't look good on me.

He was laughing as I hung up.

When I heard a hard pounding on the front door, I was still in the throes of wishing I'd taken Esme up on her offer to hunt down and kill the man. With no one here possibly knowing who I was or what I was really doing in Danger Falls, I took long strides, throwing open the door.

"What are you doing here?" My tone was nothing but a bark, heavy on the sarcasm.

"I brought you some damn groceries. What does it look like?"

Seeing Jagger standing on the porch with his arms full was a reminder that I'd tossed and turned the night before. I hadn't been able to get him off my mind. I'd thought of nothing but Cally and methods of murder, so having a man show interest in me had thrown me. He was rough around the edges and arrogant, but he had a gentle demeanor underneath all that macho bravado he wore like a badge of honor.

As a bonus, every time I looked at him, his rugged appearance set my soul on fire.

He didn't ask if he could come in, he walked in. Or maybe I should say he wasn't going to let some girl stop him under any circumstances. With four full bags in his hands, I was surprised he made it into the kitchen without dropping one.

"Why did you do that? I told you before I can fend for myself."

"Yeah?" he asked, even grumpier than when I'd seen him the night before. "Well, you're doing a shitty job of it so far."

"Mama, he cursed," Cally giggled.

"I know. He's not supposed to. You can leave now." I kept my hate-filled eyes on him. To think I'd been so stupid as to accept his hospitality burned me deep inside. Men expected something for their... generosity. My God. I needed a lobotomy.

"Not until I grab everything else. Then I'll get out of your hair, lady. Don't worry." He didn't bother unpacking a single bag and I didn't offer to help including returning to his vehicle.

I was fuming. To some, it wouldn't make any sense, but during the last few months of living with Joel he'd insisted on having a servant handle all the shopping. That had meant I wasn't allowed to pick out anything I wanted for myself or for Cally. It had just been the beginning of his controlling mechanisms. It had been the same for clothing. I'd been forced to dress a certain way when not in scrubs. I could just kick myself.

When Jagger returned with four more bags then another four, I was fuming to the point of pacing the living room. Yes, I needed food and continued to remind myself of that, but his interference and not asking me what I wanted didn't settle well in my mind.

I told myself to let it go, that he was trying to be a nice guy until he walked in with bags of toys from some toy store. The label was written in red and while Cally had just started reading, her Spidey sense picked up on the new toys within seconds.

Now I felt lower than low as her mother.

"Mommy! Look. Books. Stuffed animals. Yay!" She was jumping around the room, pulling out one toy then another. What was I supposed to do with that? Tell her no, she couldn't have them?

She grabbed a stuffed koala bear from a bag and I bit back tears. They were involuntary and unwanted, but my heart ached for her more than anything. I'd wanted a father figure for my little girl. I'd managed to hook an uncaring prick instead.

"Do you like them?" Jagger asked her. He was just as uncomfortable as I was, maybe even more so. It was obvious he had no experience around children.

At least he was trying.

I was still angry with him for being so presumptuous, but I wasn't going to dampen Cally's excitement.

"Mommy. Look. Look!"

"I see them, baby. Can I talk to you for a second, Jagger?"

He lifted his head, eyeing me warily. "Yeah. Go ahead."

"In the other room." I folded my arms, perhaps doing my best to hold in my anger. He swaggered in a few seconds later and my eyes were drawn to his stubbled face and clenched jaw. I could easily sit and stare at his eyes for a lengthy period.

"Look, I really do appreciate you doing nice things for me. I don't know how to thank you, but I don't appreciate you just assuming what my daughter and I would want or that we can't do it for ourselves. I'm a strong woman. I can do what I need to take care of my daughter. It has to be that way. I would have found the grocery store myself." My voice was cracking just a tiny bit and I hated myself more for it.

Showing any sign of weakness couldn't happen.

He had an icy glare, huffing a few seconds later. "How were you planning on making that happen?"

"I do have a vehicle. You followed me here last night. Remember?"

"You mean that pricey piece of shit with tires meant for a dry surface?"

I was shocked at his vehemence. "Piece of shit? That's a top-quality Mercedes." I was arguing with a man who drove a car worth twice what I'd paid? Yes, the Range Rover was older but still pricey.

"I call it like I see it."

"You're not a nice man."

"I never said I was."

"Then why did you assume I'd want groceries?" I asked, immediately realizing how stupid my question really was.

He grinned, but it wasn't a friendly gesture. "I thought your daughter might be hungry. I'm not a good man, but I won't allow a child to suffer because of her mother's holier than thou attitude."

Okay. Wow. That did it.

"Take them back. Every bag. I don't want anything you have to provide. Just tell me what I owe you for the cabin and dinner last night and I'll be getting out of your hair."

He was stupid enough to laugh. That only brought out the kind of rage I hadn't been able to act on with Joel.

"Have you looked outside this morning, sweetheart? The roads are about to close. You won't be able to get down that mountain with your tires, so you'll be stuck in a snowdrift somewhere or worse, you'll drop off the side of a mountain. My guess is since there are so many clueless tourists, all the guys with tow trucks will be mighty busy. I don't think you want to be stranded for hours. Do you?"

"Sweetheart?" That was all I'd gotten from his soliloquy? With my hands on my hips, I walked closer. I was instantly hit with the scent of his male testosterone, my mind almost instantly fuzzy. "I'll take my chances versus being forced to deal with a Neanderthal jerk doubling as a narcissist."

We glared at each other and the fire we shared was threatening to soften my anger. I refused to allow it.

The standoff might be considered ridiculous, but the last thing I needed was some do-gooder, even a snarly one getting in my business. With a single phone call, my nightmare would begin again.

"Come on, little princess. We have adventures to seek. I'll get your stuff."

"Mama. Where are we going?" Her little voice just about broke my heart. I sensed she was close to the edge of throwing a tantrum. Unwanted tears formed in my eyes. Lack of sleep and being in a totally new environment wasn't helping.

"I don't know yet, but we'll find some place special."

She grabbed onto the koala bear and there was no way I was going to take it from her. I'd tossed in a couple of books, her crayons and coloring books, and two dolls for her to play with. That was it. I hadn't been thinking clearly, terrified Joel would return to the house. My brain was still mush, but it was way past time to get my act together.

"Don't do something stupid," he said.

"Don't you dare call me stupid. I will never allow that to happen." Again.

"I didn't call you stupid. You're one stubborn lady and you're going to get yourself killed."

"Watch me, big boy. I can handle just about anything life throws in my direction."

Jagger said nothing else, standing right where he was like some big, dumb statue. But his smirk remained and it was driving me crazy. I scurried around, gathering our things while he was playing the wait and see game. He didn't think I'd be nuts enough to head out in this weather. I could do it. He was wrong about my vehicle. It was rated excellent in the snow.

I thought so anyway.

I'd need to try.

Staying here. With him. Was a dangerous option.

71

After shoving my feet into my tennis shoes, I tried to shove aside all the possible issues that could occur. Including freezing to death. When we'd left Baltimore, it'd been in the fifties, sunny, and no mention of snow. Damn it. I was such a bad everything, including a mother.

"Come on. Let's get you finished dressing," I said to Cally. We raced up the stairs and since I was tickling her, she acted as if this was the little adventure I'd promised her. I shoved another sweater over her top, grabbing her jacket and putting it on before we went downstairs.

"I want to stay."

Now she was going to whine.

"This was just a little stopping point along the way, baby girl. We'll find the best place in the world. I promise."

"Daddy there?"

Daddy. I'd promised Joel I'd wait until she was eighteen to tell her she'd been adopted. I'd hoped she wouldn't feel any differently, refusing to look up her deadbeat biological father. Now it just didn't matter. I was a single parent and I needed to get used to it. "Mommy and Daddy are…" How was I supposed to help an almost four-year-old turning into an adult understand her daddy didn't really care about her any longer?

Maybe he never had.

"We'll see, baby girl. Now, come on. Let's roll."

"Yay!"

Thankfully, she responded to the phrase I'd used since she was a baby. She tumbled down the stairs as I carried the bags. And wouldn't you know it, she flew into Jagger's arms, giggling as a typical happy child would do.

He was as shocked as I was, the hunk of a man tensing since he had no clue how to react. I stopped right on the bottom of the stairs when he crouched down to her level, tugging on the collar of her jacket and whispering something to her I couldn't hear. From what I could see, she nodded a couple of times as if agreeing with him.

Another flash of anger rose up like a dragon ready to breathe fire. At least this time my common sense took over and I shoved her back into her lair. He didn't deserve my full wrath. He wasn't that bad of a guy, just insufferable.

And tempting.

A lump had formed in my throat and I had difficulty swallowing. When I finally did, I tried very hard not to look at him as I grabbed my keys and purse. "Come on, baby girl. Time to go. Tell the nice man thank you. What do I owe you?"

It was said tongue in cheek and he snorted enough for me to notice. "On the house, sweetheart. Damsels in distress are my thing."

If he wanted to annoy me, he was doing a damn good job.

"Well, thank you. You've done your good deed for the year. Maybe Santa won't bring you coal in your stocking."

Ouch.

I was on a roll and I hated myself for it.

We headed outside and as soon as I planted a foot onto the first stair tread, I realized just how slippery everything could be. With tiny pellets of ice and snow hitting my face, I remained determined to find a way to leave. Or maybe happen upon a cheaper hotel to stay for a couple of days.

My nerves were frayed, but turning back wasn't an option. This wasn't the first time I'd felt all alone and destitute, but it hurt the worst. I'd failed myself and my little girl.

I got her buckled up in the backseat, tossing our bags into the back and slip-sliding my way to the driver's side.

"You shouldn't leave, Bella. You're going to get stuck," Jagger said, his deep and very husky voice sending a series of dark jolts of current down to my toes.

"I can't stay here, Jagger. No, you can't understand."

"Nah, lady. You're right. I can't." He was leaning against the railing of the porch, his legs crossed at his ankles. With his parka open and his burgundy corduroy shirt unbuttoned, I honestly thought he was the sexiest man alive.

But it couldn't and wouldn't matter.

My goal was set, my mind finally shifting from one big foggy haze to reality. I would do this methodically, the new life something I could be proud of.

Eventually.

I refused to allow Joel to take away all I'd worked for.

Bastard.

All men were bastards.

That was the thought as I put the gear into reverse, attempting yet another getaway. It was funny that I'd held it together when I'd driven out of Baltimore.

This time two tiny tears slipped past my lashes.

CHAPTER 8

 agger

Women.

What was that thing I heard countless times? You can't live with them and… you can't live *with* them. As soon as Bella rolled down the driveway, I let out a deep breath. My teeth hurt from gritting them the entire time she'd confronted me.

The woman was bat shit crazy to think she could make it down the mountain in this weather. There was no doubt my ass would need to save her.

I closed the still open door to the cabin, not bothering putting a single grocery away. Both she and the little tyke would be back here in less than an hour. I predicted it and checked my watch.

Unless she drove off the side of a mountain.

As I tromped down the stairs, my chest tightened. Nope. I wasn't having a heart attack, but the feeling was just as constricting. Why the hell did I give a shit about Bella's wellbeing in the first place? It was beating the shit out of me. She was opinionated, mouthy, the kind of gal who would kick a man in his balls, and I had a feeling she had a damn good right hook.

I jumped into my vehicle, half laughing from the vision of what I should do to her given her wild and disruptive behavior. Turn her over my knee and give her the spanking of a lifetime. Maybe if she couldn't sit for a few days, she'd finally realize she was acting like a child. Why? She was obviously highly intelligent; it was clear as much as her beauty. So why risk her life and that of her child to run away?

Was I that terrifying?

I rubbed my shaggy beard as I pulled down the driveway. Yeah, maybe I was. In the months I'd been here, I'd let myself go. No haircut. My face hadn't seen a razor since I left Maine after our father's call. Being a hermit meant you didn't have to conform to what the public wanted.

In other words, I didn't need to please people. Hunter had told me that several times.

Bella was easy to trail, but I kept my distance. The last thing I wanted to do was to scare her so she'd drive irrationally. The roads were pretty damn bad and I was thankful to see at least she was driving with caution. But with every passing second, the snow was falling even heavier than before.

A sign caught my attention and I gripped the steering wheel with white-knuckle force. The curvy pass coming up in a half a mile took out some of the most experienced drivers in the rain. I should never have let it go this far. If I'd been a decent guy, I would have locked her inside one of the bedrooms somehow, even if it had meant barricading the door.

Yeah, the Neanderthal moniker stuck. At least it was better than the one I'd gotten doing service for my country.

I adjusted the rearview mirror, taking a quick look to ensure no one was on my tail. Fortunately, it seemed even the tourists had taken heed to the warnings, stay off the goddamn roads.

Not the feisty woman with hair the color of spun gold. Damn her. I couldn't speed up for fear I'd roll down the side of the mountain. I just had to take it slow and easy.

Not my style.

When she drove around the corner, I held my breath and opened my window, straining to hear any sound.

I didn't like what I was hearing, the noise enough to let me know her tires were starting to skid. Ah, fuck me. I would never forgive myself if anything happened to her. Sucking in my breath, I kept my eyes on the road, laying off the brakes as well.

I heard a squeal and a solid thud.

Then nothing.

Shit. Shit. Fuck. Hell and damn.

I rounded the same corner, willing the goddamn wipers to go faster. Even I could barely see a freaking thing. The second corner I rounded allowed me to breathe a slight sigh of relief. She'd almost driven off the edge. Honestly, I hoped she had no idea just how close she was. The slight thud had been a slow roll of her bumper against a tree.

That purposeful maneuver or act of karma had saved both their lives.

It was treacherous enough that it took me a few seconds to be able to pull over. With every move I made cautious, I stepped out, watching the road before crossing. Bella was fighting to get out and little Cally was screaming and crying from the back.

I moved within view of Bella, lightly knocking on the window. If the little vixen thought she was going to continue playing this game with me, she was dead wrong. This time, I would lock her in the room and wait down-stairs to ensure she didn't leave.

Not that her prized Mercedes was going anywhere anytime soon. It would take me a couple of days to get a tow truck out here.

Or at least I could tell her that, convincing my buddy at the tow shop to put her last on the list. I was also grateful her SUV wasn't in the direct path of a car. Not that it didn't mean some asshole would run into it. I would need to report the incident. She had no idea what kind of trouble she'd caused me.

Her door was only slightly stuck and with a few hard pulls, I managed to open it, immediately sticking my head inside. "Are you finished with playing games?"

Maybe I was a little harsh, but her holier than thou attitude had grated on my nerves.

"I'm not playing a game. This is my life."

"You're right. It could have cost you your life. You're coming with me."

Thank freaking God she didn't argue, allowing me to help her from her beloved SUV. Once she was standing, I headed to the other side, unfastening and gathering Cally into my arms.

"It's okay, honey," I whispered, trying my best to calm her down. She was clinging to me, her little nails digging into the back of my neck.

"Do you always play the hero?" Bella asked as she slipped trying to get to the back of her vehicle.

"I'm no hero, city girl. I'm just not interested in dealing with the paperwork if you'd driven off the side of a cliff."

Cally was calmer than before, still sniffling but at least no longer hysterical.

I'll be damned if Bella wasn't struggling to get the car seat out.

"We don't have time. The roads are becoming impassible. Grab your bags. We need to get the hell out of here."

"You don't understand."

"No, you don't understand. I risked my life to save yours." I turned toward her, giving her an even harder look than before.

She stiffened, but finally nodded.

"Be careful," I told her, easing the little girl into my backseat. "Stay put, honey. Mommy will be right here."

"My bear!"

"I'll get your bear." This was such a pain in the ass, but I felt compelled to save both of them. Even in boots meant for snow, I found myself sliding given the slope of the road. I managed to grab the toy and most of the luggage, grousing the entire time back to my Range Rover. After tossing the items inside, handing off the koala to Cally, I had to fight all the nasty, chastising words I wanted to say to Bella. I reminded myself the woman was going through something she had no idea how to handle.

I asked myself for the fifth time this morning why it mattered.

But it did.

With my passengers safe inside, I said a silent prayer I could turn around and get us back safely. It was a crap shoot at this point.

Bella insisted on riding in the back, not only comforting her daughter but doing everything she could to protect her child. The pained look on her face was just another reminder that she'd been through hell and back. I should know what that looked like by simply glancing into the mirror.

There was no hiding the effects of horrific events no matter how many smiles someone might be able to plaster on their face.

I managed to get successfully turned around, but even the tires I'd had installed after moving here were having a tough time making it back up the slope. Every time we slid even a few inches, Bella moaned.

Maybe the tough time I was having making it back would be a decent reminder weather had a mind of its own and couldn't care less about anyone's issues.

I remained tense as fuck and by the time I made it back to the cabin, my leg was aching like a son of a bitch. I had no pain pills, no way of soothing the ache that was always with me. From what I knew about the roads, attempting to make it to my cabin wasn't a good idea. If even possible.

It took almost an hour to get back. When I pulled up, I felt another strong need to berate Bella, but not in front of the little girl.

I cut the engine and neither one of us said a damn thing.

"Let's get you inside," I muttered and opened the door. She gathered Cally while I grabbed the bags for the second time. I watched as she settled Cally in front of the television, removing the little girl's coat and staring down at her with a forlorn look in her eyes. Since we had satellite service, the kid was able to watch something, at least keeping her occupied for now. While I wasn't much of a talker, I needed to have a chat with her mother.

It took a minute before Bella slipped out of her jacket, shivering although the fire was still going. She finally looked at me for the first time since she'd stormed out. "Thank you."

The two words were clipped and she immediately went into the kitchen. I debated keeping my jacket on, but opted against it. The thought of spending the day and possibly the night here wasn't on my bucket list, but I wasn't a fool either.

She was either refusing to pay any attention to the fact I'd walked into the room or didn't realize I was standing in the doorway. I watched her as she unloaded groceries, both admiring her diligence in her actions as well as mentally challenging her. What would force someone to leave all they knew, including friends and family?

"What did you say to Cally before we left?" she asked in such a quiet voice I was surprised at the difference.

"I asked her to be good for her mommy because her mommy loved her." You would have thought I'd offered a few million dollars to Bella by the way she looked at me.

The hit or miss of awkward tension drove me nuts.

"Are you going to help or just stand there like a damn statue?" she barked a few seconds later.

"There's the city girl I know and love."

She wrinkled her nose. "Just get busy before we lose some of the food. And I'm no city girl. Trust me."

"I didn't think you wanted me around."

"I don't, but it appears I have no choice. Right?"

Answering her was tougher than it should have been.

She lifted her head, her nose wrinkling again as she looked at my second choice of cereal I'd purchased before shifting her attention directly on me. "Well? You're stuck here. Aren't you?"

I walked closer as I shook my head, not in answer to her question, but because the thought of disciplining her still remained on my mind. I couldn't say I knew anything about Bella, but I gathered if I tried anything so forward she'd stick a knife in my back or worse.

"Yeah, it looks that way. Don't worry. I won't bother you."

She shoved the cereal and two other boxes of food into my arms. "I'm not worried. Just stay out of my way and I'll stay out of yours."

"I'm curious. Why do you hate me so much?"

"Hate you? I don't know you," she retorted. "I just… I can't handle dealing with anything else in my life at this point, Jagger."

"Look, lady. I could tell you were in need. Sorry I bothered."

"I don't need anything hot and heavy in my life." She shoved up the sleeves of her sweater as she pulled a carton of milk from one of the bags. "It's not you."

Then what the fuck was it?

It was the first time either arm was fully exposed. The number of dark and yellow bruises struck me hard, the wind knocked out of me. Or maybe it was the hellfire in her vibrant violet eyes that knocked the oxygen out of me. As soon as she realized what I was staring at, she turned around.

The marks were clearly from a man's handprint.

"What the fuck happened to you?" I demanded.

"Don't curse around my daughter."

"I'm gonna curse all I damn well want. Who did that to you?"

"What the hell are you talking about?"

I wasn't in the mood to fight with her or have her lying to me either. I moved past the island, wrapping my hand around her wrist and tugging on her arm.

"You're hurting me." There was instant fear in her eyes, her mind slamming into a real belief I was planning on hurting her.

Of all the horrible things I'd done in my life, my soul likely ineligible to reach heaven no matter how many good deeds I performed, I'd never hurt a woman.

While I softened my grip, I refused to let her go.

She shoved her other hand against my chest. "What the hell do you think you're doing?"

"Trying to protect your ass from doing something stupid. Shoot me because I give a damn if someone hurt you." I took another look before dropping her arm, walking away with the same attitude as she'd just given me. The bruises were deep and the way she'd winced indicated whoever had grabbed her had attempted to break her wrist. My gaze flew back to her face just for an instant. But it was enough to take in her beauty in an entirely different way.

Her hair was unruly and wet from the snow, her mascara smudged from a rough night. She was still in the same clothes as when I'd met her in the hotel, yet to me, she had a warm glow about her. She was a stunning beauty who didn't deserve whatever hand had been dealt to her.

"I don't need protecting!"

We were at an impasse again. Maybe we always would be.

"What you did was reckless and stupid."

She huffed. "You're calling me stupid now? You're batting a thousand, buster."

Yeah, I was. I closed my eyes, doing what I could to slide into another personality. "Who hurt you?"

"Nobody."

"Don't give me shit about some fall or ridiculous accident. I wasn't born yesterday. Some asshole tried to break your wrist and if he's someone from the resort, I will break his neck."

For only the second time her features softened. "You'd really do that?"

"Yeah, I would." I meant it too.

"You'd go to prison for someone you don't know."

Someone I wanted to know. Shit. I wasn't entirely certain what I was saying. "Answer that for yourself. I'm going to restoke the fire." I let her go entirely, but remained furious.

As soon as I started to turn away, she touched my arm. "Jagger. Wait."

"What?"

"Thank you for all you've done. I know I said it before, but I honestly mean it. Your kindness means more than you could understand. I just can't talk about what I've been through. Okay? I'm sorry I ran out and risked your safety."

I stood where I was, unable to face her again at this point.

"Don't mention it," I grumbled. "Just promise me you won't do that shit again. I might not be around to save your ass the next time."

"I promise."

"I need to call in the stranded vehicle while we still have internet service."

"Okay."

Promises. For more than a few reasons, I wasn't certain she knew how to keep them. While a part of me wanted to grill her about the son of a bitch who'd dared touch her, I bit back all urges to continue pressuring her.

The truth was that in my world, the less I knew the better. Getting close to her wasn't an option. But I'd need to drill into her pretty little head that she needed to remain cautious, even in a small town like Danger Falls.

I knew better than most what happened to people who let their guards down.

They almost never survived.

ella

With Jagger's touch and close inspection of bruises, I'd swallowed another reminder of why I'd run.

"You're not going anywhere, Bella. You belong right here. Unless you never want to see your daughter again."

I slapped him with everything I had, keeping the hate-filled glare I'd had since he'd barged his way inside. "You son of a bitch. If you ever threaten me, I will do everything in my power to have you prosecuted to the fullest extent of the law." I spun around, prepared to walk out.

The brutal snap of Joel's hand around my lower arm brought instant agony. Using horrific force, he jerked me around to face him. "You will never talk to me that way again." As he bent my wrist, I realized he was trying to break it.

"You're hurting me, you son of a bitch."

He twisted my arm, bending it at an awkward angle. Stars floated in front of my eyes. "You seem to forget how much worse I could do to you, Bella. Don't test me."

Horrible memories and images slammed against the thick armor I'd sheltered around my mind, the steel plates cracking under the pressure. The image of Joel's face as he'd laughed from my pain was almost worse than the anguish he'd forced me to endure.

I could still feel the tightness in my chest, including the ache from when he'd tossed me into the wall, watching me fall as he'd laughed. But the moment he'd kicked me in the ribs I'd almost passed out. At least he'd had his fill, leaving after that, not caring in the least if I was curled up in sheer agony.

I stood outside on the front porch in the frigid temperatures, watching the snow fall and trying to clear my mind. The sky was dark from the heavy snowfall, making the once bright atmosphere appear as if twilight had fallen when it was only two in the afternoon.

With every deep breath I took of the cold air, the tendrils of panic slowly began to fade away. My little tyke was taking her usual afternoon nap and I had a feeling with the excitement of the day and her tummy filled with chicken noodle soup and a peanut butter sandwich, she'd be out for a long time.

That was fine. She'd been my company and my reason for making it through the long, difficult nights, but right now I needed the solace both Danger Falls and the snowstorm had provided.

With a cup of hot coffee in my hand, I continued to try to process the events of the last few days.

Jagger had been on the phone when I'd walked out. He hadn't paid much attention to me since bringing me back. I could tell he was still angry that I hadn't followed his rules without question. I should have. Then again, I wasn't particularly good with taking anyone's advice. If I had been, I wouldn't be lost in a sea of hopelessness.

The bruises would eventually fade just like the ache in my arm had, but the ones in my soul would take a lot longer. Taking it out on Jagger wasn't like me. I could be opinionated, even caustic when the need arose, but I'd never been so spiteful to someone who'd done little more than try to help me.

With steam rising from the mug, I inhaled the rich aroma of the dark roast and tried to relax. There was something so peaceful about a snowfall, especially when it was fresh. I leaned my head against the column, staring out at the snow as if the delicate flakes would provide answers. Only I could do that, but at least while stuck in an insanely nice house with a gorgeous yet surly man, I could forget all about who I was for a little while.

The door was opened and a part of me hoped it was Jagger and not Cally, who'd bugged me about reading to her from almost the moment we'd returned to the cabin. With new books and toys, her little mind was already working over-time. I couldn't lie to myself. I wanted to find more out about Jagger.

Everyone had a story. I sensed his was a doozy, and not in a good way. He'd finally gotten comfortable enough to roll up his sleeves late in the morning. That's when I'd noticed a series of tattoos on both arms. He'd caught me looking at them, immediately turning away. My personality was such that his attempt at hiding them away only made me want to learn more.

Every piece of body ink told a story just like a brooding man's eyes did.

His scent of testosterone and the forest hit me first as it almost always did. He was by far the most masculine man I'd ever spent any time with. He looked even more so standing on my front porch without his parka on. His usual glare was filtered toward the covered driveway. With his hands in his pockets and leaning against the railing, he appeared almost approachable.

He was anything but.

We'd had tension between us before, but what I was feeling right now was much worse. He must hate me. "Have you lived here your entire life?" I asked for no other reason than that the quiet was starting to become suffocating.

His chuckle was filled with his usual animosity. How dare I ask such a question? I could almost read his mind. "Does it look like this is my kind of place?"

"I think almost anyone can adjust to their surroundings if they want to."

"Yeah, well, I don't want to."

"Why? Because the townspeople are boring? Because they're beneath you?" I hated that around him I easily turned sarcastic or worse.

Jagger didn't resort to his usual nasty retort. "When you've been stuck in small towns without running water and people dying because they don't have enough food, you learn to hate the cities and towns prospering pretty quickly. Decorations. Happy people. Laughter. Quaint little shops. The townsfolk take it for granted. They have no idea their entire life could be stripped away from them in a matter of seconds."

He'd offered so little in the way of words that I was struck by how profound they were. They were also a direct reflection of the pain he'd suffered. "Maybe so, but big cities highlight every day the amount of suffering just like any small town could. So many hurry about their day-to-day tasks in their expensive clothes and fancy watches, even walking by the homeless or those begging for food, choosing not to look or care. Their complacency and lack of empathy takes almost as many lives. Unfortunately, not their own."

He seemed surprised at what I'd said, a strange tightness occurring in the thick cords of his neck. When he slowly looked down at the watch I was wearing, I'd never felt so self-conscious in my life.

I twisted it around my wrist, forcing the metal band to dig

into my skin. "I'm not going to apologize for who I was up until a few days ago. I worked hard to get where I was."

"I don't know you, Bella. What I do know is that you're running and hiding from someone, not something."

"Aren't you doing the same thing?"

Now would be about the time he'd become extremely angry, his tantrums much better than mine.

"Maybe so, but up until recently, I served my country with what I thought was honor."

His choice of words seemed odd. "You were military."

"Army ranger."

"Then that is serving with honor. Why would you think otherwise?"

"When you witness unparalleled acts of brutality, you learn that often what's disguised as honor is nothing but a lie."

"Betrayal is very difficult."

He chuckled. Where I had coffee, he'd poured himself a drink, slowly sipping on whatever he was having as he returned his stare toward the front yard. "Yeah, very true."

"Losing trust in someone you thought you knew can be the worst feeling in the world."

"One hell of a wake-up call, but sometimes that's what all of us need." He threw back his glass and I felt certain he was going to suck down the entire thing.

He didn't.

"Living with ghosts isn't good for anyone," I whispered. It was something I'd tried to tell myself to keep from falling into a vacuum of depression. As with everything else I'd touched lately, I'd failed.

"Then don't."

Invisible claws continued to slice at my chest almost every time I started to drift into panic mode. Grief and rage were usually close behind, but at least on this peaceful day I managed to curb any outburst of sadness. I must have made a noise of some kind because I sensed Jagger was studying me.

"That ink on your arm. Military?"

"Some, not all. Just reminding myself I'm alive."

"They're very attractive on you."

"You should see the scars."

I tilted my head. "I'm sorry, Jagger. I really am."

"Lady, don't feel sorry for me. I deserved what I got. I'm not good company and I'll never be confused for caring too much about anyone. But what you went through pisses me off. Whoever hurt you needs a world of hurt coming in return." He started to turn away and I just wasn't ready to let him go.

Maybe I needed the company or the heavy, almost sexual bantering. It was better than the agonizing soul searching I'd been doing.

"He's not worth it. The worry. The anger. It's just tough to put it into perspective when I thought he was something else entirely. I just was stupid enough to find that out the hard way." I looked down, forced to watch the single tear plop into my coffee. How many times had I promised myself I wouldn't cry? How many nights had I done my best to avoid the nightmares?

What little I knew about Jagger was enough to know my tiny emotional outburst would be too much for his hard-hearted soul to accept. He'd walk away just like he obviously did with most people and anything difficult drifting into his world.

He was still standing there staring at me. When he shifted directions, closing the distance between us, my heart hammered in my chest. Blood rushed to my ears from the ringing that instantly occurred. The moment he touched me, I was struck with a blinding jolt of electricity rushing straight to my core.

I couldn't like him. I didn't want to. I certainly had no business thinking of him in the way I was, but the fire within was too significant.

"What, Jagger? Are you going to make fun of the weak woman who hides behind false bravado? Well, go ahead. I've done so several dozen times to no avail." There was a snap of annoyance in my voice. Butterflies had overtaken my stomach while my legs were shaking and not from the cold.

For a man who I sensed could be brutal and even violent when necessary, his touch was tender as he cupped my chin. He forced me to look into his eyes. The hard shell encasing them had cracked just a little, fading away some of his own hatred and mistrust of everyone around him.

"What I was going to say was that the kind of man who did that to you shouldn't be taking up space on this earth. He hurt you and that's just unacceptable. But you don't need him. You're the most beautiful and beguiling woman I've ever met. Don't allow yourself to think otherwise because if you do even for a second, then the pain he caused you will fester like a vile illness and may never be cured."

There was a shared look between us that words could never explain. I found myself leaning into him. The words he'd said meant more than I could make him understand. "Jagger. I don't know what to say."

"Then don't say anything. But I will tell you this. Whoever the jerk is, he better not come around here."

My throat tightened as much as it seemed my heart was doing. While there was a distinct flutter, my nipples hardening into little pebbles, my mind was telling me this was a very bad idea.

But he wasn't giving me the option of making that selection. As soon as he slid his hand to cup my cheek, he lowered his head. The first crush of his lips over mine was something I'd remember for a long time to come. He held our lips together, taking his time to open and close them as I pressed my hand against his chest. I struggled between clenching my fist around his shirt and pushing him away.

The scent of timber and citrus tickled my nose while the light taste of whiskey infused my senses. I was tingling all over from the moment, including the way his thick beard scratched against my skin. So much of me wanted to keep him at arm's length, but I couldn't do that.

In the last eighteen hours I'd felt more alive than I had in months. The foolish girl inside of me wanted to experience more. There was almost a strange sense of familiarity with being in his arms.

As the passion rose from deep within my system, he pressed his tongue past my lips. I was already lightheaded, the kiss something out of a romance novel. The dichotomy of his roughness and such a tender kiss continued to throw me.

A perfect snowstorm as a backdrop to a romantic setting.

A rugged man in faded jeans and a corduroy shirt.

A warm cabin filled with the scent of a roaring fire.

And strong arms holding me telling me I was the most beautiful woman in the world.

Even if he was lying to me, I'd needed someone like him to remind me there was more out there than jerks. He swept his tongue into my mouth as if he owned me. His possessiveness was comforting for the moment although it had nothing to do with my personality.

Jagger pulled me closer, rocking me onto my toes. I hadn't remembered the coffee mug was in my hand until I felt his body stiffen. When he pulled away, the single look of agony on his face drove a squeal to my lips.

"Oh, shit." I jumped back, slapping one hand over my mouth as my other remained slightly tipped. The rest of the blazing hot coffee trickled down to the porch, instantly melting the snow the wind had blown in from the overhang.

I'd managed to pour more than half down his back.

He didn't miss a beat, yanking off the soiled shirt from the back of the neck. The moment he exposed his chest, I bit back a moan. This thick material had hidden a chiseled body underneath. His shoulders were so broad, as if he was wearing football uniform shoulder pads. His chest was perfectly symmetrical, his carved abdomen a true work of art. And his arms? Not only did the gorgeous ink extend all the way to just underneath his beard, but the veins on the sides were a clear indication of how physically fit he'd become.

Not from days spent in the gym. I knew better. He was the kind of man who chopped wood as exercise, preferring hard work to steel leg presses.

My mouth had to be open just slightly since he gathered an expression of amusement just before his eyes darkened all over again.

Not from anger.

From a deep, dark craving.

"I'm so sorry. Let me see if I burned you," I insisted.

His chest was rising and falling.

"Turn around. Don't be stubborn. The coffee was really hot."

He did as I asked, but kept his actions slow and methodical, barely taking his eyes off me until he was fully turned around. I gently touched the area, thankful I hadn't managed to cause even a little bit of redness. As I stroked the area, tiny vibrations drifted all the way to my inner core.

The man was a magnificent specimen.

"I think your shirt saved you. Maybe I have a tee shirt that will fit you. Then I can wash that."

As he'd done before, he shifted around to face me, taking the cup from my hand and placing it on the porch. When he pulled me into his arms, he slid one arm under my legs, lifting me against his chest.

"What are you doing?" I asked, more breathless than I had been.

"Where's Cally?" His voice was rougher than before, deep in a husky vibe that fluttered directly in my stomach.

"Napping."

"Good." He almost kicked in the door in his hurry to get inside.

"You didn't answer my question. What are you doing?"

His heated gaze swept down to me. "What does it look like I'm doing, lady? I'm going to ravage every inch of you."

ella

Jagger had managed to prove me wrong about him by the way he gently eased me in front of the fire, taking his time pushing the coffee table out of the way. His eyes never leaving mine, he snatched the furry throw from the back of the couch, bringing it with him as he returned.

I moved onto my knees, fighting my nerves while darting quick looks toward the stairs. What little passion I'd shared with Joel had never occurred out in the open. Right now, I was hopeful Cally would stay asleep. My labored breathing reflected my concern, but as soon as he dropped down to his knees, I gave him my full attention.

Who wouldn't?

He wasn't the patient kind of man, but the way he was taking his time peeling off my sweater allowed a slight insight to his soul. I was nervous, more so than I thought I'd be. Sharing intimacy when I felt so bad about myself was much harder than I could have imagined.

He'd be able to see my scars fully, including the yellowed bruise on my chest. I closed my eyes, but he wasn't having it, touching my face with the rough pads of his fingers in a caring way.

"You're beautiful, Bella. As I said, never forget that."

Hearing his kind words almost made me break. I refused to allow that to happen just like he'd suggested I shouldn't do. I was stronger than that, more resilient than I'd thought I could be. While this wasn't a new beginning by far, it was a grasp at something I wanted. Just for me.

He rubbed the side of my face, brushing hair from my eyes before rolling the tips of his fingers down the length of my bruised arm. The same hard expression was there as before, but instead of demanding I tell him what happened, he lifted my arm, gently pressing his lips against my still aching skin.

I was struck by his softness, his method of making me feel more comfortable when my stomach was still in knots. When he reached around to unfasten my bra, I planted both my palms against his chest. The feel of his skin underneath my fingertips allowed another swoon to occur, raging fire beating through my bloodstream.

My breathing was still shallow as he managed to unfasten the clasp with only two fingers. I bit back a laugh from nervousness and excitement as he slipped one bra strap down then the other. My brain wasn't functioning on all cylinders. All I could think about was how thrilled I was I'd worn sexy matching lingerie. I'd done it out of spite and my need to feel pretty again.

He took a deep breath, mumbling words I couldn't understand before cupping my breasts. With small flicks of his thumbs, he teased my hardened nipples to the point a tiny moan slipped past my lips.

A slight smile curled across his lips from the sound, his eyes flickering up to mine. When he issued a growl, I did laugh. "You're a tough man."

"Tougher than some." He took the opportunity to pinch both already sensitive buds, his eyes twinkling when another moan erupted.

"Mmm... I can see that. Maybe you need to be controlled." I fingered his nipples in return, rewarded with a soft laugh that permeated all throughout my skin.

"Never, lovely lady. No one can control me." He flexed his fingers open on one hand, slowly allowing it to drift down to my stomach. The moment he tensed again, I knew he's caught a glimpse of the yellowing bruise but said nothing. For that I was grateful.

I was so nervous the movement tickled me. Feeling more uninhibited, I kneaded his chest muscles before daring to drop my hand to the thick bulge between his legs. The moment I squeezed, he rolled his index finger around my belly button. He slipped it just under the waistband of my jeans, shaking his head.

"What's wrong?" I asked, nervous as to his answer.

"You're wearing entirely too many clothes. I'll take care of that." He fumbled with my button and zipper, cursing outright at how tight my jeans were. They were still damp, making tugging them past my hips a chore.

But he managed, sucking in his breath the moment my opaque lace panties were in full view. "My, oh my. You're wet for me."

"You have a way of doing that." I was completely breathless. My voice was no longer my own, but almost as deep and seductive as his. Since he was undressing me, I was going to touch him the way I wanted to.

His jeans were slightly looser, but I still struggled with being able to wrap my hand around his thick shaft. All I could think about was how thick his cock was and the girth huge. My fingers were long, but his shaft filled my hand. I rubbed the tip, this time biting my lower lip to show him I could be a sinful girl.

With his chest rising and falling again, he gave me the kind of look that told me clearly I would never be in charge. He proved that by easing me down onto the rug, his wry smile remaining as he pulled off my tennis shoes. The hunk even glared at them before tossing them away. "Snowshoes, I see."

"Hey, they worked."

"Not for long. We'll go shopping."

He acted as if he could demand I stay for an extended length of time. "No charity. Remember?"

PIPER STONE

"Fine. Then you can work it off at the resort." Now he was tugging on my jeans and panties at the same time.

"Doing what exactly?"

"Have you waited tables before?" His teasing continued when he slipped my wet panties under his nose, breathing in deeply.

"In college, of course."

"Then it's settled. My brother handles all the restaurants and bars in the resort. You'll work for him."

"No fraternizing with the help. Huh?"

His grin was mischievous. "None. Now we don't have to worry about it." The deep vibrato of his voice sent a wave of explosive heat through every muscle.

Waiting tables. It was something to do until I could figure out a plan. "You're on."

"Good." With my clothes removed, he crouched between my legs, lifting and splitting them wide open.

Oh, God. Another surge of embarrassment rolled though me like a tidal wave. He was already like a wild animal, every sound he made guttural in nature. How long had it been since I'd been touched this way? For-ever.

A sudden jolt hit me. "What if Cally comes down the stairs?"

He lifted his head as well as a single eyebrow before yanking the blanket into his hand, pulling it all the way over him and part of me.

104

I had to slap my hand across my mouth again to keep from laughing hard. He was creative in his methods of fucking. Still, I closed my eyes until he blew a swath of hot air across my aching pussy. Holy hell, the sensations were more explosive than before. But the first drag of his tongue around my clit was enough to push me straight into an orgasm.

"Oh, my, you are... amazing." I wasn't even certain if he could hear me under the covering.

He chuckled from my statement and shifted a single finger into position where his tongue had been. The way he kissed both inner thighs was just a telling of what was to come. I was right. The man was obviously very hungry, darting his tongue past my swollen folds.

Oh, boy. My entire body tensed as another rush of excitement tore through me. Without being able to watch him, the experience was like being tossed blindfolded into the perfect moment of nirvana. With every swipe of his tongue and every thrust of his fingers in my tight channel, I left more of my old life back in Baltimore.

Maybe there was something special about mountain men and small towns. The thought bringing a much needed smile, I allowed myself to float away as he continued licking. He had a sense of my body, realizing exactly what made me tick. His licks became fast and furious only to be pulled back, bringing me precariously close to a slice of heaven.

I glanced toward the stairs, gasping for air as his actions became rougher. My toes were curled, my heels digging into the rug. I was even shoving them up and down on the surface while clamping one set of fingers around the blanket and another trying to grip the rug.

"Jagger," I croaked, barely able to find my voice let alone recognize it.

I'll be damned if there wasn't a little bit of comedian in him. He poked his head out from under the throw. "Yes?"

"Oh, don't stop."

"I don't plan on it." He resumed what he was doing, taking even more time to drive me crazy. Back and forth my emotions flew, but the ecstasy was rolling closer to the surface. Panting, I could feel a couple of beads of perspiration sliding down my face. Soon, I would be covered in it, the heat from his body and what he was doing to me the reason.

I was losing control, my body totally in tune to his actions and the man. How I'd been able to let go this much wasn't something I wanted to question for fear of shutting down. I simply smiled as the moment of pure bliss jetted into my system like rocket fuel. There was no pretense here, no way of fighting the joy he'd just provided.

Somehow, I managed to hold back a scream of sheer delight as he continued feasting, a single orgasm lasting for what seemed like minutes. I was tingling all over, my legs shaking from the tension I'd put them under.

He didn't stop for another few minutes, which drove me to a place of utter relaxation. I hadn't realized how much I'd missed a loving touch until now. I'd lied to myself for far too long, making excuses for everything. No longer.

The moment he finally emerged from under the blanket, wearing a devilish smile, I tousled his hair. He gave me a funny look before tossing the blanket aside and standing. That was the moment I was given a slight show as he finished undressing, even tossing a couple of looks over his shoulder to ensure we weren't being interrupted.

With his jeans finally disappearing, I took a deep breath and held it. Yes, all of him was a creation made by God himself.

"What's wrong? You like what you see?" His cock was at full attention, the sight of his balls making my mouth water.

"Maybe."

He nodded once before easing back to his knees and instead of lowering himself over me, he planted his butt down on the rug.

I pushed myself up on my elbows, darting my eyes back and forth across his. "Something on your mind?"

"Yeah, it has been for a few hours."

"What's wrong?" If he was going to start grilling me again on why I was here, I'd teach him a lesson on right versus wrong timing.

"Oh, nothing is wrong at the moment, but it could have been disastrous." He decided to grab my wrists, being mindful of the bruises while dragging me over his lap.

"What the hell?" My cry was a little too loud.

"I don't take kindly to being nice to someone just for them to almost die on snow-slickened roads after not listening to my advice. My damn good advice, I might add." He brought down his hand not once but twice.

I was shocked to the point I couldn't say a thing. What did he think he was doing, spanking me like I was a bad girl or something? "Jagger. Don't do this."

"You need this. Call it a reminder that you could have gotten me killed too." He smacked my bottom a few more times and I finally reacted, trying to climb off his lap.

He was quick to the draw, wrapping his arm around my waist and throwing his leg over mine. "Hold on. This isn't right."

I struggled to see what he was doing. When he grabbed his jeans, I whimpered. The moment he tugged on his belt, I wiggled even harder. He was going to use the belt on me.

"I didn't almost get you killed." But he was right. I hadn't wanted him to follow, but I'd seen his vehicle in the rearview mirror. The truth was that I'd wanted him to follow me. I'd hoped for it. That had placed his life in jeopardy.

Four additional hard cracks of his hand and the pain finally bloomed, kicking up a thousand degrees as he picked up the pace. He paused a few seconds, folding the belt in half. His eyes were glistening. The man was enjoying this.

With every crack of the belt, I was certain I'd either die from a fit of embarrassment or from the anguish continuing to blossom. I wasn't entirely certain which. More disturbing were the tingles of my muscles and the hard throbbing deep in my pussy.

I was sucking in my breath so fast I couldn't see straight. Tears even formed in my eyes, which was ridiculous. I couldn't be over some mountain man's lap, getting spanked with a belt. But I was.

The spanking continued, the whooshing sound of the thick leather all I could concentrate on. With his thick leg over both of my own, getting up was impossible, and my attempts to crawl away only served to grind my hips into his knee. At this point my pussy was heating up even faster than my bottom. When he finally stopped, he took a deep breath. That didn't bother me as much as the way he blew it out. I sensed utter satisfaction.

"You make me crazy," I told him.

His actions quick as before, he pushed me back into position on the rug's surface, planting his hands on either side of me. "Yeah? That goes double for you, lady. I've never been around anyone so pigheaded as you." He pushed my legs apart with his knee, taking his place between them.

"Pigheaded?" I demanded. "I'll have you know that you're the most bullheaded man I've met and I assure you that I've met some doozies in my life."

"Oh, yeah?"

"Oh, yeah."

There was no talking to him. He made certain of it by capturing my mouth as he pressed his entire weight against me. His cock was throbbing and I wiggled underneath him. The pulsing sensations were just as incredible as the man.

Even if he was infuriating.

The kiss was even better than before, more passionate and slammed full of the kind of longing few ever experienced. I wrapped my arms around his neck, fighting the slight sense of guilt, which was ridiculous. I didn't owe anyone but myself anything.

If Jagger knew I was questioning my judgment he didn't show it, taking everything he wanted from my mouth. He was a marvelous kisser. Maybe he was good with everything when using his mouth.

The wave of deep vibrations and white-hot heat was over-powering. I shifted under him again and he took the hint. He pulled his lips away from mine, taking several deep breaths as the twinkle in his eyes returned.

The moment he placed the tip of his cock against my pussy, I licked my bottom lip. The small sensual move wasn't lost on him. One corner of his mouth turned up just before he thrust his cock inside.

The electric sensations were nothing like I'd expected. They were wilder. The intensity was extreme, the sheer pleasure of the vibrations tearing through my system leaving me breathless.

Speechless as well.

I clung to his shoulders, arching my back as my muscles stretched to try to accommodate his huge girth. How could a man be this large? And how in God's name had his shaft fit so deeply inside?

He took a deep breath as he lifted his head toward the ceiling, finally letting it out ten seconds later. "Amazing." The single word was barely audible, so gruff in nature that I quivered hearing it.

The second he pulled almost all the way out, I fought the covers to wrap one leg around his hip. I was trying to keep him from leaving. I could feel it in my bones.

His grin returned, his nostrils flaring as he slowly lowered his head. His eyes reflected the firelight, shimmering with flecks of gold and bronze. I could get lost in them forever. He plunged in once again, grinding his hips back and forth.

We were both careful not to make too much noise, the blanket hiding very little of what we were doing. But as he developed a rhythm, I was no longer certain I could disguise my pleasure as anything but what it was.

With my other leg now wrapped tightly around him, I squeezed my thighs. He shook his head as if telling me I was a naughty girl. He also stretched up onto his palms, switching the angle. I was instantly tossed into every girl's fantasy.

I was able to get a clear look at him, longing to run my fingers through his thick beard. I wondered if he'd allow it or bite my fingers, The silly thought brought a laugh.

"What are you laughing at, wicked lady?"

"Wicked, huh? I don't think I've ever been called that."

"You didn't answer the question," he whispered gruffly.

"Oh, just looking at a true savage. Do you forage from the woods, cutting wood like a true he-man, maybe hunting for food?" Yes, I was stereotyping him on purpose, enjoying the mischievous expression and pinched brow. I doubted anyone dared tease him. I also had a feeling my ability to do so would be rare.

He was too much of a brute.

A controlling man.

A loner.

But for tonight, I fully intended on taking advantage of our close proximity.

What in the world had gotten into me?

Jagger's response was to flip me over, his efforts tangling our long limbs in the throw cover. He didn't seem to care as he cupped my breasts, using them to push me up to a sitting position. After another quick glance toward the stairs, I planted my palms against his chest.

The touch seared my fingertips and I pressed my knees into him. I also swished my hair across his face and neck.

"Be careful teasing such a beast," he warned.

"Or what?"

"Oh... You'll find out."

I refused to allow him to try, bucking against him as I started to ride his hips like I would a bronco.

He pinched my nipples, studying them as he twisted and plucked. This time, the hint of anguish was breathtaking. With his mouth slightly pursed, I was certain he was prepared to growl like a lion.

Or roar like a bear.

That's what he reminded me of, a lumbering grouchy bear.

When he lifted his arms, planting them behind his head, his smile changed to something I couldn't read. "Give it your best shot, city girl. I got time."

He was taunting me in a way I wasn't used to. While he tried to look bored, he knew exactly what he was doing, lifting his hips when necessary and giving me the kind of heated look that continued to scream of possession.

With the fire burning so hot, we were both sweaty under the blanket. I wanted to shove it away, able to bask in our naked bodies, but I held off.

Trying to be a good little girl.

Yeah, right.

He had no clue he was yanking my real personality from the depths of my being, shoving aside all the anxiety that had wrapped me in an entirely different blanket. One with heavy chains wrapped around it. Where it had threatened to pull me all the way under the deep waters of an ocean before, Jagger's brutal display of manhood had found the right key.

I hoped and prayed it lasted.

I could tell only a few seconds later I was getting to him as I ground my body against his. But he wasn't finished yet, rolling me back over once again.

This time, I laughed, especially when he struggled to free my leg from the tight confines of the heavy material. He finally yanked it out in the open, cursing under his breath to the point I couldn't fight my laughter.

"You have no patience," I told him.

"None. When I see something I want, it's mine." The smoky heat of his voice wrapped around my shoulders, the sound both comforting and undeniably sexy.

I had no doubt that was true.

After pulling my calf onto his shoulder, he remained on his hands to fuck me. The savagery was even more spectacular, the way he was thrusting with such perfect momentum lulling me into a bubble that I prayed wouldn't burst. His entire face was pinched, his muscles starting to tense.

I wanted this to go on forever, but my body was so in tune to his that I couldn't hold back a climax of my own.

Another fierce expression was right there for me to bask in as he peered down at me. I could swear he was waiting to let himself go until I did. As I'd done before, I wrapped my fingers around his massive arms. I held onto them briefly before raking my nails down both.

He cocked his head, giving me an admonishing look, and fucked me even harder.

There was no holding back with this man. No chance I could lock myself in a cage once again.

The moment I was set free, the most powerful orgasm I'd ever had consumed me. I was floating high in the sky, incapable of thinking clearly.

Not that I wanted to.

Who in their right mind would?

His soft animalistic grunts added to the primal atmosphere and his own personal sense of freedom. As he released, filling me with his seed, it was as if the key had been tossed into murky water.

Maybe the real Bella Winters was back.

If so, look out, world. She was one demanding bitch.

CHAPTER 11

 agger

Out of my frigging mind.

I'd fucked her.

A woman I barely knew, one with a cement block tied to her ankle. I could feel that as certain as I was breathing air.

Plus, she had a kid.

A child.

Yeah, this rough and tumble asshole of a man had lost his mind.

The only good news at this point was that the snowstorm had left the area, leaving a mess of the roads and solid surfaces in its wake. I'd left the couch, where I'd insisted on sleeping, donning the same clothes I'd been in and waiting until light to start shoveling the sidewalk and front porch. That had led me to the driveway, which some might say was ridiculous. With my seventeen-inch tires, I could successfully maneuver the Range Rover out of here, but I needed something to do.

I was a jerk, but not the kind to run out after the night of passion without saying a single word to her.

I'd heard at least two plows, their quick actions meant to keep both locals and tourists safe. It was still a gray and ugly day, but at least things were looking up.

The sound of my phone jarred me out of envisioning her tempting body.

Her.

Shit. I was having difficulty even thinking Bella's name. I shoved the snow shovel into the mound of snow and ice, yanking off my gloves as I continued grousing at myself.

Danny Marcos, the tow trucking company owner was on the other line, an Italian dude who'd moved from New York in his attempt to find a better life for his growing family. He was tough as nails, a former Marine like my brother. But he understood hard times, including being overseas in a war. That's why I got along with him so well.

We'd had our share of drinks at the local watering hole, commiserating over stories that were highly embellished.

I'd left a message the night before on his phone, providing a location for Bella's Mercedes.

"Yo, buddy. How's business?" I asked as I took a deep breath. The air was crisp, the views of the trees covered in snow another reminder of a freaking greeting card.

"Busy as shit. Tourists are idiots," Danny barked. "And what the hell are you doing with a Mercedes?"

"Not mine, buddy. Just a chick who thought she could leave the area."

"Well, her damn vehicle is snowed in, a plow almost burying it in ice and snow. It'll take me hours to get the piece of shit out of there."

I grinned. The man was as rough as they came. "I'll pay you whatever you need. However, do me a favor and don't bring it to the Wyoming cabin for a few hours."

He snorted. "Got yourself into some kind of trouble, buddy?"

"Nah. Just trying to keep a headstrong woman from sliding down the mountain."

"Ouch. How did you get that duty?"

Because I was a dumbass and craved every inch of her luscious body. "Just being friendly."

"You?" he asked, laughing as he usually did when he thought I said something stupid.

"Yeah, yeah. Just do as I ask. Okay?"

"Okay, buddy, but her vehicle is in a precarious position. One careless snowplow and poof, that expensive vehicle is toast."

I raked my hand through my hair, taking another deep breath of the frigid air. "I'll take my chances."

"You're trying to keep her here." His laugh was irritating as usual, but it was good to have a buddy who understood me, never berating me with questions.

"Funny dude. Go do your job."

"That's right. Santa is heading to the Foxhead Winery and Resort. Good times. I'm bringing my kids by later."

Great. I gritted my teeth all over again. "Just do your job, bud."

"I'll do my best. Talk at ya later."

I had just ended the call when my phone rang again. This time the annoyance was from my brother Hunter. "What?"

"Does someone piss in your food every day?" he asked.

"What do you want? I'm currently shoveling snow."

"I'm reminding you that you need to be here today. Full house."

"In this shit?"

Hunter could be the most irritating man in the world. "It's the holidays, dude. Or didn't you get the memo? Tourists love this shit. Snowstorm or not."

My mind shifted to the conversation I'd had with Bella. While my gut had told me she was hiding something significant, the fact she'd agreed to consider waiting tables while the shit settled alleviated part of my concerns about her leaving. "I've got a new employee you need to meet. She's going to be working for you, waiting tables."

"Now you're interested in hiring employees?" Hunter asked, a hint of his normal arrogance sliding into his tone. I was used to that, our conversations often going off the deep end from anger and frustration.

"She needs a job. She's a smart lady and my guess is that some of your employees didn't come in today."

With the restaurants being open basically eighteen hours a day, Hunter had been forced to try to hire additional staff.

"Fine. You're right. Is she experienced? Is she any good?"

"How the shit would I know? You just need to talk with her."

"You're bringing her by?"

Another deep sigh threatened to give away the fact I knew her. "I can. If you'll get off the damn phone and allow me to finish my job."

"Fine, grouchy pants. Do your thing. Just remember Santa arrives at two."

My teeth were now aching from how hard I'd clenched my jaw. "I'll be there. You just keep your end of the bargain. Got it?"

"Oh, I got it. You owe me."

I didn't owe shit to anyone, but I let it go. After shoving my phone into my back pocket, I resumed shoveling. The shot of electricity less than three minutes later wasn't as shocking as it had been the first two times, but it was just as disconcerting.

If the beautiful lady thought what had happened the night before meant anything other than feeling good for a change, she would be sorely wrong. I would never care about anyone any longer.

"Would you like some coffee?" she asked, although I was surprised she'd waited a couple of minutes to ask.

I wasn't going to respond, acting as if I didn't hear her, but I also wasn't as young as I used to be. The actions I'd been forced into had aged my body as much as the horror of survival had nearly destroyed my mind.

"Sure. I'll be there in a minute."

My minute turned into at least ten. At least the sidewalk wasn't a hazard zone, the steps clear of a single flake of snow until the wind started blowing.

When I finally walked inside, she didn't bother looking in my direction. She was busy reading to Cally from one of the books I'd purchased. It was tough not to stare at her as she animated every page. The moment she finally acknowledged my presence by slowly glancing over her shoulder, a feeling of guilt washed over me.

Why the hell should I feel guilty about anything? Bella was a big girl. As she'd reminded me several times before, she could take care of herself.

I stormed into the kitchen with heavy feet, finding a coffee pod in the Keurig machine waiting for me to press the button. When had coffeepots become an issue? I hated these things. But I pressed the damn button, the aches and pains requiring something to warm me up.

With the damn thing happily bubbling, I took two strides toward the window. I'd never been good at pillow talk after sex, the thought of romancing the situation nothing I could handle. But the way we'd been together, the incredible amount of passion had caught me off guard.

That wasn't a good place for me to be in.

With the coffee finishing slurping, I pulled out some half and half, freezing the second she walked into the room.

She said nothing at first and I didn't move. This just wasn't going to work. I was grateful the roads were being cleared. I had nothing to say to her. Not because I didn't want to, but because I had no clue what words I could say that would matter. I liked the girl. Maybe too much. That just wasn't a smart thing for me to allow to continue.

"Were you serious about the waitress position?"

"Yeah," I said without turning around. "I just spoke with my brother, who runs the various restaurants. I'll take you to the resort in a little while. You can have a chance to talk with him."

"What about Cally?"

I knew what she was asking. Why was conversing with her so damn difficult this morning? "The company has a daycare system free for employees and even guests can drop their kids off for a day or two when needed."

"Oh. That sounds great."

The awkwardness was worse than the day before. I still couldn't face her, returning to the window to survey the amount of snow that had fallen.

Maybe three or four minutes passed in silence. "I called the towing company the resort uses. Your vehicle should be back here later today."

When she didn't respond, I finally turned toward the door.

She'd left the room.

* * *

The ride to the resort had been just as awkward as the morning at the cabin. She'd had the same kind of issue looking me in the eyes, which was fine with me. Maybe there were no words that needed to be said.

After pulling into the employee parking lot, Bella stiffened.

"What's wrong?" I asked.

"It's just been a long time since I worked in a restaurant."

"What did you do prior to coming here?" I'd paid close attention to how adept she'd been in suturing Carlos' wrist. That took skill. Skill that she refused to acknowledge and it continued to nag me.

"None of your business, Jagger. Okay?" She didn't waste any time bolting from the vehicle, ignoring me as she chatted with Cally while getting her out of the backseat.

I waited a few seconds before climbing out, hating the tension we shared, but my gut telling me it was for the best.

Bella gripped her daughter's hand as we started walking toward the front entrance. When Cally noticed a group of lit reindeer as we were getting close, she pulled her hand free, racing the rest of the way.

"Be careful!" Bella shouted. "Look both ways, young lady."

A grimace remained on my face as we continued walking side by side. But before we were even on the front concrete pad in front of the doors, she turned to face me.

"Look. I need to say something," she said.

"Sure. Go ahead."

"Last night was… Well, it was wonderful, but I can't do that again. It's not me."

"A one-night stand?" There was no reason her push off should bother me since that's what I'd wanted in the first place, yet it did. I was the guy who ran away from any concept of a relationship. If a woman I'd fucked asked for us to exchange phone numbers or what I was doing the next night, I made a beeline for the exit. The fact she was ditching me hit me hard in the gut.

"That and being with a man in general. I have a new life to build and along with Cally, those are the only two things that I plan on concentrating on. I hope you get it."

I'd learned more about her former life with her single sentence. She wasn't just running. She had left her entire world behind. "Sure. I get it."

She seemed relieved. "Good. I don't want this to be… difficult."

Yet it already was.

She touched my arm and I'd be damned if the jolt of current wasn't enough to light up the entire resort. I shrugged it off, moving to the front entrance instead. I heard her exasperated sigh, but she'd drawn the line in the sand. Not me.

Her choice.

As before, I cringed the moment I walked into the resort. Seeing that more decorations had been added meant at least some of the staff had likely been snowed in and had nothing better to do with their time. Maybe I'd take a leave of absence until spring.

"Mama. Look!" Cally was pointing to a huge banner of Santa and his arrival time that also hadn't been there the night before. The little girl was jumping up and down. I noticed she'd dragged the koala bear with her, insisting on calling him Mr. Bear. For a man who considered himself all but dead inside, I'd purposely listened in on their conversations. Why? I wasn't certain, but it had been a nudge to try to keep my emotions in check.

Cally's squeal was loud enough that several people glanced in our direction, smiling at the sight of the happy little family. Something we'd never be.

That also included my brother Hunter.

From the goddamn smirk on his face to his swagger as he approached, I wasn't certain my decent mood was going to last through today.

"Jagger," he said instead of his usual asinine greeting. "Who's your lady friend and what about this adorable little angel?"

Who'd killed my brother and sent in a body double? "Bella Winters, meet my kid brother Hunter Fox. He's also the operations manager for the restaurants. This is her daughter Cally."

"And Mister Bear," Cally chimed in.

"Well, Mister Bear is mighty handsome just like you're a beautiful young lady. I'm also part owner, Bella. Don't allow my often jerk of a brother to mislead you." He held out his hand for a typical shake.

She eyed him the same way she'd done with me the first time. "I see the arrogance runs in the family."

"Ouch!" Hunter exclaimed, acting as if he was hurt. I was going to hurt his ass if he dared flirt with her like he did every other woman under fifty who walked in through the front doors. "I think I like her. I was told you're looking to wait tables."

"It's been a while, but yes," she answered. Her lies were no better than mine.

"It's going to be a shitstorm here today and I have several employees who couldn't make it. I'll introduce you to our sous-chef and hopefully the meeting will go well and we can get you started. Chef Zimmerman is in charge of every restaurant. Just know that she's overworked and under-staffed and has a mouth on her like a sailor."

"I think I'll like her," Bella told him.

"What happened to you hiring another chef?" I asked him in my usual disgruntled voice.

He'd been harassed constantly by both Shephard and me over the last couple of months. "Good help, like decent family, is hard to find."

"Mommy!" Cally tugged at her mother's jacket, not used to remaining in one place for so long.

"I'll have one of the employees take you to daycare so you can check out the place. Then we'll get started." Hunter glanced in my direction and I could easily tell he was putting two and two together. He was the puzzle solver, the brother who most liked to meddle in other people's business.

"That's great. I didn't know what to wear." Bella had jumped into a bloody mess without a single hesitation, but she was frightened of the concept of waiting tables.

I had to admire her spunk.

"You're fine, Bella. This is a snow day around here. I'm just thrilled we have an extra body."

A part of me wanted to remind my brother he owed me a huge favor, but I resisted.

Another awkward silence pulled me back into a level of utter darkness that I'd done my best to avoid. Going back to the danger zone, as my handler had called my mood swings, wasn't in anyone's best interest.

Hunter smiled, but I sensed his exhaustion. The Fox boys had taken almost no days off since the resort had been dumped into our laps.

Cally danced around the area, amusing herself while I stood alone with Bella.

"I need you to tell me how much I owe you. If I don't have the money then you'll get paid when my first paycheck comes through," she told me. This time, she held her head high as she studied my face.

"Does that mean you're staying in town?"

"Would you care if I did?"

The answer forming in my mind surprised me. "It doesn't matter."

"That's what I thought. I'll be here for a couple weeks anyhow, if that's okay with you, Mr. Grouch."

"Mr. Grouch. Mr. Grouch. Mr. Grouch," Cally mimicked.

Lighting into Bella wasn't possible, but I moved closer so I could answer her without anyone overhearing. "You can do what you want. I'll get you the total later today when I take you back to the cabin. Fair enough?"

"Fair enough."

We were at another larger line drawn in the sand and for the life of me, I wondered how we'd gotten through the night without killing each other. We were oil and water mixed with gasoline.

Hunter approached with another girl beside him. "Are we interrupting?"

"Not in the least."

"Sure looked that way."

"Just get on with it. I got work to do."

As he'd done for months, he shook his head since we were around employees. "Bella. This is Jenny Talbot. She'll take you and the little Miss Cally to the daycare and show you around. Just don't listen to half of what she says. She's a mean sort."

"Very funny, Mr. Fox. I just keep you on your toes," Jenny stated with confidence.

"Yeah, that you do. Run along, girls, so I can talk to the other Fox in the hole."

Bella gave me another strange look as if wanting to say something to me before taking Cally by the hand and following Jenny.

I started to walk away because I wasn't interested in hearing yet another lecture from my brother. He had no business talking when he hadn't bothered trying to face his demons. This time he grabbed my arm.

"What do you want, Hunter?"

"I don't want anything, especially from you. I just wanted to tell you that Bella seems very nice. I don't know what she's doing here and we can use the help right now. Thank you for the recommendation."

"It got her out of my hair."

"What really is going on with you? You never hated the holidays before. Why now?"

I got in his face, using the anger toward myself for my actions around Bella as an explosive backdrop. "What the fuck does it matter? You have a life you seem to enjoy now. Live it. Leave me alone." I jerked my arm free and half expected him to follow me after I started to walk away.

He didn't.

But his words I heard.

"Whatever is going on with you, I get. I really do, brother. But you can't allow the nightmares and tunnel vision, the cold sweats and the rage to keep you from living in the here and now. You just can't. Being locked up inside your mind will only drive you to madness."

I laughed softly. "It already has."

CHAPTER 12

 ella

Daycare.

It wasn't like I hadn't experienced dropping my baby girl off at the hospital's daycare dozens of times. She's spent countless hours with several kind and well-trained women who'd brought my daughter out of her initial shell.

However, for some reason leaving her with strangers right now hit hard, my stomach aching at the thought of leaving her alone.

"Don't worry, Mrs. Winters. Cally will be well taken care of. She'll have playtime and a nice lady is coming in to read Christmas stories while having a snack. And after our afternoon naps, we're going to go see Santa. Would you like that,

Cally?" Zoe Drake was down on my daughter's level, already making my little girl laugh.

"Yay!"

"It's just Bella," I told her. No more Mrs. anything.

"Bella. It's a pleasure meeting you and you can check on her any time."

"Thank you."

"Welcome to Foxhead Resort. You're going to love it here," Zoe offered.

"I think it's good to be here."

I returned to the corridor where Jenny was waiting. She was speaking Russian if I recognized the language correctly. She jerked iBuds from her ears when she saw me, laughing from the way I was looking at her. "Trying to get ahead in class."

"Russian?"

"Yes, tougher than it looks," Jenny admitted.

"I don't know Danger Falls very well, but I have a feeling there's not a huge Russian population."

She laughed and guided me down the hallway. "Not a single person. I want to be in the CIA traveling the world."

"Including Russia."

"Oh, I would love to visit Moscow."

"You do realize it's dangerous. Right?"

"As my papa always told me, you only live once. Only with risks both physical and emotional can we reach the sweetest rewards."

Her words of wisdom made me think about Jagger all over again. He was the most infuriating man I ever met and likely ever would. His coldness after the night we'd shared had been somewhat expected, but not to the degree I'd been forced to experience.

"What's it like here?" I asked, trying to ignore my thoughts and improper visions so I could find my way in a town I didn't know.

"At the resort or in Danger Falls?"

"Well, both."

"Danger Falls is the kind of place where our grandmothers grew up. Everyone is polite. Few people lock their doors. Everyone waves. Sadly, everyone knows your life story. And unless you like the outdoors, it's boring as hell," Jenny admitted. "I can't wait to get out of here. But since you have a family, the town will be good for Cally and her daddy."

"No daddy. Just the two of us."

"Oh, that explains it."

Wrinkling my nose, I glanced at her. "What does that mean?"

"Oh, nothing."

"Hey. Confess."

She laughed and at least I could feel a little lighter than before. More hopeful. Waiting tables was an honorable profession and could be very profitable.

"That's why Mr. Grumpy Fox was looking at you that way."

"Grumpy Fox?"

"Jagger. I mean Mr. Fox. With three of them it's tough to be polite. They can be… difficult."

She was choosing her words carefully around me.

"I don't know if I could handle three of them. Jagger is the grouchiest man I've ever known."

"Oh, he's a bear. Don't catch him when he hasn't had his first cup of coffee. That's my first warning to you."

"What's a second one?" I asked.

She scrunched up her face as if unsure. "I know. Be careful what you say at Poppy's Diner. The gossip girls are wicked when it comes to sharing every single thing you say, good or bad."

"Then I'll eat somewhere else."

"Then you'll miss the best cherry pies in the entire world. Yummy."

Jenny's enthusiasm made me feel at ease. "Well, I'll just keep my mouth shut then."

She smiled as we rounded a corner. "Do you know which restaurant you're going to be working?"

"No clue."

"Well, this is the bar and grill, a place where the boys tend to congregate. Between the microbrewery, the burgers, and the dozens of televisions, if any of the guests are missing their male significant others, this is where you can suggest they be found."

"I'll keep that in mind as well."

"We'll head to the coffee shop and bakery next."

"Do you have any idea why Jagger is so... dour?"

She gave me a look. "That's the perfect word to use for him. Dour. All three men remain very private. Shephard has a girlfriend, which has made him open up more, but don't let Hunter's jolly demeanor fool you either. Between Hunter and Jagger, I don't know which one is gruffer than the other. I heard all three were big time military guys in three different organizations. They turned assassins or something. I don't know how much of the stories are true. But I've seen their tattoos. Shephard was a Marine. I think Jagger was Army. Not sure about Hunter. They're good guys, just..."

"Damaged."

Her nod almost added another layer of regret to my actions. What business did I have in caring to any degree? I couldn't.

So I wouldn't.

"After the coffee shop, I'll take you to meet Chef Zimmerman. My final warning. Don't allow any insult she gives you to sink in. She's just over her head with the job."

"I've been warned."

As we walked toward the brightly lit coffee shop, I noticed Jagger out of the corner of my eye. He noticed me as well and for a few cold seconds, we stared at each other. Every cell in my body was suddenly on fire as they'd been the night before. He had that kind of effect on me.

The man refused to look away, but I wasn't entirely certain his thoughts mirrored mine. He did have demons, the kind that outranked mine.

I hadn't realized I'd placed my fingers over my lips until Jenny bumped me in the arm. "Mmm… I can see you two know each other. Be careful or he might bite."

My laugh sounded foreign and as she took me into the shop, I murmured under my breath.

"He already has."

* * *

I was shocked how time flew. I'd been given the whirlwind tour, introduced to the staff, and tossed a resort tee shirt and apron. An hour later and I was serving the late break-fast crowd.

Without knowing what the hell I was doing.

At least I was lucky in that everyone feasting on homemade blueberry muffins, strawberry pancakes, and Eggs Benedict to die for were in jovial moods. They didn't seem to notice I dropped a tray full of plates, spilled a drink on a customer, and almost got a bloody nose by running into a wall.

I'd performed sixteen-hour intricate surgeries without breaking into a sweat. But this. This incredibly busy day had shown me I was out of my element so far that I was close to space. I was also exhausted. When I looked at the clock, I realized it was almost four. How had so much time passed?

"Hey, Jenny. Do you think it would be okay if I stepped out to the lobby to catch a glimpse of the kids with Santa?"

"Of course not. We're at our slow point now so I'll cover your tables. You've been working your butt off helping me. I'm grateful."

I untied my apron, meandering out of the back toward the lobby. There were at least fifty kids if not more waiting to have their special moment with Santa. I was floored at their good behavior.

Maybe it was helping they'd been smart to have a kids' area set up with a cartoon playing and toys strung everywhere. Plus, four people were dressed as elves. They were handing out candy canes and other treats. I'd been in some of the finest resorts in the last few years and I was thoroughly impressed.

As I searched the area, I finally noticed Cally. She'd made a new friend already, another little girl about her height standing next to her. The two of them were jabbering away. Every one of the daycare workers was keeping track of them, watching every little move the kids made.

I resisted interfering, longing to see how my baby did with new surroundings.

"She looks happy."

The deep voice was right behind me. I immediately tensed and folded my arms across my tee shirt. It was my effort to try to keep Jagger from noticing the kind of effect he had on me. My nipples were rock hard.

"It's a little bit of a miracle. She's bashful around people usually." The fact she'd immediately taken to Jagger told me he had a good heart even if he fought it.

"She doesn't seem shy."

"Not right now, but she just doesn't like new places. It comes from her being in the hospital on and off from the time she was born until she was almost two."

I felt him stiffen even from where I was standing. Why I'd chosen to share something so painful and personal was beyond me.

"I'm sorry to hear that." He didn't ask why and I didn't know if he cared, but I almost felt compelled to continue.

"She had a heart defect when she was born. Several surgeries, sepsis, dozens of infections later and she became my little miracle. My survivor."

"Maybe she's just like her mom." Jagger stepped slightly in front of me, which allowed for a much better view. "I'm not prying. Your business. Your life."

"You might be right, Jagger. We all learn to adapt if we want to survive."

He huffed his answer.

About that time, Cally caught my eye, waving to me like the happy kid she was. "Santa was a good idea."

"Not mine."

"Not a holiday guy, huh?"

"Not a people person. Haven't you figured that out by now?" He tilted his head enough I was able to catch the hard expression on his face.

"I don't know about that."

"Well, you'll get it eventually." As he'd done several times before, he started to walk away. Suddenly, there was commotion coming from the entrance.

Several vehicles pulled up in a hurry, people climbing out and racing inside.

"What is going on?" I asked.

Jagger shook his head. "Stay here. I need to find out."

While he raced toward the front, suddenly Hunter was jogging through the lobby, another man who looked an awful lot like him following closely behind. I couldn't avoid my curiosity, moving around the Santa display toward them.

The sky was already appearing more ominous than before, the few glimmers of sun I'd noticed fading. I had a feeling we were in for another storm.

"What the hell did you just say, Denise?" Jagger asked.

The woman was dressed in a park ranger uniform, the label on her shirt indicating her job position. She was wet, her hair stuck to her face. As men flanked her side, they appeared the same. They'd been in the snow handling a rescue.

My gut tightened.

"A partial avalanche. There was a group of tourists on Danger Cove. They didn't get the warnings and were trapped. We might have one left out there. Shephard. It's bad."

"Why the hell didn't we get the warning?" Shephard asked.

"We were trying to get them to the hospital, but the rocks and snow blocked the only road leading there."

"Shit," Hunter exclaimed. "Where are they?"

"We had no choice but to bring them here. Maybe you have a doctor among your guests. No one is likely to die but a couple have lost a lot of blood. We need to turn your conference room into a makeshift clinic." Denise was exasperated.

I found myself walking closer even though the little voice in the back of my mind told me what I was thinking was a very bad idea.

"I have no clue if we have a doctor in the resort, Denise. We can try and find out." Shephard and Denise obviously knew each other fairly well. I could tell by their body language.

"We're not equipped to be turned into a hospital," Hunter insisted.

"We have to do something, Hunter. The backside of the storm is coming in. There's no way a helicopter will be able to get in and take the victims to safety." Denise was pleading.

I was sweating.

Jagger had his hands at his sides and I had a feeling he knew I was standing behind him. He turned toward me, taking two long strides until he was in my face. "I'm not trying to pry into your business, Bella, but if you're who I think you are, we need your help."

Suddenly, all eyes were on me, eight or nine people staring at me as if they knew exactly what was going on. "I can't."

Denise pushed her way through the others. "Are you a doctor? A nurse? An EMT?"

Why was this so damn difficult? I tried to shut it down, but the oath I'd taken to do no harm kept flooding the front of my mind.

"Bella," Jagger growled.

I closed my eyes. "I'm a doctor. A surgeon. Where are the victims?"

"Thank God! They're being transported in a couple vans. They should be here in five minutes," Denise answered.

After taking a deep breath, I allowed the woman I'd been to take over completely. "Listen to me. If you have a conference room, I need every six- or eight-foot table you have in the place brought down, chairs pulled away. All the lights on. I need stacks of clean towels and a water source. However many first aid kits you have, I want them brought to the room. As far as any instruments, I may need to borrow some from the kitchen. As long as they've been sterilized. Since I don't know what I'm dealing with, this will be dicey. Can you make sure that's taken care of?" I glanced at all three brothers.

Shephard nodded. "Of course. I'll rally some employees and have what you need brought in."

"Hunter. Will you make certain all the kids find another place to visit Santa? I don't want the victims brought in front of them."

"You got it. Zoe. Let's make a new plan. We'll go into the Cascade auditorium. It's much bigger."

Zoe nodded, immediately springing into action. "Okay, kids. We have snacks and Santa is coming with us."

I turned to Jagger, needing his help and support more. "I don't know how this is going to work, but I might need you."

I'll be damned if the man wasn't gritting his teeth like he was going to say no. "Yeah, I'll do what I can. I might know a thing or two about wounds."

I bet he did.

As the entire lobby went into a quiet frenzy, I questioned my judgment. Maybe this was the best thing in my life at this point.

A grounding.

A new beginning.

A girl could hope for the best.

agger

"She's something special alright."

Shephard's voice also grated on my nerves, but at least the man was right. "Yeah, she is."

"I thought she was waiting tables."

"She is. Or maybe she was."

"But she told you she was a surgeon?"

"Nope. She didn't want to." It was late, hours having gone by. While Bella hadn't been required to perform any surgeries, she'd been working nonstop for hours with a single short break.

"I'll tell her later, but share with her how grateful we are. Okay?" Shep asked.

"I will."

"We'll talk later."

I watched him walk off and sighed.

She already knew I wasn't anyone's hero, but I'd remained by her side, helping with getting additional fresh towels and dropping bloody ones into a hamper provided by the staff members. I'd also handled a few sutures under her guidance. There'd been six victims, one of the guides minimally hurt as well. They had no idea how lucky they'd been that the entire mountainside hadn't come down on them.

They were also damn lucky there'd been a doctor in the house. She'd even set fractured bones enough to stabilize them until the road was cleared and they could be taken to the hospital. With six of the seven already comfortable in rooms, the guide refusing any rest, Bella was finally hunkered over one of the sinks in the third kitchen scrubbing her hands.

The fact I wasn't a touchy-feely kind of guy didn't mean I hadn't noticed the tension in every muscle. She'd been on her feet since ten that morning, exhaustion already taking a toll on her. She splashed her face, the slight moan tugging at me.

Here I was standing like some fucking goon admiring her voluptuous body instead of offering her some TLC.

When she reached for a towel to dry her hands, there wasn't

one. I grabbed one from the stainless-steel rack, forced to move very close to her since her eyes were closed.

"Thanks." Her voice was devoid of any emotion as it had been with me the entire day. She was obviously still perturbed with my actions from the early morning.

Maybe I was as well.

She patted her face, drying her hands and tossing the rag before bothering to look me in the eyes. It was the first time since the trauma had begun.

"Thanks for your help today. I really appreciate what you did," she told me.

"Well, I couldn't walk away since you were barking orders."

Finally, she broke out into a smile. "I guess I was. Wasn't I?"

"Let's just put it to you this way. You could be a damn good drill sergeant."

"In the Army?"

"Yeah. Imagine every male recruit following your orders. Dozens of them."

She folded her arms and leaned against the sink. "I think I like that idea. Army ranger. I bet you've witnessed and experienced more wild things than I have. I'd love to hear stories."

Instantly, the tiny camaraderie that we'd developed felt strained to me, but I ignored it. I'd already told her too much about me, but her smile was driving me crazy. She was just trying to be nice. "You could say that. I'm sure the townsfolk will likely embellish on the glorious stories and scenarios they've created about me."

"Stop worrying about what they think. It's what you know about yourself that matters. Right?"

"Yeah, but they should learn to keep their fuckin' mouths shut." I headed for the door, but her light touch stopped me short.

"Jagger. Just like you weren't trying to interfere in my past, I wasn't in yours either. I was just making conversation since we seem to have a difficult time talking to each other. I don't know why, but it does bother me."

"What do we really have to talk about? You're some fancy surgeon here to get away from life for a little while. You'll head back to your life as soon as you've caught your breath."

"That's not going to happen, Jagger. I don't have that life any longer."

Her voice held so much pain I shifted so I could see her. We'd done everything possible not to learn anything important or life altering about the other. But it was apparent we were both fractured in some ways.

"I get it," I told her.

"I need to apologize again. I shouldn't have taken my shit out on you. You've been nothing but good to me."

The way her eyelashes skimmed across her cheeks was strangely attractive to me. What was I saying? Everything about her was appealing from her small nose to her full lips. Trying to stay away from her wasn't working.

I cupped her face, rubbing my thumb back and forth in lazy motions. "You are something special, lady. Whoever let you go was a flaming asshole."

At least I made her laugh. She planted her hands on my chest and rose onto her tiptoes, pressing her lips against mine. "You're pretty special yourself."

Her whisper tickled my neck. Without thinking, I wrapped my hand around the back of her neck, pulling her as tightly against me as possible. As I captured her mouth, the tenderness and passion we'd shared before came roaring back to the surface. I could kiss her for hours and maybe that's what I'd plan on doing.

The sweet moment was short lived as Zoe crashed the party, her voice full of terror.

"Thank God, I found you," Zoe said.

Both Bella and I looked around to see what was going on.

"What's wrong?" Bella asked, pushing herself away from me.

"It's Cally. She's... She's missing. She was right there and when I turned around, she'd walked out. I don't know how that happened. There were so many kids and they were hungry."

Bella flew by me, her face harboring the kind of terror I would feel if I was a father.

"What the hell, Zoe?" I barked at her.

"I didn't mean to lose track of her."

Shit. The woman was close to being hysterical. "Did you let others know?"

She nodded, tears falling down her cheeks. "People are already searching the hotel. Ten minutes have gone by."

"Okay. Just calm down. I'm going to look for her." I raced out of the kitchen. If I thought I could think like a little girl, I knew I was selling myself a bill of goods. The kid could be anywhere.

I ran into Hunter in the corridor, the look on his face telling me everything I didn't want to know.

"What?" I snapped.

"You heard," Hunter said.

"Yeah, I fucking heard. You need to hire new staff. We need to find that little girl." I pulled away from him, taking long strides.

"Wait. We checked everywhere. Every single fucking room where she could have gone in. She's not in the hotel, but it gets worse."

"What do you mean worse?" I was in his face in two seconds flat. "Talk!"

"Where's Bella?"

"Off looking for her. Talk to me or I'll beat your ass like I used to."

Hunter was beside himself, motioning for me to follow him. "I wanted to check with you first." He led me to a door that led outside to a small patio area. It was close to the daycare center.

"What the hell are we doing out here?" The snow was lighter but still falling, the wind dying down as well. But it was still cold as shit outside.

"Does this belong to Cally?"

When he lifted the koala bear I'd gotten her into the light, my heart sank.

Dear God. She'd left the building heading out into the snow.

Now it was my job to find her.

And I would.

* * *

"You can't fucking go out there, Jagger," Denise hissed. "You're not a ranger. You don't know the area. And it's dark."

"Like hell I can't, Denise. You don't know a thing about me. I do know the area, including every inch of mountains and woods surrounding the resort." I shoved my hands into thicker gloves someone had given me, thankful I had a stash of warm clothing in my office. That included heavier boots.

"Leave him alone, Denise. He's going to go and I assure you he is one of the best trackers I've ever met," Shephard told her. "I'm going with him too."

"Like hell you are!"

I glanced at my brother, giving him a nod. Suddenly, there were several people in the room, a couple of tourists included. All were determined to find the little girl before it was too late.

When Bella took long strides into the room with a coat in her hand, I felt the same damn way Denise did about the man she loved. No way was she going.

"Don't you dare try and stop me. Don't you dare!" she yelled at me as soon as she walked into the room. "This is my child, my little girl. You don't know all that she's been through. She has to be saved. You just…" She broke down into sobs and I pulled her into my arms.

"We'll find her, Bella. I promise you that we will find her."

I could feel Hunter breathing down my neck. He'd be the first to tell me that I couldn't make promises I couldn't keep. I'd been known for doing that my entire life. No longer. This was a promise that would remain solid.

I wasn't certain Bella was strong enough to survive losing her.

"You should know Cally has a heart condition." I was looking directly in Bella's face as I made the announcement. A part of me expected she'd be furious I betrayed her confidence, but she nodded, not angry with me at all.

"Then time is of the essence," Denise stated. "Looks like we're all going. David, ride with Jagger and Bella. From the reports I heard, you should be able to use the auxiliary road behind the resort. Cally might have been drawn there since the area is flat initially, but be careful. If you know the area, you know the drop-offs."

I wasn't used to or keen on anyone telling me what to do, but Denise was sharp and knew what she was doing. "Yeah, I got it."

"Rusty. Go with Hunter and Shephard. Do you think you boys can handle the resort's snowmobiles?"

Shephard gave her a harsh look. "I think I can handle it."

"I'll have the guides go with you. Anyone who needs flashlights let me know. We need as much light on the area as possible. I'll take the tourists with me. What are your names?"

"Jack," the largest of the group said.

"Mark."

"Thomas."

"You guys know each other?" she asked.

"Yeah, we work together," Jack answered.

"Then you know how to support each other. Let's get going. Stay alert. You will all have one walkie-talkie for the group. I don't have additional consoles. Check in every twenty minutes. We'll have limited time before…"

Denise shifted her gaze toward Bella. "We got it," I told her. "But I'm not coming back until I find her." I grabbed the walkie-talkie from her extended hand, checking to ensure it was working. Others did the same.

"She has her coat with her," Zoe said from behind all of us. "She planned on going outside."

"It's light and won't offer much protection," I told them. I wasn't certain if that was a good thing or not. Exhaling, I turned toward the frazzled woman. She'd been put through the wringer, her face pale. I suspected nothing like this had ever occurred in the resort.

First time for everything. Additional safeguards needed to be put in place. I gave Shephard a knowing look and he nodded. There were times my two brothers and I could communicate without using words.

Bella almost broke down again, but moved to the door, stopping long enough to bark to everyone else, "Are you coming? My daughter needs all of us."

Shephard moved in front of me before I could follow her. "This is a crapshoot, buddy. Just be prepared."

"No, brother. That's where you're wrong. I will find that little girl if it's the last thing on this freaking earth I do. Don't try and stop me." I noticed the look shared between Shephard and Denise, but I didn't care. I meant what I said.

I stormed from the room, easily catching up to Bella. I didn't quite give a shit whether David was right behind us or not. He'd either keep up or he'd be left at the resort. Either way was fine with me.

David found us in the parking lot, jumping into the back of my Range Rover. I grabbed a duffle from the back. I'd learned long before that keeping a go-to bag with flash-lights, batteries, rope, grappling hooks, weapons, ammunition, and even survival blankets was necessary. Since moving here, I'd upped the contents with bear spray, a couple of knives, a small hatchet, and a few other items including flags to mark the way.

I'd climbed a few of the rocks around here. That meant I knew how dangerous they were. With snow on the ground and on the slopes, they should be considered treacherous at this point.

A little girl in the dark would get lost easily and quickly.

With only a few people willing to go out on a night like this, the odds were against us.

Bella was now emotionless as I drove, but one of her hands was gripping the dashboard as if she was terrified. No doubt she was.

The road was partially gravel, which helped with the traction to a point. I made our first stop only a couple hundred yards in, jumping out along with the others. I grabbed flashlights and markers, along with forcing extra batteries into their hands. My flashlights were designed to withstand heat and frigid cold, but without light, people died.

"Stay in a close radius. Bella. Come with me," I told her.

"Not a chance. We need to cover as much ground as possible."

"Fine. Mark where you are going and leave them there. Got it? Ten minutes out. Ten minutes back." I stared at her and the ache in my gut grew.

Maybe in my heart as well.

"That's not enough distance."

"We'll go up another few hundred yards. I don't think she'd make it further than that. We'll revisit this area if we can. Just follow my lead. Trust me, Bella. I do know what I'm doing."

"That's my little girl, Jagger. If I place my trust in you, don't let me down. I can't handle it."

"I don't plan on it." I pulled out the walkie-talkie. "Jagger reporting in."

Others followed.

"How's it looking?" Denise asked.

"Treacherous," I finally said after a short delay.

As we took out, my instincts were telling me we were already too late. I couldn't say that to Bella but at some point, she'd need to listen to me.

The twenty minutes were up too quickly, neither David nor Bella returning immediately. When they did, I was furious, but said nothing. Those who'd never tracked before had no understanding that disorientation occurred very quickly.

"You need to follow the rules." I issued the order in a much harsher manner than I should have. Damn it. The moment I highlighted Bella's face with the flashlight, I could tell she was ready to tip right over the dangerous precipice of emotions. "I'm sorry. We just need to keep a clear head." I tried to choose my words carefully. "Navigating this mountain is confusing to most. Myself included. It's easy to get lost in the daylight. Stay focused and we'll all get back in one piece."

"What if we can't find her?" Bella's voice was much smaller than I'd heard before. What scared me the most was that somewhere inside of her big, beautiful brain, she'd already accepted the idea her daughter wouldn't return.

That wasn't a fucking option.

Maybe if I continued thinking that, the ending would be a happy one.

Maybe...

CHAPTER 14

 agger

Another hour.

Snow still falling.

Temperatures dropping.

Hope diminishing.

We were on the higher slope, one more dangerous than the lower portion.

Both David and Bella were exhausted, Bella pushing herself, but I sensed she was completely numb at this point. We were back together in a group, no one from the other search teams having found anything. I was enraged, trying to keep my mind in the moment instead of mentally going through events in the past. It wouldn't do me any good and could possibly derail my portion of the operation.

"No. No!"

I took a deep breath as Bella dropped to her knees in the snow.

David shook his head. "It's useless."

"No!" she yelled, struggling to right herself. She lunged toward him, pulling back her arm as if ready to punch him.

"Whoa." I caught her arm just in time, wrapping my other around her waist and pulling her against what little heat my parka might offer her. "We're not doing this. Do you hear me?"

"We can't stay much longer," David chimed in once again. He wasn't winning any points.

Bella sobbed for a few seconds as she constantly swung her light from side to side. When she suddenly jerked from my arms, I aimed my light at whatever she was looking at. "There. There!"

I had no idea what she was pointing at, but she took off trying to run through the snow, falling once but continuing to press on.

"Bella. Don't go that way. Do not go that way!" I turned to David and yelled, "Stay here." I wasn't going to have the chance if forced to rescue both of them. Shit. She was headed for the blind drop-off. It was steep enough she would break a leg or worse.

"She's here. That's her shoe. That's her shoe!" Bella was yelling, the wind trying to muffle her words, but I heard them.

And I was sick inside, the rage increasing minute by minute. Losing her wasn't an option either. With my longer legs, I made some headway, but it was slow going given the snow drifts. "Bella. Just stop. Stop!"

But she didn't.

With the horrible sound of a limb snapping in two, I used every last bit of energy to rush toward her, swinging the light furiously.

She'd almost taken a tumble over the edge, stopping only because a limb had somehow broken her fall. She lay motionless in the snow, face down with her arms outstretched. Fuck.

Hearing footsteps, I was thankful David had ignored me.

"Oh, my God. Is she…"

"Do not go there," I snapped at him. "Shine the damn light right there." I pointed exactly where I wanted the beam. "And do not move."

"O-Okay," he said in a gruff voice. Hiking, mountain climbing, and tracking were entirely different. He'd had no full understanding of what he was getting himself into.

But I had.

I dropped into the snow, doing a controlled slide toward her. I'd left the damn grappling hooks inside the bag. My mistake, although there was no guarantee a single rock or crevice could be found to use.

"Okay, baby. If you can hear me, I'm coming to get you. Just don't move."

I don't know whether I should have thought of the slight lift of her head as my reward or a foretelling of things to come. I did my best to shut out my demons, inching closer. The rescue would be dangerous, but I didn't care at this point.

The truth was I had nothing to live for anyway.

With every foot gained, I felt a portion of the hill sliding away. I was almost to her, calculating the best way to bring her to the top. In daylight and in warm weather, doing so would have taken seconds. The weather hindered every movement, every single breath.

The moment David changed the beam's direction, the light shining directly down on my head, I was thrown into a moment of my past. The images were so vivid I was stopped cold, completely paralyzed. As I tried to get back to my safe zone, the words I'd learned to drag me there wouldn't come. I couldn't think of them.

"You can do it!" a call came from above.

I was the only one who could. I slammed the grappling hook into the rock, pounding it in as I'd done so many times before. But those had been for recreation. This was to save a life.

The recent snowstorm had drifted, leaving a single exposed area.

With the single member of my team hanging on to a failing rope, I had little time to react or think about my training.

I just reacted. The hook in place, I slid further down now within a couple of feet. "Tom. Listen to me. Don't move. I'm coming to get you."

"I can't hold on. I just can't."

"Yeah, you can. Just breathe for me. Okay? I'll be right there." The slope was still icy as fuck. What few places I had to place the toe of my boot were slippery as hell. Twice I almost fell, gasps from topside pissing me off.

There was no way two people could have handled the rescue operation even though our squad leader had insisted on it. I'd gone against orders while he'd been barking on the phone to someone from headquarters. There'd been no time to wait for bureaucracy.

"Hurry," Tom reminded me.

I was forced to struggle retrieving another hook. Going down much further was dangerous. Unfortunately, with the thin air, I was running out of time due to exhaustion, the heaving training in the worst conditions compromising my body's integrity.

But I pressed on, driving the hook into place. "Almost there."

We'd all been trained not to panic, but I sensed Tom was losing control. I managed another foot and was within reach.

"I'm going to wrap the rope around you, but you'll need to attach it. Can you do that?"

"Yeah, sure."

It wasn't a voice of confidence, but I had no other choice but to continue at this point. The wind was getting stronger, making the rescue that much more dangerous.

"Get up here!" the squad leader barked and others tried to calm him down. The only thing that mattered was getting my team mate to safety. I'd take the goddamn consequences for my actions, no matter what they were.

"Tom. Just listen to me. Don't fight me. I'm going to hand you down the rope now. Okay?"

"Yeah, I got it."

"The hook is on the end. All you need to do is strap it to the ring on your safety harness."

He made the mistake of looking down just as he reached up.

"Tom. Look at me. Just me. Tom. Tom!"

There was a split second as he glanced up at me when I knew his strength wouldn't hold. Everything was in slow motion as he smiled, still fighting to reach my hand. I managed to grasp his fingers, trying my best to get a better grip. That's the moment he started flailing.

"Tom. Tom!"

"Jag-ger." A small voice broke into the horrible vision and memory, jerking me back to reality. Her voice. Bella's voice.

Fuck me.

"You okay down there, Jagger?" David called.

I shook the cobwebs from my mind, hissing from allowing the horrible memory to carve even a second into the limited time I had to save her. "Fine. Going down."

I allowed myself to drop more than I should, rocks somehow finding their way through the ice and snow, tumbling into the abyss.

"Jesus!" David called from above.

Ignoring him, I reached her. "Listen, Bella. You can't fight me. We might only have one chance at this. Just lie still and I'll get you to safety."

Her moan meant she was still conscious. That was a positive.

I managed to wrap one arm around her. Now it was all about crawling toward the top. It was only two feet away, but it felt like ten at least. With the wind blowing snow in my face, I struggled just to slide her a few inches.

But I pressed on, noticing her long, gloved fingers were digging into the snow, helping in any way that she could. Inch by inch, we advanced. When we were close to the top, thankfully David was right there offering a hand.

As I pulled her safely to the surface, forcing us a few feet away, he let out a huge howl.

"Goddamn, man. That was incredible," he said, whooping into the air.

I let out a deep breath, still able to hear her slight moans. "You okay, city girl?"

She muttered something and I took another deep breath.

"We need to get her to the vehicle. Now. Keep that goddamn light shining so I can see the way." There was no time to waste. She was losing body heat.

I fumbled getting to my feet, but managed, taking another deep breath before lifting her into my arms. She felt so light, as if she'd lost half her body weight. As I cradled her next to me, she pressed her hand against my chest.

"Hold on, lady. I'm getting you to safety."

"My baby. I can't… leave my baby."

She was starting to drift off, the beginning of hyperthermia the reason. As David pressed down the slope toward the Range Rover, I continued to hug her close. I'd caught a glimpse of Cally's shoe. Time was of the essence more so now than before. I knew what I had to do.

As soon as we neared where the vehicle was parked, I stopped briefly. "David. Take the walkie-talkie. Tell the others we're bringing in Bella. Also tell them we found signs where Cally can be found."

Fortunately, the guy didn't hesitate, or I might have beaten him to death.

"Team. This is David. Bella is hurt. We know where Cally went."

While I could tell others responded, I had no clue what they were saying. All I could concentrate on was getting Bella back to the resort into warmth and safety.

I was as gentle as possible when I placed her on the passenger seat, trudging to the other side and jumping in while David climbed into the back.

The road leading down toward the resort was slippery, but I pushed it like I did with everything else. All the while, Bella was whispering words I couldn't hear, but were no doubt about saving her daughter.

I wasn't surprised the other vehicle pulled in beside me. As soon as I got out, I could hear snowmobiles heading in my direction. Everyone was returning and I was pissed.

With Bella in my arms, I stormed toward the back entrance to the resort, David opening the door so I could take her directly inside.

Several of the hotel staff were quick to respond, Zoe the one barking out orders. Bella was taken to one of the offices and placed on a couch.

"Blankets. She needs fucking blankets," I yelled to no one in particular.

"I'll get them," a male voice shouted out. I had no idea who he was and didn't care at this point. I dropped down beside Bella, brushing my knuckles across her ashen face.

I wasn't shocked when she opened her eyes, grabbing my fingers in her own.

"Save my baby." Her voice was weak yet determined.

How the fuck could I tell her the odds were falling minute by minute?

I had no plans on telling her something that would put her into a tailspin. Not a chance.

Both Shephard and Hunter barged into the room, pushing aside others. I noticed Denise's face, her expression telling me everything I didn't want to know.

Cally was likely not going to make it.

"What the fuck happened?" Shep asked.

"Bella took off on her own. Don't say it, brother. I don't need shit right now. We found Cally's shoe. I know where she went."

The blankets were brought seconds later and I stood so I could get out of the man's way.

"You could have died out there," Hunter stated, as if I didn't know that.

"We need to suspend the search," Denise admitted.

I shifted a harsh gaze in her direction. "Unacceptable and so the fuck what if I die? You got her covered, Zoe?" I asked.

"Of course. We'll take care of her."

I nodded and headed back to the door.

"You can't do this," Denise insisted.

I didn't answer, continuing my determined path.

"Where the fuck do you think you're going?" Shephard barked at me, as if it meant anything at this point. I noticed he had three walkie-talkies in his hand.

My hard stop was followed by the kind of sound most people should be terrified of. "To find the little girl." I didn't wait for any replies. I didn't care nor did I need them. After shoving my gloves back onto my hands, I took long strides toward the door, slamming my hand against it. The cold air was refreshing at this point and nothing was going to stop me.

"You're not doing this," Hunter said from behind me.

"Like fucking hell I'm not."

"Not without us."

Hearing Shephard's determined voice brought a glitch to my system and a moment of grateful relief. "Fine. Then get the fuck in. We need to do this."

"Together," Hunter said as he threw open the passenger door.

Together. Other than running the resort, we hadn't done anything together in one hell of a long time.

With the engine running, I barely waited until the two doors were closed before taking off. At least we had a basic location of where the girl had gone. How she'd managed to get up the slope was beyond me, but at this point, it just didn't matter.

Her life depended on our combined skills.

Nothing was said as I drove, skidding a few times, but correcting the wheel and the tires easily. At least I knew the strengths of my vehicle. The moment we were in position, I cut the engine and jumped out.

Shep and Hunter followed, but I was at the point of not caring. A walkie-talkie was forced into my hand that I immediately clipped to my belt.

"Where was the shoe found?" Hunter called from behind me.

I turned on the flashlight, scanning the area before I answered. "Four hundred yards up to the left."

"Come on," Shep told us both. "We fan out in a proximity, only staying a hundred yards away from each other. Talk, gentlemen. We need to do a uniformed search just like we were trained to do."

I managed to nod to both of them and took off, trying to jog and bogged down every step of the way. At least the snow had stopped falling, but an ice fog had formed. All the odds were against us.

Steps were taken, even long strides, but with every length advanced, it felt as if I was being pushed back from the wind. I wiped my eyes more than once, but kept going even though the ice crystals on my beard became a tough reminder I was losing the battle.

I kept going, searching every bank of fallen limbs and any cover that Cally might think of to protect herself with. What went on in a four-year-old's mind? I had no idea, but the instinct of survival was innate in all of us. I had to believe that.

"I got nothing," Hunter said into the walkie-talkie.

I didn't answer him, choosing to call out Cally's name instead. "Cally. Where are you? Come on, honey."

Only the wind howled.

Another ten steps were taken and I tried it again. "Cally! Cally!" I could swear I heard my brothers from the short distance calling her name as well.

Yet there was nothing.

Then...

Woof. Woof. Woof.

What the hell? A coyote?

"Cally?"

Woof.

No, it was a dog. A dog was barking. "Come on, buddy. Where are you? Talk to me." There was no way of knowing if the dog could understand, but I'll be damned if he didn't continue barking.

The dog's constant barking became a beacon of hope and a guidepost allowing me to follow his cry. "Come this way. I may have found her." There was way too much excitement in my voice even if the chances of finding her alive were slim to nil. Too much time had passed.

But I pressed on, following the dog's weakening sound. I knew when I was close, not only by his barking, but because I felt the little girl's heartbeat. I knew it.

I pushed myself through a thick group of foliage, shining the light. A dog's face appeared. Guarded relief rushed through me, but a tight tug at my heart followed. The dog led the way to a group of brush. I fought to shove it aside, the snow having drifted to partially cover it. By the time I freed an opening, the dog returned inside. The moment I flashed the light inside, I could see why.

The little girl had found the dog or vice versa, the pup doing what he or she could to keep her warm. I could tell neither were in good shape. My heart dropped when I touched Cally. She was so cold. The dog started barking again as if trying to tell me something.

"I found her. I found Cally." My voice broke up as emotions swelled within me. "You did good, puppy. You did real good." Her little body seemed so frail, so stiff as I pulled her into my arms, gently pulling us both free from the debris. But she was alive, her breathing rapid and ragged, but the soft blows indicated we hadn't lost her.

With the wind still howling, I held her close, rubbing my gloved fingers across her face. The dog was jumping and barking, which alerted my brothers to our location.

Shephard allowed the light to flow across us while Hunter came forward.

"Jesus, brother," Shep said. "You did it."

"The dog did," I told him. "I might never have found her. Cally's breathing is shallow."

"Let's get her into the vehicle," Hunter demanded.

"You drive. And the dog comes with us."

No hero, whether in animal or human form, would ever be left behind.

My brother was a damn good driver, avoiding losing control as I cradled Cally in the backseat. The entire way, the dog refused to keep his head from my lap, his nose on Cally's arm.

"No collar," Shep said as we neared the resort. "Likely a stray or dumped."

"Bastards. It's okay, pup. We got you too." I stroked his or her head, more grateful in finding Cally than I'd been with anything for a long time.

With the vehicle jerked to a stop minutes later, Shephard jumped out first, yanking open my door. By the light of the resort's back entrance, I could see the anxious look on his face.

We weren't out of the woods yet.

As the four of us and a hero dog walked into the resort, I was shocked to see at least a hundred people if not more standing in wait for our return.

Once they noticed the little girl in my arms, every single one of them started to clap, cheering for the heroes.

Only I felt like less than a hero than I had ever before.

With a group of people following us, I moved quickly down the corridor toward the office where Bella had been taken. The moment I walked inside, there was sudden hushed silence.

Bella struggled to rise to a sitting position, tears sliding down her face. She held out her arms, darting her eyes in my direction several times.

The dog pressed forward, moving to Bella's side while I kissed Cally on the head before gently easing her into her mother's arms.

There was another collective cheer from the crowd of guests before Shephard and Denise attempted to push them back. The dog was following closely behind.

I slowly lowered to my knees, offering a smile as the dog licked my face.

"You saved her," Bella said as she immediately shifted again in her effort to check her daughter's condition.

"I can only take partial credit. The pup kept her warm. He led us to her."

"No, you're my hero, Jagger."

"Nah. Not true. Not by a long shot."

She glanced down at the dog, allowing herself to smile before lifting her head toward my brothers. Her silent mouthed words of thanks nearly broke my heart. She continued rubbing her daughter's face, fighting tears and my gut told me she was praying the little girl would wake up from her slumber.

We both had our hands on the dog's head, his dark eyes confirming he'd been through the same horrible ordeal as well. In a few minutes of connection, something stirred inside of me that I'd long since thought dead.

"I think the pup is a she," I said absently.

There was a hard thumping of my heart that had nothing to do with adrenaline from taking risks or craving danger.

I closed my eyes, thankful both were alive until I heard a little voice that formed a jagged edge in my jaded heart.

"Mama?"

CHAPTER 15

"*Those who say that we're in a time where there are no heroes, they just don't know where to look.*"

—*Ronald Reagan*

Bella

I'd never really thought about heroes since I'd had none in my life. But I'd witnessed one on a horrible night when I'd almost lost the one good thing I'd ever really done since I was born. Maybe my friends would tell me otherwise, but creating a little lifeform like Cally had provided me not only with the unconditional kind of love that I'd never known existed, but also the strength to push forward with every decision and tough endeavor. The thought of losing her had almost wrapped a level of despair around me that I would never be able to abate.

Jagger was an unexpected hero, although if you really looked inside my psyche, my inner voice would tell me that I'd known what he was capable of. Even if he hadn't. Or maybe the better term to use was that he'd refused to be considered heroic under any circumstances. Why? I had my thoughts, but they were muddled like all my emotions.

A strong, resilient arm snaked down mine, a large and impressive hand shaking a glass of wine gently as a sinful offer. I lifted my head, resting it against the back of the couch and smiled.

"You read my mind," I told him. I accepted the glass, finally able to take a deep breath. I'd checked out Cally from top to bottom, much to her enthused debate. All she'd wanted to do was to hold the puppy.

Who had her muzzle and paws on my feet at the moment. With Cally's head in my lap, I was trapped, grateful for the drink. I didn't care what time it was. Time had no meaning at this point after what I'd almost lost.

Jagger moved toward the chair, plopping down and immediately staring at the fire.

There were so many things I wanted to say to him, words of gratitude that would never be enough, but he had to be the first to speak. It was an innate knowing.

"How's Cally?" He asked the question without looking at me. It was as if he was embarrassed about managing to save both our lives. Again.

"Bruised and banged up, but the dog saved her from hypothermia. As I told you before. She's a fighter."

"That's good. And as I told you, she's just like her mom." His smile was slight, but so genuine.

"What are you going to do with the pup?"

He snorted and took a long sip of his drink. Whiskey I was sure. "That's up to you. The pup is the real hero here. I don't think she has a home."

"Are you suggesting I keep her?"

"Maybe. But that's up to you."

The moment the dog moved toward Jagger, licking his face, he softened. The guy had a soft spot for animals. That was a real win in my mind. The only decent foster mother I'd had over the years had told me that I could never care for a man a dog didn't like. A dead giveaway. Maybe that had been my problem with Joel. I hadn't dog-proofed him.

Jagger sat rubbing the dog's head as if it was the most natural thing in the world. "You're really good with animals."

"They're very special creatures," he said with such reverence in his tone. Using a single finger, he rubbed the soft fur above the pup's nose.

"Where did that come from? A pet when you were a kid?"

His laugh was followed by a smile from a nice memory. "I mostly grew up on a ranch in Montana. I had lots of pets including horses and cows, chickens and roosters. My brothers and I had a dog when we were all under ten. Buck was a mutt, but sweet as could be. I'll never forget the little buddy sleeping in my bed."

175

"Nice memories."

"Yeah, they are."

"Thank you, for everything, Jagger. I honestly don't know what to say," I told him with a very quiet voice. Maybe I didn't want to disturb his train of thought or bring a barrage of chastising comments. Those I likely deserved for taking a risk. But he didn't understand how much pain I was in.

And not physically.

"You're welcome. How's your ankle?" He still didn't look over at me.

I stroked Cally's head and shifted my leg. He wasn't paying any attention. "Just a twist. Nothing more."

"Take it easy on that foot."

"Yes, sir. Any other orders you need to bark out?"

"What the hell does that mean?"

"It means you can't look at me and I don't know why."

Jagger finally turned his head. "You almost died. That bothers me. Okay? The shit didn't need to happen."

His stare was hard, but not cold like it had been so many times before. "Okay. Aren't you the one who told me that we always can't control everything?" We'd been through so many rounds of strained silence, but to me, this one was the worst.

"I never said that. I should be able to. I'm trained to do that."

Bullshit. Yet he really believed that about himself. "No, Jagger. If everyone got their way, imagine the chaotic world we'd live in."

"And we don't now?" He gave me a long and very heated gaze that tingled me to my toes.

"Not really. It may seem like it sometimes, but there could be worse things."

He huffed as if he knew I was dead right.

"You should keep the dog," he stated as if being definitive.

"What if she belongs to someone?"

"So put up flyers. I guarantee someone dumped her off like the shitholes they are." He finished his drink and rose to his feet, storming away as if angry with me. He'd been so tender before, so damn caring that I'd thought maybe his wall of armor had started to crumble a little. As usual with the man, I was wrong.

He returned with the bottle in his hand. "We need dogfood."

"Okay. We'll feed her some steak later. I know we have plenty." I tried to laugh it off since it was his choice, but he wasn't interested in breaking the mood. But I couldn't stand the wall built between us any longer. "You saved lives during your tour with the Army." I didn't really make the tangled words a question. My instinct told me I was right.

His half smile felt like a win in a battle I had no intention of losing. I was far too exhausted to pick at his wounds or his insufferable attitude.

He cocked his head in my direction again and the corners of his mouth curled in a way that sent heated shivers down my spine. Some would say he had no charm, maybe even no redeeming qualities, but they hadn't seen the side of him I'd been allowed to see.

If only for a little while.

After bringing the glass to his lips, he licked the rim before taking a sip. Maybe he was trying to entice me on purpose or just keep me on a short leash. Every scrutinizing look he offered was a direct reflection of the darkness he'd suffered.

As someone who'd also studied psychology in her effort to become a surgeon, every glance he offered made me want to learn more about his demons.

"Yeah, I did," he said. "Lost some too. Search and rescue tactical missions with a highly qualified team, but we made mistakes."

"You're trying to insinuate you made mistakes and you're having a difficult time living with that."

"Don't psychoanalyze me, Bella. You won't like what you find."

He was trying to convince himself of that fact. "Damn it, Jagger," I huffed, letting a few seconds go by. "Until what?"

"What do you mean?"

"I mean that it's easy to ascertain by your clipped answers that something happened during your military career that troubles you. Until you face what occurred, you'll never heal. That's just pointing out facts." On that damn mountain slope, I'd gathered a sense I'd lost him for a few seconds. I'd felt it, not seen it. Even now, the ugliness from something he'd thought about was eating at him. What in God's name had he been forced to endure?

His laugh was laced with the same bitterness I'd heard before as well. "Let's just say that when you fail to protect two members of your team, that takes away any chance you'll ever be considered a hero. Or it should. Forever."

"I'm sorry. I don't know what you went through, but when you join the military and are sent into a combat zone, I'm sure you and your fellow soldiers were told about what you could expect."

"Yeah, but try telling that to eager young recruits with stars in their eyes about the military."

Whatever had occurred had made him sour on his Army career. I leaned forward as much as having a sleeping child in my lap would allow. "Jagger. What you did by risking your life to save mine and my little girl's means the world to me. I won't ever forget or take it lightly. Just do me a damn favor and take the compliment."

Snuffling, he lifted his glass as if in a toast. "I know you're feeling better."

"How's that?"

"Your nasty attitude has returned."

Instead of becoming annoyed like I usually did, I tossed a pillow at him. He ducked and shook his head as I laughed softly. "You are a difficult man."

"I have my reasons."

"I'm sure you do. We all have reasons why we're soured on the world."

"Yeah? You're a brilliant surgeon making a ton of money, a beautiful woman with an insanely cute daughter and a full and amazing life ahead of you. My guess is you have an incredible and very supportive family who adores you, your Christmas holidays exactly like this freaking Hallmark card I live in. What reason could you have to hate the world?"

This was just another one of his efforts to push me away. I refused to let it work this time. "You're wrong. You're not as good at reading people as you think you are."

"Oh, yeah, lady? What am I so wrong about?"

"I don't have the perfect family. As a matter of fact, other than my daughter now, I don't have a family at all." The words I'd thought would be so difficult to say were easy around him. Few people know my background as it seemed to taint their view of me. I'd also had my share of those who felt sorry for me, acting as if I was damaged goods and wasn't capable of finding happiness. I thought I had. Maybe they were right.

"No family? They died?"

"You want to learn the truth?" My pulse was racing.

"Yeah," he admitted, but it wasn't to challenge me or attempt to shut himself down. He was genuinely interested. "Tell me."

"I never had one in the first place," I said. "My mother dropped me off right after birth into a trash bin outside a hospital. Thankfully a worker found me. It was snowing that day, or so I was told much later in my life. I was underweight, suffering from malnutrition, and close to hyperthermia myself. I was the one who found my birth mother after she died of a damn drug overdose, which means I have no clue who my father is and no one came to claim me. For some reason, I was never adopted, going from foster home to foster home until I was eighteen. I can tell you for certain that for some, our foster care system is fucked up. People want money, not children. I had my share of abusers."

I sat quietly for a couple of minutes enjoying my wine. However, I realized the intelligent, sexy, and aggravating man had goaded me intelligently into talking about my past. Damn him. I was even certain there was a tiny twinkle in his eyes. After he realized what I'd told him, his entire emotional status changed. He was like a ticking time bomb.

But dear God, I adored him for his reactions.

As I stared at the fire, I could feel the heat of his stare along with the vibration of his anger. "What the fuck?"

"Hey, I turned out okay. From an early age I was determined to have a better life. I studied hard, making straight A's in school. I worked three odd jobs all throughout high school and what money wasn't stolen from me I saved for college. Thankfully, I got a full ride, or I never would have made it through medical school without being mired in debt for the rest of my life."

At least I could laugh about my experience now.

"That's why family is so important to you."

I thought about his statement. "Yes, but I also learned the hard way that you can't pretend and hope someone loves you. It just doesn't work that way. At least with Cally, I feel something pure and sacred. You know?"

His facial muscles were contorted, his jaw clenched as I'd seen one too many times. "Yeah, I do. I'm sorry about the shit you went through."

"Don't be sorry, Jagger. I think we all go through our lives in a way that's deemed required. Maybe I'm being a little philosophical myself, but I think I'm finally starting to learn what's most important in life, at least in mine."

"What's that?"

The answer hadn't come to me until now. "Giving yourself grace."

He sucked in his breath but said nothing, yet I could tell he was thinking about everything he'd been through and the reason for his continued anger and hatred.

Maybe there was much more to being able to share a space together in utter silence than I'd given credit for. I wasn't antsy or worried he would explode into rage or bother me with additional questions. He was offering me space, much as I was doing for him. Yet I think we both felt more comfortable being around each other.

Even if the air continued to crackle with extreme electricity. A swarm of butterflies had taken up residence in my stomach, which allowed a rush of excitement where there'd been terror and fury only a couple of hours before.

I leaned my head back, thankful for our survival and for having my own private hero.

Even if they were words he didn't want to hear. I'd whisper them softly in his sleep so maybe one day he'd come to accept the kind of man he was meant to be.

A protector.

I closed my eyes, stifling a yawn. My little girl was even snoring. So was the dog. What in the world was I going to do with her? Cally had grown attached to the dirty yet brilliant and amazing pup. Her gold fur was matted, her big brown eyes full of sadness, but to me she was the most beautiful dog in the world.

As I stroked Cally's arm, I allowed myself to think about the strength and determination I'd seen in Jagger's face. He refused to let my baby go when he could have died himself trying to save her. He was... amazing.

Maybe I'd dozed off, but I suddenly felt a lack of weight on my lap. Startled, I peered up and seeing Cally in his arms all over again brought so much joy into my heart.

He pressed his index finger across his lips, shushing me. "I'll be back." As he walked around the couch, I instinctively knew he was going to take her to bed. The dog dutifully followed, trotting up the stairs after giving me a look, asking me if she was allowed.

I nodded in return.

Why was it this moment in time felt like the perfect family I'd always wanted?

Maybe I was a fool and reminded myself nothing was perfect. He'd placed my wine on the table and the fire was slowly dying down. I eased off the couch, careful putting weight on my strained ankle, but I wanted to see his reaction when he put her to bed.

It was suddenly very important to me.

I partially hobbled, but made my way upstairs, tiptoeing as much as I could toward the bedroom. The pup was patiently waiting as Jagger lowered Cally onto the pulled back sheets. There was something quite special about the way he tugged up the comforter, taking his time not to wake her, but making certain she was all tucked in. Only then did the savior dog hop into bed, placing her head on Cally's stomach.

Her tail even thumped gently as if thanking us for saving her as well.

I leaned against the doorframe, my arms folded and my heart full if only for a little while. It was tough not to make a sound as Jagger brushed his curled fingers down Cally's cheek. I did hear what he said to her and tears formed in my eyes again.

"Your mommy loves you, sweet Cally. You're a very lucky little girl to have a mommy like that."

I backed into the hallway so I could remain silent. Even breathing normally right now was hard. He'd untangled and unlocked so many feelings deep inside.

When he stepped out into the hallway, it was as if he'd

sensed my presence. He shoved his fingers into his back pockets, giving me a funny little look that I couldn't read.

"What is it?" I whispered.

"You can't follow directions. I wonder if you play by any rules."

"Rules? They bore me to death."

"Oh, yeah?" he asked as he closed the distance, taking me into his arms.

"Uh-huh." I rubbed my fingers through his beard, ending with tracing his mustache.

"Lady, I don't know what I'm going to do with you."

"What do you want to do?"

"Careful."

I chuckled as darkly as possible. "Being careful is no fun. Is it?"

His grin was absolutely adorable. "No, I guess not." He swept me into his arms as he'd done in pulling me off the mountain, taking long strides into the bedroom I'd chosen. He'd known it instinctively or he'd checked on me the night before. Either way I didn't care.

The feeling of being in his arms was incredible, almost as if it was meant to be. His eyes never left mine as he eased back the covers just as gently as he'd done with Cally, placing me on the bed.

There was no rush this time, but he closed the door in case Cally woke up, taking his time with everything. He stopped shortly after, taking a deep breath as he gazed upon my form. I wanted this crazy and rugged man to devour me and I think he'd figured that out given the way his nostrils flared.

As he advanced, I felt more lightheaded than ever. Maybe a small part of me was still a bit crazy, but I no longer cared. This felt right. His smile was devious in a dark and delicious way.

Earlier, he'd forced me from my wet clothes, insisting I put on the warm terry robe I'd brought with me. It wasn't particularly sexy, but at the point of shivering all over I hadn't cared. Everything he'd done after the avalanche had been to protect me and Cally, including trying to keep us warm and safe.

There was something about the way a man pulled off his shirt that told a woman a lot about him. Jagger was the rugged type, not caring about his attire in the least. He yanked the thick material from the back where the label was, pitching it to the floor as he'd done before.

I rose onto my elbows, which prompted a head shake from the mountain man, but his eyes remained twinkling. He knew better than to try to push me but so far.

He was right. I was as stubborn as they came.

He'd removed his boots on the front porch; however, I had the pleasure of watching as he unfastened his jeans. His nostrils flared as he pulled the dense, damp material past his hips. I could watch him do this for a long time, but I knew that wasn't an option.

The handsome guy might be able to learn a few new…
tricks, but he'd never learn patience. It wasn't even in his
vocabulary. I bit my lower lip when he finally exposed his
boxer shorts. They fit him like I'd never seen before. Cobalt
blue. I wondered what he'd look like in red ones.

Fire engine red.

My pussy throbbed as he kicked off his jeans, sliding his
thumbs under the elastic of his boxer shorts. His slight smile
was shifted to a dusky expression of lust seconds later as he
slowly lowered them down his muscular legs.

Now I was hot and wet all over.

There was no flair in his actions, no suave moment of trying
to impress me.

Just him taking what he wanted.

Which was exactly what I needed.

Him.

Every single inch of his hard body pressed against mine.

CHAPTER 16

 *agger*

Bella's hair glistened in the soft lighting. Her lush skin shimmered in the glow. After almost losing her, being this close felt entirely different. She had to be exhausted, yet the look on her face screamed of need and desire.

The fresh kiss of dawn, as my mother used to call it, wasn't far away, but neither one of us would sleep. Not with the other in the room.

As I planted one knee onto the bed, she rose onto hers. The look on her face was also different. She was no longer searching, but accepting the broken man I'd become. Maybe I had no right to think of myself in that way any longer.

The memory had almost derailed me. I'd sworn that would never happen again.

Maybe I also needed to stop making promises to myself because I sucked at keeping them. Like not allowing Bella to crawl under my skin. She had done that with the precision of a pro. Then again, I hadn't fought too hard.

I allowed my gaze to fall way too slowly down her lilac terry robe. It wasn't sexy on a hanger, but on her, a knapsack would look delicious. She had that way about her. Sexy in every moment.

Including when she had been saving life and limb herself earlier in the day.

"The robe is hot," I told her.

"It is a little warm in here." She fanned her face.

"That's not what I mean, lady."

"What do you mean?"

"I mean," I said as I reached for the sash, slowly untying it, "that you look damn hot in it, but you'd look better completely out of it."

She lifted her arms to the sides, allowing me to completely untie it. The look on her face was one I adored, full of mischief. "You think so, huh?"

"I'm a fortunate man. I know so."

I also craved seeing her smile and even after everything she'd been through, she managed to provide a bright one. How was this woman so resilient after everything she'd been through? Not just tonight, but during a good portion of her life. I had no idea, but maybe she could teach me a thing or two.

Right now, I planned on doing that for her.

Only as soon as I pushed the material off her shoulders, the robe pooling around her knees, she dropped onto her hands. Very slowly she crawled the few inches forward, using the tips of her fingers in sliding them along the insides of my thighs. "Well, I must admit you look better without clothing as well."

"Yeah?"

She purred like a kitten, the sound permeating my eardrums. With a single gaze she could turn any man on. But right now, she was mine. Maybe being possessive was in my nature.

My cock was aching, throbbing to the point I could feel it in the pulse on my neck. Yet she took her time, ignoring my shaft as she fingered my muscles. She'd already gathered I didn't like to wait for anything, but she was tormenting me on purpose.

I sucked in and held my breath, placing one hand on her head.

My other hand curled into a fist, pushing it into my mouth to remain as silent as possible. Damn. It was rough around her with what she was doing.

Bella was concentrating, finally blowing across my cock-head just once.

"You don't heed warnings very well."

"What warning?" she asked so innocently.

"To be careful teasing me. I'm a bear when I reach a point."

"I like your gruff and obnoxious side. And you've been a grizzly since I met you."

The woman also had a way of putting me in my place. The moment she wrapped her hand around my dick, I jerked.

"Did I hurt you?" she asked with heavy concern in her voice as she looked up.

"No, of course not."

"Then what?"

"Your touch causes burning heat. That's what. Too much for you?"

"No, just enough." She lowered her head once more, taking the tip of my cock into her wet mouth.

I'd experienced different and incredible sensations around her, electricity that could light a forest fire, but her mouth was so blazing hot every muscle immediately tensed. She just had something about her that kept me fully aroused even during the times she'd irritated the hell out of me.

I found myself fisting her hair, tangling my fingers in her long strands. My eyes were heavy as she managed to begin seducing me within seconds. Every nuance of her touch, every hot breath that washed over me was more enticing than the one before. I was forced to take scattered breaths, trying to put a heavy control mechanism on my deep longing. If I didn't, I'd take her like some Neanderthal.

Although that sounded pretty good right about now.

She took more of my shaft into her mouth, using her jaw muscles to clamp around it. I was shocked at her incredible skill, pushing forward and arching my back as a way of taunting her myself.

If she took the hint, I wouldn't know, although she did cup my balls, rolling them delicately through her fingers. The haze that formed over my eyes was just as fantastic as what she was doing with her mouth. This was just about the best thing in the entire world. A smile broke out across my face even as she squeezed my balls. The friction was exactly what I needed, my thudding heart taking over my pulse as well.

I couldn't stop my lips from twitching as hers were working to provide far more pleasure than a man like me deserved. But damn if I wasn't enjoying myself. The smile remained as she pumped up and down with her mouth, swirling that long tongue of hers like she was a fellatio expert.

Maybe she had a second career. No. She wasn't that kind of woman. She was a true lady with a bleeding heart made of gold. If she wasn't careful, I'd manage to tarnish it, but not right now. Every moan she issued I matched with a deep growl. My body started to convulse from the building pressure. I wasn't entirely certain I wouldn't blow my load without warning.

I didn't want that to happen.

But I couldn't stop her, the joy of having her mouth wrapped around my cock like a dream come true. I took over for a short period, pumping into her mouth as the sound of her sucking filtered into my fractured brain. It was like music even though I couldn't care less about songs or verses.

It was all about the woman she was and how she continually dragged me from my shell. I should hate her for it, but I felt more alive now than I had twenty years ago. Imagine that.

Her soft mews continued and she was still trying to take back control by twisting her hand around the base of my shaft. I was going to lose my mind from the extreme friction. There was no chance I could hold back much longer and lord, I wanted to drive myself inside her sweet pussy. Nothing was going to stop me at this point.

Even my own desire.

I gently but firmly pushed her away, issuing another growl as she licked her lips in appreciation.

"You taste divine," she told me.

Even those three words were enough to turn me into a bad man, not taking my time with her. "Mmm… You don't take warnings well at all."

"Nope." The way she popped the 'p' did me in. So playful. So stunning.

I desperately needed to thrust my cock inside. She didn't try to stop me as I tossed her onto all fours, immediately dragging my flexed fingers down her back. "I'm going to fuck you like every woman deserves to be fucked. Long and hard."

Her heavy breathing was her acknowledgment. She kept her head tilted over her shoulder as I kicked her legs apart, still rolling my fingers down to the crack in her ass. I used a single finger to finish, ending up driving it into her glistening channel. God, she was tight. More so than before.

And she wasn't going anywhere for a very long time.

I continued teasing her as she'd done to me, using a second and third finger as she shifted her hips back and forth. But I couldn't take it any longer, placing the tip of my cock against her swollen folds. Her long hair was begging to be used so I did, wrapping one hand around the silky strands.

The second I plunged every inch deep into her channel, she let off a ragged moan. Her body was shaking, her fingers clawing at the sheets. Yeah, this was heaven on earth. I started fucking her slow and easy at first, picking up speed as her juice slickened my shaft.

Bella did what she could, meeting every thrust even though I wasn't providing her with much leeway. But she was making me addicted to every inch of her body. I picked up speed, my fucking heart beating like a son of a bitch. Lights pulsed in front of my eyes. What was the woman doing to me?

The slight beating of the headboard against the wall made her giggle and me slow down. The last thing I wanted was the door to come flying open. I had a feeling the pup wasn't fast asleep just yet, every sound clear as day.

With a grin on my face, I did what I could to control myself, enjoying the sound of her ragged breathing. I sensed not long afterwards she was about ready to drift into a moment of ecstasy.

"Come for me, lovely lady. Come hard and fast." My words were clipped, the sound just as husky as hers had been. Her muscles continued to constrict and I gritted my teeth to keep from erupting in her.

Her moans were soft but penetrating, every sound pushing me into a strange haze.

"You are so... amazing," she whispered as her entire body tensed, a climax rushing in seconds later.

A part of me was relieved because I knew I couldn't hold back much longer and I wasn't finished with her yet.

Not by a long shot.

She clawed the bed, gasping for air and half laughing. I had a sense she wanted to scream from the pleasure she was experiencing. When she slumped as much as my hold would allow, I let go of her hair. However, the moment I teased her dark hole with my finger, she threw her head over her shoulder.

"What are you doing?"

"What do you think?" I grinned at her and she scowled, deciding it was best to torment me all over again. When she undulated her hips, pushing back against me, a wave of her incredible scent rushed into my nostrils.

The woman was going to make me drunk with her fragrance alone. I wasn't taking the bait, pushing my thumb all the way inside as gently as possible.

I did crave hearing her moans and was rewarded all over again with a series of them.

"You're so... bad."

"I thought you said I was amazing," I told her as I pumped in and out several times.

"I lied."

"Lying is a sin."

"So what?"

I shifted my cockhead against her asshole, taking my time pressing it inside just an inch at first. I read her body movements afterwards and paid attention to her soft moans. When I sensed her body had finally relaxed, I pushed two more inches inside.

The lovely doctor wasn't going to allow me to remain in absolute control. She drove her body against me, forcing my cock almost all the way inside.

"Oh, shit," she whispered and threw her head back. "That is fabulous."

"I'm glad you like it. I'd hate to disappoint." I pulled out, pushing in again. When I did it a third time, she arched her back. Everything about her was far too inviting. We might be stuck in bed for hours.

I used a softer rhythm this time, but I was still fucking her with a roughness to my touch. I was gripping her hips, thrusting mine forward. The warmth was invigorating, the softness of her skin enticing. If I could keep my stamina, I'd do this for hours, but I'd had a tight leash on my level of control for far too long.

Four more savage thrusts and I couldn't take it any longer, erupting deep inside.

Time would tell if this meant anything or if she'd bother

staying, but after saving her life, something had changed inside of me. Not just wanting her or needing her touch.

I wanted her to remain.

* * *

"You snowed in with that doctor of yours?" Shephard asked.

"She's not mine, Shep. Besides, I doubt she's staying in town for too long."

"I wouldn't be too certain of that. I saw the way she was looking at you."

"Only cause I saved her daughter." I'd returned to the front porch under the guise of taking out the dog, but I'd needed a little space. Not from her. I could have easily remained in bed with Bella if circumstances had allowed, but there was still work to be done.

Plus, my mind was creating an entirely new set of demons.

We'd arrived back at the house in the pitch black to find her Mercedes had been brought back safely. Folks from the department of transportation had also cleared the debris on the road leading to town.

One of the things I did like about Danger Falls was that everyone in town knew the tourist industry was the reason they were thriving. Every business had taken a huge leap into the black the moment the resort and winery had become fully operational after our parents had spent millions renovating it.

No one wanted to go back to the days of worrying about foreclosure, so things were done quickly. I'd been told that's why every holiday was celebrated with such ferocity.

"Bullshit. She has a thing for you."

Shephard knew how to tease me better than Hunter did. Or maybe I just allowed him to get me more.

"She's been through a lot, Shep. I can't think about anything at this point."

"I never knew you to shy away from something."

I wasn't about to acknowledge his statement. Sometimes the things we craved the most were the ones we should stay away from.

His sigh was the usual one he gave me indicating he was certain I'd back out, not following through with allowing my guard to fall. I'd yet to share with him that I admired the fact he'd fought his demons and won, but I couldn't. That would get into a long conversation about the ones I carried around like a steel anchor.

"I'll be late getting to the resort today. Need to get some dogfood." My voice was gruffer than before.

"So you're keeping the pup then?"

"I don't know what Bella has planned, but the dog needs to eat while we got it. Plus, there's a good chance it belongs to somebody."

"I don't think so. I'll have the staff ask around and maybe if you go into town, you can talk to Poppy about it. She knows all the animals in the area."

"Poppy. Yeah, not a bad idea. Cally will like the diner." Poppy's Diner served good food in a pleasant atmosphere that allowed pets. She even cooked up homemade dinners for them and offered incredible treats not available in any commercial outlet. But it was also the place to find out every little dirty secret one of the locals tried to keep.

That's why I very rarely frequented the place no matter if I did enjoy a home-cooked meal. I had enough issues with the sheriff breathing down my neck.

"See? A family man already."

"Shut the fuck up. Okay? Not on my agenda." That single thought had come to me in the middle of the night regarding a possible future. I could actually see myself with someone. However, I wasn't ready to admit that to anyone. Not at this point.

Including the man inside.

"Why the hell did you call me?"

"To tell you not to come into the damn office. You were the town hero last night. Hell, everyone in the resort is already talking about the lives you saved."

"Don't you dare call me a damn hero, Shep. You better than anyone know I hate that shit."

"Jesus, bud. You need to chill out."

Why did I have a feeling there was something going on he wasn't telling me about? "Just talk. I know you too damn well. Spill it or I'm hanging up."

He laughed. "You do know me far too well. Here's the deal. You didn't check the computer when you took the cabin for your gal."

"She's not my damn gal. Okay?"

"Whatever you say. Anyway, I have a group coming in late tonight. It's been booked for over two months. With the roads clear, they can get in. I know it's shit news, but they requested the Wyoming cabin in particular."

Well, fuck.

"Fine, what about another cabin?"

"They're all booked as is every room in the resort itself. I'm sorry, buddy. You're going to need to figure something else out."

"Fuck. I doubt the damn inn or bed and breakfast has any rooms either."

"I took the liberty of checking for you," Shephard told me.

"Don't say it. None are available because of the freaking holiday. Goddamn it. What am I supposed to tell her? I don't have any suggestions."

Shephard cleared his throat. "Well, I do, but you're not going to like it."

"What?"

"Your place. You have plenty of room and you know it."

I had to really think about what he'd just suggested before I issued a retort that neither one of us would appreciate.

Certainly not this early in the morning. "That's not possible."

"Not possible or you just can't get your head out of your ass long enough to grasp you like this girl and want her to stay?"

Hissing, I pulled the phone away, whistling for the dog. The gorgeous but way too thin pup popped out from a section of pine trees, bounding in my direction. Her tail was wagging and my heart ached for the girl. "It's not a good idea."

"Other than that you're a slob, tell me why."

He knew I didn't have a good answer. My cabin was huge, even larger than this one, which made me feel uncomfortable as hell. Living there had reminded me how alone I was. A part of me hated my hesitation, but I wasn't good company and knew that. "I gotta get off the phone so I can tell her."

"Buddy. When are you going to learn it's okay to want a different life? You deserve one. Just reach out and take it."

"I'll keep that in mind, but I'm not you. I'm incapable of letting the past go. I'll stop by later."

"No, you won't. Take a damn day off. Please." He laughed and my gut told me he was still holding something back.

"What else? What the hell aren't you telling me?" I growled this time, irritated he was dragging this out.

The exasperated sound he made was a clear indication he

was hiding something. "I didn't want to tell you this, but you need to know."

"Know what?"

"After last night and how Bella handled the tragedy, I was curious about your guest."

Instantly, my hackles were raised. "You were checking up on her? What the fuck is wrong with you?"

"Hey, you're my brother and she saved our butts, but both of us are required to care about anyone who steps foot into our operation. You know, insurance? Lawsuits?"

"I get it, Shep. I'm not a fucking idiot."

"No, you're not, but I saw your face too. I checked on her credentials. There's a buddy of mine who can look up anyone on this planet. He owed me a favor."

"And?" I felt every muscle in my body tensing.

"And there is no one by the name of Bella Winters who graduated from college let alone medical school."

While the news hit me hard, I knew there was more to the story. "Did you check to see if that was a maiden name?"

"It should have popped up if that's what she was formally known as. I don't know what it means. Maybe there's a real explanation for the lack of information, but like I said, you needed to be told."

A new flash of anger hit me straight in the gut. I'd known she was hiding something from me and it hadn't been my place to pry. "Who doesn't have a secret, bro? Tell me that."

"Yeah, but the difference is that if anyone learns she isn't a real doctor, we could be sued every six ways from Sunday. She's already a goddamn local hero. You know how people are in this town. They're going to ask questions. Is Bella prepared to answer them?"

I had no answer to that. "Let me handle my business."

"Not just your business," Shep reminded me. His tone reflected his concern and increasing agitation. He had no idea just how irritated I was.

"I got it. I'll deal with it."

The call ending was my choice. I held the phone to my head. What the hell was I supposed to do?

"Tell me what?" Bella asked from behind me.

"Nothing important." How long did I think I was going to keep the news from her? And how long was she going to keep lying to me? As I looked into her beautiful violet eyes, I not only noticed continued pain and sadness, but a solid conviction to keep herself protected.

Including from me.

"Don't do that. I overheard some of what you were saying. This place is rented, isn't it?" she asked. She was searching my eyes.

Exhaling, I was momentarily distracted by the dog hopping onto the porch, happily shaking snow off before running inside the open front door. "Yeah, it is. There's nothing else available."

She studied me, maybe waiting for me to say something else. "Well, then. Fate has decided I need to move on." Her look forlorn, she turned and headed inside.

"Wait. Don't do that," I told her.

"What? Now I'll be out of your hair, which is obviously what you want."

"No, that's not true, Bella. I just... I'm not used to this. Okay? But you're not leaving yet. I have a huge place and plenty of room. You're coming to stay with me."

"Why?"

"Why? You know why." Well, fuck me. This was a damn good time to distance myself from her, but for the life of me, I couldn't do it. Maybe she'd somehow already put a leash on my balls.

"Not good enough, Jagger. Why should I bother coming to stay with you if you don't want me there?"

In two strides I was directly behind her, turning her around by the shoulders. At least she allowed me to do so without running off. She needed an answer and deserved a decent one. "Because I don't want you to go. I like your company and I'm not sure if you leave that I won't hunt you down. I don't think you'll like the cage I'll put you into when I find you and I think you know by now, I will find you."

Her frown slipped, a slight smile forming. She wrapped her arms around me for a hug, lifting her head seconds later. "I'd like to stay." Her whisper was sultry like the night before.

"Good." I lifted her chin with a single finger.

"Mama. I know what to name her. Xena. She is a princess warrior. Right?"

Cally's little voice brought smiles to both our faces. "I guess you have a dog."

"You mean we have a dog," Bella said. "As long as no one claims her."

As she turned around, crouching down and having a discussion with her daughter, I realized that I'd just placed myself in a predicament I wasn't certain I could get out of.

But even stranger than allowing myself to do that was that I suddenly felt happy.

I only hoped it all didn't come crashing down when she realized I really was a bad guy.

Then she would run and I'd let her.

ella

My phone chirped indicating a text.

Instantly, I was on edge, my nerves crawling with anxiety.

I ignored the sound, staring out the windshield.

"Xena didn't like her bath, Mama," Cally said from the backseat.

"Maybe not, but she wasn't getting in this vehicle without one," I told her. I had a feeling when the housekeepers came to get the cabin ready for the next guests, they wouldn't be too happy either. The entire downstairs smelled like wet dog. "She was smelly like you are when you play in the mud."

Cally giggled, which brought a sense of relief. I'd been anxious all morning. The text only made it worse.

Another text came in and my skin was crawling. There was a chance Esme was chastising me over not telling her everything about where I'd landed, but my gut told me otherwise.

Joel was taunting me again, keeping me on edge on purpose.

While my phone was in my purse, I hadn't turned off the ringer. What was wrong with me? The answer was far too complicated.

"I don't like baths either," Cally admitted.

Hearing her happy laughter was exactly what I needed. Especially since Jagger was brooding, even though he was doing much better at not hiding his emotions after the night we'd had.

I wasn't certain I'd done the right thing in agreeing to stay with Jagger for whatever number of days or weeks I remained in Danger Falls. He wasn't entirely certain his offer was the right thing to do either. I could tell by his brooding demeanor.

He knew I was an imposter. I could feel it in my bones. That's why he remained quiet, fuming because I'd lied to him.

Whatever he'd learned about me was akin to dynamite waiting to be lit. And the fuse was short. Could I trust him? How did I know he wouldn't pick up the phone and contact Joel or the man's equally horrible attorney?

I didn't.

That's why our silence was easier to deal with.

When another text came in, Jagger finally shifted in his seat. Had he heard the sound? Of course he had. The man was like a radar beacon, catching every sound.

"Aren't you going to respond?" he asked.

"I'm sure it's nothing important."

"Right," he huffed.

I did my best to ignore both my phone and his snide comment, but when another text came in, the angry side of me took over. With one hard jerk, I pulled my phone into my hands.

The text was ugly and very clear as to Joel's intentions.

Joel: *Do you really think you can run away from me with my little girl?*

Joel: *I will find you and when I do, you'll be very sorry you crossed me.*

Joel: *I will release that video. Do not think I won't.*

Joel: *You crossed the wrong person.*

Me: *She's not your little girl. She's mine.*

I'd never felt so uncomfortable, the understanding that Jagger was in the seat next to me reinforcing I could never run away from my past.

. . .

208

Joel: *I'm going to find you, my little bitch. And when I do, you will pay for trying to leave. You are my wife. And I assure you that anyone close to you is going to hate the fact they helped you.*

Why did he care? Why did he act like he wanted me back?

Me: *I'm not your wife any longer either. You fucked it up when you slept with her. If you touch a single one of my friends, I will make certain you go to prison for a very long time.*

I started to shake. He was threatening my best friend.

Me: *Esme doesn't know where I am.*

Why was I bothering?

Joel: *It's fascinating what a scalpel can do in slowly and effectively destroying nerves and tendons.*

Me: *Leave me alone. You got what you wanted. You touch her, you die.*

I waited to see the three little dots floating across the screen, but there weren't any. A couple of minutes passed and I knew he wasn't going to answer. He'd played me again and won. He wasn't outright threatening anyone, although a decent detective might be able to make a case from what he'd said. But in Baltimore, Joel Brockford was a prominent man, someone to be feared because his daddy owned everyone who had any desire to make something of themselves.

I turned my phone off at that point, refusing to fall prey to Joel's almost perfect method of manipulation. He was the master at it, keeping me on edge even during surgery.

"Something wrong?" Jagger asked.

"Nothing I can't handle."

While he didn't respond, I noticed his chest rising and falling as it did every time he was annoyed or angry. Besides, the shake of his head indicated he didn't believe me.

We were headed into town to pick up a few things, both of us not working after the traumatic night we'd experienced. I'd been forced to admit to myself when I crawled out of bed that I was exhausted, every muscle aching.

But my condition wasn't totally due to almost falling down a mountain slope or attending to tourists who should have listened to the weather forecast. Or even my emotional state when I'd thought my beautiful baby daughter might never be found.

It was mostly because of hot sex.

I bit my lower lip as he made a turn, slowing down as we approached the area where the road had been blocked off the evening before. One lane had been cleared so far, flagmen allowing people to go in turns.

Was it terrible of me to be thinking about my sexual escapades with a sexy man instead of continuing to try to piece my life back together? Maybe. The useful word was 'try.' So far, I wasn't doing a very good job. Now that everyone knew I was a surgeon by profession, I had a feeling the townspeople wouldn't leave me alone.

But I would remain steadfast in my decision to stay away from medicine for the time being. It was too painful all the way around.

"Mama. Can we get some toys for Xena?" Cally asked.

I very slowly looked over at Jagger. Every time my daughter spoke, I noticed a tiny crack in his armor. Very tiny, but I knew underneath the grizzly bear of a man was a heart that continued beating to his own rhythm. The conversation I'd overheard had pulled me back into my own mental reclusion.

He didn't know if he wanted me here.

Then why offer his cabin? Or maybe his brother had made the suggestion. Whatever the case, I could tell I was already crowding his space.

We passed the flagmen and Cally had to kneel in the back-seat, waving to them frantically. She had such a good heart that I was constantly reminded why all of this was worth it.

"We should give them some water, Mommy."

"Maybe we will on the way back," I told her. "Plus, I'm certain they have some." She loved all creatures big and small, acting as if she could save the world. I'd felt that way at her age even if I'd had no one to nurture me. I would do everything in my power while I remained alive to provide her with all the tools she needed to succeed.

How many times had I thought I would die? Too many. I dropped my head, the unexpected attack of emotions not what I needed right now.

I felt the heat of his gaze as he made another turn, the two-lane road turning into four. I could see the city limits sign including the population stats. I concentrated on that, biting my tongue to keep from issuing a stark sob.

Jagger had no idea what to say to me. For a man like him to stutter after coming inside meant he was clueless. Maybe I just needed coffee. Lots of coffee. I could handle an IV drip at this point. I was still afraid I'd be lost in the terrifying memories. Why was I so emotional today?

You know the answer.

He will find you.

Joel would need to make guesses about the last name I was using. After taking two years to finally learn my mother's identity—including her last name, which I'd adopted—I hadn't told him I'd been searching for her. Let alone what I'd found. However, I hadn't offered to testify against my ex so no protection had been offered to me. My single report of abuse had been met with being made to feel like the attack had been my fault. I'd learned then just how deep the Brockford family pockets were. Using my mother's name had seemed like the only choice.

Still, even if the odds of Joel finding out were slim, I worried he'd find a way.

"Mommy. Can I get an ice cream cone?"

"Ice cream?" Jagger finally piped in. "It's like thirty degrees outside."

"There's no bad time for ice cream," Cally and I said together. It had been our little mother-daughter motto since she'd managed to formulate sentences. I was amazed how adult she sounded at almost four. Like a big girl with even bigger dreams.

I remembered being that girl.

"Well, then. I think we can make that happen. If your mother approves," he told us.

"Yay! Mommy. I've been good."

Exhaling, I almost reached over and squeezed his leg, but thought better of it. We weren't a couple. That's what I had to keep telling myself. "Yes, honey. You have."

Woof.

Xena piped in and I said a silent prayer Cally's world wouldn't need to be shattered with the loss of the pup. I had no clue if I could take her with me wherever we ended up. Or if she belonged to someone who was desperately looking for her.

"We'll stop at the pet store first for a collar and leash, some food too," he said, returning to his quiet space. "And maybe a few toys!"

"Okay. Is there a place we can ask around about whether Xena has been missing?" I tried to keep my voice low so Cally wouldn't hear. She was so lucky to be alive, the few scratches and bumps, bruises and abrasions not keeping her down for long enough in my mind. The little girl had no idea how close she'd come to dying.

Oh, God.

I pressed my hand over my face, praying I could hold it in. Small towns were the kind of place where news traveled fast. I had a feeling I would be forced to go over the events again and again. I couldn't handle that.

"Sure. Poppy's Diner. A good place for all four of us to get something to eat."

He didn't seem happy about it either. "Including Xena?"

"Danger Falls is dog friendly. Almost every business and store. There isn't a single person who won't stop and pet a dog. Crazy shit."

"He said a bad word."

I bit back a laugh. "Yes, he did and he needs to apologize."

Jagger finally cracked a smile. "I am very sorry. I was a bad, bad boy." When he threw me a look this time, a moment of closeness erupted between us.

I adored this man, but how could I help him lose the anchor around his neck? If he wasn't careful, it would soon become a noose.

The moments of awkward silence between us could be measured in miles or gallons. I wasn't certain which fit the situation the best. At least the town limits came into view and I could absorb myself in the quaintness, buildings that indeed reminded me of those seen in holiday movies or television series that seemed to have no real point to them.

I was a pessimist when it came to romance even though I craved it with every inch of my soul.

With every building painted a different vibrant color, including the brick facades, I could see the town plopped in a tropical atmosphere. "Danger Falls isn't what I expected," I told him.

"Every tourist says that," he admitted. "My parents had a hand in redecorating the town so the place would seem friendlier."

"Your parents?"

His laugh held meaning and one he wouldn't discuss with me. "Yeah, they bought Foxhead Resort, determined to bring life back to the dying town."

"It looks like they did a good job." The place was crawling with people, the remaining snow on the ground adding a Christmasy feel. The sidewalks were already cleared. I found that amazing. Wreathes were hung from every door, every streetlight adorned with garland and lights, a repre-sentation of Santa or a snowman capping each.

"Look, Mommy! Santa."

My heart ached since the holidays meant so much to her. Christmas brought heartache to my world, but I'd tried in her few short years to bring her the joy of the season.

When she started singing her favorite Christmas tune, I stifled a laugh. "Don't mind the baby girl. She can't get enough of the holidays. I know you hate them."

"Yeah, I do," he admitted. "I have reasons."

"I get it." I did. Either Joel or I had always had to work, never truly enjoying the holiday season other than the typical company party he'd forced me to attend.

"More than you know."

He added the last part as if an afterthought and so many questions formed in my mind. Too late. I noticed the pet store marquee and sighed. Today just might be the most difficult day of all.

* * *

Jagger

Secrets.

Danger.

Both were ubiquitous in my world. I'd become the master of keeping secrets close, doing my best to ignore them while they ceremoniously attempted to destroy my life.

I'd become damn good at being able to shove them aside.

Bella wasn't capable of doing so. Maybe because of Cally. Whatever the reason, her suffering kept my anger fresh and just under the surface.

Whoever had texted her was at least part of the reason she was petrified with every shadow. Somehow, I would need to figure out what I was dealing with since Bella refused to tell me.

"Look, Mommy," Cally squealed again. "Santa Claus."

We arrived in town and it seemed the entire population was out in force. My muscles tensed all over again at the thought.

I hated shopping.

Purchasing groceries was a pain in the ass.

But here I was in the middle of a thriving pet store, far too many tourists and locals fawning over treats behind the doggie bakery case and stuffed animals that had hefty price tags. But it was something I had to do. Just seeing the joy-filled look on Cally's face almost warmed my heart.

Almost.

"Xena stays in the car until she has a collar and a leash," Bella told Cally as the little girl tried to get the dog out of my Range Rover.

"Ah, Mommy!"

"Nope. We don't want her running away. Do we?" Bella pinched her daughter's chin.

I noticed again that neither one of them had a decent coat on. Their two were far too flimsy for this kind of weather.

"Come on. Let's get the two of you inside." I opened the door, ushering Cally into the store, waiting to see Bella's reaction.

She was more pensive than I'd seen her. Before she had a chance to slide past me, I blocked her entrance.

"What are you doing?" Her tone had returned to being demanding.

"I could ask you the same question. What's going on?"

"I don't know what you mean."

"I think you do. What was in the text and who was it from?"

Bella glared at me. "None of your business."

"Since you'll be living in my house, it is entirely my business."

She huffed, the sound exaggerated. "Then I guess I need to look for a place so I can get the hell out of your life." Bella sidestepped me, but I thwarted her attempt.

"Don't do that, Bella. You're going through something and I have a feeling it's dangerous. Now, confide in me."

"Why should I? I don't know you."

I snagged her wrist with a little more force than I'd intended.

"Let me go or so help me God."

Exhaling, I released my hold, holding back on my typical self-righteous stare as she peered up at me. "Is someone threatening you?"

"No. Why in God's name would you think that?"

Because I knew when someone felt panic that swept up through every ounce of their being. "Because you were rattled by the text."

"Just a friend from back home hassling me for not calling her."

She tried to laugh it off.

I could easily see through her bad attempt at lying to me.

"You're certain that's all it is?"

"Absolutely. Stop worrying, Jagger. Last night was last night. I'm fine."

"Uh-huh. Come on." Her reasons for lying to me were her own, but I could smell her fear.

"I just need to make a quick phone call. Will you keep an eye on Cally for me? Please?"

I didn't need to be some damn mind reader to know she was in serious trouble, more so than I'd originally thought. "Sure. Happy to."

Happy?

The woman was far too frustrating, but I would find out what she was hiding.

A little girl and a dog. I had no clue what I was doing. As soon as I was noticed by the owner of the store, she flew out from behind the bakery counter. "Jagger Fox. I never thought I'd see you here."

Betty Barker had been the owner for a few years, taking the insurance money left over from her husband's tragic ski-lift death to open the place. I'd met her once at the resort when a pet adoption event had been held there. It had been my mother's doing, insisting we could help. The day had meant our parking lot had been filled with vehicles and people who would likely never rent a room or cottage at the resort. I'd tried to stay away, but the older lady had sought me out.

With her garish jet-black hair and thick blue eye shadow, she almost reminded me of Betty Boop.

"Yeah, well, we got a stray who needs a collar and leash. Some dogfood."

"What kind of dog?" Her eyes flitted toward the pup, her hands clasping together. "The hero dog. Oh, my God. I am so honored. And this must be little Cally."

"Yes, ma'am," Cally told her.

"My, such manners for a special young lady. Why don't we go and look for the perfect collar for that very good girl who saved you?" Betty asked, already holding out her hand.

"Xena. Princess warrior."

Cally's voice would always dig out a portion of my heart and I didn't know why. I hadn't spent time with a kid in as long as I could remember. Maybe because she was the spitting image of her mother. The same flaxen hair. The same violet eyes.

"Well, then. The collar must be extra special for a princess. And treats."

I had to hand it to Betty; she knew how to handle children where I failed miserably.

"By the way, Jagger. I just wanted to tell you that the whole town is proud of you. What you did to save that little girl just warms my heart like it does everyone else." She planted her hand against her heart. "You have a good heart. I'm sure your mother is very proud of the man you've become."

I wasn't certain about that.

She didn't wait for me to respond, trailing behind Cally and Xena, the little girl touching everything within her reach. When the three were safely a distance away, I returned my attention to the front of the store.

Bella was pacing the sidewalk, animated as she talked on her phone. Only after she moved to the edge of the sidewalk facing the street did I head out the door. I leaned against the exterior of the building, the excessive traffic preventing me from overhearing what she was saying.

But I could tell by the pained look on her face that whoever she was talking to was important to her. I had one foot on the wall, trying to act as if I was enjoying the brisk weather.

Bullshit.

As soon as she turned around, her pointed look confirmed I sucked at acting. She spun around again, her hand motions more animated than before. Soon, she was off the phone, but her screen remained lit. I was going to use that to my advantage before her iPhone locked down.

When I confronted her, this time she allowed a few seconds of fear to show on her face. "What are you hiding from me?"

"Stop asking me. You couldn't understand and I just want to leave it alone. Don't you get it?"

"What I get is that you're pretending nothing is wrong when you're terrified of every shadow."

"That makes two of us."

Her words were biting and I gritted my teeth. Soon, I'd have no enamel left on any of them. "Fine. Have it your way."

"By the way. We need to get you a new shirt at least. My treat."

She tugged at my rumpled, ruined shirt and I laughed. "Yeah, we can do that."

Her expression softened, hope flaring in her soft purple eyes. It was the same look she'd given me the moment I'd brought her daughter back to safety. The same expression that had slayed me then just about broke me now. "I just need some peace. Please try and understand."

"What about happiness?"

She scoffed and threw open the door. "I gave up on that when I left Baltimore."

ella

"Two brothers in one day, Jagger. I think I died and went to heaven." The lady behind the counter appeared shocked at seeing Jagger swaggering through the diner's door.

"Look who's here, Lois," another older woman said as she fanned her face. She slapped her lunch companion on the arm from across the booth.

"Jenny. Be still my heart. Like icing on a cake. If only I could lick it off," Lois said. She had on huge glasses, lifting them and I'd be damned if she didn't lick her lips in appreciation.

A laugh bubbled to the surface, but Jagger gave me a dirty look.

"Would the two of you stop it," the woman behind the counter snapped. "That's no way to talk to my customers.

Jagger. Such a pleasure. Hunter dropped by earlier for one of my famous cherry pies."

I could tell he didn't care. There was such animosity between him and his brothers. Competition?

"You got a free booth, Poppy?" Jagger said in a grumbly voice, ignoring her sexual innuendo.

"Sugar. I'll toss out one of our regulars if I need to." She was a hoot, throwing a haughty look over the counter at the various booths and the workers who took up every stool at the counter.

"Don't be that way, Poppy," a guy finally piped in.

"Shut up, Mike. My place, my rules."

Mike threw up his hands.

Spitting out a chuckle, I narrowed my eyes as I studied Jagger's contorted expression. I had a feeling I was going to like this place. Of all the men I'd known in my life, he was the worst with people coming up to him or even saying hello. He suddenly reminded me of a man being told he needed his incisors removed without Novocain.

Poppy's Diner was packed, at least three other dogs taking up positions at their owner's feet by several of the colorful booths. The place reminded me of a restaurant you'd see in the fifties. Colorful. Quaint. Pictures adorning the walls. And garish lighting. Neon if I was correct. I was easily able to envision the place lit up at night. A customer would be able to see it a mile away.

My tummy immediately growled just with walking in. I gathered a whiff of baked apples and cinnamon, fresh coffee brewing and vanilla. Cally was already tugging on my leg, pointing to dog biscuits that were artfully placed on a cake pedestal, the glass covering preventing dust or unwanted, unwashed hands. How she knew about doggie treats was beyond me other than watching television.

"Look, Mommy, look! For Xena! Pwease. Can we get one?"

"I'll get one for the pup," Jagger said, already pulling his wallet from his jeans pocket. At least he'd allowed me to purchase him a nice long-sleeved Henley. The caramel color accentuated his deep chocolate hair. In turn, he'd insisted on ensuring I purchased a few items, including snow boots and warmer coats for both Cally and me. At the last minute, he'd tossed his credit card on the counter, refusing to allow me to purchase anything.

It had been the same at the pet store, the hardware store for a few items to 'ensure our comfort' as he'd called it and when he'd purchased fluffy towels because his at the cabin were ratty. I'd finally stopped trying to stop him from spoiling us. It wouldn't have done any good.

"Nonsense," Poppy said. She tossed a towel she was wiping her hands on behind her, coming out from behind the counter. An older lady, her bright smile suited her outfit, which reminded me of an eighties movie: fluorescent pink accented with various shades of purple, her tight-fitting pants shimmering with silver stars.

"You don't need to do that, Poppy," Jagger said. "Bella doesn't like charity."

He was just trying to annoy me and I'd decided not to allow him the chance to do so.

"Pft," she hissed. "Don't mind him, sugar. The Fox boys are notoriously grumpy all the time." She plucked two biscuits from under the covering, bending down to Xena and making googling noises. "A little heroine. Xena for a princess warrior. Right?"

"Yes. Yes!" Cally jumped up and down, doing what I'd started to call her signature dance move.

Suddenly, there wasn't a customer in the diner who wasn't watching us with an amused expression. I felt a flush rush to my cheeks. I didn't need to be in larger crowds right now. The women were trying to be polite, but I could swear they had daggers in their eyes. Evidently, Jagger was a hot catch around town. I could see why.

"John, bring another bowl of water," Poppy called over her shoulder. "We have a new furry guest amongst our midst, a true heroine. Fix her up a cheeseburger too."

Cally gasped as only she could do, so melodramatic I had to smile.

"Thank you, Poppy. You're very kind."

"Nonsense, girl. You must be Doctor Bella," Poppy said. She held out her hand, her smile far too genuine to resist.

"Just Bella. Okay?" I shook it and instantly felt warmth.

"I'm Poppy Danfield. I own this fabulous establishment. I'd like to purchase the three… um, four of you lunch on me."

"No, Poppy. We can take care of our check," Jagger insisted.

She flapped her hand at him. "Don't mind him, sugar. Like I said. Grumpy."

"Yes, he is. Mrs. Danfield. Do you know anything about Xena? I mean, she wasn't wearing a collar. We haven't gone to a veterinarian yet to see if she's chipped, but I was just wondering if you knew her."

"Poppy. Please. She does look kind of familiar." Poppy rubbed her jaw and glanced toward a man sitting at the end of the counter. "Doc Welby. This is Bella and Cally and you know Jagger, I think."

I caught the look the doctor gave Jagger. It would seem my roommate wasn't well liked by men, only the ladies appreciating the eye candy they'd been presented in town. I could easily read the minds of every single woman in the place no matter their age. They wouldn't mind a nice roll in the hay with the man.

"Yeah, I know him. Nice to meet you two ladies," the doctor said.

John came out from a swinging door with a gorgeous ceramic dog's bowl full of water. He had a huge grin on his round face as he squeezed through the opening from behind the counter. I hadn't noticed he had a placemat in his hand, little pictures of dog bones all over it. He first petted Xena before placing the mat and the bowl down in front of her.

She'd been offered water and treats at every store we'd gone to, yet she lapped up the water as if she was parched.

Cally immediately picked up on the conversation, her anxious breaths concerning me right away. I dropped to the floor, lifting her chin with my hand. "Are you okay, honey? Can you breathe?"

Ever since she'd gotten out of the hospital the last time, I'd feared a relapse. Even the cardiologist, a man highly respected in the country, had told me the likelihood of my little girl falling prey to a heart attack was at a much higher percentage than a typical healthy person. I'd panicked with every cough and sneeze for the first year.

"Just sad, Mommy. Please don't take Xena away."

I was so relieved I let out a small moan. "We talked about this, honey. If Xena belongs to someone else, don't you think they're going to be missing her? Even crying about her?"

While my daughter got her stubborn streak from her mother, she was a caring, sweet girl who'd once asked me to bring a dead squirrel back to life. "I know. I just... I love her."

I squeezed her arms and I could swear everyone in the diner was now listening intently. I tweaked her nose before standing, completely embarrassed as I glanced around the diner.

"Don't you worry, honey. Aunt Poppy will get to the bottom of this. Doc Welby. You said you've seen this pretty pup before? I think I've seen her in town. I just don't remember from where."

Doctor Welby. The name suited him. With his shocking, neatly trimmed white hair and kind eyes, I had a feeling his patients trusted him instantly. He shuffled over, the lack of movement showing his age. "Poppy. So you think you know this little fellow as well." He glanced down at Xena.

"She's a girl, Doc," Poppy admonished.

I stole a quick look at Jagger. Even he was slightly amused, the corners of his magnificent lips turned up.

"Xena," she added.

"Princess Warrior!" Cally sang out.

"Oh, well then," Doc Welby said. He bent down, stroking the pup's head. "I do know her. It's good to finally see her too."

My heart sank and I was surprised that Jagger placed his hand on the small of my back. As soon as he did, a shock-wave of electricity swept up from the base of my feet. I just couldn't stand to see Cally's heart broken.

Doc Welby continued to stroke Xena's head, remaining quiet. I felt Cally was about ready to throw a tantrum, but not just one a typical almost four-year-old would have. Her panic attacks were few and far between now, but when they hit, they were terrible, painful to watch. She'd grown way too attached to the pup.

"Xena belonged to a friend of mine. Remember Steve Young?" he was asking Poppy.

Poppy snorted. "That old coot? He used to make a pass at me every time he came in. Whatever happened to him?"

"He died last month. From what I heard, the dog ran away when the EMTs arrived and no one was able to find her. She hasn't made an appearance since. Now, she's a heroine. Steve would love that." He shifted his attention toward

Cally. "I think, little lady, that you have yourself a new pet, but you must promise to love and care for her for the rest of her life."

Cally's eyes were huge, her little mouth opening wide as she gasped. "Mommy. Xena is ours!"

I was so relieved my heart started racing.

Doc Welby was grinning from ear to ear. "I'm glad she found a good home." He lifted his head, paying more attention to me. "Jagger. I heard this lovely lady saved a whole bunch of tourists last night. I had my daughter in and wasn't taking calls."

"She did a great job, Doc," Jagger managed. I was certain the man was ready to eat nails at this point.

"Great job? I got the play by play from a couple buddies of mine who heard all the details from a niece of one of them who works there. She said it was a streamline action. Then all that happened after that. Whew. You're a very lucky young lady to have such a strong man like Jagger by your side."

"Oh, we're not together," I insisted.

Why was it that his grin was almost similar to the way Poppy's eyes were lighting up? I felt another heat from a blush warming up my skin.

"Well, whatever the case, it's obvious he cares about you and the little one here. Anyway. Folks know around here I'm getting ready to retire. My daughter was harassing me something fierce last night." He scratched his head, laughing as if he'd taken a full berating. "I'll have to close shop if I can't find anyone to take my place and that will mean folks needing to travel a good ways just to see a doctor for a cold, the flu."

Oh, no. I could tell where this was going.

"I was just passing through," I insisted.

"Trouble is," he continued and I had a feeling he was going to ignore me, "no young folks want to move to a place like Danger Falls. Vacation here? Sure thing, but they feel like it's going back in time."

"I love it here. The buildings are adorable and everyone is so nice." By the look shared between Poppy and the doctor, I could tell I'd fallen head over heels into a setup.

"That's good to hear. You'd fit in real nice around these parts. Wouldn't she, Jagger?"

Jagger didn't answer right away, grumbling yes when he did.

"I'd like to offer you a job. You can lease or buy the clinic from me and I'll give you a damn good rate if you choose to buy it. I promise you that you'll love the place. Just needs a woman's touch."

To say I was flabbergasted was an understatement. "Um, that's really sweet of you, but you don't know who I am or my credentials. I didn't bring a resume with me." What was I doing?

He shrugged. "If the stories about last night are even half true, then you're right for the job. I also know good people when I see one. Maybe you could stop by in the next day or two."

Why was it everyone in the diner was hanging onto my words, waiting to hear what I would say? "Doctor Welby. I'm really just passing through. I don't know what I want to do with the rest of my life. I just…"

"Just think about it, Bella." He touched my hand, his shaking. I could tell he'd wanted to retire for a long time. "You'd make an old man real happy."

"I'll… think about it." How had I gotten roped into this?

"Good. Jagger. Do your best to rid yourself of that surly attitude and show the lady a good time. Take her to all the best places in town. I know you can afford it. Don't be a cheap guy. We need her." He grinned and winked at Poppy before returning to his barstool. I had a feeling he'd been a staple at that very one for years.

Jagger grumbled once again. "I'll do my dam… darnedest to keep her here." I was surprised he caught himself before cursing.

I didn't really know small towns. I'd lived in one during foster care, but the only reason I'd been allowed outside the house was to go to school. When several of the customers started to clap, I shrank back. A couple of people even tried to take pictures. I was the one coming close to a panic attack. Without realizing what I was doing, I fled the diner, a wave of terror rushing into me.

Immediately, I felt like an idiot, but I was perspiring, my heartrate much higher than normal. I hadn't experienced such a rush of suffocation in a long time. I walked to the edge of the sidewalk, staring out at the traffic. I was right in front of the diner window and I sensed every face plastered or neck craned to gawk at the crazy person.

I tensed the moment I noticed a shadow coming up behind me. My throat tightened immediately and I almost took off running.

Stop. Don't. You're safe.

But was I? I'd tried not to allow Joel's text to bother me, but I was failing miserably.

Jagger was damn good at coming up behind someone, likely without them noticing, but I wasn't just anyone. And he wasn't just another guy. Our connection was somehow profound, something I'd never thought I'd want again. But I couldn't stand lying to him much longer. The burden was too significant, the ache I felt by doing so hitting me far too hard.

He stood by my side, donning his dark shades and doing exactly what I was doing. Staring out at nothing. There was no tension this time between us. This was his way of giving me more than just space. He'd listened to me about needing peace.

I couldn't help myself, every few seconds looking over in his direction. He didn't move a muscle, but his facial muscles twitched a couple of times. For a man who didn't like to talk much, I sensed he had a whole lot to say at this point. His stubbornness was keeping him silent for now. The mischievous girl in me wanted to egg him on to see how long that lasted.

Just him being here meant he cared at least about my well-being. At this point, it was all I could tolerate.

"They think I'm nuts. Huh?" I asked, maybe a little more contritely than I'd planned.

"A little."

"Great."

"But you fit the townsfolk. They're all certifiable."

He still had a way of making me smile. "Well, good then."

"Poppy grew up here. She moved away for college and to get married, but eventually came back. She and her husband ran the bed and breakfast for a long time until his death, but she's happiest running the local gossip column and the diner. And I don't mean a newspaper," he said, allowing himself to laugh slightly. "Lois and Jenny are harmless, both widowed and between the two of them and their friend Camilla, you can find out everything you ever wanted to learn and shit you didn't about every person living in Danger Falls and half the tourist population."

"They seem nice."

"Yeah, a pain in the ass all the way around, but wouldn't hurt a fly. The hardware store has been around since the very beginning of this town somewhere in the early nineteen hundreds. Doc Welby has been here almost as long, as you can tell. He's a good doctor, although he certainly doesn't have your skills. But there isn't a local around here who won't go to him for just about everything."

"Sort of like Doc Hollywood?"

He finally stared at me with his dark and brooding look. I could see his eyebrows shooting up over his sunglasses.

"Never mind. It's an old movie."

"Oh. Betty Barker used to be a showgirl way back when. She has stories that keep the tourists enthralled. While Denise's boss, the head of the park ranger service Greg Young has been here only a few years, he's said that there's no place he'd rather be."

"You don't need to give me their resumes, Jagger. I really do like everything I've seen and the people are all very nice. I just… I'm in a tough spot and need to be careful with where I end up taking root. I want to ensure it's what's best for Cally."

"What about your medical career?"

"I don't know any longer. That's the truth. It's really weird. The joy of helping people is no longer there. I used to love the feeling of being able to end a surgery, telling the waiting families that their loved one was going to be just fine. But the surgeries were constant, the issues getting worse, and I felt like I was losing a battle I shouldn't have been involved with in the first place. Maybe that sounds selfish."

"Not selfish. Self preserving. A shame though. You are good at what you do."

A quiet sigh escaped my lips. "That means a lot coming from you."

"Tell me something. Why did you run out a few minutes ago?"

Finding a good answer was going to be difficult. "I don't know. I felt as if claws were being wrapped around my neck. Not because of the job offer. Maybe because I'm not who people think I am. Like you, I'm no hero."

"You're wrong," he told me.

"I'm never wrong."

He shook his head as if completely frustrated with me.

"Maybe just the thought of living in a small town is too suffocating."

"Maybe. I never wanted to move here. For the first three months I felt like I'd been forced, removed from my life, but I came to realize the people are genuine. A pain in the ass sometimes, but they mean no harm. The vast majority know I like to keep to myself."

"You must be a great celebrity."

With that he folded his arms. "Fresh blood. Someone new to talk about."

"Whatever you say."

"Mostly they're good with allowing my privacy. They'd be that way for you too. I don't know what you're looking for, Bella, but I don't need to scrutinize your past to know you're running from something. I'm an expert at it. I kept myself away from people on purpose and I was perfectly happy. But it was all a lie. I'm never going to sit at that diner and chitchat, but at least I can appreciate that these people welcomed me into their lives and if I was ever in need, they'd welcome me into their homes."

"That's wonderful. I have trouble trusting and that comes from years of practice."

"I got it. I ain't pushing nor will I ever. But I need to ask you one more question and I want an honest answer." He turned to face me.

"I'll try." When I didn't shift around immediately, he forced me to gently, even removing his sunglasses. Dear God, there was such a serious look on his face. "What is it?"

"I need to know who the hell you are. There's no Bella Winters listed as a doctor anywhere in the world. You have a goddamn professional crossbow in a duffle bag you try and keep hidden from me. You received a threat on that text and don't you dare tell me otherwise. You're not Bella Winters since she doesn't exist. So why are you lying to me and to the good people of this town?"

CHAPTER 19

 *agger*

I'd put my foot into my mouth plenty of times in my life until I'd mostly stopped talking altogether.

With Bella, I'd betrayed the limited trust she'd placed in me, which hadn't been my intent, but her stonewalling had broken through some barrier. I couldn't understand completely my level of determination to break through her barriers, yet I felt more compelled to do so than I had with almost anything in my life.

She hadn't uttered a single word after returning to the diner to have lunch. After I'd questioned her real identity, she'd remained unblinking for thirty seconds before turning around and returning inside. She'd found an empty booth before I'd gotten back inside.

While she had chitchatted with Poppy, Lois, and a few of the others, she'd purposely not bothered to address me at all. Fortunately, Cally hadn't noticed since she'd been enjoying her new puppy as a little girl should.

Poppy had noticed, I could tell, but for once she kept her mouth shut.

I'd struck the kind of nerve I wasn't certain could be fixed.

Even when we'd gone back to the cabin to grab the groceries and pack up her things, she'd acted as if I wasn't in the room.

At least she hadn't driven in the opposite direction, returning to my house at the same time. Little did she know if she'd chosen to do that, I would have hunted her down.

We were safely tucked away in my cabin, Bella standing out on the deck in the snow with only a single outside light on with a glass of wine in her hand. She'd been there for almost a half hour. For all the quiet times I preferred, I'd grown used to our conversations and her lilting voice. I couldn't stand not hearing her laughter.

With Cally safely in bed with Xena, logs just added to the fire, and the kitchen cleaned up after dinner, I could either go to bed and leave things this way, or act like a goddamn man for a change. Apologizing wasn't in my nature, but I knew no other way of trying to get her to open up once again.

If that was even possible.

I grabbed my jacket and glass of bourbon, heading outside. She'd turned on the outdoor heater that had come with the house, even brushing the snow off one of the chairs so she could sit down. I moved to the other end of the expansive deck where the hot tub was located. It was the one thing I'd enjoyed about being forced to move here.

A goddamn hot tub to soothe my aching muscles.

It also was therapeutic enough to yank the anger from me for a limited time.

My parents had spared no expense when purchasing the various cabins, adding to the resort's footprint. I couldn't say I'd spent much time here, but I knew other people would love being backed up to the mountains, a lake only fifty yards away.

Tonight, I had a different feeling about being here than I had the entire time since moving to Danger Falls. It felt almost right. How strange was that?

"Why did you move here? I know you mentioned your parents and what's going on with your dad, but your two brothers seem quite capable of handling the resort between the two of them." she asked. She'd returned to having no emotion in her voice whatsoever.

"Because it was the right thing to do for my family."

"But you're not close, especially with your brothers."

"Not really. We all went our separate ways."

"Each into the military."

"Yes," I told her. "We'd been preparing for it our entire lives, our father basically insisting. We weren't given a choice like normal kids. He was an ex-Marine and told us at an early age college could wait until we'd done our time."

"A hard man."

"You really have no idea. But he taught us to respect our country. I'll give him that. Just too bad it didn't last."

"Because of everything you were forced to do and what you witnessed."

"Yep." I took a gulp of my drink.

She shifted in her seat, but said nothing for a couple of minutes. "That's very sad. Let me guess. You couldn't leave the job in the Army you had, at least not in your mind. You found one similar to follow that one, but the tasks became more dangerous, more volatile until you couldn't take it any longer. Now the nightmares are tearing you apart."

Why lie to her? "You're psychoanalyzing me again. Yeah, something like that." In order for her to trust me enough to tell me the truth about herself, she needed something from me. I wanted to tell her to be careful what she was asking for, but what was the point? "I was hired by another military organization to handle covert operations throughout the world. They made it appear seamless. Instead, the missions were complicated as fuck."

"Top secret?"

She was asking the questions in a matter-of-fact way, acting as if my choices were normal. "Yes."

"Cleaning up their messes no doubt."

I hadn't really looked at it that way, but she was right. "In a manner of speaking."

"How bad are the nightmares?"

"How did you know?"

"Because you flailed last night, mumbling in your sleep. I stayed awake to make certain you were okay. Did you know that?"

Fuck. My throat almost closed up.

I shifted around, leaning against the railing. She was sitting in the dark, but I could almost read her mind. "No, I didn't. I'm sorry. I hope to God I didn't hurt you."

"Of course not. I was terrified you were going to hurt yourself."

"Why would you think that?"

Her sigh was deep and long. "Because the one decent foster family I was in, the husband had been in the military. He came back a different man. His nightmares were controlled at first. But they manifested themselves into violence. Finally, after a horrible incident where he nearly destroyed the house, he killed himself. As you might imagine, I was shipped out of there very quickly."

"Jesus. You've been through hell and back."

"What I've been through is nothing in comparison to what I imagine you have. Yes, I had difficult and very lonely times, but I was lucky in that none of the homes took away my spirit. All ten of them."

Holy shit. "The nightmares are bad at times, but not always."

"All because you couldn't save someone."

"And because I'm a bad man."

"Meaning what, Jagger? What makes you such a terrible man that you refuse to allow anyone in your life? The life you led was honorable."

"You're wrong, city girl. It was anything but. In my mind, what I was doing was nothing but being given a license to murder people." She might as well know who she was sleeping with.

"Then you condemn every soldier in every military organization."

"Not at all," I told her.

"You can't have it both ways, Jagger. I have a strong sense that the organization you worked for after your military career ended didn't necessarily follow all the rules. But you did. Their rules."

It was like telling me if I was a mafia hitman told to take out an entire restaurant then I got a pass. "More complicated than that."

"So is just about everyone's life. I know your surly moods aren't just about hating people or feeling sorry for yourself. You're terrified you're going to hurt them. So what makes you such a terrible man?"

A strangled sound erupted from my throat. "Because I've killed enough people to fill up this house. Don't you get it?"

I wasn't certain if I expected her to run or to laugh. When she stood, I accepted that learning the truth was too much for her to take. But she surprised me as she'd done so many times, moving to the railing only inches away. "Did you enjoy the kills?"

"No."

"Did you kill women?"

"Hell, no. Women are meant to be cherished. I would have refused a direct order and left the organization had they asked."

She seemed relieved at my answer. That put up additional red flags. The bastard had hurt her more than once.

"Do you want to kill again?"

"Only if I felt it was honorable, and I'm no longer certain that's possible. Maybe now you get what I was trying to tell you."

"You came to Danger Falls because your father is dying. You didn't really have to. You were off touring the world, I would imagine in your endeavor to keep democracy intact. But you did. Don't kid yourself that you're doing someone a favor other than yourself. And you're not a bad man, Jagger. You're one of the best men I've ever met in my life."

Her words sent a chill down my spine. "Then you don't know me."

"Not as much as I'd like to." She tilted her head. "Not nearly as much."

"You might not like what you find."

244

"What if I already do?"

We had a way of communicating even when silence seemed to be the main objective. She was struggling with telling me anything, but I sensed her need. The same damn need I had. Two strangers had found each other, coming together during a period in both our lives that anyone might run from. Only she was about the strongest woman I'd ever met. I'd been able to see that within her more every day.

"The crossbow was something a foster father showed me how to use. It was the single Christmas gift I ever received until later in life when I had friends. I wasn't around long enough in any single home to enjoy holiday celebrations. He made certain I respected it as a weapon, providing invaluable lessons. I was even on a crossbow team in high school. I kept it throughout college and when I went to medical school, maybe for sentimental reasons, but I do know how to use it and I won't hesitate to do so if I need to."

"To keep your daughter safe."

"To keep anyone I care about safe, which only accounts for two people."

"Including her father," I said.

"Hell, no. He's dead to me and has been since he refused to acknowledge he was the biological father. I mean my daughter and you."

The closeness we shared was still strained yet I craved touching her. As I cupped her face, the warmth I felt in my hand tingled my fingers. "That means a lot to me, but as you might imagine, I can take pretty good care of myself."

"I've noticed that." She nuzzled into my hand. "As far as why you couldn't find my graduation certificate, it's because I'm using my maiden name. Well, my mother's name. I never formally used it until I had to."

"Does anyone else know?" Including whoever had beaten her.

"No. It was something I knew I had to keep to myself. I was forced to use every last name in a foster family when enrolled in school. I don't know if it was a requirement of the agency who farmed me out to people or not. Maybe since they hadn't bothered to look for family, they thought the choice better than giving me a fake name like Smith or Jones. I just went with it. I had almost nothing of my mother's, except for a letter she'd written me about why she'd dropped me off in a hospital trashcan. No name. I had it safely stored in plastic and had a friend who was able to get DNA off it. One thing led to another and I was given her information."

"I'm sure that gave you relief."

"I don't know, Jagger. She didn't want me. She preferred sticking a needle in her arm. But she had a name and I had a connection to someone who had my blood. So after all the shit with my ex, I adopted it when I left Baltimore. I do have my diploma. I locked it away in a safe box inside the Mercedes, a vehicle you hate."

"I didn't say I hated it." I knew she was teasing me, but I was far too angry with circumstances to feel anything but fury.

"Yes, you did," she retorted, her laugh returning. "But that's okay. I don't blame you. I hate it too."

"Then we'll get you a new one."

"With all that money you earn?"

Now I laughed. "You'd be surprised what a hired mercenary earns, sweet lady. I didn't need much either so I'm worth a pretty penny."

She inched closer. "I'll keep that in mind. Maybe I'll marry you for your money."

"I don't think I'd mind."

"Don't tempt me." She even rested her head on my chest.

I stroked her hair, feeling her entire body shivering. "Why are you running, baby? Why is this asshole texting you with threats?"

It took her a full minute to lift her head. "I'm married, Jagger."

I immediately pushed myself away. "Married?"

"Separated, the divorce final any day. I'm sorry I didn't tell you sooner. I just wasn't certain what this was or if I could trust you. You don't know how powerful my ex is."

"What's your married name?"

She hesitated before telling me. "Bella Brockford."

Brockford. The name sounded vaguely familiar.

"You couldn't trust me with sharing you were married?" Something was very off about this.

"With telling you he's a monster."

"What do you mean, a monster?" The tension immediately shifted into every joint in my body. I fisted my hands even though I made certain to keep her close.

"He wants custody of Cally and he didn't adopt her, but he's threatening to force the adoption papers through without me being there to sign them."

"He was the one who hurt you, wasn't he?"

She looked away.

"Bella. Tell me the truth. Did he hurt you? The bruises. The pain you had. He did that. Didn't he?" I couldn't even recognize my own voice. I held her face again, forcing her to look in my direction. "Didn't he?"

"Yes, Jagger. He did. And he's still contacting me. That's why I can't stay here. That's why I can't care about you. If I do and he finds out, he'll kill you too."

* * *

Kill.

Some snot-nosed lily-white surgeon thought they would take the life of such an incredible woman? And try to take me out in the process for standing in his way? The fucker had another think coming. "Fuck that. He'll get a bullet in his brain."

"Don't do this. This is exactly why I didn't want to tell you," Bella said sharply.

"I won't let him hurt you or Cally. Not a chance on this fucking earth." I wasn't certain if I'd ever been so angry in my life. I was pacing the deck, already on another glass of bourbon. All I could see was blood in my eyes.

"Please, Jagger. Just calm down. Joel is in Baltimore."

"But you think he'll manage to find you so he can ruin your life? Let him come here."

"You just don't know what he's capable of or what his father is capable of. Plus, they have police and even members of the FBI in their back pockets. I won't be safe anywhere."

"That's where you're wrong, lady. You're safe here. With me." Yeah, I had plenty of guns in the house, all of which I'd need to ensure were locked up because of Cally.

She moved away, holding her glass close to her face. Soon we'd perfect the art of silence. I was beginning to hate it with everything I had inside of me. "I don't want you hurt. Your brothers either."

"You don't know my brothers very well. Maybe we'll have to change that. There are things that can be done to ensure Joel won't be able to find you and if he does, I assure you the sheriff will have his ass locked up."

"I don't know if I can do that."

"Then you're going to allow him to win by running."

"Which is exactly what you did, right?"

Ouch. "I deserved that."

"No, you didn't."

Yeah, I did. I closed my eyes, rubbing my hand through my beard. "I have friends who can help."

"No one can help. No one." When she turned around to face me, she tilted her head to the side. "Is the hot tub on because I'm freezing." She took a purposeful step away, crossing her arms over her chest and making a 'brr' sound.

Lord, God above. We could go from having a frank, difficult conversation to overheated in the matter of seconds. That intrigued the fuck out of me. She had two distinct sides.

Just like I did.

And tonight, I planned on taking full advantage of this one. Who wouldn't?

But after tonight, I would hunt the fucker down.

"Yeah, it's on. And very hot. Just like someone standing in front of me." To prove a point, I moved to the cover, flipping it off in two moves. Steam rose into the air.

She cocked her pretty little head, daring to fold her arms. I reached down to the controls, turning on the colorful lights and the jets. Within a few seconds, the water was bubbling.

"Do you think that's hot enough for you, little lady?"

"Mmm… Let me think. I don't have a swimsuit." Her words were little more than a ragged whisper. If she was trying to arouse me, it was working.

"Who needs a swimsuit?" I tugged on her coat, yanking her against me with enough force that she smacked her hands against my chest.

"What are you doing?"

I tilted her into a slight arch. "Do we need to keep going over that? Taking you. Which is all I want or need right now. Say no and you'll see what happens."

"I think I'll tell you no just to do exactly that."

"So you're telling me no?" I challenged.

"That's exactly what I'm saying, grumpy guy. Do I need to spell the word for you?"

Dropping my head, I blew across her face a few times. She moaned, but the sound was meant to tease me. My balls were already blue from the intense craving.

"Your actions and disobedience have consequences."

"Oh, yeah?" Her two little words were nothing more than a purr.

"Oh. Yeah."

Bella rose onto her toes, planting one hot kiss on my lips, her actions forceful enough she managed to open my mouth, driving her tongue deep inside. Why was it that the taste of her was somehow better in the frigid temperatures? I wasn't usually the kind of man to enjoy all this taunting foreplay, but my mind needed the break from the dark craving.

I would handle Joel Brockford myself. She would never need to cower in fear or worry the bastard would ever touch her daughter again.

But there was nothing I could do right now.

It was time to play.

And show her who was boss.

I allowed her kiss, enjoying the way the light breeze whipped across my skin, the softness of her lips and the building excitement from both of us letting go. But as usual, my patience was waning.

She shoved me away, slip sliding on the snow immediately. Her laugh floated into the night sky, the sound sweeter than ever before. As soon as she started to rip off her clothes, her boots going first, I did the same.

We might be nuts doing something like this, but it almost felt like I was a young man again, experiencing the joy of tasting a woman for the first time. She had that kind of effect on me.

When she was completely naked, she jumped through the remaining snow in her attempt to get to the hot tub. I was having none of it. She was such a tiny thing in comparison to my big, bulking body that all I had to do was reach out with one arm, lifting her off her feet and crowding her against me.

I had a distinct advantage.

She was naked.

I still had my boots on.

No cold feet.

"Oh, no, you don't!" she squealed softly so as not to wake the sleeping child.

"Oh, yes, I do." I started humming, another first in my lonely world, and brushed snow off the railing of the deck. When I planted her over the edge, the look she gave me was a clear indication she would lay in wait.

But without a doubt she would get me back.

"You wouldn't dare," she hissed.

"Wouldn't I? You'll learn I'm a man of my word."

With that, I brought down my hand on her naked bottom.

ella

The brutal crack of his hand not once but twice was jarring.

Maybe I was in shock, but I didn't move. Heck, I couldn't breathe from the frigid air.

Prickly points of electricity jolted every nerve and tendon in my body. I kicked out, trying to plant my foot on any part of his body to drive him off. However, with a man like Jagger, when he put his stubborn mind to something, there was no turning back.

He would always be successful in getting what he wanted.

His hum intensified the moment, making it almost surreal. Here I was, outside on the night after a deep snow, ice crystals all over the railing from limited melting, steam from the hot tub washing across my back.

If this wasn't a sinful moment, I didn't know what was.

Jagger was having a good ole time spanking me like a wayward child, bringing his hand down in a perfect rhythm. I wanted to scream and throw a tantrum, but even with the roaring noise of the bubbling water, I held back.

I could only imagine what people would think if they saw us.

Maybe we were a little nuts.

I wiggled and gyrated my hips to no avail, the cracking sound of skin connecting with skin becoming a strange but powerful aphrodisiac. Panting, I finally dug my nails into the wood, the pain jetting through me irritating and deliciously enticing.

My pussy already ached, throbbing deep to my core. Whether from cold or arousal, my nipples were hard like diamonds. But one day soon I would get the man back.

"Ouch!"

"Hush, little girl. This is exactly what you need and deserve."

"No fair."

"All is fair in my world when I say it is."

His big he-man attitude was attractive. Maybe a little too much so. I'd seen the look of fury in his eyes. He would never allow Joel to get away with hurting me in any manner. I liked that.

Who was I kidding? I adored his vicious need to break my ex's neck.

A smile flew across my face and I finally closed my eyes, accepting my punishment. I could easily get used to this man.

Maybe far too easily.

He rubbed my aching bottom, likely gathering heat in his hand. But he started up again, one brutal strike coming down after another. I was almost in awe, a strange place to be when someone spanked you. Maybe a small part of me believed I deserved such harsh punishment.

Whatever the case, I was shivering all over and there was no way the electric sensations were for any other reason than being with him.

"Four more, lovely lady."

My heart fluttered when he called me that. It was a term of endearment, one I doubted he'd offered to anyone else in his life. I really did want to get to know more about him, but that would take time as well as peeling layers away from the onion.

I was certain he felt the same about me.

The four strikes were equally as savage, the heat on my bottom a direct conflict of the chill in the air.

When he lifted me off the railing as if I weighed nothing, a rush of air was pushed from my lungs. He cradled me against him as he'd done so many times, the sound of his boots thumping against the deck somehow comforting. He didn't seem to care as he dropped to one knee, easing me into the water with utter gentleness.

If only I could take a picture of the naked man in boots and nothing else. I was certain the town gossip would be hotter than normal. Exhaling in appreciation, I moved to the other side of the oversized hot tub, already basking in the warmth of the water.

Even if my butt hurt and likely would for a few hours.

He knew how to provide a decent spanking.

The thought made me blush.

Jagger was still in the mood to taunt me, taking his time removing his boots. The lighting presented a gorgeous figure of perfection for a few precious seconds before he slipped into the water.

We swam around each other for a full two minutes before he advanced. He was without a doubt a true predator, the look in his eyes confirming my belief. But I was a girl who wanted to be caught, captured, and kept for a long time.

Could I stay here and be happy?

I'd been so uncertain before, but I knew I could find a fabulous life here. If only I allowed myself to do so. Maybe things would work out. Maybe…

He pushed me back against the solid surface, his growl a clear indication of what he had planned for me. I teased him by rubbing my leg against his thigh, pursing my lips on purpose as well.

The way he spun me around in the water made me laugh. "What do you want, big man?"

"Not grumpy dude any longer?" he asked.

"Oh, you're grumpy as hell, but I kind of like that. You're a bit ruffled."

"I've been called many things, lady, but not ruffled."

I brushed the back of my hand across my face. "There's a first time for everything. Right?"

"Yes." When he captured my mouth, I moaned immediately into the kiss. Just the way he held me was special, entirely different than before. We'd bared our souls, allowing the other to learn our darkest secrets.

The thought of doing so was still painful, but as he kissed me as if I'd never been kissed before, all the fears slowly started to melt away.

I slipped my arms over his shoulders, delighting in being able to tug on his long hair. His thick beard scratched me more than it had before, which allowed a bubbling laugh to surface. It broke through the kiss and I pushed him away by a few inches.

"You don't like my beard," he said gruffly.

"I don't think there's much about you I don't like."

Our lips were so close together, only centimeters apart. He was breathing heavily, his haunted eyes dipping down low.

"Where is this going?" I asked, which shocked me. Only hours before I'd done everything in my power to shove him away.

"I don't know. Does it matter?"

"Not right now." The admittance was freeing. Whatever this would turn into had allowed me to feel something I'd never felt before.

Someone who truly gave a damn.

Not because he wanted to have arm candy on the side or because he needed a family to show off to the press and his associates. Jagger was real and we were right here together.

He kissed me again, more roughly this time, acting as if maybe this was the last time we'd be able to connect. As our growls and moans filled the night sky, I wrapped both legs around his waist. The warmth was incredible, but the feel of his weight was even better.

As the pure intimacy continued, I felt every muscle that had remained tense since I'd gotten here fall away, relaxing because I knew I was safe.

Even if just for now.

His tongue dominated mine, pushing a level of heat I'd never known existed before. They were dancing together, but I knew he would completely dominate mine. That was the kind of man he was.

With the sky clearing, the moment he broke the kiss, I glanced up at the stars. I used to make wishes to them, only to find out not one had come true. But I made another one, my mind hopeful.

That I could make Danger Falls my home.

Jagger shifted his hand between us, pressing the tip of his cock against my pussy. He wasn't blinking, barely moving as he studied me with such emotion in his dark eyes. The moment he slid his shaft inside, I clung to his shoulders.

On this night and for whatever time we could carve out, we were as one. No matter what happened, I would remember this very moment as one of the best in my life.

"So tight," he whispered and drove the last few inches deep inside.

"So huge."

His grin was lopsided and, in the twinkling, vividly colored lights of the hot tub, I could tell he was lost in his own level of pure ecstasy. I never would have believed he could find such peace in sharing something between a man and a woman. Maybe first impressions weren't my strong suit.

As he pulled out, I jutted my hips forward. I needed him inside of me as much as I did the air I was breathing. He sensed my longing, driving inside with careful actions. But I pressed him harder. I needed the roar of excitement and the rush of adrenaline. He repeated his actions, still watching me carefully as if I was going to break into a thousand pieces.

I knew now I was much stronger than that.

So many emotions rushed into me as we fucked... no, we made love. There was no other way of looking at the tenderness laced with the rough need we'd both shared. He still never blinked, his entire face contorted in worry and confusion.

About how he was feeling.

He spun me around again and I shivered to the core, even throwing my head back as a beautiful sweep of ecstasy began a powerful journey from my toes to my core. In those incredible seconds, I did what I could to drive the orgasm away. Losing this moment would be painful.

But my body refused to obey my deepest thoughts and needs.

The dazzling sensations rocketing through me were even better than the climaxes he'd provided before. How could a man so insanely gruff be this amazing in... hot water? The thought brought another smile to my face.

His smile as he watched me was wry, as if learning my body meant he had full control over me.

I wasn't certain there was a single ounce of me that minded.

As our fucking heated to an explosive point, bubbles splashing over our bodies, the orgasm hit me harder than I'd believed possible.

There was no way to bite back a slight scream and instead of me being forced to slap my hand over my mouth, he did so for me with a rough kiss.

I couldn't get enough of the taste of him, floating directly into nirvana as my shattered body responded to the pure ecstasy. Only when I started coming down from the spectacular high did he let himself go, falling into his own state of nirvana.

Squeezing my pussy muscles, I was able to bask in his moment of bliss as he threw his head back. I felt the moment he erupted deep inside, filling me with his seed.

Whatever the future would bring, this moment belonged to us and us alone.

From being around Jagger, I'd learned that life wasn't just about everything being black and white.

Or good and bad.

Right versus wrong.

Gray was allowed to seep in and those who were lucky and in tune with the world around them could appreciate it.

In a short period of time, he'd taught me all about seeing the different shades of evil, providing a light I thought I'd never see again.

If only this could last forever.

CHAPTER 21

The sound was jarring. So much so I jerked up from a deep sleep. Something inside told me I'd been in a nice slumber, but the darkness in the room was instantly terrifying. Had someone broken into the house?

"Jagger. There's someone inside." Fear tore through me as I struggled to unearth my arms from the tight covers, immediately reaching over to his side of the bed.

Even though I was starting to see shadows in the room, I had to feel his pillow to realize he wasn't in bed. Maybe he'd heard the intruder.

Oh, dear God. Cally!

Still fighting the covers, I managed to jerk my feet from under them, placing them quietly on the floor. If someone was in the house, I would need to remain very quiet. Where was Jagger? Inching into the bathroom, I resisted turning on a light. Half my clothes were still outside, the towel he'd used to wrap around me when carrying me to his bedroom thrown somewhere against one of the walls.

Maybe I'd get lucky and he was the kind of man to wear a robe. A slight breath escaped my lungs when I felt one on the back of the door. I slipped into it, fighting the terrified girl inside even more. I'd never been this way, forced to take care of my own battles my entire life. Joel had taken too much from me and that was going to stop right now.

I took cautious steps toward the door, hopeful he would dash in and tell me everything was okay.

But I sensed that wasn't going to happen. My stomach was in knots as I opened the door, slipping into another wave of shadows as I made my way to Cally's room. Very quietly I turned the doorknob, grateful Cally had to sleep with a light of some sort on. The lamp on the other side of the room had a low wattage bulb, which allowed a slight view of my sleeping baby.

Xena lifted her head, but as soon as I placed my finger across my lips, she lowered it again. There hadn't been any disturbance in the room I could see. Since I'd left my phone in the kitchen, I couldn't call 9-1-1. That meant I had to find out what I'd heard.

As soon as I closed the bedroom door, I heard another noise. This time I sensed it was something being tossed against the wall or on the floor. Where the hell was Jagger? Why wasn't he hearing this?

I remained as quiet as possible as I made my way to the top of the stairs. I only had a limited view of downstairs, able to tell the fire in the fireplace was mostly embers at this point. But with every light being off, I could barely make out the furniture. Maybe I was being foolish, but I started to descend the stairs.

When I'd walked down four of them, another noise startled me more this time. But it wasn't a thud. The sound was a deep, haunted moan.

Jagger.

I hurried down the rest of the stairs, waiting on the landing as I tried to figure out where the sound had come from. There were several rooms on the bottom floor including a study toward the back I'd peeked my head into.

He wasn't in the kitchen or the living room. My gut told me Jagger was suffering from a nightmare he'd experienced. I moved cautiously down the hallway, passing two darkened rooms and a bathroom. The door to the study was partially cracked, a source of light streaming from underneath.

I was still cautious as I approached, unsure what I could do for him. When I pushed open the door, my heart broke a little. The moment he tossed two heavy books across the room, I cringed deep inside. I should have heard him having a nightmare.

He ripped at his hair before plopping down in one of two leather chairs, dropping his head in his hands. On the table to the side was a bottle of booze and a glass that only had a swig left in it. From what I remembered of the bottle from before, he'd had one too many in trying to exorcise his demons.

For the first time since we'd met, he didn't sense my presence, which was almost as concerning as the fact various items had been tossed around the room, several books with broken spines laying haphazardly on the floor.

"Jagger." I didn't dare take a step inside. I'd had a few psychology classes, but that in no way made me qualified to deal with PTSD. It was obvious he was suffering from the horrible deeds he'd seen and been forced to do during both dangerous occupations.

A mercenary.

I hadn't allowed myself to think about what he'd done until now. He'd killed people for a living. Yes, maybe bad people who others believed deserved to die, but that didn't change the fact he'd used them for target practice. A sudden cold shiver slammed down my spine.

Whatever organization he'd worked for had likely lied to him or worse.

Left him without support.

He jerked his head up, his entire face contorted from an extremely heightened level of anger.

"What the fuck are you doing here?" he asked and he immediately reached for his glass, finishing off the last of his bourbon. It didn't take him two seconds to refill his glass.

"Don't, Jagger. Just don't."

His laugh sounded bitter. "What don't you want me to do, sweetheart? Drink myself to death or pull out a handgun?"

Was he trying to terrify me with threatening to kill himself? If so, he was doing a damn good job. But I was also angry, furious in fact.

"Both." I walked toward him, folding my arms. "What the hell do you think you're doing?"

"What do you think? Finding an escape."

I had two different ways of dealing with this. Coddling him or telling him exactly what was on my mind.

I chose the latter for good or for bad. I wasn't in the coddling mood. "How fucking dare you."

His eyes flickered with confusion at first, but his mask was firmly shoved back into place. "How dare I do what?"

"Act like you don't give a damn about anyone else but your-self. You're a fraud. An asshole. A jerk and I thought you were completely different."

"I guess you thought wrong."

"Bullshit, Jagger. You risked your damn life to go on that mountain to locate my daughter. You kept me from falling off a goddamn cliff. In my mind that shows you have grit, a salt of the earth kind of man. It also tells me that you have integrity. You have the entire world at your feet. Money. A fabulous resort to work in. A town of friendly fucking people who think the sun rises and sets on your ass and… And a woman who gives a damn about you, but you'd prefer to wallow in self-pity. I call that bullshit."

I held my breath, waiting to see what he would do. As anticipated, his rage flared once again and he jerked to his feet. A part of me was momentarily on edge, but my gut told me and the inner voice whispered that he would never dare raise his hand to me. Not once. Not under any circumstances.

He fumed, his chest rising and falling and his face turning red. I saw hatred in his eyes. All for himself. But he remained quiet, just the little bit of ice rattling in the shaking glass creating any sound.

We glared at each other until I was certain I had to try yet another tactic.

"Fine. Have it your way, Jagger." I turned to leave and as I'd hoped, he refused to allow me to get out of the room. He planted his flexed hand on the door, slamming it closed before picking me up. "Let go of me."

"No." His single word was filled with agony. He sat down again, planting me on his lap. The single act told me he'd survive this panic attack.

But there would be more. How would I be able to handle the next one? And the next.

The man was a bundle of nerves, the cords on the side of his neck thumping from his increased pulse. My doctor side almost took over, but I tamped her down. What Jagger needed right now was someone to listen. Not to bark orders or tell him how he should be feeling. While he'd admitted his previous job, information most people wouldn't understand, there was much more to what he'd endured. Something more personal.

He had one arm around the base of my back, keeping me in place while allowing me to know his intentions weren't harmful. Sadly, his eyes were dilated as memories plagued every thought. "Let me help you, Jagger."

"I don't think anyone can." He took another sip of his drink as he stared off into space.

I wrapped my fingers around his and the glass, stretching them out so I could rub the tip of my index finger back and forth across the top of his hand. He allowed me to take the glass from his hand, finally able to look me in the eye as I took a sip of his drink.

He was starting to come down from the fog that had hardened his mind and his heart. But not enough that it would mean anything the next time he had an episode.

"A nightmare?" I asked.

His nod was so forlorn. "Nothing unusual except I thought you were…"

"Someone who hurt you."

"Yeah. I can't do this to myself any longer or to you."

"You're not going to hurt me."

"You don't know that!" The right corner of his lip curled.

"Yes, I do. It will never happen. You won't allow yourself to do that."

He retrieved his drink, laughing more bitterly than before. "I wish I had your confidence." In an unexpected move, he kissed my cheek. It was also a slight dismissal. He wanted to try to shove his experience under a rug.

"I don't know any longer." He placed his glass on the table. Every time he looked at me, I could see another layer being peeled. He'd been so caught up in hating himself that he'd forgotten it was okay to live. To enjoy.

As he slid a strand of hair from my mouth, his face contorted and he looked away. "Few people could ever understand what it's like to be a prisoner of war."

Oh, shit. Another reason he hated the world. He'd experienced the worst of mankind.

"I wouldn't want my worst enemy to try and fathom what it's like to be deprived of sunlight, food, and water. I'd never wish the kind of torture I'd endured on anyone no matter what they'd done in their lives. There are fates worse than death. All you do is pray that death will take you, and a part of you is lost in the darkness forever. But I've come to understand what I had to face was nothing in comparison to the loss experienced by the families of those I killed. I deserved the months in captivity."

He made the statement in such a cold, calculated way that I wasn't able to come up with a decent response. At least not until I was able to process what he'd told me.

"No one deserves to be tortured, Jagger. Some, however, deserve to die for the terrible things they've done to others either for fun, financial or political gain. What you did as a soldier was make the world safe for others, keeping democracy alive. What you did as a mercenary was the same, only you were forced into even more dangerous situations because you were very much alone. It wasn't your fault you were captured by some terrible people either. But do you want to know something?"

His eyes were glistening as he studied me. "What?"

"You're not alone right now. I'm here. And unless you have other plans, this is where I intend on staying." He was holding back some of the details, but I couldn't press him. My heart was heavy for him yet grateful that he'd shared his horrors with me.

He'd opened himself up, making his needs and anxiety vulnerable to me, someone he barely knew. Some might not understand how special that was. Maybe my thinking was twisted, but I'd been the one to discuss murder options with my best friend so who was I to justify myself?

There was no real cure for anyone suffering from the mental turmoil he was going through, but there were support mechanisms, people who could help ease his anxiety. Right now, his first task was acceptance of his deeds and that they didn't reflect on the man.

He also had to forgive himself.

It was something we both needed to do. Maybe fate had brought us together for a reason.

Healing.

Understanding.

Survival.

CHAPTER 22

agger

The afternoon sun had a warming effect, the thick snow slowly fading into a memory. I pulled into the parking lot of Shackles, a favorite local watering hole, the grip on my steering wheel tight.

Two days had passed since I'd lost my shit and Bella had found me. I knew I'd seemed like a madman to her, likely ranting and raving. I remembered only some of what I'd told her. But what I knew was that she'd held my hand for a solid two hours after I'd told her I'd been captured, finally falling asleep on my chest.

The closeness had been the nearest thing to heaven I'd ever experienced.

I'd carried her up to bed, tucking her in and watching her sleep for the rest of the night. As soon as dawn had broken through the gray horizon, I'd heard both Cally's and Xena's feet romping through the house. At least the sweet little kid had allowed me to pour her a bowl of cereal for breakfast. She'd chattered away like she did every minute she was awake while I'd fed the pup.

It had tugged at my heartstrings more than any time before.

The reason why had become clear to me. Because everything seemed normal. A normal family. A normal house. A normal morning.

When nothing was truly normal in my world or in Bella's.

My anger was still fresh, my mind anticipating what I would do to Joel if he stepped foot in Danger Falls.

At least work had taken up the better part of the last two days, which had kept me from going off the deep end. With Bella still on the job waiting tables, and Cally and the hero dog Xena the hit of daycare, I had the early evening to myself. What did I do instead of going home to an empty house?

I asked both brothers to meet me at a goddamn bar. It wasn't my usual behavior by a long shot, so I knew they'd have questions.

I'd had more trouble sleeping, only able to stay with Bella for a couple of hours. At least I'd waited until she'd fallen asleep before heading downstairs, pulling out my computer and searching for every scrap of information I could find on the Brockford family. She hadn't been lying about their power.

Joel's father had come up through the illustrious ranks of being one of the top surgeons in the country to running a highly profitable charity for extreme medical conditions. The money he'd managed to bring in was astounding. He appeared charming in the photographs, always smiling and shaking hands. However, I could read between the lines.

People were afraid of him.

Some notorious criminals had also been included in a couple of the photographs. That gave me an indication there was some type of a relationship with the Brockford family.

Maybe the patriarch had a way of saving the lives of powerful people who would then owe him a favor or two, including eliminating anyone getting in his way. It was just a crazy theory of mine, but one that wouldn't leave my mind. Joel was shadowing his father's footsteps, also highly respected and considered the quintessential surgeon on the East Coast.

As with every family, dark secrets lay in wait for the right person to find them. While a significant part of me wanted to resort to my previous convictions on handling a target, I also knew the problems killing Joel could create.

I'd come to terms with the thought of destroying the man instead.

Unfortunately, I would need help in doing so. Something I wasn't used to either.

After parking the Rover, I climbed out, scanning the parking lot. It was early, but there were already a solid three dozen vehicles, which meant the place was going to be packed. The damn holidays again. Plus, the snow hadn't dampened anyone's spirits.

Cally had started talking about what to get the dog for her stocking and I'd been forced to walk out of the room. My attitude had been bad enough that the little girl had taken to calling me Mr. Grumpy. And every time Bella had burst into laughter. Meanwhile, both girls as well as Xena also had added light to the house that hundreds of lamps hadn't been able to do.

I strolled into the bar, glancing at the bartender who I knew. While I might not frequent the place that often, people paid attention to the Fox boys. The whole town had watched us like hawks for weeks after our arrival. In addition to the sheriff throwing shade given our backgrounds, there'd been real fear we'd sell or shut down the resort. I couldn't blame them for their concern.

We'd looked pretty rough around the edges when we'd walked into town, our people skills lacking.

I'd barely walked past the bar when the bartender shoved a glass of my brand of bourbon across the bar top. "I take it my brothers have arrived?"

"Back table. I guess they don't want to be seen." Mark grinned and was shouted at from the other end of the bar.

As I pushed my way through the crowd, I had one too many congratulations. Praise was getting old, especially when in my mind I didn't deserve it. Poppy had even dropped off muffins, for God's sake.

"You did good out there, cowboy," Tyler Florence said as I tried to pass him. "Saving that little girl. I didn't know you had it in you."

Tyler was a deputy, a nice enough guy, but he was a sheep following his boss, Sheriff Adam Young's dislike of the Fox family. Since we'd never had a run-in with the sheriff's department, the only two reasons for the hatred would be our reputation and the fact Adam's family had tried to purchase the resort. His father had a land development company and from what I heard, had plans on turning the resort's side into condominiums.

But his personal conviction to run me out of town or put a bullet in my gut was something else altogether.

"Just doing what any good person would do in helping out a fellow man." It was best not to provide but so much information to Tyler. He'd take whatever I said directly back to the sheriff. I wasn't in the mood for some pissing contest over God knows what.

"Yeah, so I heard. I also heard the girl's mother is staying at your place. I guess you think you're the only hero around here. Shacking up with the sordid woman."

It wasn't a good idea for any man to goad me, period. But in speaking about my woman that way, he'd crossed a final line.

Now the dude had me pissed. I was in his face in a second.

"You don't talk about a lady that way. What's it to you if she is staying with me anyway?"

"I was just jiving you, man," he said, real fear in his eyes.

"I suggest you remember this is a public place, gentlemen." The newer gruff voice was just as irritating.

I slowly turned my head in the sheriff's direction. I should have known where there was one, the other would follow. "I think that's something you should mention to your man here, Sheriff."

"I don't like you, Jagger. As you know, I don't like the three of you boys. I think you bring shit onto this town and if I had my choice, I'd kick you out."

"Not your call. But I'll keep that in mind. Maybe I'll see if the other boys would like to purchase a few more pieces of property around here. I think you have your heart set on a few. I wouldn't get your hopes up." Maybe I was just fueling his guns, but I couldn't help myself.

There'd been tremendous speculation about the jobs my brothers and I in our former lives had performed, stories including we were part of some big mafia family. At least most of the townies had stopped googling our names in hopes of finding some dirt.

I had a bad feeling the sheriff was keeping a file on the family.

Of course he had a reason to hate me. I'd only found that out after moving here. Because of his hatred for me, I continuously egged him on. But that didn't make it right that he was gunning for my entire family.

277

"You shouldn't have come here, Jagger," the sheriff said quietly, as if for my ears only. "One mistake and I'll lock your ass up."

I stopped only briefly, resisting all the nasty words that came into my mind. "Maybe you're right, but I'm here now. I'm staying. Just try and force me to leave and you'll regret it."

"Don't threaten me, boy. I have friends in all the right places." He laughed one of those maniacal sounds that likely put the fear of God into all the locals. Not me. He could threaten all he wanted, but he had no idea what I was capable of.

No man was going to push me away from anything or anyone ever again.

No matter how much he hated me.

He was huffing behind me as I turned and headed toward the back of the bar. I couldn't care less, but we owed it to the staff to keep the man and his family away from the resort. There were always bad business deals and while our father had taken great strides to keep the integrity of the resort, I'd had a feeling all along the Young family was planning something under the table.

"What the hell was that all about?" Hunter asked as soon as I sat down.

"My typical run-in with the sheriff and one of his goons."

"Boy, that man hates you. What did you fucking ever do to him?"

I shook my head toward my brother. "I don't know. I think it's all about my sterling personality."

"He's an asshole. We should ensure he's not voted in at the next election." Hunter had no idea how dangerous Sheriff Young could be. However, he was small potatoes in comparison to the Brockfords.

"Both of you, just lay low. Okay? We don't need to come up against the man. He has some powerful friends and you know how ruthless his father can be. Plus, with our father's past history, we don't need any unwanted attention drawn to the resort."

Past history. Our father had provided a trumped-up story about working from the ground up with a company where the other executives had turned rogue, engaging in criminal activity. He'd taken his share of the proceeds and skipped town to avoid possible prosecution, pretending he was someone else while raising three boys in Montana. Then he'd up and sold the place prior to bankruptcy, somehow managing to purchase the resort and spending millions of dollars in renovations.

The three of us had decided to let it go, not grilling him any longer since he had only months to live. But I knew in my gut whatever bad deeds he'd done would come back to haunt the family one day.

However complacent we'd become, I was surprised at Shephard's declaration of peace. "I'll keep that in mind." I sat back, surveying the crowd and enjoying a few sips of my drink. I noticed the sheriff was talking to a few men in the crowd. My hackles remained raised. He was going to cause trouble. I felt it in my bones.

"Not that this newfound brotherly love isn't good for our mental stability, but why the hell did you want to meet us?" Hunter pushed after clearing his throat on purpose.

"You got a hot date?" I asked him. "Another tourist fascinated by your engaging eyes?"

"Very funny, but as a matter of fact, yes." He grinned and I shook my head.

"Your dick is going to fall off if you aren't careful," I told him.

"I didn't say I fuck all of them."

"Louder so the entire bar can hear you. Jesus, brother."

Hunter snorted. "At least I get some. Maybe things are changing for you though, huh?"

I glared at him.

"The two of you make enjoying a cold beer a moment of torture. Now, I have other plans as well so cut the chitchat. Denise is meeting me here for a couple drinks, maybe dinner. Unless you want her knowing your business and bugging you about getting together for a holiday thing, spill it."

What I wanted to avoid was her taunting me about being best man and any questions she had about Bella. Since she was an ex-detective, she never stopped asking questions.

Seeing the many ways my brother had changed over the last few months had initially pissed me off. Now I knew why. Shephard had found true happiness and I'd been jealous.

I laughed halfheartedly. "Then I won't keep either one of you. As much as I hate to say this, I need your help."

Shephard placed his hand against his heart. "From us? We should be honored."

"Fuck you," I grumbled.

Shephard laughed. "Stop being so much like some grizzly bear stuck in a trap. Does this have anything to do with your houseguest?"

"How is Bella adapting anyway" Hunter asked, but I knew the man was fishing.

"She's fine. She's taken over the place. Even ripped down the goddamn curtains I hate." At least I could smile. "Yesterday she came home with flowers for the kitchen table and made freaking chocolate chip cookies, for God's sake."

"And so it begins," Shephard mused. "Just wait until you're seriously involved. Don't forget to pick up your socks and underwear. What's up?"

The man was way too happy.

"I need this kept quiet and I also mean from Denise. Okay? Bella needs help and we're the only one who can provide it to her."

Shephard took a deep breath and leaned over the table. "You found out why she dropped in on our little town. Did you grill her on her last name too?"

"Yeah, on both. She's running from her soon to be ex-husband. He was abusive to her. I've seen the bruises. He also threatened her career, cheated on her, and is trying to take her daughter from her." Bella had told me more of the sordid details, including finding her best friend in their bed with the man.

"Ouch. Real nice guy," Hunter hissed.

"Yeah, he took a video of them engaging in some pretty kinky stuff and is threatening to release it like it's from a porn movie."

Shephard coughed, spitting out part of his beer. "What the hell? Who does that shit?"

Hunter gasped. "And why? He was the one who fucked up."

"She thinks there's some contractual reason Joel asked her marry him," I told them.

"Like an arranged marriage? Is that what you're thinking?" Shephard wiped his mouth with his sleeve, sitting back in his seat after doing so.

"Yeah."

"She's still married?"

I glanced at Hunter. "For now. They are legally separated and the divorce should be final any time, but yeah, still married."

"You know the fact you're hooking up could create difficulties for Bella." Shephard waited so I'd absorb what he was saying.

"We're not hooking up." I felt the agitation rising.

"Then what are you doing?" Hunter had a damn smile on his face.

"Trying to learn to live again." My answer was at least honest. "And I am going to protect her. No matter what it takes or what it means to my life."

Shephard raised his glass. "A toast, Hunter. To our brother who just returned to life."

CHAPTER 23

 agger

Maybe neither one of them understood what lengths I would go to in order to keep Bella and Cally safe.

"The bastard had already texted and called her, threatening her," I added to the conversation. "I think it's only a matter of time until he does everything he can to track her down. He had ammunition to try and take Cally away and from what she's told me, he'll make good on his threats."

"Is he the child's biological father?" my older brother pushed.

"No. And he didn't legally adopt Cally, but is trying to push that through the court systems as well. I think he and his father own people in Baltimore. They will try and get it shoved through. That will devastate Bella. I won't allow it to happen."

"Blackmail is a powerful tool." Shephard looked away. "You know, maybe Denise can help. She's from Charlotte but maybe she knows something about the Brockfords."

"No," I said way too vehemently. "Not that I don't trust Denise, but I want to keep this between us for now. Until we see what we're dealing with."

Shep was none too happy, but nodded.

"The boy is in love."

I knew Hunter was just messing with me, but his frivolous attitude was the last thing I wanted to hear. "She's a good person. She doesn't deserve to lose her career and her daughter over a two-timing asshole."

Shephard nodded. "Agreed. What do you need from us?"

"You guys have deeper contacts than I have. I want every scrap of dirt found out on the Brockford family."

"Why does that name sound familiar?" Hunter was asking himself more than he was of either one of us.

"Big names in Baltimore. I don't know otherwise. All I've found is glow and show. But they're both associated with some corporate moguls accused of a few crimes of their own. A lot of corruption in Baltimore."

"Birds of a feather..." Shephard didn't need to finish the statement.

"What happened to your people, Jagger? Your handler should be able to help provide some information." Hunter lifted his eyebrows after asking the question.

I twirled the glass on the table. "Let's just say I burned a bridge or two." And I had. There was no way I could go back to the organization I worked for as a mercenary and when I'd been discharged from the Army, pretty much everyone was glad to see me go.

"You do care about this girl. Don't you?" Shephard gave Hunter a hard look as if cautioning him to lose the jokes.

"Yeah, I do. She makes me feel alive again. I can't explain it."

Shephard's smile was almost embarrassing. "You never will, not really. When you're used to living alone for so long, having someone invade your space leaves you anxious at first, breathless the next, and finally you find yourself head over heels in love. And you don't even know how you got there."

"Well, shit. Now I know the signs to look for so I can run far away from any chick I start feeling that way with." Hunter was thoroughly amused.

Maybe I was feeling a little that way, but love wasn't in the cards. "I'm not good for her, Shep. You know that."

"Why the fuck would you say that?"

"It doesn't matter," I insisted.

"Yeah, I think it does. You retreated back into that shell of yours after the first goddamn few weeks of living here. Why?"

I shrugged as an answer. Meeting them wasn't about analyzing my mental condition.

"Nightmares?" Hunter asked and this time, there was no look of amusement on his face.

According to the contracts we'd each signed with different organizations, we weren't allowed to discuss anything regarding the missions. All three of us had turned our military skills into a mercenary position, but I had no clue who they'd worked for or in what parts of the world they'd been. The three of us had tried to bury our experiences, but even though Shep was happy as could be, I sensed his darkness remaining.

Was there a way to exorcise the demons that were covered in blood? That was the million-dollar question.

"A few." My answer was controlled.

"Maybe you need to talk to someone," Shephard suggested.

"I don't need a damn shrink." My tone was harsher than I intended.

"No, but you need to talk this out. Maybe Bella can help with that."

My laugh sounded anything but happy. "She has too much shit on her plate right now. She needs our help. Are you willing or am I going this alone? I don't fucking care if I need to fly to Baltimore, I'll get that asshole to stop hassling her one way or another."

I could tell by Shephard's grin I'd hit all the hot buttons in his mind. Fuck that. My only intention was to get her the help she needed. Period.

"Don't do anything stupid, brother of mine. Let me make a few phone calls." Shephard took a long pull of his beer. "But I can't promise anything. I burned a few bridges myself. I'm going to get another beer and a glass of wine for my girl. *You* were fashionably late." He laughed as he rose from the chair.

"She has you wrapped around her little finger," I told him, trying to pull the conversation back to something lighter.

Hunter was staring at me like he used to do as a kid. He'd once told me I was the weirdest human he'd ever met. I had a feeling he still felt that way. Not that I could blame him.

"Does Bella know you're looking into her ex?" he asked.

"No."

"You can't start off a relationship with a lie."

"It's not a damn relationship and it's not a lie."

He laughed and lifted his glass. "You act like you have it all figured out. She'll call you not sharing this with her or worse, killing the man, a lie and let me ask you something. Is she sleeping in your bed in your house where she currently resides?"

I just glared at him.

"That's what I thought. You're in a relationship." He gave me a drawn-out smile before gulping his drink. "I'm just jiving you, man. You've been way off lately. More so than when we arrived. I've noticed you a couple times sparring with the sheriff. Is he giving you a hard time?"

"Always. I think he has something on Pops."

Hunter breathed out. "Then we can't let him destroy our future."

Future. I still wondered what kind of future I really had. "Yeah."

"Is there something else?"

I twirled my glass. "Nothing that needs mentioning."

"Careful with all those secrets, bro. They will eat you alive. So with Bella, I can see some light in those angry eyes of yours. What's wrong with enjoying her company?"

"What's wrong? I'm afraid I'll hurt her," I admitted. I'd woken up several times to find a lamp broken or a bottle smashed against the wall and I had no memory of doing so. What if I did something terrible in the middle of the night? I would press the barrel of a gun against my temple.

"Then don't. But that means you might need some help. It was forced on me after a few… incidents."

It was the closest he'd come to talking about his life before the resort. I knew better than to ask questions. The different ordeals the three of us had gone through would mostly die with us. It was not only a requirement, but the shit was way too personal.

"Easier said than done. I think I'm violent during the nightmares."

His eyes drilled into mine. "Bella is a doctor, bro. She will understand if you talk to her. Maybe she can offer some psychological help, even if you don't think you need any. If you're worried about hurting her in any way, you need to ask yourself why the fuck you think you don't need anyone's help. Besides, I have a feeling she already cares a hell of a lot about you."

"How could she?"

"You didn't see her face when you rescued Cally."

I snorted. "Being grateful for performing a rescue and caring are entirely different." I knew she cared. I wasn't certain why I was lying except my brothers would continue nagging at me. Just like I'd done when Shephard had gotten involved with Denise.

"I'm no expert in the love department. You know that, but you need to face your feelings and your fears. There's nothing wrong with caring about someone."

"Not true."

"Oh, come on," Hunter hissed. "Tell me why."

"It's not true if you were the reason the only other person you ever cared about is dead. That's why." I hadn't intended on spouting out those words and as soon as I did, I instantly regretted doing so.

Hunter's eyes opened wide. "Wow. No wonder you've been keeping that armor on. I bet it's getting pretty heavy."

"Let it go. I don't want to talk about what happened."

"Shephard is right. You definitely need to talk to someone, but I suggest Bella. Does she know how anxious you are and anything about what you went through?"

"Only what she's gleaned, but she's good at picking me apart. That shit is not fair to her."

"No matter what you think of me, Jagger, the worst thing you can do is to allow your past to interfere with your future. Plus, keeping closed off and away from everyone will never allow you to sleep at night. I tried that. I failed. I can't tell you the number of times I had my service revolver in my mouth. The only thing that kept me from pulling the trigger was the knowledge that maybe one day things would get better."

That was the most Hunter had told me about what he'd suffered. He may be the jokester and the playboy, but I sensed a much darker side that neither Shephard nor I had any clue about.

I noticed Denise walking in our direction, Shephard prepared to meet her halfway. I chuckled under my breath and Hunter glanced over his shoulder.

When they kissed, I groaned. He shook his head.

"There's nothing wrong with affection, bro," Hunter told me. "Including in public. Maybe take your non-relationship woman out and you might be surprised how good it feels."

"Said by a guy who's never been in a relationship." Whether or not I knew Hunter's personal demons, I sensed my comment had pinched a nerve.

What would we be like if we'd become doctors or attorneys? Would we be any closer?

Hunter stood to greet her and I did the same. Why did it feel so damn formal?

The lovebirds headed to the table and Denise immediately hugged Hunter first before heading in my direction. She was a hugger and that was fine. I just wasn't into it.

"At least this time you didn't flinch," Denise told me when she pulled away. As a park ranger, she was all business and barked orders, but around my brother she was all lovey-dovey.

Just like he was.

"I don't do that."

"Yes, you do," the three of them answered.

There was something to be said about having family.

Annoyance.

At least I could smile. "I should get going."

"Hold on," Denise told me. "You need to commit to bringing Bella and Cally over for dinner. Then we can finish having our discussion that we started in the grocery store."

"What discussion?" Shephard pushed.

I ignored it.

"I gave you my answer and they don't go anywhere without Xena," I said, hoping the fact she owned a huge Malinois would deter her thinking.

"Xena and Pepper will get along just great. I'll consider that a formal yes to my invitation. And we will finish that discussion." Denise gave me a pointed look.

Shephard was standing behind her and threw up his hands.

I managed to keep the slight smile on my face. "I'll talk to Bella. I'm not promising anything."

"Good. I will bug you until you make it happen."

"We'll talk in the next couple days. Okay?" Shephard nodded as I pulled out a twenty, dropping it on the table.

"Fair enough."

"Think about what I suggested," Hunter called before I got out of earshot.

I would. Then I'd toss it aside. My one goal was to help her with the situation. Then I'd help her find a place of her own.

It was best for both her and Cally.

CHAPTER 24

The phone had lit up twice during my drive. I was terrified to look at it.

But I had.

And regretted it.

It felt as if a noose had been wrapped around my neck, slowly stealing my life's breath. Soon, I would be driven in a darkness that I'd never recover from. Either madness or death. Or maybe prison at this point.

I stood all by myself in front of Poppy's Diner, still trying to make up my mind what to do. With life. With Joel. With Cally.

With Jagger. Sweet and damaged Jagger.

Up until this point in my life, I'd been determined and had a single path laid out ahead of me. I'd reveled in the organization and that had kept me from ending up on drugs or on the streets. I'd become so focused that no one had been able to break through my emotions. The plan had been perfect in my mind.

Graduate high school with honors with scholarships in hand.

Graduate college at the top of my class.

Head to medical school.

An internship on the East Coast at the best hospital.

After that it was all about working to become highly respected while buying a nice condominium that I could call my own.

Never had I entertained becoming anything but a surgeon. I certainly hadn't entertained working in a small town, but that's what I was doing.

I also hadn't anticipated marrying an asshole.

Was it the appeal of Danger Falls?

Partially.

Suddenly, I felt homesick, although Baltimore had never really felt like home. It was more like a stopping place where I could spread my wings before moving on. The whirlwind romance with Joel had changed everything. He'd orchestrated that happening. But at least I'd met a wonderful, goofy chick and developed a lifelong friendship.

I needed to talk to her like I used to, sharing our hatred of certain people and laughing over silly rom-com movies while drinking wine. The feeling became overwhelming. I backed away from the crowds of people purchasing holiday gifts and munching on cookies while they walked, pulling out my phone.

The ugliness of the text I'd received nearly broke my resolve.

Unknown: *Soon, you little slut. Soon.*

Unknown. Why was Joel bothering? Because he was smart. He knew that I'd start taking screenshots of everything he sent, maybe even recording the phone calls. I'd been too shaken up before to do so. Hissing, I shifted to Esme's phone number, trying to break the cycle of abuse with just one text to start.

Me: *Hey, girl. I need wine. Lots of wine. I have so many things to tell you. You should take a vacation and come visit. It's beautiful here. Call me later.*

She was likely busy with the late lunch crowd, her skills as a renowned chef garnering her accolade after accolade. I was so proud of her accomplishments. I felt a little comfort, a slight tether to the life I'd once had. I shoved my phone away, taking a deep breath of the crisp air. It was a beautiful afternoon and I refused to allow any asshole to spoil my new adventure.

As I walked the sidewalks leading to the diner, people waved, many people I didn't know saying my name. I'd seen the article in the local newspaper, something they still produced on actual paper. I'd even seen a few old-style metal boxes on a couple of corners where you could slip in a few quarters and purchase a copy.

Then there was the scent of fresh pastries and coffee, colorful flags and of course every store was decorated to the hilt for the upcoming holiday. If you were the kind of person who didn't get a warm feeling in your heart, then it wasn't beating. But that wasn't the reason I was considering staying and abandoning my entire life's plan.

The reason was Jagger.

Were we in a real relationship? I had to think no at this point, but it seemed we were headed there. I felt truly comfortable in my own skin when I was around him. That told me a hell of a lot about the man.

His strength.

His determined actions.

His heated passion.

Even his gruffness.

Maybe I would thrive with a different atmosphere. And allowing the possibility of finding love. Maybe.

There were a whole lot of maybes and even more questions, but if I didn't consider taking the position of the town doctor, I'd never know. In the few days of waiting tables, my feet and legs were killing me. Even more than when I'd stood on my feet for an entire day doing surgery. Plus, as embarrassing as it was to admit, I was a klutz when it came to serving food. For all the intricate surgeries I'd performed, I couldn't walk a tray full of food through a busy dining room to save my life.

I glanced inside the entrance door to Poppy's, already seeing some familiar faces. At least with Poppy and the others, I could get the truth on Doc Welby's place.

And maybe sneak finding out a little information on Jagger in the process.

I walked in and my mouth instantly watered from the delicious smells floating through my system. From baked apples to homemade Christmas cookies, this was one of the warmest and most welcoming places I'd ever walked into.

"Bella. Good to see you again. Would you like a cup of coffee?" Poppy noticed me immediately.

"I would. It's still chilly out there." While Jagger had insisted he purchase me some warmer clothes, for some reason the wind was biting today.

"Move over, Gerald," she told one of the customers. There was a seat in between him and the guy he was talking to. "Let a lady and true hero sit down."

Gerald glanced over his shoulder and gave me a toothy grin.

But he moved.

Poppy wiped the area and placed a new coffee mug down just as I sat down. She was eyeing me the entire time she was pouring coffee. "Are you settled into the town?"

I laughed. "First time I've ventured out by myself." Thankfully, my SUV hadn't been damaged from my stupid antics of trying to get away.

"Well, perfect time of year. Of course summer is good too. The whole town is talking about you guys."

"Ugh. Don't tell Jagger that. Or as my daughter calls him, Mr. Grumpy."

"He can be a little obtuse."

"That's a word," I told her.

"Where's that adorable daughter of yours?"

"At daycare at the restaurant." I poured in some cream, taking a few seconds to stir it. "Can I ask you a question, Poppy?"

"You can ask me anything, honey. Shoot."

"Doc Welby's office. Is it nice? Will I be happy taking over his practice?"

She laughed and I could tell she was brimming from excitement. "Doc Welby really was the doctor for almost everyone in town. Sure, they went to Roanoke or Salem if they needed specialists or a hospital, but he knew everybody by their first name. Hell, he birthed some of the people who still live here as adults. He just had a way of making you feel special, especially when he used to make house calls. Those were the days."

"House calls?" I thought about the medical bag I'd carried with me for years. Maybe the chaotic mess of my life was really a moment of serendipity.

"He sure did. It's been a while, but I know some of his older patients were grateful. I think you'll like his place. His wife made certain there were some feminine touches. You're thinking about taking him up on his offer?"

"I'm still thinking. I thought I'd just drop by and see the place."

Poppy refilled several customers' coffee before returning to me. "That's exciting news. He'd love to see you and we'd love to keep you here."

"Why? If you don't mind me asking."

"I don't mind at all. Easy answer. You're good for Jagger. I know. I'm a bit of a mother hen, but with his dad's cancer, Jagger's mom right by his side no matter what country they're in, Jagger needs someone to look after him."

How many times had I blushed since arriving in town? More times than I could count and I'd never felt compelled to blush before. I'd never really had a reason. "Why do you think I'm good for him?"

"Oh, come on. That man is so broken the pieces are rattling around in that rugged body of his. His dad once said he'd suffered the most. I mean to be captured near Christmas and then watch his fiancée die at the hands of the insurgents who'd taken them captive does split a person in two. You know? He's blamed himself ever since."

It was obvious she thought he'd told me. I was horrified that he'd suffered so much, trying my best not to react when my stomach was doing flipflops. I nodded, but felt the color drain from my face. There was no sense in letting her know he couldn't set the ghost of this girl free just yet.

"Why blame himself? He didn't lure them to these bastards. He didn't perform the ugly deed."

"You like him a lot." Poppy grinned in a knowing way. "I'm glad to see that."

"Yes, I do, but no one deserves that level of guilt."

"No, they don't. I don't know all the details, but evidently Jagger took her off the base, which was considered unsafe. He was almost court-martialed for it. His dad didn't tell me everything."

My God. Why the hell had the man mentioned the tragedy to anyone in the first place?

"Anyway, pretty much everyone in town thought Jagger might die a lonely man. Then you came into town and suddenly there's life inside him. A bright light just waiting to come out and shine. All because of you and that cute little girl of yours."

She had me laughing. "He's kind of special."

"I'm glad you think so," she said, winking. "Go see the doc. You have a good man on your hands, just one that's a little rusty in being a human being. Can I get you anything to eat?"

"No, but I wouldn't mind taking one of your famous cherry pies home for dinner."

I was still sick inside, finally starting to understand why he felt as if he would hurt me.

"Of course, girl. Let me get it boxed up for you."

As she walked away, I couldn't help wondering whether he would ever be free of her ghost. If not, I wouldn't be able to compete with that.

302

ella

With the cherry pie safely on my passenger seat, I headed to the doctor's clinic. Poppy had provided me with an address and directions. I found his place easily enough, although when I pulled into the parking lot, it appeared like a lovely house adorned in white with turquoise shutters. There was a front porch with flowerpots, but the flowers were all dead and no one had pulled the carcasses, tossing them into the trash.

Still, I had a feeling it was going to be quaint inside.

I wasn't disappointed, the small but accommodating reception area adorned with lots of magazines and pictures of the mountains surrounding the town. There was a single patient inside, the younger woman flipping through an issue of *Women's Day*.

"Can I help you?" an older lady asked from behind the reception desk.

"Hi, I'm Bella Winters. I don't have an appointment, but Doc Welby said I could stop by and see his clinic. I'll wait."

Her eyes opened wide. "You are very much welcome and the doc indicated maybe you'd stop by. He's finishing up with a patient, but I'll tell him you're here."

"Thank you." I suddenly felt suffocated, almost leaving as she walked away. No. I refused to walk out now. I was taking control of my life, but I had to do this for me, not just because of how I felt about Jagger.

I couldn't sit down while waiting. I was far too nervous. My pulse was racing, my hands clammy. There hadn't been a single surgery I'd performed where I'd felt this nervous. Why now? Because the decision I ultimately made would be the most life-changing event I'd ever gone through by far. My gut told me that.

Was it a positive decision?

I was leaning a certain way at this point.

At least ten minutes passed until I heard two voices. Doctor Welby walked out from the back alongside an older lady. She was laughing and my keen eyes told me she was flirting with him. That brought a smile to my face. He was a good-looking older man with a full head of hair and other than slight paunch in the front, lean and mean.

He'd make a good catch for anyone.

He showed the lady to the door, his smile remaining as she walked out. "Mrs. Jensen. I'll be right with you."

The other woman sitting in the chair offered him a huge smile. "Doc Welby, you're worth waiting for and remember, I'm no longer flirting."

This time I bit my tongue to keep from laughing. This was definite flirting. Poor guy. I wasn't certain whether to feel sorry or happy for him that he was so popular with the ladies.

He shifted his attention in my direction and it seemed as if relief flooded his gray eyes. "Bella. It's so good to see you. Please come back to my office and we'll chat."

I followed behind him, noticing out of the corner of my eye the receptionist was watching me intently. My decision would alter her future as well. She had every right to be nosy.

Doc Welby's office was tiny, every wall surface covered, his desk a complete mess, and I noticed there wasn't a computer in the room. Still, I had a feeling the man was completely organized. He'd have to be if he knew all the patients' first names without looking at charts.

"Have a seat, my dear," he told me, pointing toward the single one in front of his desk. The chairs were likely from the seventies, the desk more ancient than that, but his furniture suited him.

"Thank you for seeing me on such short notice."

"Nonsense. For a pretty lady like you, I'll make all the time in the world."

"I don't think you have any issues with the ladies."

I'll be damned if he didn't blush. "They're just gold diggers."

He was adorable and this time I did laugh. "Maybe so."

He plopped his folded hands on the surface of his desk. "So, what do you think of my little place?"

"Very… quaint."

His laugh was heartfelt. "I know there needs to be some updates, but I do have a new computer system installed, not that I've been forced to learn to use it, but it's state of the art. I have almost three thousand patients, most of which come to me on a regular basis. I get to make my own hours, enjoying a longer lunch. And I have terrific views. What more do you need in a profession?" His eyes were twinkling.

"Well, since you put it that way."

I adored the sound of his laughter. He pulled out a file and I sensed he'd been certain I'd take whatever the deal was. Or maybe I was his only potential buyer. Either way, he opened the file and started going over all the figures. For an old-timey doctor, he certainly had everything in order. His excellent financials were all there, as well as a layout of the building including the original plans and what he'd done to renovate the building. He had receipts from recently purchased medical equipment and full documentation on the computer system he'd purchased.

He was dead serious about selling.

The terms were more than fair. In fact, I'd be an idiot if I didn't seriously consider purchasing his practice.

The only issue was that my money had been tied up by Joel. The bastard would stop at nothing to keep me from having a new life. Yes, I could ask Esme for a down payment, but I really didn't want to possibly burn my friendship. "I think you've done an amazing job building a practice. I just don't know if I can swing it. My past is haunting me. I might not have any money until it's no longer tied up in the courts."

Maybe it was small town life or the fact the doctor had been witness to others having difficulty, but he placed his hand on my arm. I tensed from the light touch.

"I'm certain we can work something out."

"I don't take charity."

"Trust me, I won't give it to you. One of my daughters was just like you, hungering for more in the big world, including romance. She didn't think she could find it in Danger Falls. When she moved to San Francisco, I supported her decision, but I knew she'd never find happiness. Sadly, I was right. Sometimes you find happiness where you least expect or want it."

"Was your daughter a doctor?"

His features softened, his eyes reflecting his adoration of his daughter. "Just like her old man. I was so proud."

"Is she thriving?" I was hopeful with his answer, but I could instantly tell the subject was a sad one.

"No, Bella. She fell in love with a man who wasn't good for her."

"I'm sorry."

He sat back, looking out the window in his office instead of at me. "She was a bright shining star snuffed out by a man who didn't love her."

"What happened?"

His words hit me harder than I'd anticipated.

"He killed her."

* * *

The sun was no longer bright in the sky as twilight approached, the darkening atmosphere matching my sinking mood. I'd spent more time with Doctor Welby than I'd thought, enjoying watching him with a patient after looking around the place.

The filing system was antiquated, but with some time spent by hiring a college kid, the computer system could be up and running in no time. It had everything a growing clinical practice could want, including patient appointment reminders.

As I headed to my SUV, I found myself dipping my head when people passed. They continued waving or saying hello, but I felt more like a stranger than I had before.

Or maybe I was just more cognizant of my surroundings, constantly tugging the lapel of the jacket closer to my neck.

So few people understood how a person's life could change so quickly, going from hope for the future to broken glass shattered by violence and anger.

I felt that more today than I had before. Maybe I'd finally come down from a hopeful high in my attempt to navigate through the muck that my life had become. The doctor's anguish weighed as heavily on my mind as Jagger's former life and experiences. I was no longer certain I was the strong woman I'd built myself up to be.

Making tough choices was more difficult than I'd believed. So much so I was numb inside. However, decisions were vital if I wanted to regain control of my life.

"Ms. Winters."

The voice was one I didn't recognize and I immediately bristled. As I turned around, I was somewhat shocked to see a man in uniform. A sheriff's uniform to be exact. "Yes? Is there something I can do for you?"

The man was older, maybe in his late sixties, his law enforcement uniform somewhat ill fitting. While he wore a smile, his eyes reflected the intent for malice. I knew the look well. I could write a paper on staring down a person with malevolent eyes. He scanned the street before walking closer. "I thought I'd offer you a piece of advice."

A fresh breath of anger washed through me. My instincts were still working pretty well. He had no intention of offering me solid recommendations.

He was prepared to offer a warning.

At least I hadn't lost all my feisty personality. I folded my arms and purposely closed the distance between us. "Well, sure, Sheriff. I do so love locals who don't know shit about me trying to guide my existence in this beautiful little town. Go for it."

I could tell he was surprised my tone was biting. So what? I was finished with being told what to do.

He took his time, acting as if what he was about to tell me was gospel. "My advice is to get out of town when you can."

Admittedly, I hadn't planned on laughing, but since I'd never met him, I wondered why he felt compelled to assert whatever authority he had. "I'm curious, Sheriff. Why?"

"You seem like a nice girl, Bella, although it's obvious you're hiding a dubious past. Everyone knows that."

"There isn't a person alive who doesn't harbor some dark secrets. I have a feeling you have more than one."

The man didn't like my answer, his entire face darkening more than his eyes had before. "I know you're shacking up with Jagger Fox. You should learn to choose your companions more wisely. The man is bad news."

"And why is that?"

"Because he's killed people. Lots of innocent people."

"Haven't you, Sheriff?" As before, he was put off by my question.

His anger exploded and even though he was fighting to keep from making a scene, he threw his index finger in front of my face. "If you don't want your entire life destroyed, I suggest you heed my advice. You have a little girl to consider."

I'd been challenged so many times by arrogant pricks who thought they were holier than thou that my reaction was second nature and done without thinking. I was in his face, only a few centimeters away. The man was repulsive, his strong aftershave disgusting. While parts of my body were shaking, I refused to allow him to know he'd bothered me to any degree.

"I suggest you back off, Sheriff. I'm not the wayward waif you might believe I am. I can take care of myself and the people I care about, including Jagger Fox. And especially my daughter. No one will ever try and hurt them, or I will retaliate. And no, that's not a threat. That's a promise."

He took a deep breath, but it took him a few seconds to do so. "Be very careful, Ms. Winters. I have family in Baltimore. But you should really be careful of Jagger. The man is a true monster."

The last threat stole my breath. He grinned since he obviously noticed the sudden fear creeping into my system. With that, he backed away, tipping his ugly cowboy-style hat.

"Have a good day now, Ms. Winters. Just remember what I said."

Oh, I would. Only nothing was going to stop me any longer from getting what I wanted.

At least the asshole helped me make my decision. As he walked away, I took another deep breath of the air in the small town. I deserved happiness. I was more determined than ever that no one was going to derail my world.

Not for another second.

CHAPTER 26

 _agger_

Bella was late.

No, I hadn't tried to call her. I'd given her space, which was what she said she needed. More. Fucking. Space.

Meanwhile, I was ready to burn down the entire town in order to find her.

I'd been pacing the floor, my mind drifting to the worst possibilities. Had something happened to her?

The moment the door was thrown open, utter relief flooded through me.

"What the hell is it with this town?" Bella huffed as soon as she walked inside the front door of the cabin. She walked toward the kitchen with a pie in her hand, grumbling the entire time.

"Not sure what you mean."

"I mean some of the people are amazing, but not all of them." She'd returned to the room, her entire body as tense as mine.

All I'd thought about the couple of hours she'd been gone was how to protect her. I'd even put in a call to an old contact, an act I considered one of desperation.

Or a telling moment I was in extreme danger.

I'd broken the one rule I'd given myself after leaving my last job: never to contact my handler again. There was far too much bad blood, but my instincts were telling me that Bella's trouble would soon find her. Since she was still using her old phone, the asshole could have found a way to track her. Or, he might be cunning enough to know she'd use a different name. He had to know her story in that she'd grown up in foster care. What kid who had been didn't want to learn about why they were given up in the first place?

My contact had yet to return my call and there was no guarantee he would. I wasn't well liked in the organization I'd worked for. Maybe because I hadn't managed to remain a killing drone like they'd wanted.

Or maybe it was because the man had been a sore loser given I'd won our physical altercation.

As Xena ran toward her, Cally following, Bella took a few seconds to greet both, her voice changing from the anger I'd heard seconds later. "I missed you guys too." She was smiling, but I sensed she was not only experiencing fury but also deep concern.

What the hell had occurred?

"Mama. We played out in the snow," Cally said, her little voice excited. "Jagger threw snowballs."

Bella gave me an appreciative nod. "He did? That's wonderful. Do you mind heading up to your room with that furball of yours? Just for a little while."

"Okay, Mommy. Jagger said you're going out tonight."

I shook my head and chuckled. Kids couldn't be trusted with anything.

"Well, I guess we'll see about that. Scoot, baby girl."

Cally huffed exactly like her mother did when she was frustrated. "O-tay. No fair."

Bella waited until Cally was almost all the way up the stairs before approaching. "Going out, huh? I think Cally will like that."

"Not with Cally and don't think you're getting away from your outburst. What happened?"

She sighed and took off her jacket, tossing it over the back of the couch. "It seems the sheriff in your little town doesn't like me too much."

"What the hell did he say?" I immediately bristled. If that motherfucker did anything to her, I wouldn't care he had the law on his side.

"He acted as if I didn't belong in this town, telling me that in no uncertain terms. He also acts as if he knows about my life in Baltimore. How is that possible? Oh, who am I kidding. My guess is the smear tactic has already started. Today Joel sent an anonymous threat."

I tried to relax, but with Sheriff Young, I wouldn't put anything past him. "The sheriff is using his hatred of me against you, and remember, your name was on the local news. He's an asshole."

"You're right. He hates you. He called you a monster."

I was.

The words almost left my mouth. "Don't mind him. He doesn't like anyone since his wife ran off with the mailman."

At least her face brightened. "You're kidding me."

"No. It was the local week's gossip when I arrived in town." Which wasn't a lie. What I didn't decide to share with her was that since the mailman had ended up dead only a couple of weeks later, the gossip had gone off the rails. The mailman had died of a heart attack. Some believed it was because of rough sex while others had been certain the guy had been poisoned.

By the sheriff himself.

At least it had taken scrutinizing eyes off the Fox brothers' arrival in town for a little while.

Did I think Adam Young was capable of murder? You bet. But I'd learned in my years of traveling the world that every single person had a button that if pushed would drive them to doing bad things.

"Well, he made it clear I should leave."

"Are you?"

She finally relaxed enough that her smile wasn't forced. "For me to know and you to find out."

"I purchased a burner phone today. You might want to think about disconnecting your old one."

As she eyed me warily, she nodded. "I'll think about it. Now, what did you cook up if Cally isn't going with us? I can't leave her alone."

Her comment was right on cue to a knock on the door. "I took care of that. I think we need some time out of the house."

"You? Did you hire a babysitter?"

"Something like that." I wasn't positive I'd done the right thing, but I'd heeded my brother's advice. Staying cooped up in the house wasn't good for anyone, least of all Bella. I moved toward the door. My choice in babysitters was meant to be an olive branch of sorts. It surprised me that I'd bothered. Why would I care about whether people got along and there were no hard feelings?

I opened the door and immediately glanced toward Bella. She was none too thrilled to see Zoe standing in the doorway.

Zoe immediately sensed the tension, but I encouraged her

inside. "If you don't want me here, Bella, I completely understand."

Whether or not Bella blamed Zoe for Cally running away I wasn't certain. I could easily tell on Bella's face she wasn't prepared to place her trust in anyone.

"This was a mistake." Zoe started to head for the door. "I just want you to know how sorry I am. I was overwhelmed that night. I feel terrible."

"No. It's fine. Really, Zoe. It wasn't your fault. The entire scene was chaotic, so much so I'm surprised how amazing you were keeping the other children calm. Cally is fine. She's a tough little girl," Bella told her. "It's just been a few difficult days. Getting out will do me some good. Please stay."

I could tell Zoe was relieved as she turned around. "Take your time tonight. I love kids and Cally is such a great little girl."

"And I hope you love dogs," Bella added. "Soon, we might have a menagerie."

"Of course." Zoe pulled two bags from her purse. One contained a few pieces of chocolate and the other dog bones. "I always come prepared."

Bella seemed more at ease. "Well, Cally will have fun not being forced to be around her overprotective mother."

"I think you're a great mother and I've been around a lot of them."

"Thanks for that. Sometimes, I just don't know." Bella smiled.

"Trust me," Zoe said. "I've seen some real wingdings."

Bella burst into laughter. "I bet. So, where are we going?" Her smile was more relaxed than before, the look she gave me forcing my balls to tighten almost instantly.

"Dinner and maybe a hot spot in town. Well, as hot as it can be in Danger Falls, I guess." My answer surprised me. What did I know about hot spots? Until moving here, I hadn't been inside anything more than a total dive in over ten years.

She glanced at me with a funny look on her face, even wrinkling her nose. "Then I guess I'll dress up."

I didn't want to tell her that almost no one in town bothered to wear anything more than jeans in the winter and shorts in the summer. Maybe the testosterone-filled male inside of me wanted to see what she'd come up with. "Take your time. We'll leave whenever you're ready."

"Cally's upstairs in her room. I'll show you the way. If you don't mind making her dinner, that would be helpful."

"Absolutely."

As the two women headed up the stairs, I immediately moved into the kitchen, pulling out my phone. No message from the man I used to trust with my life. Funny how that kind of camaraderie ended when one of the two tried to kill the other. Kirk was many things, including a good friend, but when push came to shove, he'd followed orders.

Just like I'd been doing for years.

The organization had mentioned that you couldn't trust anyone. That had been something I'd reminded myself of more times than I could count. Still, after the dust had settled and the misunderstanding was brought to light, we'd resumed our friendship and he knew he owed me.

Which was why I continued to be furious. He'd obviously forgotten we'd both left the organization in disgust after learning of their involvement with some unseemly people from other countries.

It was obvious favors meant nothing.

There was one more person I could contact, someone who had the muscle, the money, and the soldiers to start a war. He was also one of the most dangerous men in the world. If I asked for his help, I'd owe him a favor.

It would be well worth it.

I glanced toward the kitchen doorway before locating the man's private number.

While this wasn't a good idea, I didn't care. I'd do anything to protect Bella.

Anything.

CHAPTER 27

ella

"A country bar?" I asked as we walked to the entrance of the bar. We'd had dinner at a quaint and very quiet Italian restaurant close to where Doc Welby's clinic was. We hadn't talked about my past or his, just spending time getting to know each other.

For the first time since we'd met, we'd been completely relaxed, bantering like kids and enjoying the food tremendously. He'd even dressed up in a jacket with black jeans and without a doubt, Jagger had been the most handsome man in the entire place.

No, in the entire town.

"Only part of the time," he answered as he opened the door.

"Then what's with the music? I don't do the two-step."

"Don't worry, city girl. I don't either."

The music was loud, the crowd huge for a weekday. A Monday no less. I was shocked to see so many people dressed in jeans and cowboy boots. This wasn't the Wild West.

Shackles felt welcoming as soon as I walked in. There was a long bar on one side of a massive room, a raised stage on the other, and in between were dozens of tables. With three bartenders working, I sensed they'd been prepared for a busy night.

"There's the band," I said wistfully. They were checking their equipment, getting ready for the show.

Jagger grinned as he pushed his way through the crowd, heading for the bar. "At least four nights a week. You'd be surprised the number of smaller but decent artists who appreciate the venue."

"No, I don't think I'd be that surprised."

"Hey, buddy," a bartender called from behind the bar. "You're beginning to be a regular. This must be that famous gal I've been hearing about. I'm Mark, this man's favorite behind the bar dude. What can I get you? On the house. You worked on a buddy of mine the other day. Might have saved his life." He threw his arm across the bar for a handshake.

"Regular, huh?" I poked Jagger in the stomach with my elbow. "I was just doing what I could to help. Maybe a glass of merlot if you have it?"

"Sure do. From a pretty fine vineyard. I know what you

want, Jag." Mark winked and moved to fill our drink orders. "From a certain famous vineyard in town."

The Foxhead Winery.

"I guess you're well liked," I told Jagger. "And Jag?"

"Smalltown stuff."

"Uh-huh." At least I felt freer and more comfortable than I had in a long time. I pressed my hand on his chest and peered out at the crowd. "Don't look now. I think your brother and that park ranger spotted us. Are they together?"

"Engaged. Shep wants me to be his best man."

"And?"

"Hell, no."

I smacked his arm. "You're a curmudgeon if I ever met one."

"Hey. I'm in shock," Shephard said as he approached. "Good to see you both. We got a table. Why don't you join us?"

"Please. We'd love to have you."

Jagger acted like he was going to say no. I poked him again and at least he smiled. "Fine. We'll join you for a little while."

After answering me, he locked eyes with mine and did something that instantly shocked me. He took my hand.

As he led me through the crowd, I could feel all eyes on us; they weren't gazes of anger or hatred, but ones of admiration and respect.

"You look amazing," Denise said as soon as we sat down.

"Doesn't she?" Jagger piped in.

"The only dress I brought with me. Thank God I had a decent one to wear. Although by the looks of things, jeans and cowboy boots would fit in nicely." Maybe I was a tad bit overdressed. I laughed and continued studying the bar. "This is interesting."

"You should see it on a Saturday night. It's insane in here. Never come unless you want to be hassled by tourists. Summer is worse. Hopefully, you'll find out." Denise shook her head. "But a place that frees the soul. After today, I need that."

"Meaning what?" I asked her.

"I had to tackle a tourist trying to take up close and personal pictures with a bear."

My laugh continued, but I could tell she was serious. "Really? Who would be that stupid?"

"Tourists," all three of them said together.

"Hey, we aren't all bad," I told them.

"Except what I hear is that you're no longer a tourist," Shephard suggested.

Shephard glanced at Jagger, a grin crossing his face.

"We'll see." I could feel Jagger's eyes on me.

Jagger's brother leaned forward in his chair. "I guess I'll have to work my magic on this little lady since my brother is having a difficult time convincing her to stay."

"No pressure, honey bunny," Denise told him.

"Honey bunny?" both Jagger and I asked at the same time.

Shephard growled. "Be careful, flowerpot."

"Ohhh…" The two were adorable together, but I sensed it made Jagger somewhat uncomfortable.

Mark found us at that point, placing the drinks down without asking if we wanted to run a tab. I had to admit it felt good to be out like a normal person.

Even though I wasn't certain I could ever consider myself as one again.

"I wanted you to know I checked with the hospital. All the patients have already been released. You did an amazing job, Bella. I can't thank you enough. Cally doing okay?" Denise leaned over the table.

"Better than okay now that Xena is in our lives."

"I think you're creating a home here." As soon as Shephard gave her a look, she shook her head. "Hey. There are mostly grumpy guys or older women in town. I'd love to have a friend."

"You won't if you keep pressuring her," Shephard told her.

"Yeah, don't pressure Bella. She doesn't like being told what to do."

Now it was my turn to glare at Jagger. At least he was grinning. "Very funny. Besides, I have some news. I might as well spill the beans now."

Jagger twisted in his seat. "You're keeping more secrets."

"Just for a few hours. I'm taking Doc Welby up on his offer."

Denise squealed and clapped her hands. "That's fantastic! I am thrilled and I know Jagger is." She gripped his hand and Jagger immediately tensed.

I was surprised when I felt his other hand on my leg. The little squeeze made me swoon. Conversation was cut short when the band took the stage, and the entire crowd started clapping.

He leaned over, nipping my earlobe. Another sign of affection. I was hot and wet all over at this point. "You're really staying?"

I nodded.

"I'm glad. Real glad."

Without a doubt I'd made the right decision and as the band made a few announcements to the audience, I wasn't paying any attention, instead leaning my head on his arm. Being around him, able to savor his amazing aftershave and feeling close to someone I cared about deeply made all the problems seem easy to solve.

I knew better, but at least tonight had been special and it wasn't over yet.

"You two should dance," Denise yelled across the table.

"Not a chance," Jagger retorted. "Not in the mood right now. Too much shit going on."

"Then why are you here?" Shephard taunted.

Exhaling, I fiddled with my wine, but was tired of his hot and cold. "Nope. We're dancing." Even if it was a country song, which I ordinarily couldn't stand, I refused to allow anyone to destroy this moment of joy. I stood and held out my hand, challenging him with my expression to deny me.

He lifted his eyebrows and instead of turning into the surly man he was so famous for becoming when times got tough, he grinned. "Careful what you ask for, lady."

"I'm not asking. I'm telling you. Get up and come on." Of course I said the words so the others could hear.

"Woo-hoo! I like this girl," Denise shouted.

Laughing felt good. Being with people I might be able to consider friends one day was amazing. If only Esme could be here, enjoying the view.

Including the hot guys.

She would go nuts.

I made a mental note to hunt her down in the morning, but for now, it was a nice date evening with a grumpy guy turned hero. I dared not call Jagger that again, but I could think it in private.

He didn't fight me as I led him through the crowd, groups of people already dancing. When I found a spot where we could squeeze in, I turned to face him, curious as to what he would do.

As expected, he seemed uncomfortable, easily noticing the couples who either nodded in our direction or used his name directly. He'd never be the kind of man to enjoy the spotlight. But he managed to break through another barrier, taking me into his arms.

I wrapped my arms around his neck, swaying my hips in time to the music. His steps were awkward, moving one foot to the side then the other. "You really don't like dancing?"

Snorting, he took a few seconds to glance around the bar. "Does it look like I know what I'm doing?"

"I have a feeling you're holding out on me. You have many hidden talents." I tried to move us around in one small circle, but his body was stiff as a board. No go. At least I could enjoy that he'd allowed me to take control for a little while.

"Nah. I've never been good at this shit. Music ain't my thing."

"No prom dates?"

"Hell, no."

"No wedding receptions?" I hadn't realized what I'd said until he got a faraway look in his eyes. Thoughts about Poppy's declaration seized my mind. I'd betray a trust if I mentioned a word and this bar wasn't the place.

He snickered. It was another attempt to hide behind his thick mask. "I don't have friends who'd invite me."

"Well, maybe we need to change that."

"You can't change me, lady. What you see is what you get."

"Oh, yeah? I think you're lying to me." I pushed his chest playfully, throwing back my head and even belting out lyrics to the music. The band had taken a hip rock song and turned it into a country mantra. I was pleasantly surprised that I enjoyed the sound.

"You're calling me a liar?"

"Yep. I am, big he-man. What are you going to do about it?"

He puffed up and I just knew he was going to ruin the evening with his usual prickly self, storming off the dance floor as if I'd committed the greatest sin.

When he yanked me against his body, tugging one arm out and clasping our fingers together, I didn't know what to think. But as he shifted his body, moving around the dance floor with precision as if trained by the finest dancers, twirling me around not once but twice before dipping me so low my head almost touched the floor, I shifted into a state of shock.

As he pulled me up slowly, it was as if he knew the band's music and how they transitioned from one song to another. A downtempo beat took over, which allowed his dance moves to become slower, much more sensual. He kept our heated bodies close, so much so I could feel his throbbing cock between my legs.

I was still in that wonderful haze of surprise as he continued to showcase talent that was so unexpected I was tingling all over. He twirled me around again, tugging me close and onto my toes. His grin was the most mischievous I'd seen and I was completely in awe of the man and his talents.

Not just on the dance floor.

"You are calling me a liar, lady?" he whispered into my ear, instantly dragging his tongue down the side of my neck after issuing a harsh growl.

"Uh-huh." I couldn't find words.

"I think you need to be reminded who is in complete control of you. Including that hot body of yours." He twirled me around again, every step a telling statement that there was nothing he couldn't do.

"Never," I breathed, so lightheaded stars were floating in front of my eyes.

After dipping me again, he held me that way, nestled against his massive body, his arm firmly planted around my waist. He was telling me in a different way that he'd never allow anything to happen to me.

The moment he slowly pulled me to an upright position, people around us began to clap.

Denise and Shephard's sudden appearance beside us didn't annoy Jagger as I would have believed. Instead, he was concentrating on staring into my eyes.

"Bro," Shephard yelled above the music. "I didn't know you had so much talent."

Without breaking our locked connection, one so electric every muscle had tensed, he answered his brother with all the tart grumpiness I'd grown to adore. "It's obvious you don't know much about me."

"I guess so. Wow."

"The most adorable couple on the dance floor," Denise added.

I had to agree with her, although I couldn't be certain since I'd only had eyes for the man holding me as if I was precious and cherished.

"Just so you know, I have it on good authority the bathroom is a hot make-out spot."

Denise's teasing words brought us both out of our sexual haze.

We both laughed as Shephard groaned, even swatting Denise on the butt a couple of times. "You are a bad girl."

"I think it's the only way to handle you boys. We need to keep you on your toes at all times," she countered. "Am I right, Bella?"

"So right. But I was considering a leash," I said to egg Jagger on.

He responded by pulling me close once again, the whisper in my ear one that set my soul on fire. "I'm going to spank that bottom of yours until it's rosy pink before tying you to the bed and drenching your hot body in whipped cream. After that, I'll feast for hours."

For a man who didn't seem as if he could be playful, he'd just pushed me onto a plateau of happiness and hunger I never wanted to come down from.

"You just think you can tame me," I whispered in return.

"Oh, I know I can. As a matter of fact, I already have."

"How's that?" I asked. We were once again moving as if we could both dance.

Jagger took his time answering, taking deep breaths and issuing another series of growls. "Because the moment you came into my life, I began to unravel every inch of you, allowing you to feel something you'd never felt before. Now that I've reeled you in, you should know you're mine."

"For how long?" I wasn't certain my feet were touching the floor any longer.

"From now until the end of time. And if you dare try and escape my hold, no one will be able to stop me from hunting and finding you. Something for you to remember."

CHAPTER 28

 *agger*

Passion.

I'd found it once in my life but not to this degree.

I'd shared a closeness with a woman only to find myself shutting down, incapable of providing what anyone would ever need.

Then Bella had dropped into my life like a wrecking ball, shattering my pristine but boring world and refusing to let go.

Hell, I'd done everything I could to push her away including acting like the biggest asshole in the world. But she'd refused to buy my bullshit. She'd seen past the anger and hurt to find what I really needed.

A soulmate.

Okay, so I wasn't the kind of guy to believe in the crap about love at first sight. It was more like complete disgruntlement. We were nothing alike. She was sunshine in the middle of a thunderstorm. I was the thunderstorm capable of turning into a tornado. Maybe someone would call us enemies at first, although that might be a little harsh.

But if so, all those love experts out there who believed they had all the answers did say something right.

Enemies made the best lovers.

I couldn't get enough of her. Every time she walked into a damn room my cock reacted first, my mind second. I'd had no idea that was possible. The moment I'd seen her in the purple dress, I'd been certain we wouldn't get out the door. The light material hugged every voluptuous curve as if she'd been poured into it.

And besides Shephard every goddamn man in the bar was watching her, hungering for her. There wasn't a single male pair of eyes that wasn't on her.

I'd never been the jealous type because I hadn't given enough of damn before, but the moment some jerk had asked her to dance, I'd overreacted.

She was still somewhat miffed, that cute nose of hers wrinkled. As she sat beside me, she acted as if I was the last person on this earth she wanted to talk to. I knew better. She was calculating how she was going to get me back. I honestly couldn't wait to see what she did.

The roads were dark and given the way I'd decided to drive back to the cabin, I couldn't see her beautiful face. But the time allowed me to make plans for how I was going to handle her when we got home.

Every inch of her would be hot and wet before we got upstairs.

I was such a jerk, but I couldn't help issuing a smile in the dark.

"You're going to be your brother's best man," she stated.

"Not possible."

"Why? Because you don't care about him?"

That was as far from the correct answer as possible. "No, because it's just not me." I couldn't put into words how I felt about the honor of being asked, so as usual, I avoided the question.

"You think you're all that and a bag of chips. Don't you?" Bella's question came out of the blue.

"Yep."

"Not easily frazzled?"

"Nope."

"Uh-huh. As with most things," she purred, "you're wrong."

"I'm never wrong. When are you going to get that through your pretty little head?"

She exhaled, the sound exaggerated and dared to place her hand on my leg. When she squeezed her fingers around my tight muscles, my cock immediately responded. "I suggest you find a safe place to pull over."

"Oh, yeah? Why's that?"

I heard the click as she unfastened her seatbelt. When she scooted closer, my breath caught in my throat. She delicately placed her hand across my groin and my grip on the steering wheel tightened. "Because I don't want to be involved in an accident."

The little vixen continued teasing me, yanking on my belt before doing her best in an awkward position to unbuckle it.

My mind drifted into a thousand places, all of them wrapped in my hungry needs. "You're a bad girl."

"We've already established that. Now I'm going to show you just how bad I can be." By the time she managed to unbuckle and unbutton, I was lost in a haze of lust.

I tried to continue concentrating on the road, my mind muddled as I attempted to think about a place to pull over.

Ah.

I found the perfect location.

She wasn't holding back, unzipping and tugging on my jeans until she freed my cock, her hand hot as Hades. I barely managed to pull the Rover into the parking lot of what would soon be her clinic before she wrapped her long fingers around my shaft.

"Fuck me," I whispered and pulled into a parking space where I left the engine idling. As she shifted backwards so she could bend over, I shook my head and tried to ensure we were all alone.

It was late enough that the traffic was sparse, with barely any cars passing by. I turned off the lights, already gasping for breath. Thankfully, the parking lot wasn't well lit, the other businesses in close proximity not adding any additional spotlight to our sinful act.

Bella took full control, tugging on my jeans until they were partially down my hips. When she blew across my cockhead, I twisted my hand on the steering wheel. But the second she took the tip into her mouth, using her jaw muscles to suck, my hips were driven off the seat.

"Shit, woman. You're just…"

She mewed in response, managing to drive her hand between my legs so she could cup my balls. I wasn't certain if I'd ever had a blowjob in a parking lot before.

First time for everything.

"Woman…" I whispered, every muscle already tensing.

"Yes? Do you want me to stop?"

"Not a chance in hell." I pushed her head back down, smiling involuntarily from the extreme pleasure. "You can do this all night long."

"Mmm…"

My gut told me I'd never last that long. The way her tongue was swirling back and forth could drive any man into sheer madness. Just being able to tangle my fingers in her long hair kept my senses on the high side of crazy, my need to plunge my cock inside her sweet and tight pussy almost all I could think about.

Except for her hot and wet mouth.

At this angle, I couldn't indulge in sliding my fingers inside her tight channel. The bratty woman was doing this on purpose.

She took my shaft down inch by inch, the electricity and fire in the vehicle creating steam on the windshield. Soon I wouldn't be able to see outside. What the hell? Who cared?

The sound of her sucking and licking filtered into my eardrums; it was sweet music, but it would be better if I was thrusting inside. Panting, I eased my head back onto the seat, fighting stars that threatened to steal my vision.

Every moan she issued added to the sexual atmosphere, keeping me on edge. Even my boots felt tight from the tension. Her lips were perfect, her tongue becoming a weapon. Holy crap. If I wasn't careful, I'd lose my load within seconds.

I did what I could to drive down my need to erupt into her mouth, even tugging on her strands of hair.

However, soon I couldn't take it any longer and pulled on her arm. Bella finally released her hold on my cock, lifting her pretty little head and pouting those lips of hers.

"What's wrong, lover?" she asked in a husky voice.

"More. I need more." I was like some true savage in the wild.

She eased her long fingers through her hair, studying me intently in the shadowed light. "For always."

It was as if she was confirming what I'd told her inside the club. I couldn't blame her given my odd moods. "For always." I pulled her onto her knees, fighting the tilting steering wheel to get it as far out of the way as possible. As soon as I did, I dragged her across my lap. At the same time, I yanked her dress up to her waist and fought to lower my jeans another few inches.

Damn, it was hot in here.

"What do you have in mind, big boy?"

Her teasing voice was enough to push me beyond the very edge I'd fought hard to keep. "Fucking you. What do you think?"

"But I'm wearing panties."

Was she really telling me that? "So what?" While I considered ripping them off her body, I changed my mind, shoving them aside instead. There was no need to waste precious lace and silk.

Her breathing ragged, she gripped my shoulder with one hand as I lifted her by her hips. With her other delicate fingers, she placed the tip of my cock just past her swollen folds. Goddamn, her scent was the perfect combination of jasmine and vanilla mixed with her fragrance of crazed desire.

We both moaned as I yanked her body down, her bottom planted squarely on my legs. She threw back her head, swishing her hair back and forth.

Just like she'd done on the dance floor.

I jutted my hips upward, driving my cock even deeper inside. The feel of her muscles and wetness, the heat of our bodies and the sin we were performing was more than just a powerful aphrodisiac. It was allowing another part of me to awaken.

While the angle was difficult, I still fucked her long and hard, our breathing so labored I was certain she was going to scream. She clawed at the roof of my vehicle and I sensed she was close to a delicious orgasm.

So I thrust in more roughly than I'd done before, gasping for air just like she was doing. The entire vehicle was rocking from our raucous actions. Every sound was exacerbated, moans and growls mixing together brilliantly.

There was no way I would close my eyes through this special moment, no matter how filthy or sinful. I needed to stare her directly in the eyes. I'd meant what I'd said to her and it was important for her to realize I wasn't lying. Hearing she was purchasing the clinic had sent a ray of warmth through me.

It also allowed for additional concern.

Tomorrow I'd deal with the issues.

One way or another.

As she pressed her lips against mine, I was ready to swallow her tongue. I thrust mine inside, capturing her taste and her essence with my mouth. Every beautiful moment we were together I wanted more.

There would never be enough.

Her moans escalated as she was swept into a sweet orgasm. Her entire body shuddered in my hold, her knees tightening against my hips as her body swayed. As soon as she came down from the clouds, she pulled away, laughing as if suddenly nervous around me.

The way she bucked against me was too much to take. My stamina lost to my close to desperate need to fill her with my seed.

With my body shaking violently, I fulfilled my duties. For a few precious seconds, we were once again as one.

Coming down from the rafters was hard to do. I was still hard, still pulsing inside of her. The scent of our sex was extreme, so overpowering we both laughed.

"Whew," Bella whispered and raked back her hair with both hands. "One hot man."

"You're the fiery woman who started this."

"Yes, I did. Keep that in mind," she purred. "So hot."

It was sweltering inside. As soon as she tried to climb off, I maneuvered her stomach across my lap. Without wasting any time, I ripped down her panties and I brought my hand down on her naked bottom.

"You can't do that. What if someone sees?"

"You weren't worried about that a few minutes ago." I had a huge grin on my face as I cracked my hand on one side then the other. Her buttocks were already hot, my fingers tingling with every swat I gave her.

The way she was wiggling kept my cock semi-hard, but that could change into full arousal at any second. She had that strong of an effect on me.

I even whistled as I spanked her, also enjoying the steam on the windows. Defrosting would take a few minutes.

"Ouch."

"You can complain all you want," I told her. "That won't stop me." I continued, thrilled I had her as my captive. When I stopped long enough to caress her cheeks, she wiggled until my balls started to swell.

Four more hard cracks of my hand and I finally stopped.

Bella remained where she was for a few seconds, grousing under her breath. When she fought her way until she was on one knee, she shifted her weight but a few seconds later, she groaned. "We've got company."

"What? Here?" I glanced in the mirror outside my door, cursing under my breath since the window was fucking fogged.

But I didn't need to see the vehicle clearly to know what we were about to deal with.

The goddamn sheriff's office.

Sure, either the horrible man or his deputies were required to cruise the roads, ensuring our tourists and locals remained safe, but my gut told me the sheriff had been watching us.

"Move to the passenger seat," I told her.

"What's wrong?"

"Just do it, city girl. Some unpleasant business."

She moved over, fixing her clothes then trying to fasten her seatbelt as the vehicle in question entered the parking lot. While the windows were still steamy, I turned on the defroster, hoping it would help in time.

I didn't need to have a perfectly clear glass to realize the moment the man stepped from his law enforcement vehicle that our unwanted visitor was the sheriff. Laughing softly, I rubbed my jaw and rolled down the window.

"The sheriff?" she asked.

"In the flesh. Asshole."

"Why doesn't he like you?"

"Myriad reasons including bringing bad karma into this town."

The asshole was swaggering slowly, shining a flashlight over every inch of the Rover.

"There's more to it," she insisted.

"Maybe cause I'm not such a nice guy including to jerks wearing a uniform."

Bella sighed. "That would do it."

"Evening, folks," the sheriff said, directly shining the light over both of us.

"Howdy, Adam." I knew he didn't take kindly to me calling him by his first name. My personality was such I just didn't

PIPER STONE

give a shit about authority figures. That had almost tanked me in the Army.

"What are you doing out here? It's after hours. I'm certain Doc Welby is closed for the night. That would mean you're trespassing."

I sensed immediately that my little warrior woman was none too thrilled at being accosted. To prove my point, she leaned across my lap, her long hair nestled in my crotch far too enticing. The scent of sex given the slightly humid air was sticky and sweet, just like my cum slickening her inner thighs.

He took a deep whiff, grinding his teeth as soon as he did.

"Sheriff, see, here's the thing. I'm purchasing the practice from old Doc Welby. He and I got along famously and he talked me into moving to this little town. Fabulous place with mostly decent people. You aside, of course. Now, I realize you all but threatened me to leave before it was too late, but here's the thing." She hesitated, dragging just the tip of her tongue across her bottom lip on purpose.

My. Wasn't I proud of my feisty vixen?

"I don't take kindly to anyone's threats. As a matter of fact, I get a little crazy. You know the kind I mean. I'm the type of girl who just can't seem to control her actions. Besides, the mayor and his entire family are good buddies of the doc. Doesn't he control your career?" Her smile was bright, her cleavage on full view.

Part of me wanted to drag her over my knees for a second hard spanking. We didn't need any trouble from the man

344

on top of everything. But the other part was cheering her on.

He lowered down until he could look her in the eyes. "I'd be very careful if I were you, Ms. Winters. I know things about you. Bad things. I wouldn't want to ruin your new life. Welcome to Danger Falls. I hope you find what you're looking for."

He stormed away, slamming his door and revving the engine.

After he'd sped out of the parking lot, I slowly turned my head toward her. "The mayor? How in God's name would you know that?"

Bella sat back in her seat, smoothing down her dress. "Well, I don't."

"What do you mean you don't?"

"I have no clue if you have a mayor so I couldn't know if the position is held by a man or a woman."

I sucked in my breath. "You were bluffing?"

She shrugged and blew me a kiss. "I'm a damn good actress when I need to be."

Just feeling free and alive enough to wrap my hand around the back of her neck, jerking her toward me reminded me of something Shephard had told me.

That I deserved to live.

"I don't know what I'm going to do with you," I told her in a gruff voice before crushing my lips over hers.

She gently placed both hands against my chest, arching her back as I plunged my tongue inside. Just like before, I couldn't seem to get enough of her, savoring every tiny lick of her tongue.

After easing back, I shook my head. "You need discipline in your life."

"I guess you think you're going to provide that as well."

"You bet." I laughed and shifted the gear, heading out onto the road. Forced to adjust the rearview mirror, I glanced quickly at the road behind us.

The sheriff was parked on the other side of the road.

Watching.

Waiting.

Whatever trouble he intended on bringing wouldn't be directed toward me alone.

He'd now placed the woman I cared about in the bullseye.

Maybe he'd need to learn a hard lesson about manners.

CHAPTER 29

ella

Exhaustion and joy.

Was it possible to experience both at one time?

That was exactly the way I felt on this beautiful morning. Being tired was worth it. I felt like Jagger and I had gotten closer.

Nightmares.

Jagger had experienced another one and his ranting had awakened me. For all his worry that he'd display violence, the most I'd seen was tossing the books out of frustration.

He'd allowed me to talk to him and to listen. He'd mentioned his captivity and the months he'd endured, including over the Christmas holiday. He'd also told me the only soul he'd told had been his dad. It would seem his father had also been taken a prisoner of war, although for a much shorter timeframe.

What he hadn't mentioned was anything regarding what Poppy had told me and I'd decided not to ask. Not only would it break the building trust between us, but I had a feeling doing so would push him back into a deeper level of darkness and I wouldn't be able to drag him back into the light.

The secret was churning in my stomach, but I was determined to let him tell me when he was ready.

At least another two glorious days had passed without any additional difficulties. Almost as if things were getting back to normal.

The black cloud was still there, but I was better able to deal with my fears.

I'd enjoyed spending time at the house and had even taken the opportunity to forward my mail to Jagger's address. It was risky, although Joel shouldn't be able to find anything out about the post office box I'd rented in Baltimore. Although I wouldn't put anything past him, fighting the post office regulations shouldn't be in his purview.

I could at least admit I'd enjoyed almost every minute of my time spent in Danger Falls. It almost felt like home. Between spending time at the clinic, still helping Hunter at the resort and fabulous nights with Jagger, the anxiety was starting to drop off.

With a new burner phone, I'd had zero threats. Now, besides Jagger and Hunter, the only other person I'd given the number to had been Esme.

And the wench hadn't called me back. It wasn't like her not to return my call. That was the only thing on my mind as I jumped into my SUV after dropping Cally off at daycare. As soon as I had my seatbelt on and the gear in drive, I dialed her number, the Bluetooth hands-free kicking in immediately.

"Hello?"

Esme's voice sounded like her phone had been dropped in the middle of a trashcan full of water, but I knew her sexy tone when she was exhausted. "How many hours did your asshole of a boss make you work?"

"Don't ask," Esme said, her yawn loud. "Why are you calling me so early? What time is it?"

"Almost ten and that's not early. Time to rise and shine, little spitfire."

"Well, since I didn't get into bed until six in the morning, not too bad."

"The last time we talked about your fabulous job, you weren't open for breakfast."

"We still aren't. That doesn't mean Jeff wasn't in the mood to berate the entire staff after an almost botched dinner with a bigwig. The bossy mysterious jerk stayed until almost three in the morning. He and buddies were drinking up a storm and the kitchen staff couldn't leave since he kept ordering food."

"Let me guess," I told her as I glanced into the rearview mirror. My old habits of feeling like I was being followed and watched would be tough to break. "You almost poured a bucket of water on him."

"I came close but settled for a shot of expresso. He was none too happy since my aim at his crotch was a direct hit."

"Ouch! I'm surprised you have a job."

"Oh, I'm sure the lectures will continue, especially since the Middle Eastern jerk and his entourage spent almost sixty thousand dollars."

"What? Is that even possible?"

Esme chuckled. "Darling, I do create the finest food on the East Coast. Expensive too. But you gotta pay to play."

It was so good to talk to her. "How about taking a few days off and coming to visit?"

"You know I'd love to, but Jeff would kill me."

"Aren't you due some vacation time?"

"I've been working here four months. I doubt it. Why? I can tell you have something up your sleeve."

The girl knew me too well. "It's just the resort needs a chef and I thought of you."

"And live in a place called Danger Falls? I don't know if the town could survive if I took the job."

"I'm here, remember. They're surviving me." I headed to Poppy's Diner to pick up a few muffins for the doctor, his one nurse, and sweet receptionist. It was the least I could do for the time Doc Welby had taken with me while still performing his duties.

"Oh, good point. Hey, if the job's online I'll take a look at it, but I love it here, even if I have plans on castrating Jeff at some point. I wonder if human testicles would be considered a delicacy?"

"You are cold and cruel, which is why I love you. Think about trying to get away for a weekend. The drive is really beautiful. Plus, you'll have a fabulous place to stay in."

"Would I get to meet your hot roommate?"

"You would."

"I'm as good as there. I'll see what I can do. But I can't promise anything at this point."

"And you call me a party pooper."

"You are, but I hear happiness in your voice," Esme told me.

I made a turn into town, enjoying the view more than I had before. Bright sun. Not a cloud in the sky. It was all just about perfect.

Even if I did feel like a black wave was threatening to drag me straight into hell. "I am."

"I'm so glad."

Her tone was entirely different. I heard noise and if I knew her, she was trying to create an IV coffee drip. "What's wrong?"

"There's nothing wrong."

"I don't believe you. Did Joel do something?"

She sighed and it was her dramatic sigh, the one I learned the first week I'd met her that I needed to be concerned about.

"Joel came in for a drink last night."

"Oh, he did, did he? Let me guess. He was intimidating as hell to you, his second method of trying to get his way."

Esme snorted. "He tried but he failed. But he did say something weird. He told me to tell you to watch the news in the next few days. He wouldn't provide a date or tell me anything about what he's talking about. Do you have any clue?"

Shit.

"I'm not certain." It was time to hire an attorney, although at this point, I wasn't certain what one could do unless he or she was a shark. And law enforcement wouldn't help since he hadn't openly threatened her. I didn't want to alarm her any further.

"Well, I'll keep my ear to the ground. I gave him a piece of my mind, but he is just a smug asshole."

"Yes, he is. Just stay away from him."

"I don't plan on seeking him out, girl. But be careful. He was just... Different. Strained. I don't know. It was like something happened. Did you hire an attorney or something?"

"Not yet, but I plan on doing that in the next week or so." I'd also spent time searching for one in Danger Falls only to realize I'd need at least a law firm out of Roanoke at this point. The initial phone call had allowed me to know I was in for the long haul with Joel's attempt to push forward the adoption, but I had a few elements on my side.

Maybe, somehow, he'd gotten wind of any inquiries they made.

"Good. I'm glad to hear that. Let's talk in the next couple of days."

"I'd like that. Remember. Don't give this phone number out to anyone."

Esme laughed. "Not a chance. Wild horses couldn't drag it out of me."

"Of that I have no doubt." I pulled into the community parking lot just a block away from Poppy's, already taking a deep breath to calm my nerves. "Think about coming out."

"I definitely will. Just take care of yourself and that sweet girl of yours."

As I ended the call, a slight sadness washed over me. I missed our fun times together. It was so good to feel a connection to my past.

Grabbing my purse, I headed into the diner, thrilled that a couple of people passing by knew my name. How silly it was to feel happy that I was being recognized. That didn't happen in Baltimore even in tight social circles. Not that I'd ever considered any of Joel's friends anyone I could trust.

In this tiny town, everything was different.

Poppy waved as soon as she saw me. I headed for the small

but luxuriously packed bakery case, breathing in the delicious aromas of freshly baked goods.

"You're exactly the person I wanted to see," Poppy said as she approached.

"Uh-oh. What did I do?"

She laughed. "Not a thing, darlin'. I wanted to talk to you about the engagement party I'm organizing for Shephard and Denise. They haven't had the time with their work schedules and I thought it would be a nice touch since they've both done so much for the community."

"That's a great idea. Now, if I can only convince Jagger to be Shephard's best man."

"I have a feeling you're the only person he listens to."

I rolled my eyes. "I don't know about that. How can I help?"

"All you need to do is get them to the restaurant. That's it. You can tie Jagger on the hood if he argues with you."

She could have me laughing for hours. "I just might need to do that. When is the party?"

"Saturday night. Eight sharp. I got my ladies making sure everything is decorated and we have a few surprises in store for them."

"Be careful. Shephard is still a bear according to you."

"I can handle Shephard Fox. I handled his dad just fine. Maybe I'm an old lady, but I still know a thing or two about men."

"I know you do, Poppy, and you're not old. Happy to help. Now, you can do me a favor. Where's the best place to purchase a sexy dress in town?"

She leaned over the bakery counter, giving me the kind of look that said she had an entirely different wardrobe away from the diner.

I wasn't going to ask.

* * *

Jagger

"You were right," Hunter said as he walked into my office. Shephard was close behind, closing the door after him.

"What was I so right about?" I leaned back in my chair, folding my arms behind my head.

"Remember I mentioned I'd heard the Brockford name before?" Hunter asked as he moved to one of two chairs in front of my desk, plopping down. He had his usual grin on his face as well.

"Yeah. You found something out."

"I found out how connected Joel's father is. He's funded several major projects in Baltimore, provided campaign donations to the tune of millions, and even helped design the new children's wing at the hospital where his son works. He's all over the social pages as the do-gooder. However, you are correct in that he is tied to some pretty bad people."

"How bad?" I asked, although I could guess the answer.

"Let's just say I wouldn't cross them if I were you. No one dares try. If they do, they tend to find themselves in various vats of hot water or worse. I've seen it myself."

I glanced at Hunter. He wasn't joking.

"And what does Joel provide for them?"

"Didn't you know? He ventured into several other interests with regards to surgery." Hunter gave me an odd look.

A light turned on over my head. "He's a goddamn plastic surgeon for the right money."

"Bingo."

"Well, shit," Shephard said. "He's changing identities of those very bad people when the pressure is on."

Hunter nodded in his direction. "Yep, and since he never actually went to medical school for that particular skill, it's kept a great big secret."

"I'm curious, brother. How do you know?" I asked.

He didn't appear eager to be forthcoming, so when he sat forward in his chair, I was eager to hear what he had to say. "The people I worked for after I did my stint in the military were little more than criminals themselves. I'm not going to share with you any names, but my targets were also some unsavory people considered their enemies. I had an up close and personal run-in with my target. He wasn't too happy to see me. But in the end, I completed my mission."

Hunter was grinning, the memory obviously a fond one.

"Even my handler wasn't interested in going up against the Brockford family."

I glanced at Shephard. I had a feeling he was the single brother who'd remained loyal to a mission that had started the moment he'd entered bootcamp. Until now, I'd had no idea Hunter had fallen into the same darkness I had. The two of us would never be considered saints.

Even more reason we didn't usually share stories amongst the three of us. "With that kind of muscle, Joel is going to track her down. I still can't figure out why he gives a shit. A foster kid with a child spawned by someone else."

Shephard and Hunter looked at each other.

Tension swept into my system. "What is it? Talk. One or both of you."

"You're not going to like it," Hunter said and shook his head to reiterate what he was saying.

I pounded my fist on the desk. "Tell me. Secrets will destroy her."

"Because she's more important to Joel than you think. With her on his arm, his power will ultimately increase."

Hunter relayed the information as if reading off a dossier given to him regarding his target. Much like I'd been given. It would seem there truly was very little difference in those hoping to tread the gray line and those preferring the evil endeavors done by monsters.

I wasn't certain where I fit in.

But with another secret revealed, another reason Joel would stop at nothing to get Bella back, I knew what had to be done.

Maybe karma was on my side, but if I had to sell my soul to the devil again, I was finally doing it for a good reason.

"What are you going to do, brother?" Shephard asked. "I'll help you any way I can."

"I'm going to do what's required to keep her safe."

"Don't do anything stupid," Hunter suggested.

I laughed. "My entire life has been a lie. I thought I was doing the right thing. But in the end, I was a fool, wasting years that I can't get back. I found the one thing that makes me happy and no one is going to take her from me. No one." I gave them both a hard look.

Shephard nodded. "I understand. Know we'll have your back."

Where I was going, they couldn't help. Maybe it was for the best.

They left my office and I closed my eyes, rubbing my temple. A headache was forming and it had Joel's name all over it. I took my phone and dialed the number.

"Silencer." It was the name given to me more in jest than anything, my use of a silencer the only thing ever noted by police or other law enforcement agencies throughout the world. I'd been forced to use that method since so many of my targets remained in high profile areas. Creating a stampede could have possibly kept me from exiting the location safely.

"I have considered your request," he told me.

"And?"

"I will handle the operation, but you will owe me. You do understand that, do you not?" His English was fluent although it had been a long time since he'd set foot in the United States. I'd never met the man, few people had, but he was considered one of the most lethal men in the world.

He'd also been my mentor.

"I understand."

"What level do you prefer?"

We'd used codenames for everything including missions. At this moment, I wanted to put a bullet in Joel's brain myself, but that meant choosing today to return to my old life or staying in my new one.

I chose what was most important to me.

Bella.

"Level two."

"You're certain."

Joel would be destroyed, giving a clear warning, but would be allowed to live. I'd prefer he wallow in sanctimonious bullshit and the loss of his reputation and maybe his career. Prison wouldn't be bad. "Yes."

"Then so be it. Just remember the deal you made."

"Yes, I will."

The veil of secrecy was required to be kept. It was written in blood by those who'd joined the organization. That same blood would be spilled if any treachery occurred. It was my cross to bear, but right now, one I would do so without issue.

Salvation wasn't in my vocabulary.

The call ended and there would be no further discussion until the deed was done. What I'd done would come back to haunt me in weeks, months, or even years.

One day I'd be dragged into the past.

If only for a little while.

I only hoped it would be something Bella could forgive.

CHAPTER 30

ella

"*Secrets,*" a former teacher had told me, "*will always end a relationship.*"

I had too many of them to count.

So did Jagger.

We were mired in them. For all the joy I'd been able to experience over the last couple of weeks, a heavy weight was coming close to crushing me.

"Stop fidgeting," I told Jagger as I adjusted his tie. "You look debonair."

And he did. In fact, he looked as if he'd just walked from a hot male magazine meant to drive women nuts. It was working for me.

"Yeah, right. Why the hell am I wearing this shit?"

"You mean a jacket and tie? Because the event is slightly more formal."

"Do you think Shephard isn't going to know something is up? He ain't wearing a tie."

I grinned and stood back, admiring the look on him. He'd even shaved, allowing me to watch as he'd cut off his long beard. "You look much younger and sexier without that Brillo pad on your face."

He yanked me into his arms. "I thought you adored my beard. The way it scratched that sweet pussy of yours. Huh? Tell the truth."

"I'm not saying a thing." When he pushed me over the back of the couch, swatting my behind, I squealed, which caused Xena to bark like crazy. I had to laugh. He was much more playful lately, although I still sensed there was a darkness in him that would haunt him for many years to come.

"I can't believe you roped me into this," he grumbled as he returned me to a standing position.

"It's good for you to get out. Makes Mr. Grumpy a nicer guy."

He rolled his eyes, not something he normally did. "Let's go. Where do they think we're going?"

"A fabulous restaurant."

"And how did you convince them to go?"

I backed out of his reach. "By telling them you had a little announcement to make."

"You did not."

"Yes, I did." I grabbed my coat, heading out the door before he could grab me.

He waited a few seconds before emerging from the house, as grumpy as ever. "You will get it for this."

"Promises. Promises."

Jagger was still grousing as he climbed into the Range Rover, huffing as he started the engine. "Just remember, your hours are numbered."

"It will be fun. Besides, everyone can use reasons to celebrate."

I knew I did. Christmas was around the corner and I honestly had no idea how well I'd handle the holiday. Or if I could. Time would tell.

The clock was ticking.

He said very little as he drove, although he kept his hand on my knee. But I was very observant, noticing he continuously glanced into the rearview mirror. He'd also checked his phone several times, never mentioning a word of what he was doing.

Secrets.

I sat back in the seat, trying to calm my nerves. This was a celebration, a beginning of a new life together. I was happy for the couple, even though I was wondering if I'd ever

PIPER STONE

experience something so incredible like marriage again. I refused to allow Joel to sour me on the subject.

As he pulled into Shephard's driveway, he grumbled another long list of reasons the engagement party was a bad idea. I'd gathered the distinct feeling his bad mood had nothing to do with the party and more to do with the question hanging over his head.

Would he agree to be his brother's best man?

"I'll be right back. Do not go anywhere," he barked, although his expression softened after peering back at me from the driver's door.

"Where am I going?"

"Knowing you, anywhere you want."

I noticed Denise giving him a big hug and whispering something in his ear before they headed to the vehicle.

"Where the hell are we going?" Shephard asked as soon as he slid into the backseat. "And why am I wearing this getup?"

"Are all three of you nothing but grumpy bastards all the time?" I asked.

"Yes," Denise confirmed. "They are. But that's why we love them. Right?"

The two of us could laugh while the men bristled. I could also breathe a little easier for tonight. I'd be amongst friends.

"We're going to a dress-up place," I told them.

Shephard grumbled just like Jagger always did.

The ride to the restaurant only took a few minutes. For some reason I was thankful for that. It seemed oppressive sitting next to Jagger, as if another shoe was going to fall. When he kept his hand pressed against my back as we walked toward the entrance, constantly scanning the parking lot, my gut told me he was preparing for something to happen.

I sucked in my breath, only able to give him a strange look before walking inside. This was a surprise party after all. I couldn't pull him aside and grill him on what was going on until later.

At least Jagger took over, mentioning the Fox name for our reservation while I studied the people inside the restaurant. I suddenly had a feeling we were being watched, studied as we were walking toward the back of the location.

My skin was crawling. Although I attempted to tell myself I was being foolish, the ugly sensations remained.

"Right this way," the hostess told us, heading for a set of closed doors.

"Why do I feel like this is a setup, bro?" Shephard asked.

"Don't fucking look at me," Jagger said, grinning as he looked in my direction.

"Hey, I was just the decoy," I told them.

Denise smacked her hand on her waist. "To what?"

The doors were opened and as everyone inside screamed surprise, any possibility of responding was lost in the gleeful whoops and hollers of the fifty or so people. Instantly, music began to play, almost everyone coming up to congratulate them. Poppy had pulled out all the stops, creating a breathtaking environment. There were waiters walking around with silver trays full of flutes of champagne, the delicious scent of food wafting throughout the room.

Candles were everywhere and there was a small band that was lively and already creating a warm atmosphere. I also noticed a group of video equipment pushed against one wall. The event was going to be videotaped. An instant wave of nausea rolled through me. The thought was far more difficult to shove away than normal.

"Champagne, city girl?" Jagger asked.

"Sure." I could tell the instant he realized something was off, his brow furrowing and as he'd done before, he swept the room. "What are you looking for, Jagger? Do you expect someone to crash the party?"

"No, of course not. What's wrong? You look like you've seen a ghost."

"Just a nagging feeling like you obviously have. Why do I have the notion you're hiding something from me?"

"Why don't you relax for tonight," he suggested.

"Jagger. Please don't patronize me. I know you at least well enough at this point to realize you're doing everything you can to protect me. I think that includes using whatever contacts you have from the past in an effort to destroy Joel. If I'm right, I appreciate the thought, but I need to fight this battle."

"I don't think you understand what you're up against."

"Meaning what?"

"Meaning your marriage was arranged. Did you know that?"

I took a step away from him. "I already mentioned that's what I believed. The way you just said that is like you know it's true for certain and why. Is that true?" I was right. He'd done some searching. What could he have learned that I didn't know?

Whether or not he was going to answer I'd never know, as Denise broke through the crowd of well-wishers, pulling me into a tight embrace. "Thanks for this."

"I can't take any credit. It's all Poppy's doing."

"I'm surprised you were in on this, but it's a nice surprise." Shephard reached out, waiting for Jagger to shake his hand.

Jagger and I locked eyes. I had a feeling this was going to be a very long night.

"Come on. This is a party you helped orchestrate. Don't stand here like wallflowers," Denise dictated. I could tell she wasn't going to take no for an answer.

"We better follow her orders, bro," Shephard piped in. "Thank you."

"Sure. Anything for the happy couple." Jagger grabbed my arm before we were absorbed into the crowd. "Do me a favor. Stay by my side tonight. Don't go anywhere without me."

PIPER STONE

While I'd been afraid before, the concerns were nothing in comparison to the way I felt at this moment. "Okay. But you need to explain what you meant."

"I will. I promise."

As we meshed with the partygoers, everyone in town I knew joining in the festivities, I continued to look over my shoulder. The apprehension remained, but slowly over the next half hour, I started to relax.

Maybe I was a fool, but if I didn't let go of my past, I'd never have a future here.

Poppy was suddenly at the podium that had been brought to a small makeshift stage. She clapped her hands first, finally tapping the microphone.

"Ouch!" someone called from the audience.

"Well, I had to get your attention somehow. We have the entire night to drink and dance, but now, it's time for the show."

"Oh, no," Denise hissed. "I don't think I like where this is going."

Although I had an indication of what Poppy had collected, the story of their love affair a sweet touch, I found myself continuing to glance at the door to the auxiliary room. I don't know what I was expecting, but I was glad Cally was staying with Zoe for a little girl party time.

Jagger remained closer as everyone crowded closer to a screen that suddenly dropped down from the ceiling.

"Did you have anything to do with this?" Shephard growled at his brother.

"Do I look like I'm the kind of guy to be involved with something like this?" Jagger shook his head. "No. Hell, no."

I remained where I was, although as soon as the first slide was presented, I was pushed forward. Jagger wasn't right behind me and my throat instantly closed.

"Do you want to see how this love affair began?" Poppy continued.

The guests cheered.

"Then please roll the video."

The lights were lowered, leaving me far more uncomfortable.

I was only partially paying attention as I pushed my way past a few people, finally locating Jagger talking with Hunter. He noticed I was searching for him, giving me a slight nod. At least he was within sight.

I took a deep breath and tried to pay attention, but I couldn't seem to find a way of concentrating. Maybe it was because my head was aching, the dull throb behind my eyes making it difficult to keep a haze from forming over my eyes.

After grabbing a second glass of champagne, I found a spot where I wouldn't be noticed. The urge to leave was strong, so much so I was fearful I'd hyperventilate.

I held my purse close, doing my best to shake off the dread almost consuming me. When my phone buzzed indicating a text, I shivered. Even Zoe didn't have my number, Jagger providing his instead in case there were any issues. Maybe it was Esme with a surprise. I fumbled to grab my phone, doing everything I could to keep from dropping the glass.

But the moment I pulled the burner phone from my purse, the light in the room began to fade.

Unknown: *You thought you could run and get away with destroying me. You thought wrong. Get prepared, little bitch, your day of fame is going to be a doozy.*

My hand shaking, I lifted my head, once again searching for Jagger. The entire world seemed to be in slow motion.

He noticed me, immediately breaking away from Hunter.

The lights went out, the projector as well, the entire crowd roaring their disapproval.

And Poppy cursing at the top of her lungs.

But the moment the projector popped back on, I braced myself for what was to come.

As my face appeared on the screen, the video Joel had taken in full and very vivid display, I couldn't move.

Couldn't breathe.

My new life and the love I felt I'd finally found were over.

Forever.

Scenes.

Memories.

Laughter.

Shock.

Every emotion rolled through me, flashes of light providing a horrible haze in front of my eyes. I could hear my name being called. Feeling faint, I tried to push my way through the crowd.

"Don't," Denise said from behind me, grabbing me into a bearhug. "It's okay. It's going to be okay."

"Ladies and gentlemen," a growl emitted throughout the room.

"How is it going to be okay?" Tears stung my eyes, the dirty deed Joel had performed far too low. How could he do this? Why? Was it all about the fact I refused to stay married to him?

I broke away from her, tearing to the front.

"We're not done yet," the gravelly voiced man shouted again.

But there was more, the film cut off after only thirty seconds, a deep voice taking over the presentation.

"The dazzling couple you've fallen in love with aren't the golden boy and girl you believed. And do you want to know why?"

Was that the sheriff?

Oh, my God. It was. In his hand was a microphone, the townspeople crowding even closer.

I shrank back, every inch of my body shaking.

Jagger broke through the crowd, finding and taking me into his arms. "Stay here."

"No. Don't leave me. What's he doing?"

"I don't know, but I need to find out."

Commotion roared as the sheriff continued. "Jagger Fox is a murderer. And do you want to know how I know that? Because he killed my daughter."

As pandemonium broke out, the guests going wild, everything remained a blur. The words echoed in my ears, my vision remaining cloudy. Yet one image played into my mind.

Jagger jumped through the crowd, pushing and shoving, his brothers right beside him.

And with one brutal punch to the sheriff's jaw, the man was knocked to the floor.

 *agger*

"What the fuck?" Hunter barked out for the fiftieth time.

I paced the floor, barely looking in his direction. The house I lived in didn't seem large enough for the five of us and one special damn dog.

Bella remained curled up on the couch, Xena right beside her. She'd said absolutely nothing since we'd left the police station after the deputy had finally let me go. I'd been arrested for assaulting a police officer, but in my mind, not only would I do it again, I'd break his fucking neck.

Denise tried to hand me a glass of whiskey, but I refused to take it. Undaunted, she lifted my arm, forcing me to accept the gesture. "You need this and you need to calm down."

"How the hell am I supposed to calm down when that bastard tried to destroy my life and Bella's as well?"

"And you allowed that son of a bitch to get to you. What he did was as close to extortion as I've seen, but you assaulted him in front of a hundred witnesses. You could get jail time." Shephard's wise words went in one ear and out the other.

"So the fuck what?" I challenged.

"That bastard deserved what he got," Hunter added. "I'm curious if there's anything going on in Baltimore right now. Maybe we're missing another motive." He reached into the duffle he'd brought into the house, yanking out his iPad.

"What the hell difference can it make?" I bellowed at him. I knew he was only trying to help, but my mood was all about revenge.

"The three of you need to calm down. Hunter is right. The more information we have the better. You all know that. Joel is using what he can to try and keep his reputation alive. If there is any truth to some marriage arrangement, it could be tied to a big business deal including a criminal one."

I nodded. "True." I'd yet to mention my source and had no intention of it. In my mind, I couldn't help but allow my instinct to take over. I had a distinct feeling whatever the man had done to destroy Joel and his family had already begun. That would be the reason for the release of the video. Why not ruin the happy couple?

"We need to think this through. How did the sheriff gain access to that video? Wasn't it still a private matter with Bella and this Joel Brockford dude?"

"Yes, but the sheriff has been nosing around, threatening both of us," I told them.

Shephard hissed. "And you didn't fucking tell us? That's police harassment. The judge won't like that in the least."

"You damn well know the judges in this area are partial to law enforcement."

"Not always," Denise piped in. "They've learned a few lessons. It's who Sheriff Young knows in the rest of the state, including Richmond. Or beyond. Baltimore isn't that far away. Didn't you say the Brockfords have a long sordid history with various criminal activity?"

"Not proven, but yes." I shifted my attention to Bella, my heart aching.

"Well, we can't put anything past Joel at this point I guess."

I'd been forced to relay the story. There'd been no other choice since it had been made public. Bella hadn't objected, but she hadn't said anything either. That's why I was surprised when she rose from the couch, her arms folded as she headed in our direction. She was still in the same emerald green dress she'd purchased for the event, her long hair framing a haunted face yet her eyes remained bright.

At that moment, I thought she was the most beautiful woman alive, even in sadness.

"Joel sent me a text on the new burner phone seconds before the sheriff attempted to destroy us. I think with the sheriff obviously asking questions, trying to find out who I was so I could be used against Jagger, the two had a conversation, Joel releasing the video to him."

"I think she's onto something," Hunter said as he moved closer. "Take a look at a piece on the front page of the largest newspaper in Baltimore."

He handed me his iPad first. The headline said it all.

Is the Brockford Empire Funded by Criminal Activity?

I didn't even need to read the article to know the truth had started coming light. Where my source would take it from there, I wasn't certain. But we would find out soon enough.

Bella took a deep breath. "Who is Joel Brockford really?"

There were too many details about her life that she needed to fully comprehend, but I was hesitant to add to the night's horrible experience. Just seeing the look on the locals' faces had torn her apart.

I was angry with them too for not rallying around us.

People loved a loser more than they did a winner. I'd learned that the hard way.

"A very bad man with even worse intentions," Denise answered for me. "With both your blessings, I'm going to do some investigation of my own. I have buddies that will provide me with every ugly scrap of information about suspicions involving that family. Maybe they've yet to be proven, but it's obvious someone else is out to get them."

I glanced at Bella and she nodded. "Fine. Go for it." She'd never find out anything about my source or that I was behind the method of destruction. Not that I gave a damn right now.

Bella crowded closer, Xena suddenly realizing her new mommy dog wasn't right by her side. As she rushed over to Bella, I could tell the woman I adored softened. Enough she leaned into me.

"Now, what about the goddamn elephant in the room, bro?" Shephard pushed. "Why the hell does Sheriff Young think you killed his daughter?"

"Because I did." The words hung in the air and both brothers looked at each other.

"How? Line of duty?" Hunter asked. There was no animosity in his voice, only disbelief.

"She was captured off the base because of me," I told them and it was difficult to change positions so I could look in Bella's eyes. However, her breathing was no more labored than before.

"How is that your fault?" Hunter pressed.

"Because I went against orders. I knew the area surrounding us was considered dangerous, but we hadn't seen any insurgents in almost a week. We'd just gotten engaged and I didn't have a ring. I knew a guy in the small town near our camp I'd talked to dozens of times. He had a beautiful diamond that had been in his family for years. He was willing to sell it to me because the war had nearly destroyed every possession. I made a mistake. We were captured together. I had intel and the bastards wanted it."

"And you couldn't give it to them," Shephard stated. It wasn't a question. Both my brothers knew the score. We'd given our oath to the military.

"No. If I had, the entire operation that eventually led to their defeat would have led to the destruction of our base. I couldn't allow that to happen. Sheila knew that. She was an army nurse and well aware of the danger."

Bella placed her hand on my arm, squeezing in solidarity.

The sudden silence in the room brought yet another ache to my system.

"They tortured both of you and forced you to watch her die." Hunter gave me a respectful nod.

I hung my head, struggling with the knowledge that her last dying breath had been when in my arms. "Yeah."

"You're not to blame," Bella told me.

"Not the way I see it or her father."

Shephard looked at me, shaking his head. "Did you know Sheriff Young was her dad?"

"Not before I moved here. But Pops told me as soon as I arrived. That's why I almost left, but you can't run from your past."

"No, you can't," Hunter admitted. "All three of us have tried."

This had occurred so many times when we'd been kids, we needed no words to provide understanding. Our lives had been shaped by countless decisions that hadn't been our own. Were we to blame for any of them?

"No one will blame you for Sheila's death other than her father. Losing someone is tough for anyone." Denise offered a kind smile.

"Yeah, well, that doesn't give him the right to do what he did," Hunter snapped.

Shephard put his hand out. "We're a family. We'll work through this together."

A family. I'd done my best over the years to try to forget everyone from my past, including Sheila. But it wasn't about hating where I'd come from or disliking my heritage. I was proud to have been born into a family who respected honor and integrity.

Even if our father had crossed more than one morally gray line.

However, subjecting Bella and Cally to my mistakes was unforgiveable.

And always would be.

Maybe it really was best to let her go.

The buzz on my phone was the distraction I needed. I headed outside onto the front porch before answering.

"Silencer."

"It's done. Confirmation on the woman's father."

"His name?"

My source sighed. "That's breaking protocol."

"I don't give a shit. This is important to me personally."

"Michelangelo Ross. And Silencer? I hope she's worth it."

"Yeah, she is."

I closed my eyes.

There was no mistaking the name or how powerful Mr. Ross had become. He was more influential and dangerous than any mafia organization or cartel. That's because he was considered the head of a First Family, his ancestors arriving centuries before. Not only did his corporation own almost two dozen hospitals throughout the United States, they also owned dozens of other businesses, including pharmaceutical companies and laboratories. In other words, his family could control diseases as well as cures throughout the world if so inspired.

The Brockfords wanted a piece of the pie and would stop at nothing to get it.

Including Joel marrying Ross' illegitimate daughter.

What if her father came looking for her? Maybe he hadn't been alerted. It was likely he had no clue he had a daughter, which added to the sense of urgency. Maybe the man should be alerted. If what I suspected was correct, the Brockfords were planning on using the marriage to either get close to the man or challenge his power in their way.

After all, the Brockfords had a powerful group of backers as well.

An entirely different take on a business that could truly rule the world.

The connection was ended. My source had completed his end of the deal.

There would be no further conversations until or unless my services were needed. I breathed a sigh of relief, holding the phone to my head. Maybe the veil of secrecy and fear would be lifted. I took a deep breath before staring up at the sky. The stars were bright. If only I was the kind of man to wish upon one, but in my life, dreams and hopes had never come true.

"You suck at playing the hero."

Her voice provided a much needed reason to feel grateful for at least a couple of minutes. "Oh, yeah? Well, you suck at playing the martyr."

"How am I playing the martyr?"

"You sacrificed something terribly important to you. Your career."

"But careers don't make a life, Jagger. People do. They are the reason for true happiness. Yes, I loved what I did, but it's nothing unless you can share it with someone. I was hoping I could do that with some rugged mountain man, but it still seems he'd prefer to keep his distance."

She wrapped her arm around my waist, joining me next to the railing.

"You can get your life back now."

The slight tilt of her head added to my continued angst. Without knowing exactly what my source had done, I wouldn't know if any damage control was needed. But I would protect her with my life.

"I have a life, a new one and in case you haven't figured it out over the last few days, I love it. I'm not certain if I'll be welcome in Danger Falls any longer, but home is where the heart is. You're my heart."

Her words touched me more than I should let them. I pulled her close, pressing her face into my chest as I held the back of her head. "You'll be surprised about the folks living in this town. They won't let you down."

I only prayed I was right.

She lifted her head, pursing her lips. "Did you know you have a know-it-all smugness about you?"

"So I've heard."

"I find it desperately cute."

I wasn't certain why she'd chosen that moment to tell me, but I had a feeling she was doing what she could to drive away the ugly visions.

"You're the one who's desperately cute."

She clung to me as we remained on the porch. "Joel isn't going to stop. I contacted an attorney out of Roanoke. I don't know if they're a big enough firm, but they acted as if they can help me. I'm going to call them again on Monday and give them the go to ensure the divorce is final, the adoption papers ripped up, and my money returned. I might need to push off purchasing Doc Welby's place for a little while. But that's okay. Waiting tables is just fine for now."

Waiting tables.

Not that the honest job was beneath her, but she'd shrivel up and die at some point without being allowed to do what she wanted.

"An attorney?"

"Yeah, Williams and Mullins. They have an office in Richmond too. I'm hopeful at least."

"Maybe there's another choice," I told her. "Joel isn't going to bother you."

"You sound so convinced. Let him. I'll fight him with everything I have. I'm stronger than I've led anyone to believe. I just got caught up in his lies and all the nasty things he said to me."

"Understandable."

"Not for a woman like me. I'm better than that."

"Yeah," I told her. "You are."

She brushed her hand across her face and I noticed her entire body was still quivering. "Why did Joel wine and dine me so that I'd say yes to his marriage proposal?"

"I wish I could say because he cared about you."

"You know why. Don't you?"

"I don't think you need to hear this right now."

"Jagger. I'm tired of living a lie. Besides, you promised. That's what I've been doing for years. I had to lie about being a foster kid because a lot of people still look down on it as if what happened was my fault. I thought I'd found a home after being offered a job during my internship by Joel's father. He was in charge of the hospital at the time. Then I met Joel, and I truly believed I'd found my soulmate. Only I now know better. So please, don't hide anything from me, especially about my life. I can take whatever it is. I no longer want to feel like one great big imposter."

The feeling was one I knew too well. I took her hand, intertwining her fingers. "You were targeted because of who your father is."

"No one has any clue who my father is. How in the world would they find out?"

"Just like you found your mother. A trail is always there and with enough time and money, information on anyone in the world can be found. Do you want to know who he is?"

She thought about my question and I saw all the new ones popping in her mind. Every concern, every new question forming was reflected in her eyes, even in the shadows. They were equally as painful. She was also searching my eyes for both answers and advice. I wasn't certain I had any to give to her.

"Not yet. Maybe. But not until I embrace who I am. I just need a little space, Jagger, and I hope you can understand."

I nodded and pulled her close for a second time, pressing a kiss on the top of her head. There was too much to be done so she'd be allowed to enjoy her new life. But not tonight.

Tonight was for forgiveness.

Not of each other, but of our own personal sins.

ella

My entire life had been built on lying to people.

What I'd learned since arriving in town is that included lying to myself.

I was the master of pretend, and had been even from kindergarten through high school. It had helped provide a wall between me and everyone else. I'd felt impervious to bullies and there had been dozens of them.

Sadly, I hadn't learned my lesson that not all bullies grew out of their need to torment others. Some just became much better at their methods of inflicting pain.

Joel was that way.

I'd fallen for his bullshit every step of the way.

Maybe that's why I'd insisted on locking myself inside the cabin for almost seventy-two hours. It was crazy. I hadn't wanted to talk to anyone except for Cally and Jagger. Even then, our conversations had been stilted. I'd taken walks in the cold with Xena, enjoying the quiet and peace. Sometimes Jagger joined us, knowing some of the most gorgeous locations for hiking I'd ever seen.

He'd neglected saying much about Sheila, but I think he knew he didn't need to. What I noticed and was thrilled about was that he hadn't experienced a nightmare in two sleeps. Maybe that was nothing to celebrate just yet, but hopefully, now that the secret that had eaten him alive was out in the open, he would slowly start to heal.

I'd told myself I was reflecting on my life so I could be a better person and make better decisions. The truth was that I was a damn coward and I'd finally had enough of my personal pity party.

Denise had been bugging me to meet with her and I'd pushed her off. It was past time to find out what she'd learned as well as who my father was.

All in due time.

Plus, I had another deal to make with Doc Welby. I didn't care what it took; I'd find a way to make the payments we'd already agreed to.

As my first test of will, refusing to remain the pretender, I chose to meet Denise at Poppy's Diner instead of some hole in the wall coffee shop just so I could try to hide.

Yes, I hesitated after parking, taking gulping breaths and trying to convince myself I was still as nuts as I was when I came to this small town. But what struck me every time I did was how strong I felt in comparison to that night when I'd tried to get a room.

I was much stronger, only this time I wasn't pretending. Was it the clean mountain air, the kind people, or the fluttering that continued in my stomach every time Jagger walked into a room?

Maybe a little of all three.

While I'd face condemnation the moment I walked in that door, I was prepared for it. I wasn't to blame for the video even though I'd agreed to be a part of it. For two pairs of eyes only.

Another deep breath, a shift of my hands down my jeans, and I opened the door.

As expected, every single person in the place took a beat, including Poppy. But soon afterward she smiled, pointing to a booth at the end of the row. Maybe Denise was the one who'd been more embarrassed since she was sitting as far away from people as possible.

I felt as if I was walking down a row of shame since I felt the heat of everyone's stare. But I did it and was proud of myself. As soon as I slunk into the booth, Denise lifted her eyebrows, giving me a nod of approval.

"Well done, girl. You're stronger than I am," she told me.

"I highly doubt that. But it's time to live again."

"I'm glad to hear you say that." She was keeping her hand on top of a manila file. No good things came in manila files. I knew that to be true.

How many cases had I worked on where I'd used my paper file when talking to a family about a complicated surgery? More than using my iPad. Paper was comforting to those who had no idea what was going on.

But to me, I was terrified at what was lurking underneath the thin cover.

"How's Jagger holding up?" she asked.

"Jagger is a tough man, but he's suffering."

"Hopefully, he can start to live again."

I nodded. "I think he's more worried about me."

"Because he loves you."

"I don't know about that."

"All you need to do is to look in his eyes to know what he's thinking. It's obvious the way he feels. Do you share that same feeling about him?"

I could tell she was fishing. Poppy brought coffee before I could answer.

"Don't be a stranger, honey," Poppy said. "You're too good for this town."

"No, the town is too good for me maybe."

Poppy sighed. "I gave that fucking asshole a piece of my

mind. Thank God he's being shipped out of here. We don't want his kind here. Any cherry pie this afternoon?"

"Not today, Poppy. But thank you. Jagger didn't even get a piece the last time."

She winked. "We'll need to take care of that. You okay, Denise?"

"Just fine, Poppy." Only Denise's voice suddenly held a tenseness that hadn't been there before.

As soon as Poppy left, I leaned forward. "Sheriff Young is leaving his position?"

"Yes, and internal affairs out of Roanoke is looking into his behavior as well."

"How did that happen so fast?"

She shrugged and I wagged my finger at her.

"You did something. Didn't you?"

Denise winked. "I just told the chief of police in Roanoke what was going on. They run the show down here. I ensured they knew I was a former detective with the Charlotte Police Department since I registered a formal complaint."

"You are so bad."

Her laugh allowed some tension to be released. "Maybe so, but I wasn't going to stand by and watch my family be persecuted for things that they weren't responsible for."

"Jagger is lucky to have you. He needs family."

"I hope maybe one day you'll think of me as a sister. You'll need to after Jagger asks you to marry him."

It was our short time for girl talk and I felt myself blushing. "He's not that type. You know that."

Her turn to wag her finger. "Never say never." I could tell she was itching to discuss whatever she was holding onto.

"I know about my father, other than his name."

"Jagger knows one too many people. That's obvious."

"What does that mean?"

There was something almost ominous about her deep sigh. She tentatively pushed the file across the table. "No, I'm not certain Jagger had anything to do with this, but it happened very quickly."

As I opened the file, I realized I was looking at copies of police reports. "What am I looking at?"

"Joel Brockford and his father William are being investigated along with six other men from a group created about ten years ago. They are trying to monopolize aspects of the healthcare system by using alternative methods than what William has led everyone to believe. Yes, there are contributions, but the charity that William is fronting was funded by blackmail and extortion. Or so the FBI believes. It seems there is big business in medical care, including scams with insurance companies."

I shook my head. "That makes sense. I wanted to be a part of the charity, but Joel refused. He said I had way too much on my plate."

"Maybe that's because he was fearful you'd learn they were attempting to eliminate their only clear enemy, Michelangelo Ross. Does that name ring a bell?"

"Vaguely. But I wasn't into medical politics. I met him briefly at a dinner he came to where I was forced to dress up and act like arm candy. He was the special guest."

My gut told me the man was my father. I glanced at the photograph again, my heart and soul telling me I was right. I wasn't certain how I felt about it. But I had questions for him if what I was thinking was true. Lots of questions.

"Probably a good idea and I'll just bet he was. Anyway, from what my buddy tells me, someone tipped off the FBI. And provided copies of detailed records indicating their criminal activity."

"To whom?"

Denise cocked her head. "No one seems to know. Plus, some malfeasance was uncovered as well. Something about botched surgeries performed by Joel, the victims paid handsomely to keep their mouths shut."

"Why do I feel like there's another 'but' in your story?"

"Maybe because two of the three ended up dead."

I took a deep breath, holding it for some time. "They were going to talk."

"Perhaps so. Any other juicy details are on lockdown. But I think your problems are going to go away."

"From your mouth to God's ears. Thank you for making some phone calls."

"It was the least I could do. I just hope Jagger can find it in his heart to forgive himself."

"Yeah, I do too." I glanced out the window as a stream of people walked by. They all seemed happy, laughing and talking, so many with shopping bags full of goodies in their arms. "I really do."

My heart was fluttering as much as the butterflies were doing in my stomach. I knew in my heart Jagger had been the one to call in a favor from some influential person. He'd done that for me.

Maybe for us.

Either way, I couldn't wait to get home and thank him. He was my rock. He was my friend. He was my lover.

And he was becoming the true love of my life.

"What now?" Denise asked.

"Now, I go purchase a business."

She clapped her hands. "I'm glad you didn't change your mind."

"No, I couldn't be more certain of my decision than I am. Danger Falls is where I'm meant to be."

* * *

"What did you just say?" I asked, shocked at what I'd just heard. I was sitting across from Doc Welby and instead of a sheepish look, he seemed pleased with himself.

"I'm sorry, Bella. But it was an all-cash offer I couldn't refuse."

The clinic had been sold to someone else. "But we had a deal."

"As I said, I'm sorry, but it was too good to pass up."

I knew what was really happening here. Poppy had been able to put on a good face, playing an actress, but I wasn't wanted in this town. Not after…

Swallowing, I tried to collect both my thoughts and my emotions. "Is there any chance the buyer will back out?"

"I don't think so. I already have the money in my bank. I tried to call you, but all I got was voicemail."

He had my old phone number. I'd been the one to fuck this up.

"I see. Well, thank you for your time."

"Of course, Bella. I just hope… Well, I just hope you can find happiness. You seem like a very nice girl."

A nice girl who'd made a porn film. Why would anyone bring their kid to be examined by me?

I couldn't get out of his office fast enough. The knot I'd felt before was nothing in comparison to what had permanently attached itself to my stomach lining. I made it to my vehicle, but I had a feeling I'd stumbled half the way.

Tears had already formed, angry and bitter ones that stung as they leaked from my eyes. After everything, Joel had won a portion of the battle. I'd be damned if he was going to win another one.

Thankfully, Cally wasn't here to see this, still in daycare. I wouldn't be able to pick her up for another couple of hours. Right now, I needed the comfort of being alone.

Very much alone.

Even Xena was with her. I had the house to myself in case I needed to throw a tantrum.

Heading back to the cabin was really my only option.

Only it wasn't my house. No matter how many subtle changes I'd made.

I allowed the tears to fall as I slipped into the SUV, taking no comfort in the plush leather seats or the fact a part of my nightmare was over with. Now, if I stayed, I had no idea what I'd do and how I'd make a better life for my daughter.

The drive was terrible, my vision blurry from tears and all I'd wanted was to catch a little break. All the bad decisions I'd made had come back to bite me.

Maybe it was best if I moved on, but how could I leave Jagger?

I passed his driveway, forced to go another mile before I could turn around. At least I could laugh at myself for being so stupid.

I finally managed to pull in, taking it slow up the slight hill. Seeing Jagger's vehicle in the driveway had an entirely different effect than before. How was I going to tell him I wasn't certain I had any choice but to leave town?

Idling in the driveway wasn't a good thing to do. Only when I noticed an express package on the front porch did I finally cut the engine. Who knew. Maybe there was some good news inside the envelope.

My legs felt heavy as I walked up the stairs. But when I noticed a logo from Williams and Mullins, I was pushed into another layer of emotions. My hand shaking, I picked up the package, forced to sit down on the step before opening the flap.

The stack of papers was fairly significant, but inside was a final copy of my divorce decree and notification from the adoption courts that the adoption would not be going through as requested. There was also a letter stating my funds were in the process of being returned. It was the last line of the letter that brought another wave of surprise.

My bill had been paid in full.

Jagger.

It had to be.

He'd done this.

Another lurch of emotions brought a single sob. No. I wasn't going to do this. He did care about me. At least I could take comfort in the incredible thought.

A moment of utter joy and relief swept through me. Did it destroy the utter despair from losing the clinic? To a small degree. Eager to tell Jagger about the new information, I jerked up and rushed inside.

Instantly, I knew something was terribly wrong.

Joel was making good on his threat.

The back door was open.

Furniture knocked over.

The house had nearly been torn apart.

And blood.

CHAPTER 33

agger

A fool's walk.

That's what I was currently taking by allowing the fight to escalate.

I'd met Harrison Young, the sheriff's son only twice, neither time worth writing home about. However, he was a frequent flyer at Shackles, including the day his father had been in the place. He didn't like me and that had been apparent the first time I'd met him. He looked just like the sheriff, only a younger version.

He was also just as surly, his father having to keep him out of jail given his record of fighting to solve situations.

However, Harrison had never come across as particularly violent.

Until moments before.

The second I'd opened the front door, he'd declared me a murderer and issued two hard punches. Things had gotten out of hand after that. He'd attempted to use a knife, managing to stab me in the arm. That's when I'd taken it away from him.

Only the blade hadn't been his only weapon. He kept a Ruger pointed at me as he forced me to walk deep into the woods. I'd only gone to buy time.

"So what's your plan, Harrison? Kill me out here and bury the body?"

"That's a good plan. Don't you think?"

"I didn't kill Sheila."

"You as good as did."

"You weren't there. You have no clue what we'd both gone through." For both Adam and his son to find out any details of her death and my subsequent rescue would mean the sheriff had friends in the Army. Of course the fact I'd nearly been court-martialed hadn't helped.

"It doesn't matter what happened to you. I hope like hell the enemy tortured your ass."

I gritted my teeth, carefully scanning the area. I'd walked these woods a few dozen times in sunlight and in the snow. There were miles of forest, the two closest houses still a mile away on either side. No one would hear the shot or if they did, they'd just think a hunter was out killing deer.

With my weapons locked up, I had nothing to defend myself with.

The only thing I could try to do was disarm him.

That was dicey given I'd smelled alcohol on his breath. He'd likely taken a couple of shots for courage.

The fucking coward.

When I slowed down, he hissed from behind me, shoving me forward using the barrel of his weapon. "Keep fucking walking."

I did but spun around, throwing out my arms as I backed away. "Why not just do it here?"

"Because I have a special spot where you deserve to die." The gleam in his eye was telling.

The cliff. He was planning on walking all the way to the drop-off that was another two miles from here. "Look, what the hell do you want?'

"Isn't that obvious? Your death. You deserve to die for what you did to my sister."

My patience was reaching the end. "I loved Sheila. We were going to get married."

"You sure know how to show your guilt and remorse. By shacking up with some porn star?"

I instantly bristled. "I suggest you shut the fuck up."

"Oh, don't worry, killer. I'm going to enjoy spending time with her. When I get finished, she'll never want or need another man."

The hard snap of my anger was instantaneous. I swung around, lunging toward him, easily able to knock him to the ground.

With the gun flying out of his hand, I issued several brutal punches, catching him under the chin and in the stomach.

He was stronger than he looked, kicking me in the face. I was pitched backward and he immediately scrambled for the weapon.

"No!" I yelled, throwing myself at him again. As we both fell to the ground, I rolled to one side, immediately clambering to my feet. Four savage punches later and his body was teetering back and forth. The hard crack meant I'd broken his nose. Blood streamed from his nostrils as well as his mouth.

He'd managed to punch me in the eye with enough force stars were shimmering in front of both. "I suggest you stop right now and you can live."

Harrison grinned. "I think you got this wrong."

We both dove for the weapon, our hands colliding. As we wrestled, he managed to yank it from me, both jerking to our feet at the same time.

I backed away, calculating what the hell I could do at this point.

He lifted the weapon, pointing it at my head. If I could rush forward at the right time, I'd pin him to the huge tree behind him, maybe able to get the gun from his hand. "You don't want to do this, Harrison. You know I didn't kill her. They did, the monsters who captured us."

"It doesn't matter, buddy. You weren't supposed to take her off the base. You did this to her. My baby sister died because of you and now, it's time to meet your maker." His hand was shaking, but I sensed he intended on following through with his plans.

Years before, I honestly hadn't cared if I died on duty or elsewhere. I'd had nothing to live for.

Now, I did.

The woman I'd fallen hard for, the one I wanted to spend the rest of my life with.

Bella.

As he pressed his finger against the trigger, I heard a crunch of leaves behind me. When his gaze was lifted for a brief second, I dove to the ground.

And I immediately heard two things.

A primal yell from a decidedly female voice and a whooshing sound.

A split second later, a bolt punctured his upper arm, the force of the weapon used tossing him against the huge oak, the sharp point driven past the bark into the heart of the tree.

As I looked up, Bella remained with the crossbow in her hands, already reaching for another bolt.

"Bella," I called.

She darted her gaze toward me, but followed through with grabbing another metal arrow, placing it on the bow in position.

"Don't do it, city girl. He's not worth it."

Bella took a deep breath, taking another aim, this time at the man's chest. "I won't let him win. I will never let anyone win again. He will not hurt you."

"Fuck you, bitch." Harrison writhed in pain, struggling to get free. I took long strides toward him, yanking the weapon off the ground where it had landed in front of him.

The ugly name used only fueled the fire I noticed in her eyes.

Panting, I wiped my mouth and walked toward her, still holding out my arm. "Lower your weapon, Bella. For me. For us."

She held her head high. "Jagger is not a killer, you asshole. He's a goddamn hero. Get it through your head."

Harrison laughed and she continued debating firing the shot.

"Bella. Baby. Come on," I whispered, able to inch a little closer.

"You will pay, you monster." Thankfully, she lowered the bow and I was able to take it from her hand, shoving the gun in the waistband of my jeans before taking a deep breath.

With the bow in one hand, the arrow in the other, I pulled her into my arms. "It's all over. It's going to be just fine."

She clung to me for a few seconds before pushing herself away. When she started walking toward him, I took another deep breath. "What now?" she asked.

"Now, he's going to be arrested."

Harrison laughed. "I don't think so."

Bella wasn't the kind of woman to handle asshole men without retaliation. With everything she'd been through, she had less patience and care than I did. Taking long strides, she issued a hard crack against his face.

The bastard laughed again at the same time he used his other arm, wrapping it around her neck. He instantly started to strangle her.

"Let her go," I yelled at him.

Her choking sounds indicated how strong the man was. I dropped the bow and arrow, yanking his weapon into my hands.

"I said, Let. Her. Go."

His hold was tighter, Bella flailing as she struggled to free herself. Her eyes were pinned on mine, her mouth twisted as she gasped for air. When he grabbed the side of her face, ready to twist at a brutal angle, which would snap her neck, I had one chance in ten of making a clean shot.

"Bella!" I yelled.

Maybe there was something to be said about two people being able to read each other's minds. Maybe the connection we shared was all we needed. Love. Yeah, it was all about love. Time was precious and my sweet city girl jammed her elbow into his stomach.

As his hold weakened, she pushed herself free, flinging her body onto the ground.

And I took a shot.

* * *

Bella

"Esme!" I squealed the moment she walked into the clinic. "You came."

"Do you think I'd actually miss the opening of my best friend's new clinic in smalltown USA? Not a chance, girl-friend. A little surprise."

I hugged her tightly against me, giving Jagger a sly grin. "A wonderful one. I'm so glad you're here. I'm a nervous wreck."

"You shouldn't be. You are a brilliant doctor. Danger Falls is lucky to have you." She pulled away, immediately lifting her sunglasses in a seductive way as she turned around to glance at Jagger who was leaning against a wall in the corner. With his muscular arms folded, his black-on-black outfit, he gave off a sexy and dangerous aura.

Which would always make my mouth water.

"And who is this handsome fella?" she cooed.

"Jagger, the hero," Cally answered.

"Oh, little munchkin. It's so good to see you. And this must be the infamous Xena, the bestest hero of all."

"She's mine, Auntie Esme. All mine."

Esme bent down, giving my baby girl a bear hug. As she chatted with Cally, rubbing Xena's head, I took the opportunity to walk closer to Jagger. Maybe I was swaggering a little bit just like he did. "What do you think, big man? Is the place colorful enough for you?"

He scowled as only he could do. "Bright colors."

"There needed to be a change from the bland tan in every room. Come on. Show me that gorgeous smile of yours. I know you have one."

He scowled even more.

His huffing was done in jest. He'd finally started to lighten up over the last couple of weeks. When I'd found out he'd not only made payment to the attorney's office but had also bought the clinic for me, I'd almost been angry.

Until my common sense had taken over.

He wasn't just my hero. He was the only man for me.

I bopped his nose and he took me into his arms, swinging me around. Cally had finally gotten used to the fact this was our new home and our hero was my new guy. She'd looked me directly in the eye when I'd told her and said, "Duh, Mommy."

"You're pretty amazing, lady," he told me. "Still a very bad girl, but I know how to handle it."

"I think you're the amazing one, but you will never tame me."

He shook his head. "Bet me, sunshine. And you saved my life."

"You saved mine. Several times, but who's keeping count?"

As he lowered his head, nuzzled into my ear, nipping my earlobe, I closed my eyes briefly. The last few weeks had been incredible, except for the reporters that had kept hounding us for an interview.

Harrison survived his ordeal given Jagger's calculated gunshot, already in the hands of the Roanoke Police Department. Somehow, I didn't think Sheriff Young would be able to get him out of the attempted murder charges.

"A spanking later. You are way overdue," he whispered.

I blushed.

He pressed his lips against mine.

I swooned.

He pulled me into his arms.

I melted.

He'd even enjoyed spending the holidays with his three

girls, as he liked to call us. We filled his house with laughter and dirty dishes.

At least that's what he liked to remind me.

"Now, you did agree to being best man. Right?" I gave him an evil eye.

I did so adore his heavy groans. "Yes, dear."

After flashing him a grin, I pecked him on the lips again.

"Okay, you two. Save it for later. We have doors to open and a party to host," Esme said from behind us.

Laughing, I bit Jagger's lower lip before turning around. The fact she had her hand over Cally's eyes made me laugh. "She's seen us kiss before."

"Yeah, Auntie Esme. I'm a big girl," Cally blurted out and ceremoniously removed Esme's hand.

Woof. Woof.

"See, Xena is in agreement. We have five minutes. Hopefully, we have a huge crowd waiting to join us. We have plenty of drinks and cookies as well." I winked at my friend and fluffed up the fresh flowers I'd brought just this morning. I'd enjoyed painting and purchasing new pictures for the clinic. But mostly, everything else would stay the same. Including the two employees. And Doc Welby promised to be around if I had any questions.

This would take some getting used to, but I was excited and eager.

"Did you hear?" Esme asked as he moved closer, trying to keep her voice low.

"Hear what? I don't watch or read the news any longer."

"You should have. Joel's no longer performing surgeries. The medical board revoked his license. I guess he botched a few and was caught doing plastic surgery. Can you imagine? And that's the least of his worries."

I darted a glance in her direction. "Well, I won't wish ill will on the man."

She planted her hands on her hips. "Oh, come on."

"Okay, remember that conversation we had weeks ago at your place? I might take you up on calling that cousin of yours."

We both laughed. Joel definitely wasn't worth it.

"Now, how long are you staying?" I asked.

Esme shrugged. I could tell the woman had something up her sleeve. "Well… It depends on if I get the job at the resort or not." She sucked in and puffed out her cheeks as she waited for my response.

"Oh, my God. You'll get it. His brother Hunter is supposed to be here any minute. I'll introduce you. You will adore the resort. I know you will."

"Brother, eh?" She licked her lips. "Honey, if he looks like that gorgeous man, I will never leave."

"Don't get any ideas. No fraternizing with the hired help."

"Oh, come on. Don't want to be my sister-in-law?" She batted her eyelashes.

"We're not getting married."

"You are if the looks that man gives you are any indication."

"No girl talking over there," Jagger piped in. He was pretending to be grumpy, but I could tell how happy he was.

I gave him a watchful eye anyway.

The door was opened and Denise burst in with Hunter and Shephard in tow. In her arms was a huge bouquet of roses.

"To the great new doctor in town." Denise pushed them forward, immediately motioning for Shephard. "Take a picture."

For the next couple of minutes, photographs were taken of the monumental occasion, the precious time reminding me of what families were supposed to be like.

While they were still talking, I decided to allow any guests who'd showed up to come in and see the place.

I'd invited about thirty people and almost all had said they'd come. I was eager to get my practice started and it seemed like the best way to do so.

When I walked out onto the porch, a few things struck me, including how beautiful the flowers were that Jagger had hunted down, going to several stores in and around Danger Falls. Pansies. They would survive the early January cold.

The second was just how perfect the day was. It was cold, but there wasn't a cloud in the sky.

And the third was that there wasn't a single person waiting to join in the celebration.

Not one,

Not Poppy or Zoe, Carlos or Jenny, or even the gossip girls from the diner.

Or Doc Welby either.

I was stunned, but I knew why. I wasn't wanted in this town.

A sob threatened to give me away and I did what I could to hold it back, ready to bolt back into the clinic.

Jagger grabbed me, turning me around to face the street. "What do you see?"

"What do you mean?" I snapped. "Other than the fact there's no one here? No one cares? Everyone thinks the same damn thing? I'm a porn star."

"Shush," he growled as he popped me on the behind. In broad daylight. "Okay, let's try this. Close your eyes for me and what do you see?"

He even placed one hand over my eyes to ensure I'd follow his instructions. I huffed and puffed, but knew there was no getting out of this. "A quaint town with beautiful buildings and smiling people."

"Keep going."

"A place where the love of my life lives and my little girl, my beautiful puppy and where I have a home. Although we need new drapes."

"Ugh. Anything else?"

"A nice family and a building clinical practice. Possibly. Maybe one day I'll have patients."

"You are such a grumpy pessimist," he told me. "I have news for you."

"Oh, yeah, Mr. Grumpy?"

"You have a man who loves you even when you leave your coffee cup in the living room or forget to turn out the lights. A guy who adores your little snores at night."

"I don't snore."

"Oh, yes, you do. But I adore them. I especially love the looks you give me when we're making love. You're a beautiful person inside and out and everyone knows that."

"I don't think everyone. They're not here, Jagger. I failed."

His sigh was way too exaggerated. "Think and look again, city girl. The townies know good people when they meet them."

As he slowly removed his hand, it took me a few seconds for my sight to once again adjust to the light. When they did, I was shocked at what I was seeing.

Signs of 'congratulations, Dr. Winters' were everywhere, all done with vibrant magic markers. Tables were being set up, food and beverages coming from vans and trunks of cars.

There were balloons and suddenly music was blaring from an unseen source.

Zoe was here and Poppy too. Doctor Welby and a young woman that had to be his daughter. And the gossip sisters.

And there were people I didn't know. Lots and lots of people, all waving to me as they set up for a huge festive party.

"See? They love you and so do I. This is your home."

I noticed a man standing by himself, far removed from the crowd. Behind him was a gorgeous, sleek black Maserati. He stood in a dark suit and shades, his salt and pepper hair providing a debonair look.

"Who's that?" I asked.

"Michelangelo Ross." Jagger turned me around to face him. "I thought it was time to meet your father. Don't be angry with me. Please. He had no idea he had a daughter. He wanted to be here today and I thought you needed to know you have dozens of people who care about you."

"Angry? How could I be angry?" Nervous? Yes. Excited? Yes. "I'm never angry with you." I pulled him into a hug and Jagger sighed.

"Go say hello. I think you might like what he has to say."

As I pulled away, the cheering continuing, I blew the love of my life a kiss.

As I breathed a sigh of relief, the others from inside joined him on the porch. Danger Falls. Home. Family. Friends.

Love.

The End

AFTERWORD

BOOKS OF THE MOUNTAIN MEN OF DANGER FALLS SERIES

Shephard

On a dark, stormy night, a stranger stripped me bare in my own hotel room, spanked my ass red, and then pinned me to the bed and turned my most shameful fantasies into raw, filthy reality.

No names. No commitments.

Then I returned to my life, thinking I'd seen the last of the gorgeous Marine turned mountain man who rutted me like a beast while I screamed loud enough for the whole building to hear.

But fate had other plans.

With a killer leaving a trail of death in Danger Falls, my job as a park ranger required me to hire a tracker, and the man turned out to be the same chiseled god who made me his once already.

And this time he's not letting me go after just one night.

BOOKS OF THE MONTANA BAD BOYS SERIES

Hawk

He's a big, angry Marine, and I'm going to be sore when he's done with me.

Hawk Travers is not a man to be trifled with. I learned that lesson in the hardest way possible, first with a painful, humiliating public spanking and then much more shamefully in private.

She came looking for trouble. She got a taste of my belt instead.

Bryce Myers pushed me too far and she ended up with her bottom welted. But as satisfying as it is to hear this feisty little reporter scream my name as I put her in her place, I get the feeling she isn't going to stop snooping around no matter how well-used and sore I leave her cute backside.

She's gotten herself in way over her head, but she's mine now, and I protect what's mine.

Scorpion

He didn't ask if I like it rough. It wasn't up to me.

I thought I could get away with pissing off a big, tough Marine. I ended up with my face planted in the sheets, my burning bottom raised high, and my hair held tightly in his fist as he took me long and hard and taught me the kind of shameful lesson only a man like Scorpion could teach.

She was begging for a taste of my belt. She got much more than that.

Getting so tipsy she thought she could be sassy with me in my own bar earned Caroline a spanking, but it was trying to make off with my truck that sealed the deal. She'll feel my belt across her bare backside, then she'll scream my name as she takes every single inch of me.

This naughty girl needs to be put in her place, and I'm going to enjoy every moment of it.

Mustang

I tried to tell him how to run his ranch. Then he took off his belt.

When I heard a rumor about his ranch, I confronted Mustang about it. I thought I could go toe to toe with the big, tough former Marine, but I ended up blushing, sore, and very thoroughly used.

I told her it was going to hurt. I meant it.

Danni Brexton is a hot little number with a sharp tongue and a chip on her shoulder. She's the kind of trouble that needs to be ridden hard and put away wet, but only after a taste of my belt.

It will take more than just a firm hand and a burning bottom to tame this sassy spitfire, but I plan to keep her safe, sound, and screaming my name in bed whether she likes it or not. By the time I'm through with her, there won't be a shadow of a doubt in her mind that she belongs to me.

Nash

When he caught me on his property, he didn't call the police. He just took off his belt.

Nash caught me breaking into his shed while on the run from the mob, and when he demanded answers and obedience I gave him neither. Then he took off his belt and taught me in the most shameful way possible what happens to naughty girls who play games with a big, rough Marine.

She's mine to protect. That doesn't mean I'm going to be gentle with her.

Michelle doesn't just need a place to hide out. She needs a man who will bare her bottom and spank her until she is sore and sobbing whenever she puts herself at risk with reckless defiance, then shove her face into the sheets and make her scream his name with every savage climax.

She'll get all of that from me, and much, much more.

Austin

I offered this brute a ride. I ended up the one being ridden.

The first time I saw Austin, he was hitchhiking. I stopped to give him a lift, but I didn't end up taking this big, rough former Marine wherever he was heading. He was far too busy taking me.

She thought she was in charge. Then I took off my belt.

When Francesca Montgomery pulled up beside me, I didn't know who she was, but I knew what she needed and I gave it to her. Long, hard, and thoroughly, until she was screaming my name as she climaxed over and over with her quivering bare bottom still sporting the marks from my belt.

But someone wants to hurt her, and when someone tries to hurt what's mine, I take it personally.

Holed up in my cabin with her bottom burning and a snowstorm raging outside, there's no denying the spark between us, and we both know she'll soon be screaming my name as I take her in the most shameful of ways.

But when her past catches up to her, the men who come after her will learn a hard lesson.

She's mine now, and I protect what's mine.

MORE ROUGH ROMANCES BY PIPER STONE

Eagle Force

Debt of Honor

Debt of Loyalty

Debt of Sacrifice

Standalone Romances

Captured and Kept

Taming His Brat

Roughneck

Torched

Hostage

Kept

Hard Ride

Bounty

Big Rig

Owned

Seized

Cruel Masters

Hard Men

Rough Ride

When I tore Chantel's clothes off on that dark balcony and gave her exactly what she needed, I didn't know the girl screaming her surrender into the night should have been off-limits to me.

Not just because I'm old enough to be her father, or even because my half-brother raised her.

Because she's too innocent for the wicked things I would do to her perfect little body, for the way I would make her beg and writhe and come over and over again with her hair gripped tight in my fist and her ass sore from my belt, then flip her over and claim her even more shamefully.

But I don't care.

She's mine now, and I'm keeping her.

BOOKS OF THE RUTHLESS EMPIRE SERIES

The Don

Maxwell Powers swept into my life after my father was gunned down, but the moment those piercing blue eyes caught mine I knew he would be doing more than just avenging his old friend.

I haven't seen him since I was a little girl, but that won't keep him from bending me over and belting my bare backside… or from making me scream his name as he claims my virgin body.

He's twice my age, and he's my godfather.

But I know I'll be soaking wet and ready for him tonight…

The Consigliere

As consigliere of New York's most ruthless crime syndicate, Daniel Briggs rules with an iron fist. But here in Los Angeles, he's just my big brother's best friend, forbidden in every way.

This stunningly handsome billionaire may be the most eligible bachelor on the West Coast, but to him I'm still just a little girl in need of protection from men who would ravage her brutally.

Men like him.

But he'll soon realize I'm all grown up, and then it won't be long before my teenage crush finally shows me the side of him he's kept hidden from me—the savage side that will blister my bare ass for talking back and then take what has always been his with my hair gripped in his fist.

I don't know what comes after that. I just know everything he does to me will be utterly sinful…

The Underboss

When Francesco Arturo helped me escape an unwanted arranged marriage three years ago, I didn't know he was the underboss of the most powerful mafia organization in New York.

I was just an eighteen-year-old virgin on the run, and he was the handsome savior mesmerizing me with eyes the color of the Aegean Sea before carrying me off to his bed to make me his.

He could have taken my innocence that day, but he didn't.

I gave it to him.

But this isn't a fairy tale. When that perfect night came to an end, I was still the daughter of a Chicago crime boss with a father set on marrying her off to whatever vile man paid the most.

Now he's finally found a suitor for me, but there is something the brutal bastard doesn't know.

I already belong to someone else, and he's coming to take me back.

BOOKS OF THE BENEDETTI EMPIRE SERIES

Cruel Prince

Catherine's father conspired to have my father killed, and that debt to the Benedetti family must be settled. Just as he took something from me, I will take something from him.

His daughter.

She will be mine to punish and ravage, but when she suffers it will not be for his sins.

It will be for my pleasure.

She will beg, but it will be for me to claim her in the most shameful ways imaginable.

She will scream, but it will be because she doesn't think she can bear another climax.

But when she surrenders at last, it will not be to her captor.

It will be to her husband.

Ruthless Prince

Alexandra is a senator's daughter, used to mingling in the company of the rich and powerful, but tonight she will learn that there are men who play by different rules.

Men like me.

I could romance her. I could seduce her and then carry her gently to my bed.

But that can wait. Tonight I'm going to wring one ruthless climax after another from her quivering body with her bottom burning from my belt and her throat sore from screaming.

She will know she is mine before she even knows she is my bride.

Savage Prince

Gillian's father may be a powerful Irish mob boss, but he owes a blood debt to my family, and when I came to collect I didn't ask permission before taking his daughter as payment.

It was not up to him... or to her.

I will make her my bride, but I am not the kind of man who will wait until our wedding night to bare her and claim what belongs to me. She will walk down the aisle wet, well-used, and sore.

Her dress will hide the marks from my belt that taught her the consequences of disobeying her husband, but nothing will hide her blushes as her arousal drips down her thighs with each step.

By the time she says her vows she will already be mine.

She will be used mercilessly, over and over, and every brutal climax will remind her of the humiliating truth: she never even had a chance against me. Her body always knew its master.

Claimed as Revenge

Valencia Rivera became mine the moment her father broke the agreement he made with me. She thought she had a say in the matter, but my belt across her beautiful bottom taught her otherwise and a night spent screaming her surrender into the sheets left her in no doubt she belongs to me.

Using her hard and often will not be all it takes to tame her properly, but it will be a good start…

Made to Beg

Sierra Fox showed up at my door to ask for my protection, and I gave it to her… for a price. She belongs to me now, and I'm going to use her beautiful body as thoroughly as I please. The only thing for her to decide is how sore her cute little bottom will be when I'm through claiming her.

She came to me begging for help, but as her moans and screams grow louder with every brutal climax, we both know it won't be long before she begs me for something far more shameful.

King of Depravity

King of Savagery

King of Malice

Lords of Corruption

Lord of Punishment

Lord of Vengeance

Lord of Retribution

Lord of Ruin

Lord of Vice

Lord of Debauchery

Tainted Regime

Cruelest Vow

Twisted Embrace

Captured Innocence

Carnal Sins

Required Surrender

Demanded Submission

Compelled Obedience

Bent to His Will

Broken by His Hand

Bound by His Command

Royal Players Club

Royal Mistake

Royal Flush

Royal Pain

Edge of Darkness

Dark Stranger

Dark Predator

Standalone Romances

Caught

Ruthless

Prey

Given

Dangerous Stranger

Millionaire Daddy

Indebted

Taken

Bratva's Captive

Hunted

Theirs as Payment

Ruthless Acquisition

Bound by Contract

Dangerous Addiction

Auction House

Interrogated

Vow of Seduction

Brutal Heir

Bed of Thorns

Morally Gray

Vicious Intentions

Scandalous Liaison

Ruthlessly Mine

Scandal

Cold-Hearted King

Strictly Forbidden

She Belongs to Me

BOOKS OF THE ALPHA BEASTS SERIES

King's Mate

Her scent drew me to her, but something deeper and more powerful told me she was mine. Something that would not be denied. Something that demanded I claim her then and there.

I took her the way a beast takes his mate. Roughly. Savagely. Without mercy or remorse.

She will run, and when she does she will be punished, but it is not me that she fears. Every quivering, desperate climax reminds her that her body knows its master, and that terrifies her.

She knows I am not a gentle king, and she will scream for me as she learns her place.

Beast's Claim

Raven is not one of my kind, but the moment I caught her scent I knew she belonged to me.

She is my mate, and when I claim her it will not be gentle. She can fight me, but her pleas for mercy as she is punished will soon give way to screams of climax as she is mounted and rutted.

By the time I am finished with her, the evidence of her body's surrender will be mingled with my seed as it drips down her bare thighs. But she will be more than just sore and utterly spent.

She will be mine.

Alpha's Mate

I didn't ask Nicolina to be my mate. It was not up to her. An alpha takes what belongs to him.

She will plead for mercy as she is bared and punished for daring to run from me, but her screams as she is claimed and rutted will be those of helpless climax as her body surrenders to its master.

She is mine, and I'm going to make sure she knows it.

BOOKS OF THE CENZAN MATES SERIES

Conquering Their Mate

For years the Cenzans have cast a menacing eye on Earth, but it still came as a shock to be captured, stripped bare, and claimed as a mate by their leader and his most trusted warriors.

It infuriates me to be punished for the slightest defiance and forced to submit to these alien brutes, but as I'm led naked through the corridors of their ship, my well-punished bare bottom and my helpless arousal both fully on display, I cannot help wondering how long it will be until I'm kneeling at the feet of my mates and begging them take me as shamefully as they please.

Capturing Their Mate

I thought the Cenzan invaders could never find me here, but I was wrong. Three of the alien brutes came to take me, and before I ever set foot aboard their ship I had already been stripped bare, spanked thoroughly, and claimed more shamefully then I would have ever thought possible.

They have decided that a public example must be made of me, and I will be punished and used in the most humiliating ways imaginable as a warning to anyone who might dare to defy them. But I am no ordinary breeder, and the secrets hidden in my past could change their world… or end it.

Hunting Their Mate

As far as I'm concerned, the Cenzans will always be the enemy, and there can be no peace while they remain on our planet. I planned to make them pay for invading our world, but I was hunted down and captured by two of their warriors with the help of a battle-hardened former Marine. Now I'm the one who is going to pay, as the three of them punish me, shame me, and share me.

Though the thought of a fellow human taking the side of these alien brutes enrages me, that is far from the worst of it. With every searing stroke of the strap that lands across my bare bottom, with every savage thrust as I am claimed over and over, and with every screaming climax, it is made more clear that it is my own quivering, thoroughly used body which has truly betrayed me.

MORE SCI-FI AND PARANORMAL ROMANCES BY PIPER STONE

Alpha Dynasty

Unchained Beast

Savage Brute

Ruthless Monster

Ravenous Predator

Merciless Savage

Dark Wolves

His to Claim

His to Possess

Standalone Romances

Claimed by the Beasts

Rogue

Primitive

Harvest

Fertile

Defiled

ABOUT PIPER STONE

Amazon Top 150 Internationally Best-Selling Author, Kindle Unlimited All Star Piper Stone writes in several genres. From her worlds of dark mafia, cowboys, and marines to contemporary reverse harem, shifter romance, and science fiction, she attempts to delight readers with a foray into darkness, sensuality, suspense, and always a romantic HEA. When she's not writing, you can find her sipping merlot while she enjoys spending time with her three Golden Retrievers (Indiana Jones, Magnum PI, and Remington Steele) and a husband who relishes creating fabulous food.

Dangerous is Delicious.

* * *

You can find her at:

Website: https://piperstonebooks.com/

Newsletter: https://piperstonebooks.com/newsletter/

Facebook: https://www.facebook.com/authorpiperstone/

Twitter: http://twitter.com/piperstone01

Instagram: http://www.instagram.com/authorpiperstone/

Amazon: http://amazon.com/author/piperstone

BookBub: http://bookbub.com/authors/piper-stone

TikTok: https://www.tiktok.com/@piperstoneauthor

Email: piperstonecreations@gmail.com

Made in United States
North Haven, CT
18 January 2025

64602941R00251